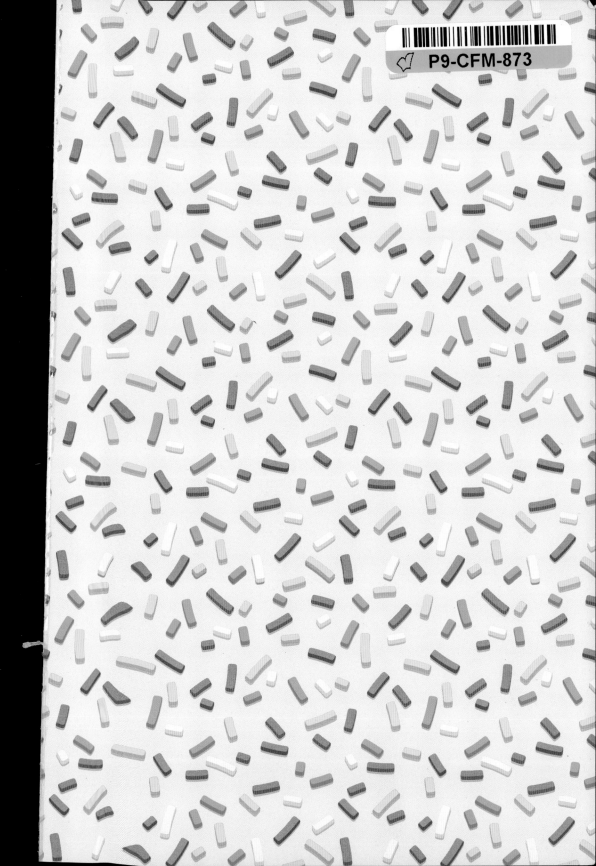

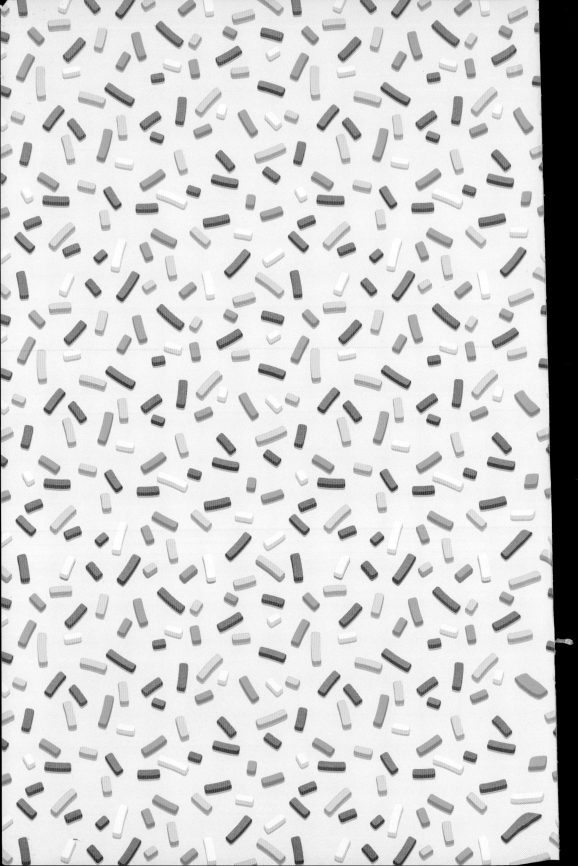

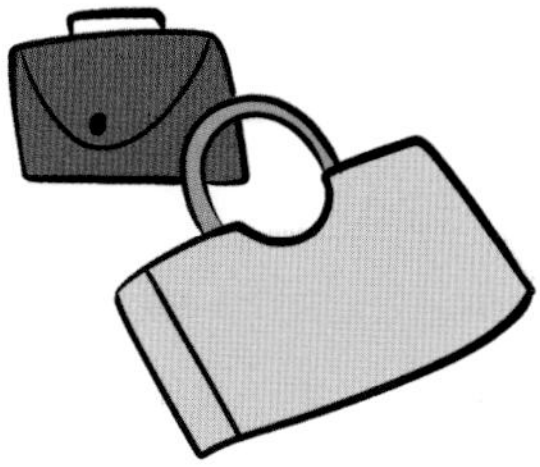
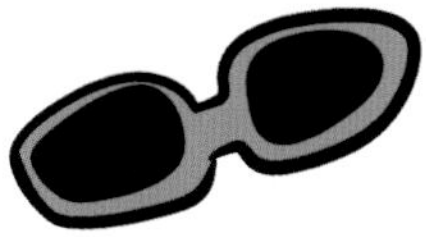
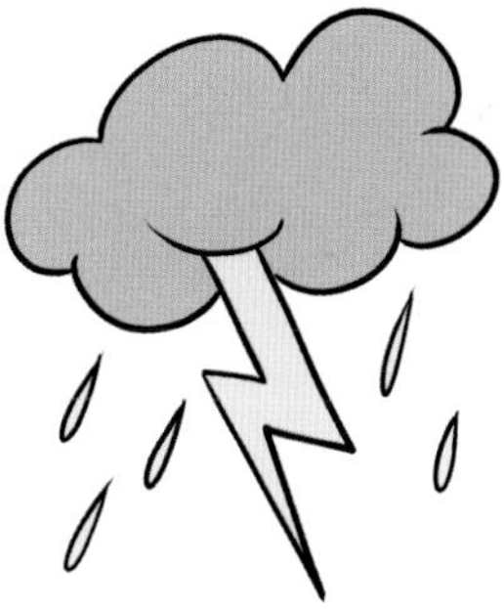

Mia in the Mix

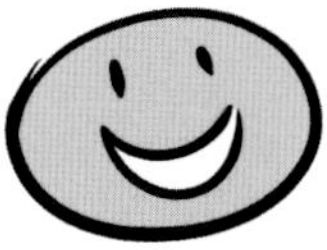
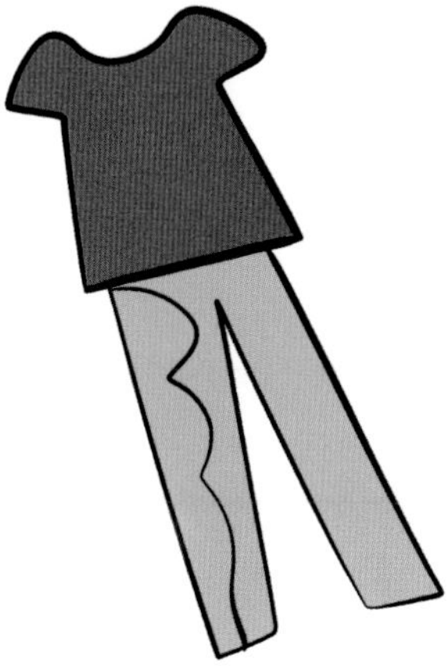
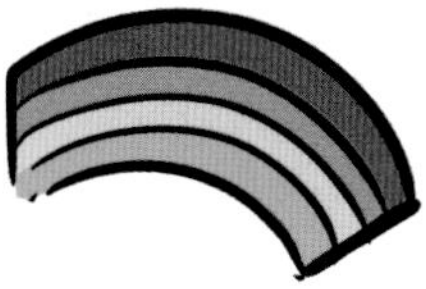
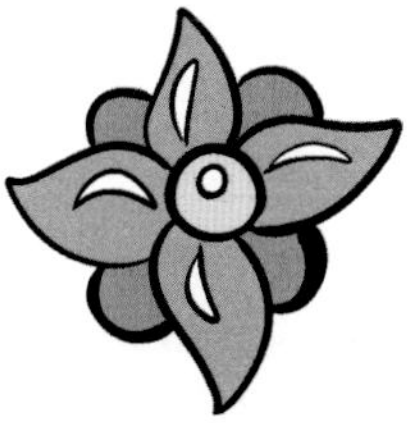
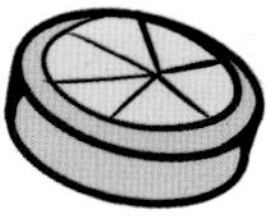

SIMON SPOTLIGHT
An imprint of Simon & Schuster Children's Publishing Division
1230 Avenue of the Americas, New York, New York 10020
This Simon Spotlight edition November 2022
Copyright © 2022 by Simon & Schuster, Inc.
All rights reserved, including the right of reproduction in whole or in part in any form.
SIMON SPOTLIGHT and colophon are registered trademarks of Simon & Schuster, Inc.
For information about special discounts for bulk purchases, please contact Simon & Schuster
Special Sales at 1-866-506-1949 or business@simonandschuster.com.
Text by Tracey West
Cover and Character Design by Manuel Preitano
Art Services by Glass House Graphics
Pencils by Giulia Campobello
Inks by Giulia Campobello and Marzia Migliori
Colors by Francesca Ingrassia
Lettering by Giuseppe Naselli/Grafimated Cartoon
Supervision by Salvatore Di Marco/Grafimated Cartoon
Designed by Laura Roode
The text of this book was set in Comic Crazy.
Manufactured in China 0323 SCP
10 9 8 7 6 5 4 3 2
ISBN 978-1-6659-1416-1 (hc)
ISBN 978-1-6659-1415-4 (pbk)
ISBN 978-1-6659-1417-8 (ebook)
Library of Congress Catalog Card Number 2022934413

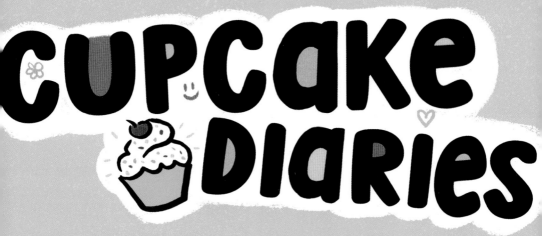

CUPCAKE DIARIES

Mia in the Mix

By
Coco Simon

Illustrated by
Giulia Campobello
at Glass House Graphics

Simon Spotlight
New York   London   Toronto   Sydney   New Delhi

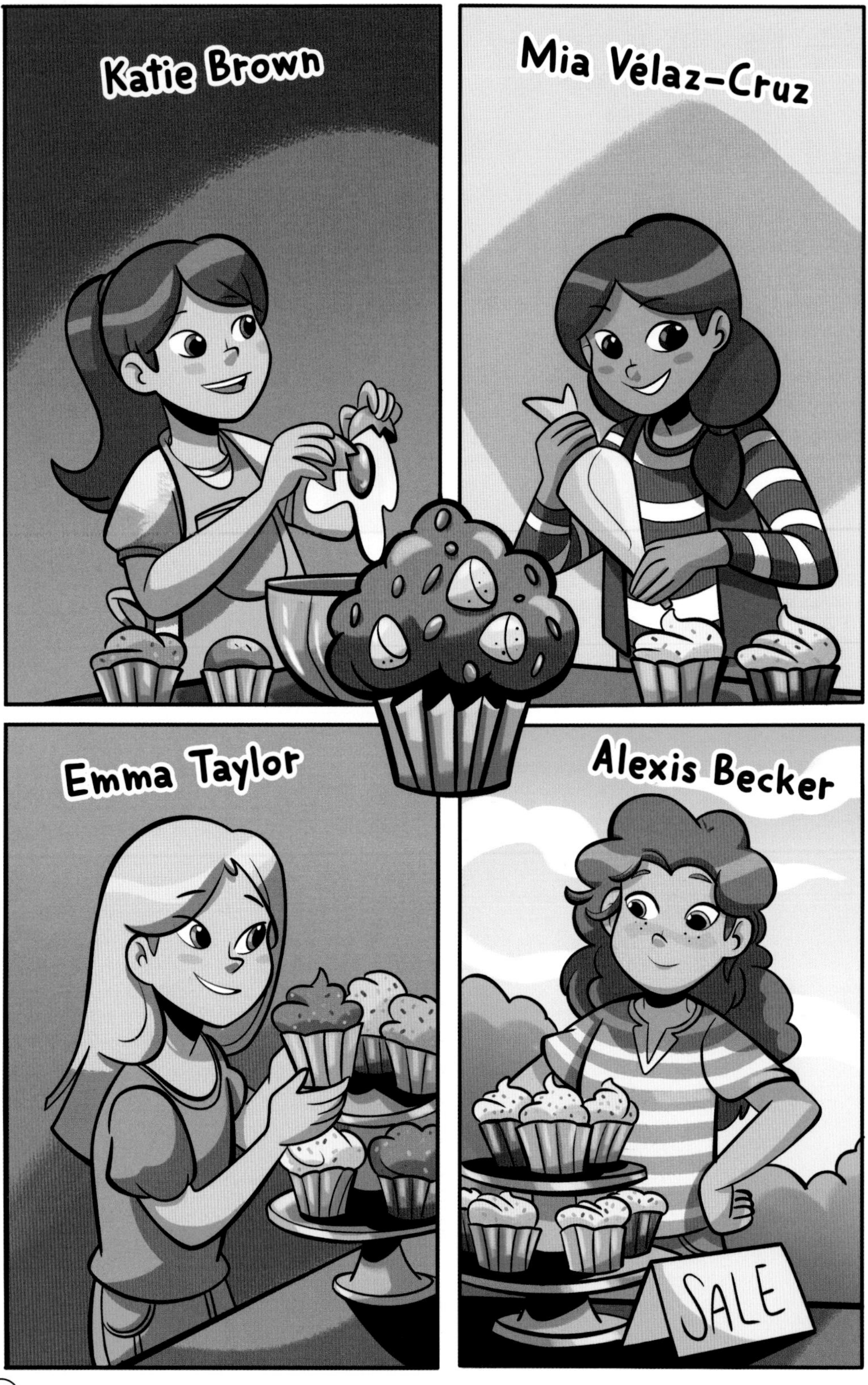
Katie Brown
Mia Vélaz-Cruz
Emma Taylor
Alexis Becker
SALE

Chapter 1

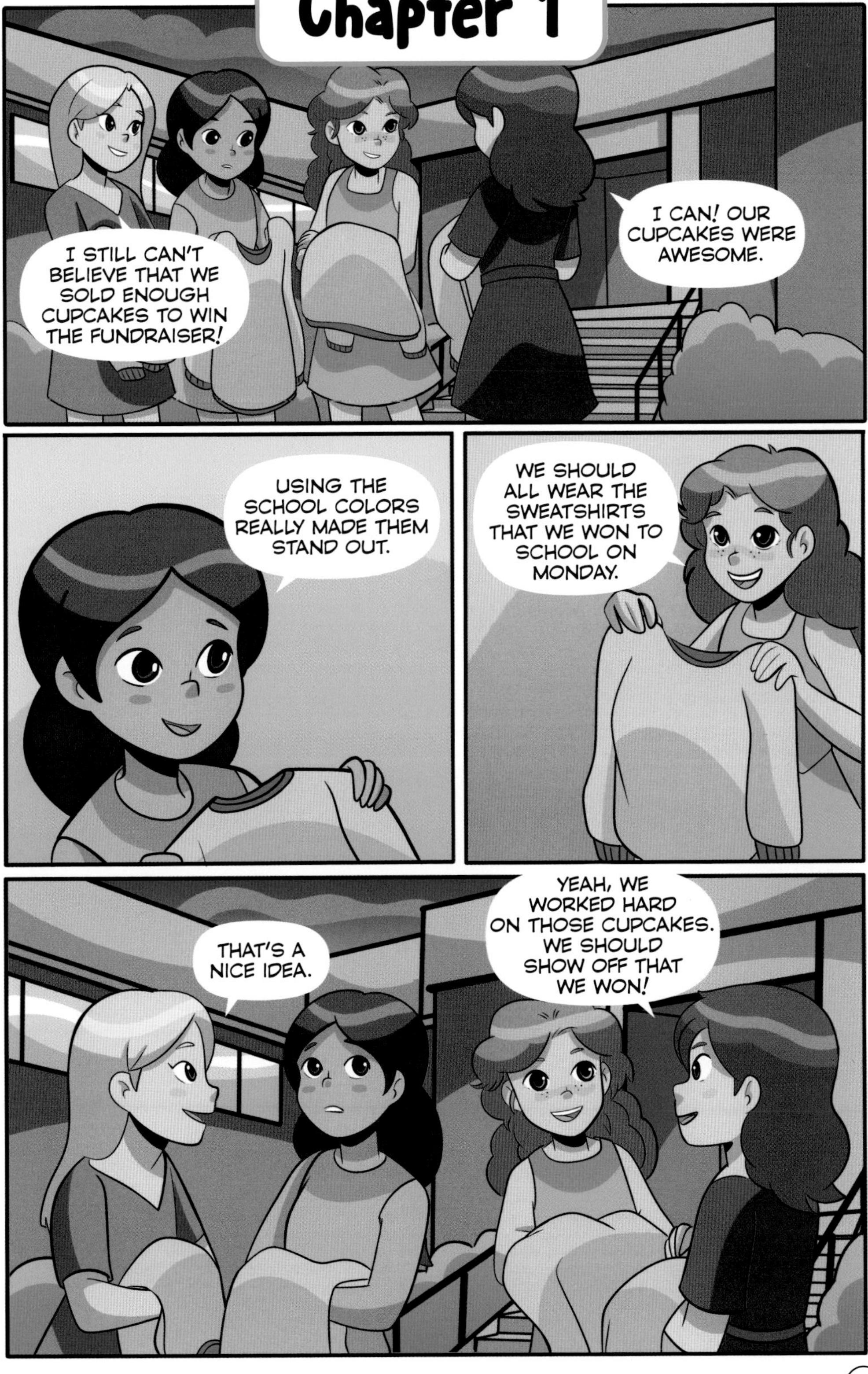
I STILL CAN'T BELIEVE THAT WE SOLD ENOUGH CUPCAKES TO WIN THE FUNDRAISER!
I CAN! OUR CUPCAKES WERE AWESOME.
USING THE SCHOOL COLORS REALLY MADE THEM STAND OUT.
WE SHOULD ALL WEAR THE SWEATSHIRTS THAT WE WON TO SCHOOL ON MONDAY.
THAT'S A NICE IDEA.
YEAH, WE WORKED HARD ON THOSE CUPCAKES. WE SHOULD SHOW OFF THAT WE WON!

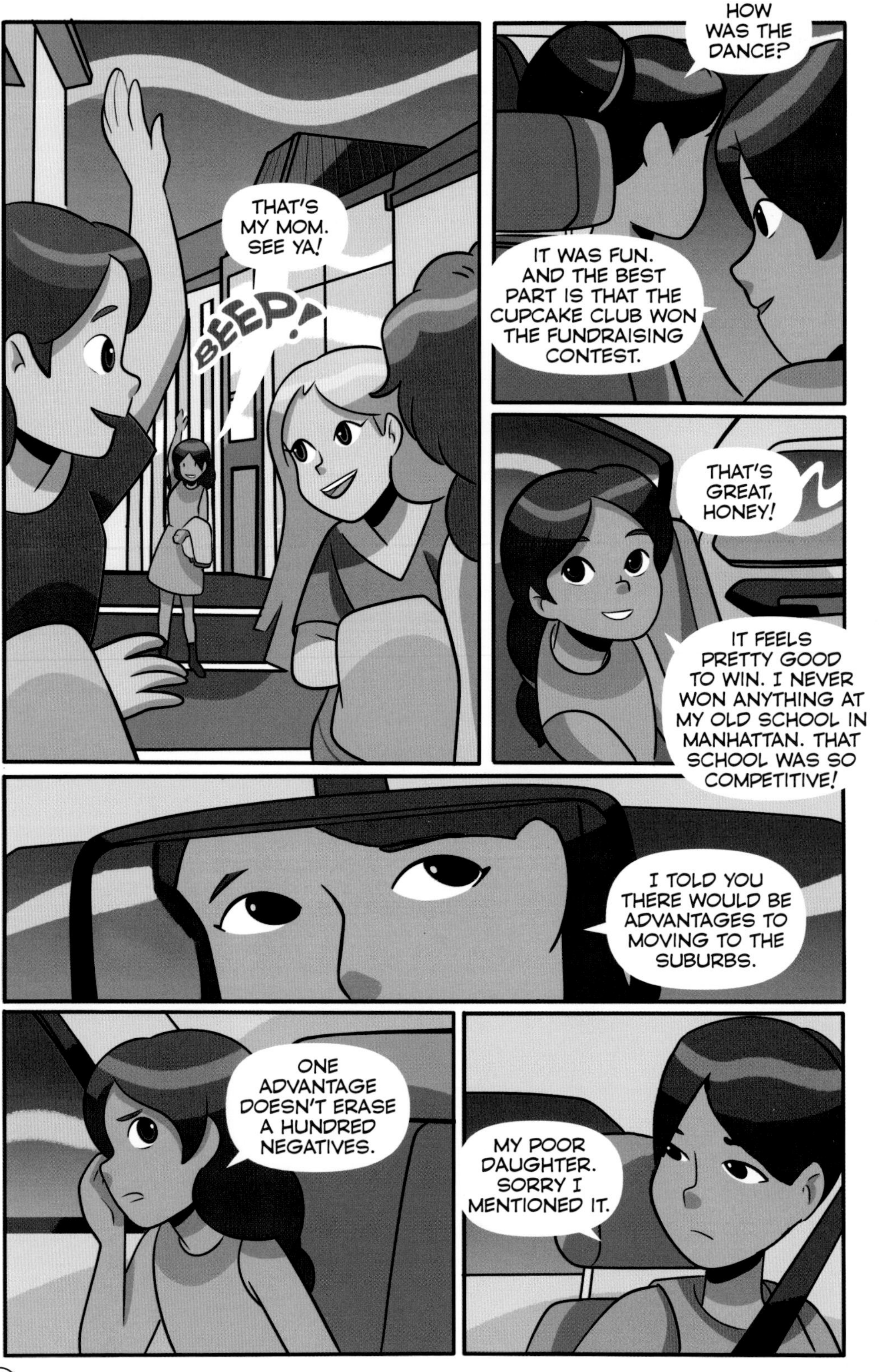
THAT'S MY MOM. SEE YA!
BEEP!
HOW WAS THE DANCE?
IT WAS FUN. AND THE BEST PART IS THAT THE CUPCAKE CLUB WON THE FUNDRAISING CONTEST.
THAT'S GREAT, HONEY!
IT FEELS PRETTY GOOD TO WIN. I NEVER WON ANYTHING AT MY OLD SCHOOL IN MANHATTAN. THAT SCHOOL WAS SO COMPETITIVE!
I TOLD YOU THERE WOULD BE ADVANTAGES TO MOVING TO THE SUBURBS.
ONE ADVANTAGE DOESN'T ERASE A HUNDRED NEGATIVES.
MY POOR DAUGHTER. SORRY I MENTIONED IT.

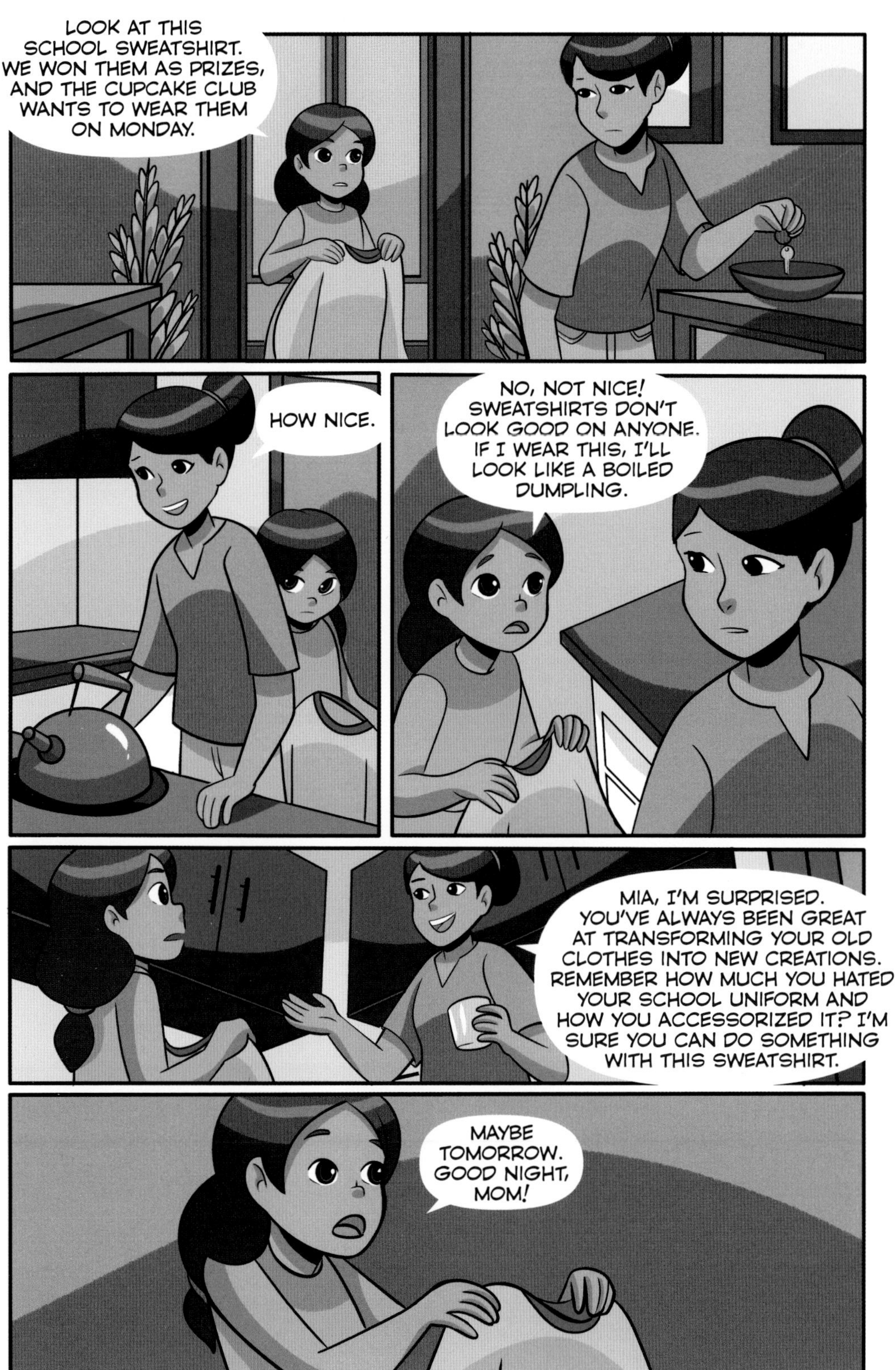
LOOK AT THIS SCHOOL SWEATSHIRT. WE WON THEM AS PRIZES, AND THE CUPCAKE CLUB WANTS TO WEAR THEM ON MONDAY.
HOW NICE.
NO, NOT NICE! SWEATSHIRTS DON'T LOOK GOOD ON ANYONE. IF I WEAR THIS, I'LL LOOK LIKE A BOILED DUMPLING.
MIA, I'M SURPRISED. YOU'VE ALWAYS BEEN GREAT AT TRANSFORMING YOUR OLD CLOTHES INTO NEW CREATIONS. REMEMBER HOW MUCH YOU HATED YOUR SCHOOL UNIFORM AND HOW YOU ACCESSORIZED IT? I'M SURE YOU CAN DO SOMETHING WITH THIS SWEATSHIRT.
MAYBE TOMORROW. GOOD NIGHT, MOM!

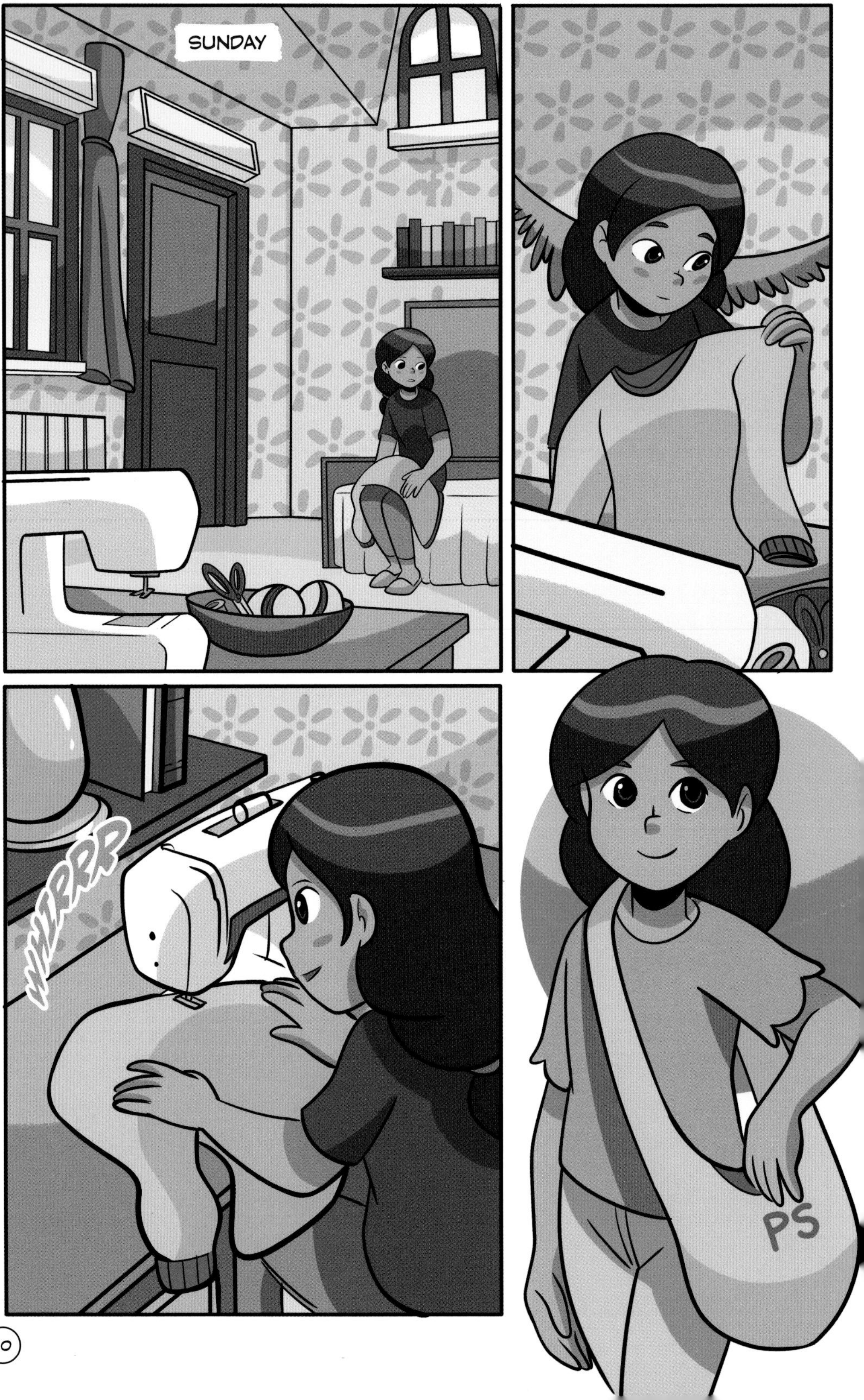
SUNDAY
WHIRRR
PS

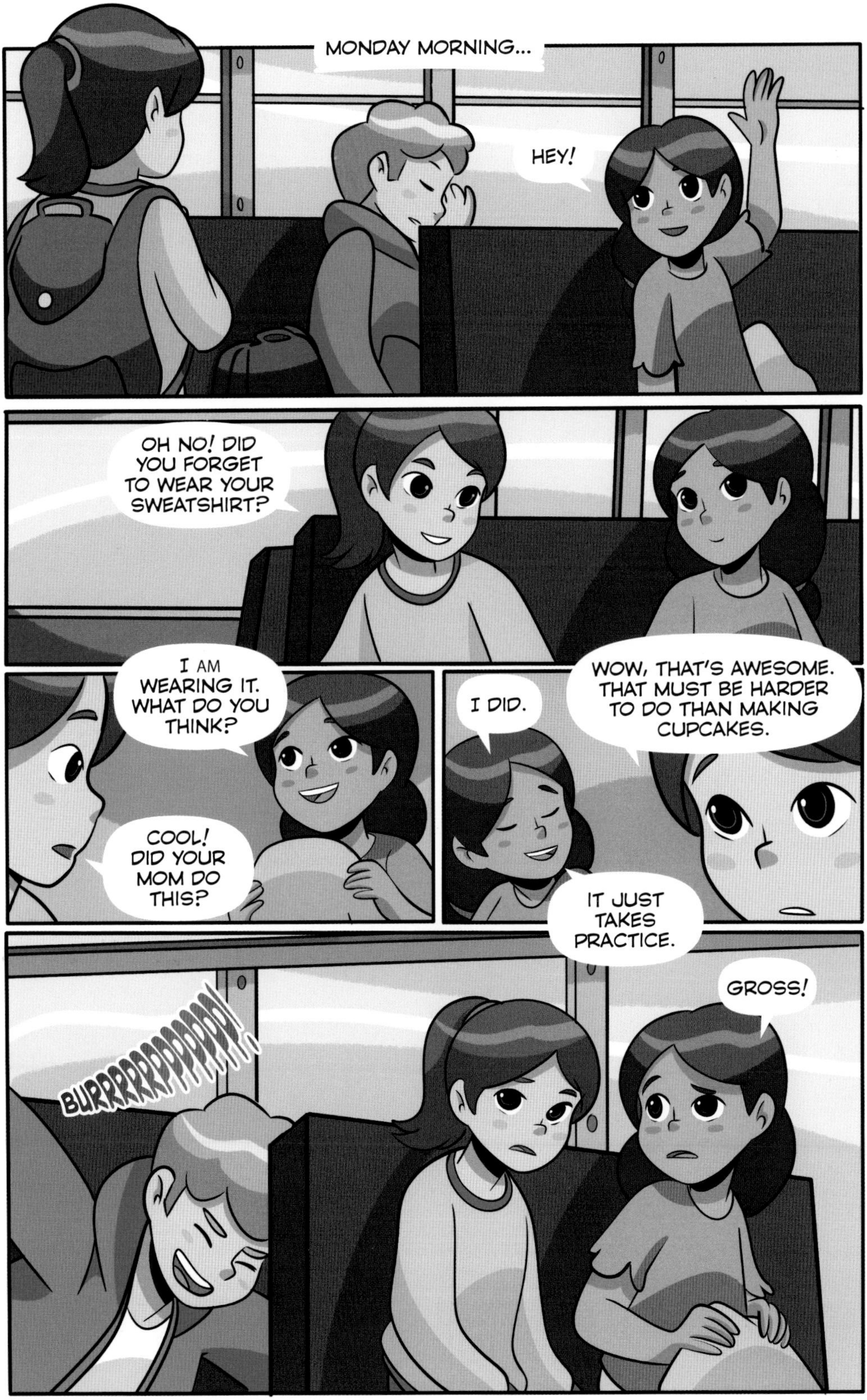
MONDAY MORNING...
HEY!
OH NO! DID YOU FORGET TO WEAR YOUR SWEATSHIRT?
I AM WEARING IT. WHAT DO YOU THINK?
COOL! DID YOUR MOM DO THIS?
I DID.
WOW, THAT'S AWESOME. THAT MUST BE HARDER TO DO THAN MAKING CUPCAKES.
IT JUST TAKES PRACTICE.
BURRRRRRPPPPPP!
GROSS!

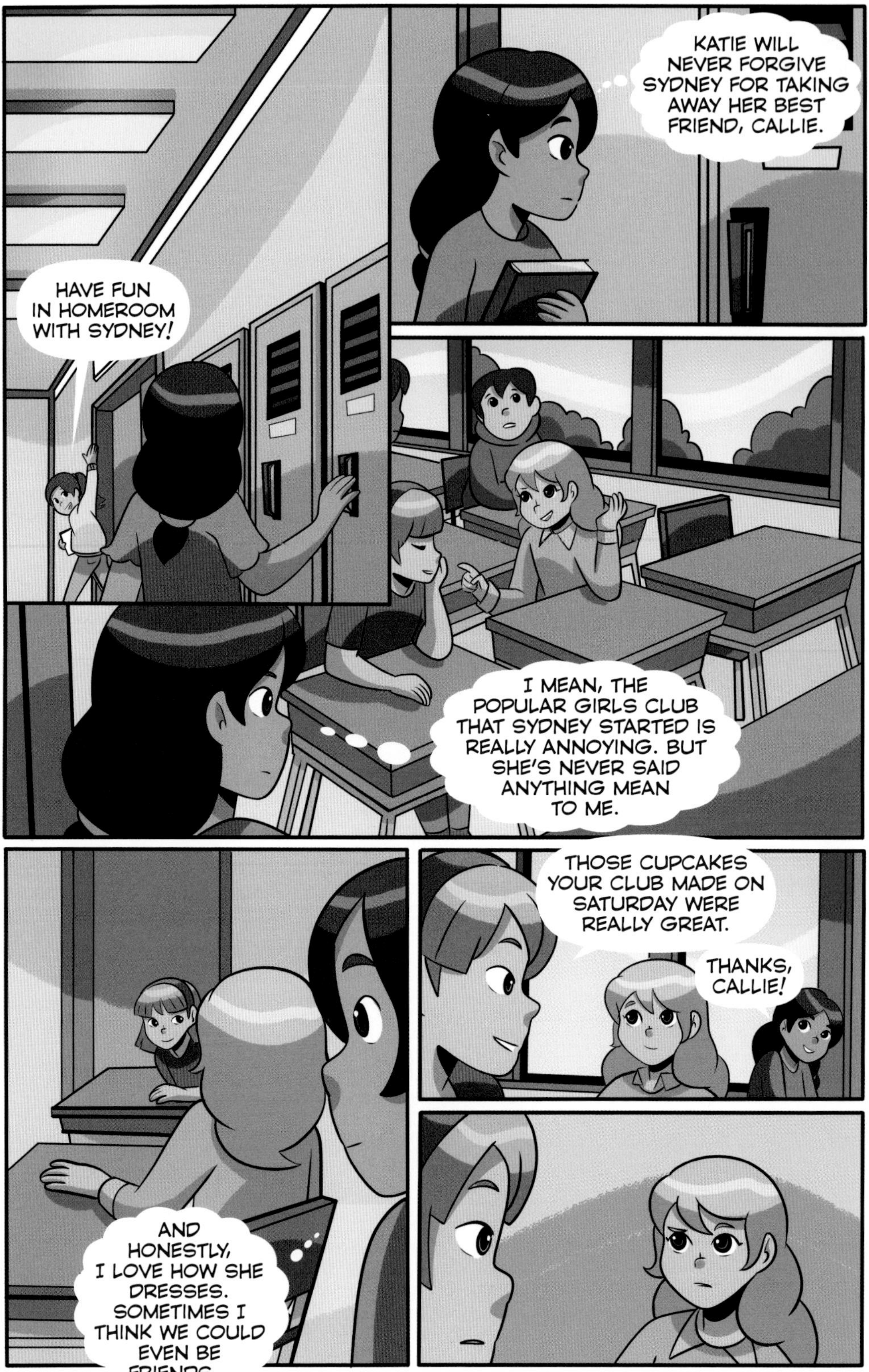
HAVE FUN IN HOMEROOM WITH SYDNEY!
KATIE WILL NEVER FORGIVE SYDNEY FOR TAKING AWAY HER BEST FRIEND, CALLIE.
I MEAN, THE POPULAR GIRLS CLUB THAT SYDNEY STARTED IS REALLY ANNOYING. BUT SHE'S NEVER SAID ANYTHING MEAN TO ME.
AND HONESTLY, I LOVE HOW SHE DRESSES. SOMETIMES I THINK WE COULD EVEN BE FRIENDS...
THOSE CUPCAKES YOUR CLUB MADE ON SATURDAY WERE REALLY GREAT.
THANKS, CALLIE!

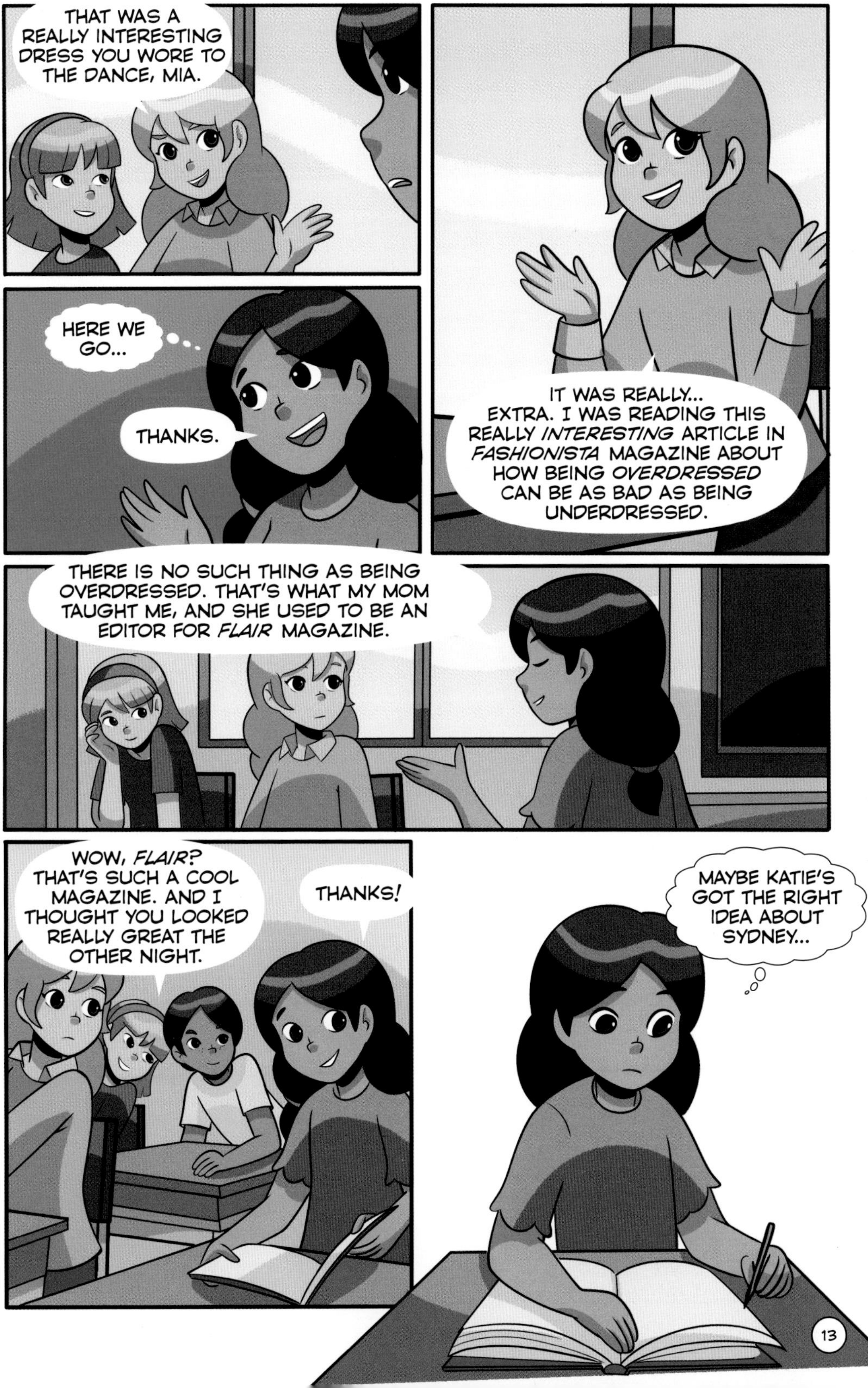
THAT WAS A REALLY INTERESTING DRESS YOU WORE TO THE DANCE, MIA.
IT WAS REALLY... EXTRA. I WAS READING THIS REALLY *INTERESTING* ARTICLE IN *FASHIONISTA* MAGAZINE ABOUT HOW BEING *OVERDRESSED* CAN BE AS BAD AS BEING UNDERDRESSED.
HERE WE GO...
THANKS.
THERE IS NO SUCH THING AS BEING OVERDRESSED. THAT'S WHAT MY MOM TAUGHT ME, AND SHE USED TO BE AN EDITOR FOR *FLAIR* MAGAZINE.
WOW, *FLAIR*? THAT'S SUCH A COOL MAGAZINE. AND I THOUGHT YOU LOOKED REALLY GREAT THE OTHER NIGHT.
THANKS!
MAYBE KATIE'S GOT THE RIGHT IDEA ABOUT SYDNEY...

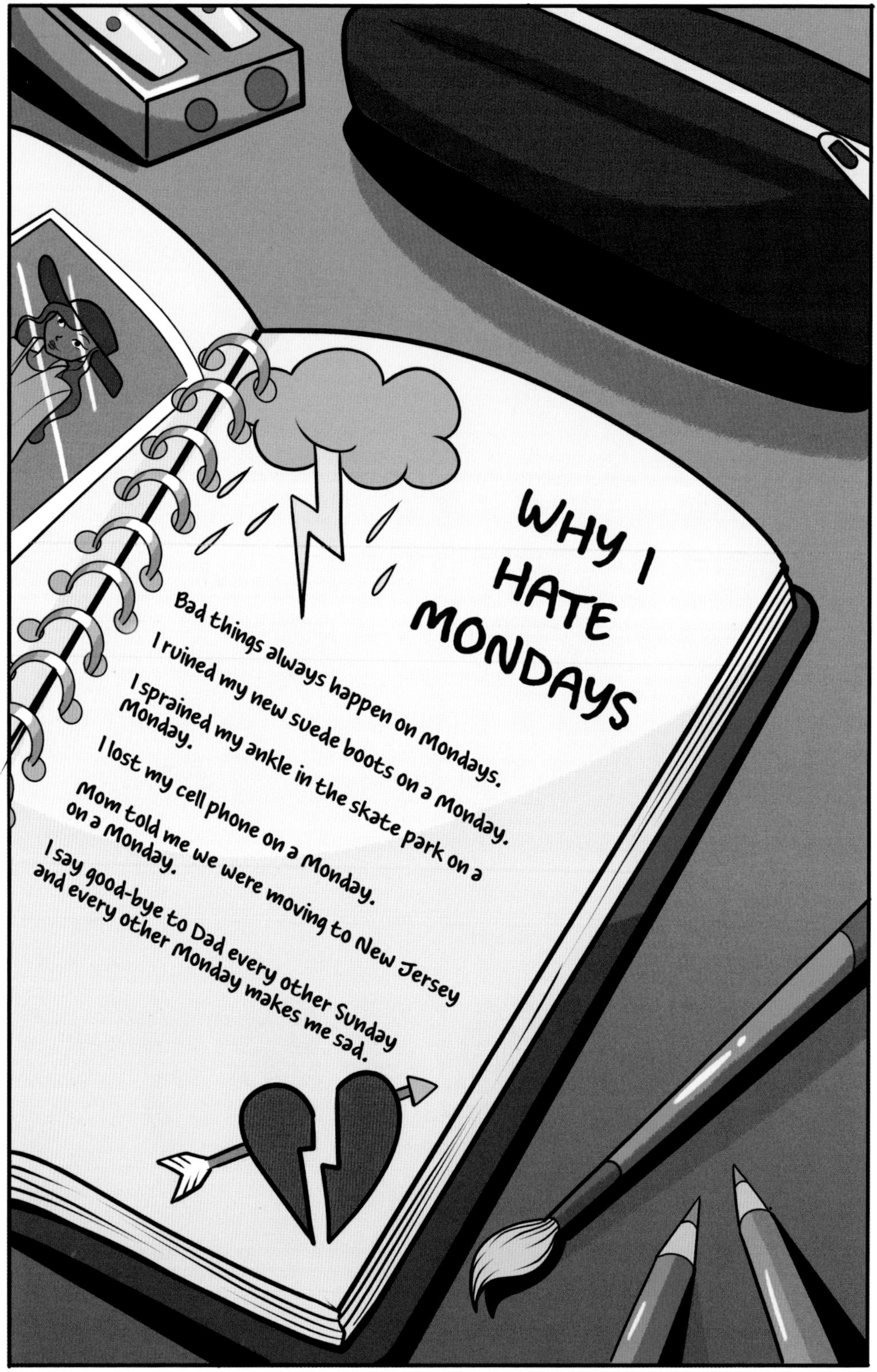
WHY I HATE MONDAYS
Bad things always happen on Mondays.
I ruined my new suede boots on a Monday.
I sprained my ankle in the skate park on a Monday.
I lost my cell phone on a Monday.
Mom told me we were moving to New Jersey on a Monday.
I say good-bye to Dad every other Sunday and every other Monday makes me sad.

Chapter 2

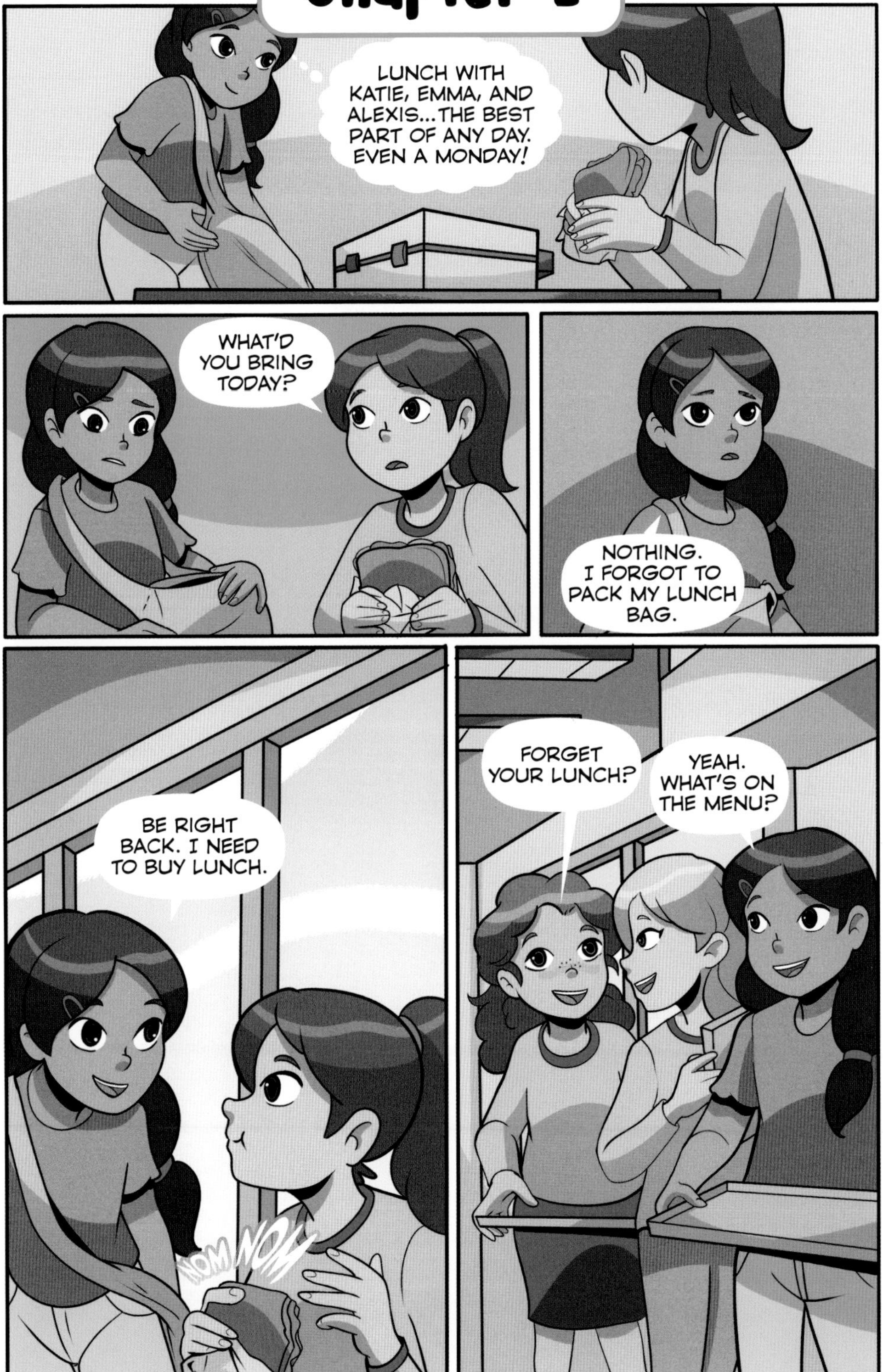
LUNCH WITH KATIE, EMMA, AND ALEXIS...THE BEST PART OF ANY DAY. EVEN A MONDAY!
WHAT'D YOU BRING TODAY?
NOTHING. I FORGOT TO PACK MY LUNCH BAG.
BE RIGHT BACK. I NEED TO BUY LUNCH.
NOM NOM
FORGET YOUR LUNCH?
YEAH. WHAT'S ON THE MENU?

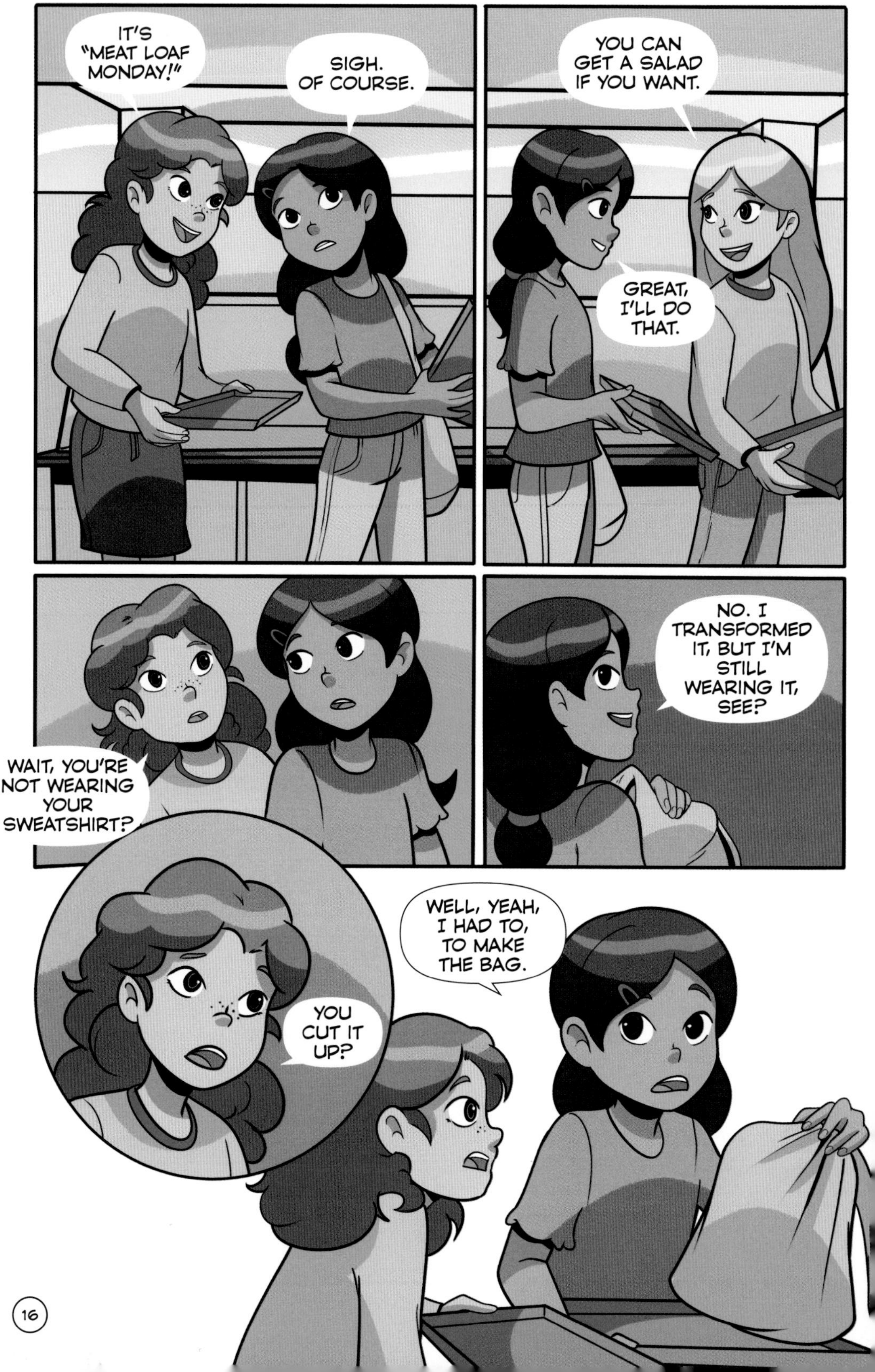
IT'S "MEAT LOAF MONDAY!"
SIGH. OF COURSE.
YOU CAN GET A SALAD IF YOU WANT.
GREAT, I'LL DO THAT.
WAIT, YOU'RE NOT WEARING YOUR SWEATSHIRT?
NO. I TRANSFORMED IT, BUT I'M STILL WEARING IT, SEE?
YOU CUT IT UP?
WELL, YEAH, I HAD TO, TO MAKE THE BAG.

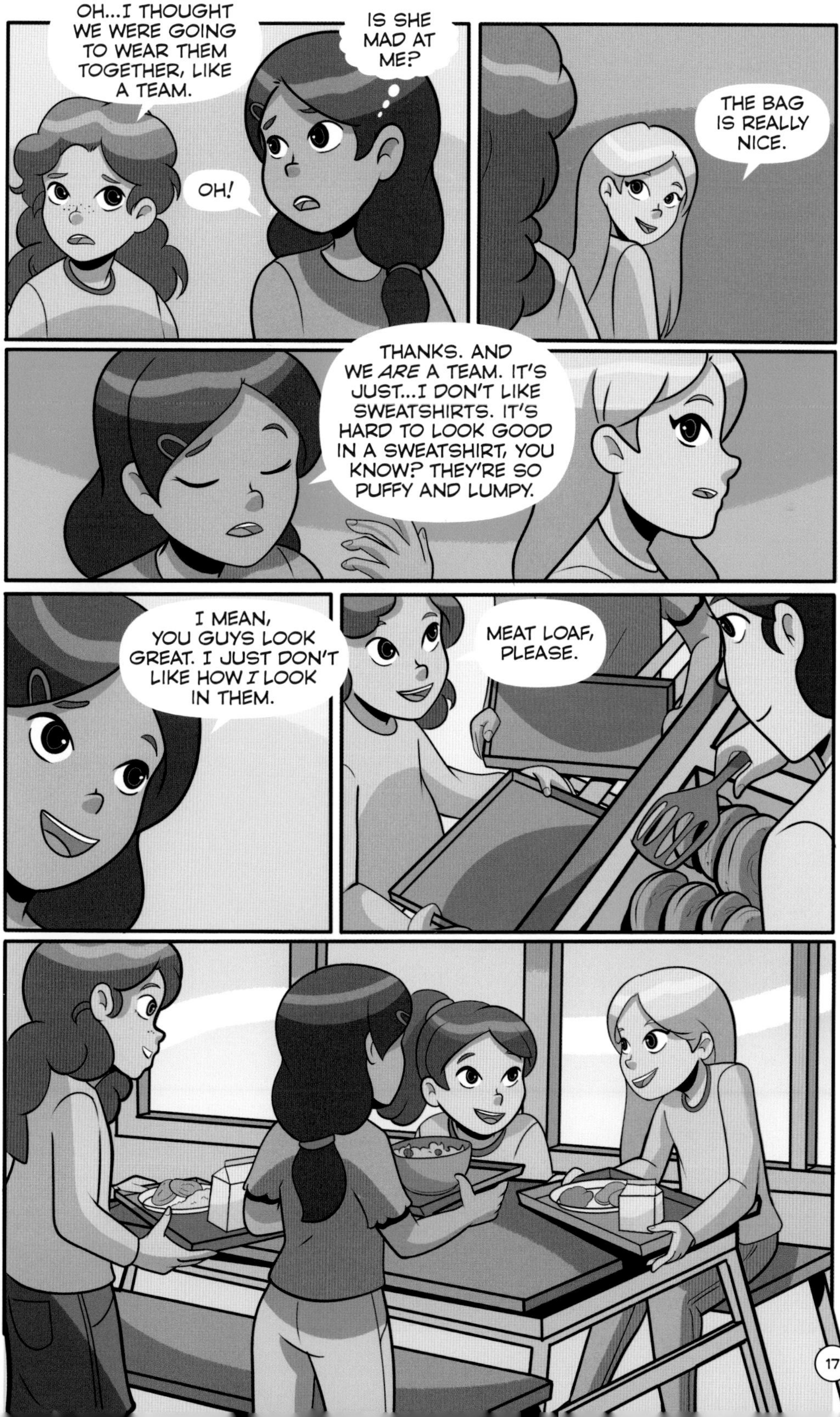
OH...I THOUGHT WE WERE GOING TO WEAR THEM TOGETHER, LIKE A TEAM.
IS SHE MAD AT ME?
OH!
THE BAG IS REALLY NICE.
THANKS. AND WE *ARE* A TEAM. IT'S JUST...I DON'T LIKE SWEATSHIRTS. IT'S HARD TO LOOK GOOD IN A SWEATSHIRT, YOU KNOW? THEY'RE SO PUFFY AND LUMPY.
I MEAN, YOU GUYS LOOK GREAT. I JUST DON'T LIKE HOW *I* LOOK IN THEM.
MEAT LOAF, PLEASE.

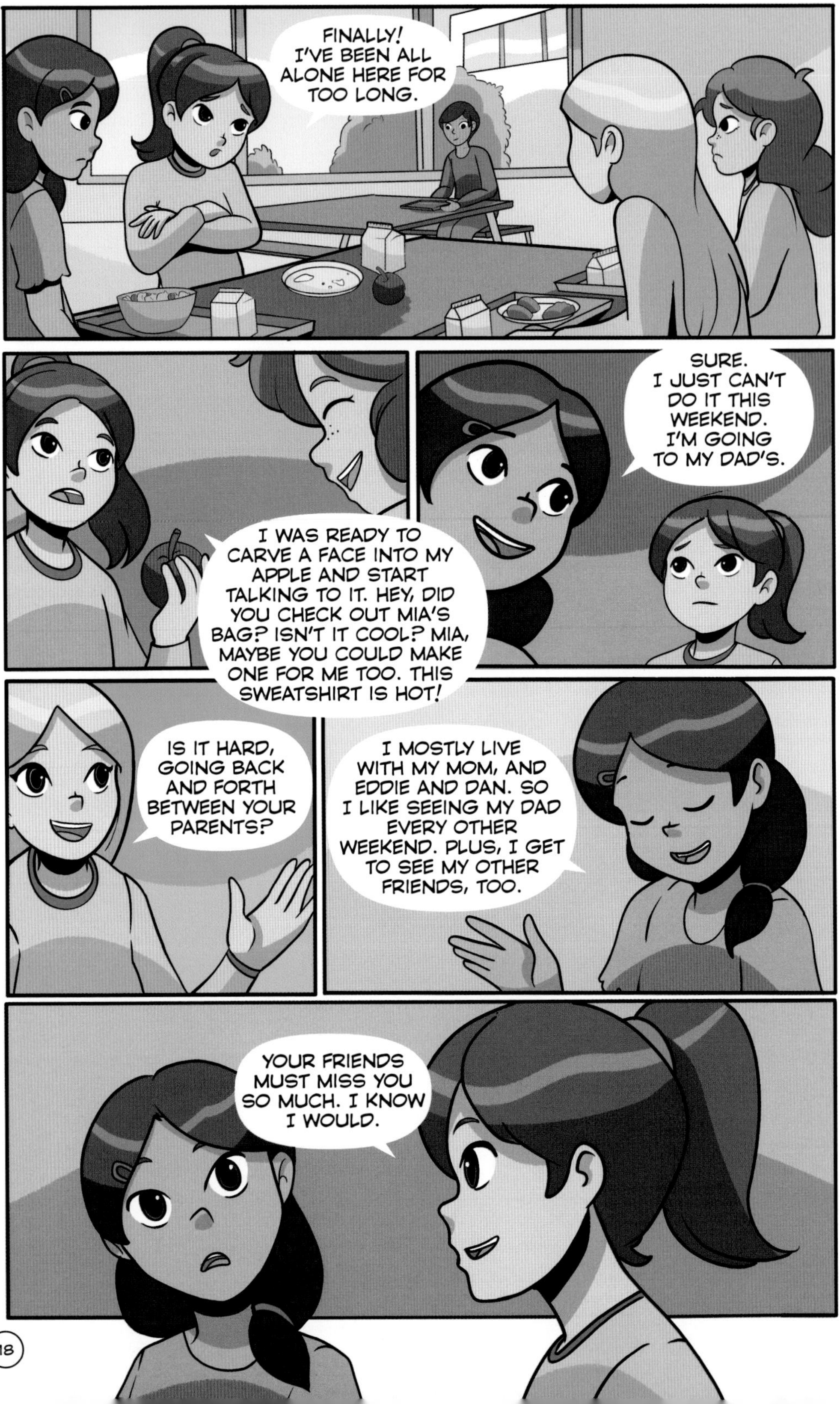
FINALLY! I'VE BEEN ALL ALONE HERE FOR TOO LONG.
I WAS READY TO CARVE A FACE INTO MY APPLE AND START TALKING TO IT. HEY, DID YOU CHECK OUT MIA'S BAG? ISN'T IT COOL? MIA, MAYBE YOU COULD MAKE ONE FOR ME TOO. THIS SWEATSHIRT IS HOT!
SURE. I JUST CAN'T DO IT THIS WEEKEND. I'M GOING TO MY DAD'S.
IS IT HARD, GOING BACK AND FORTH BETWEEN YOUR PARENTS?
I MOSTLY LIVE WITH MY MOM, AND EDDIE AND DAN. SO I LIKE SEEING MY DAD EVERY OTHER WEEKEND. PLUS, I GET TO SEE MY OTHER FRIENDS, TOO.
YOUR FRIENDS MUST MISS YOU SO MUCH. I KNOW I WOULD.

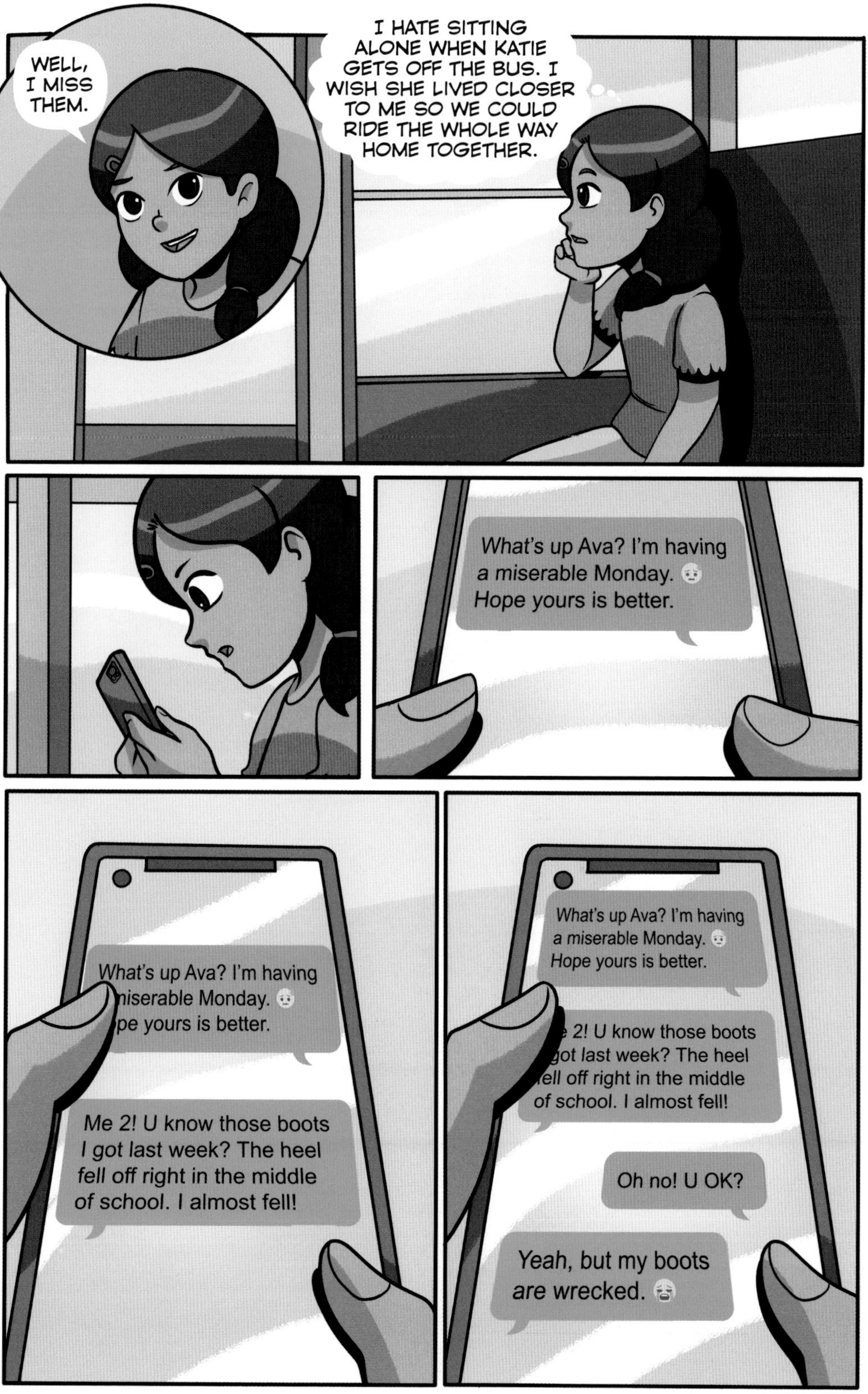
WELL, I MISS THEM.
I HATE SITTING ALONE WHEN KATIE GETS OFF THE BUS. I WISH SHE LIVED CLOSER TO ME SO WE COULD RIDE THE WHOLE WAY HOME TOGETHER.
What's up Ava? I'm having a miserable Monday. Hope yours is better.
What's up Ava? I'm having
iserable Monday.
pe yours is better.
Me 2! U know those boots I got last week? The heel fell off right in the middle of school. I almost fell!
What's up Ava? I'm having a miserable Monday. Hope yours is better.
e 2! U know those boots
got last week? The heel
ell off right in the middle
of school. I almost fell!
Oh no! U OK?
Yeah, but my boots are wrecked.

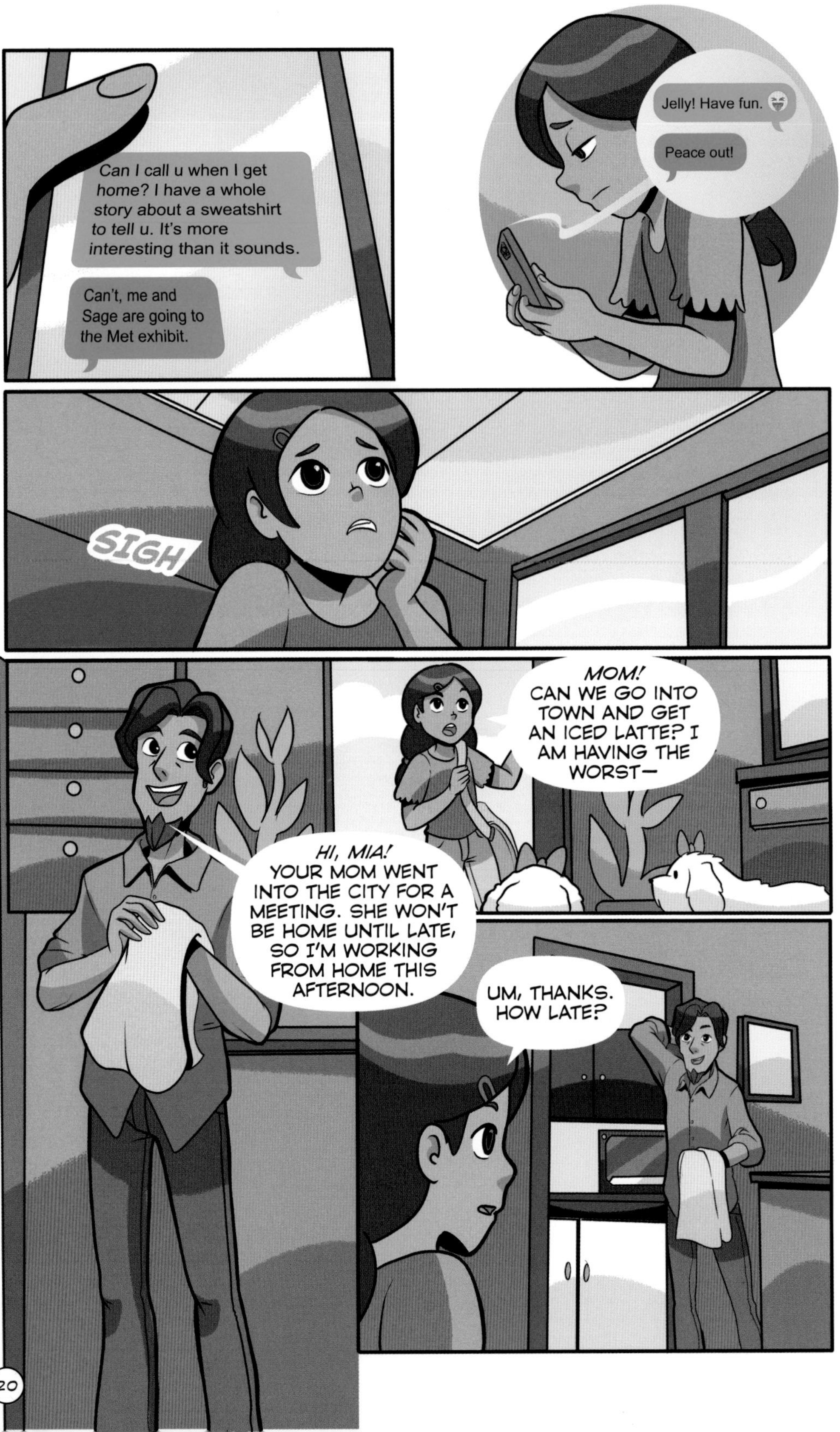
Can I call u when I get home? I have a whole story about a sweatshirt to tell u. It's more interesting than it sounds.
Can't, me and Sage are going to the Met exhibit.
Jelly! Have fun.
Peace out!
SIGH
MOM! CAN WE GO INTO TOWN AND GET AN ICED LATTE? I AM HAVING THE WORST—
HI, MIA! YOUR MOM WENT INTO THE CITY FOR A MEETING. SHE WON'T BE HOME UNTIL LATE, SO I'M WORKING FROM HOME THIS AFTERNOON.
UM, THANKS. HOW LATE?

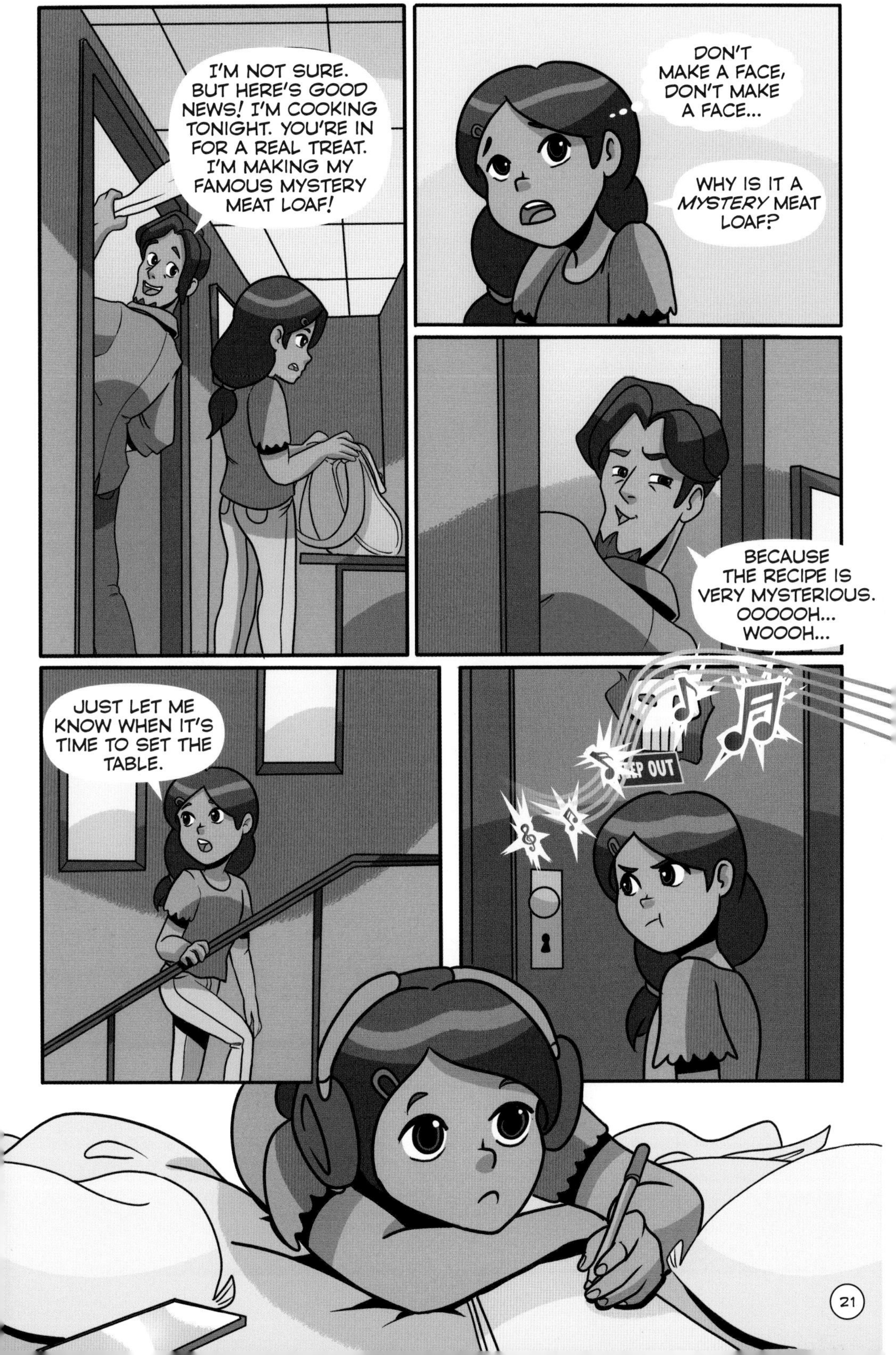

I'M NOT SURE. BUT HERE'S GOOD NEWS! I'M COOKING TONIGHT. YOU'RE IN FOR A REAL TREAT. I'M MAKING MY FAMOUS MYSTERY MEAT LOAF!
DON'T MAKE A FACE, DON'T MAKE A FACE...
WHY IS IT A *MYSTERY* MEAT LOAF?
BECAUSE THE RECIPE IS VERY MYSTERIOUS. OOOOOH... WOOOH...
JUST LET ME KNOW WHEN IT'S TIME TO SET THE TABLE.

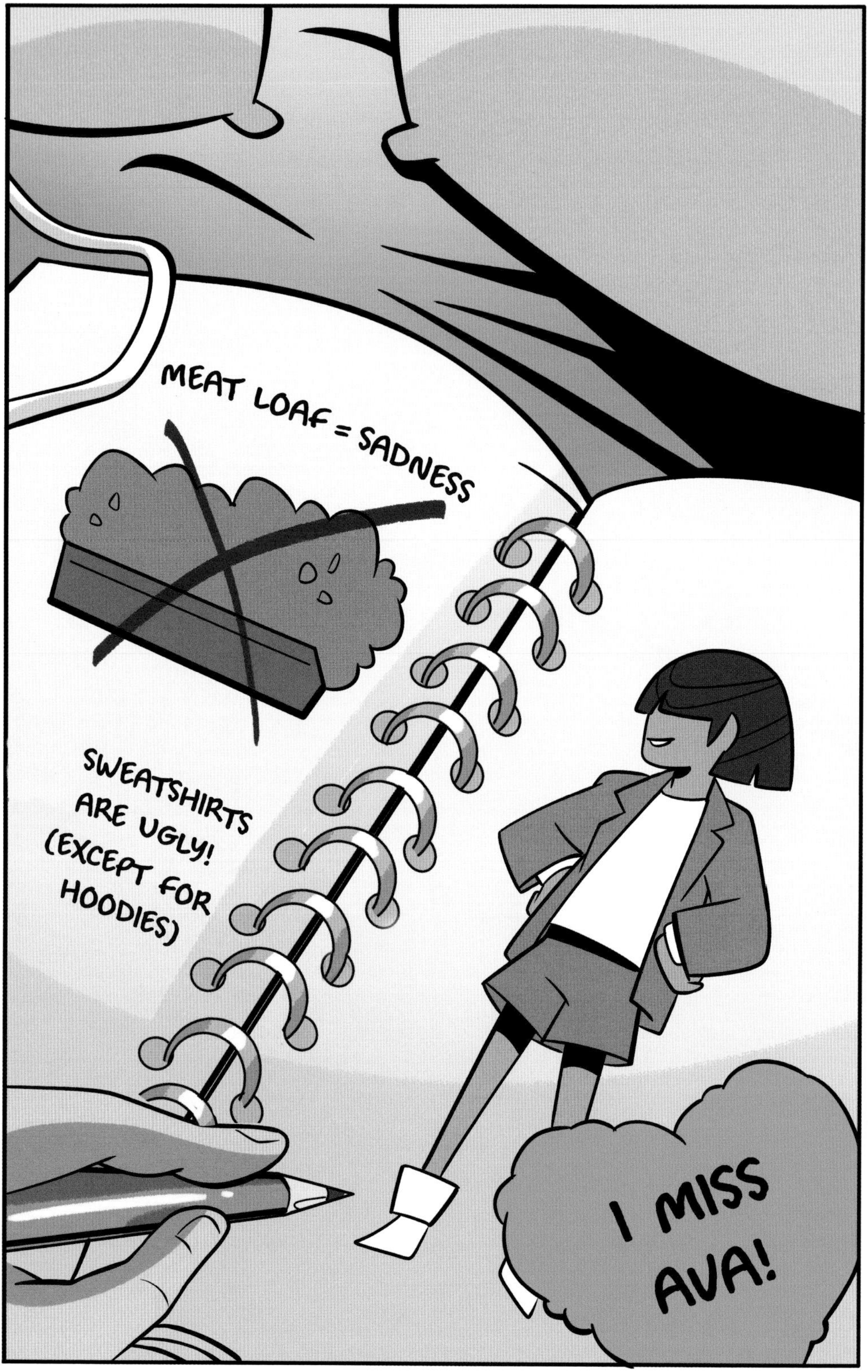
MEAT LOAF = SADNESS
SWEATSHIRTS ARE UGLY! (EXCEPT FOR HOODIES)
I MISS AVA!

Chapter 3

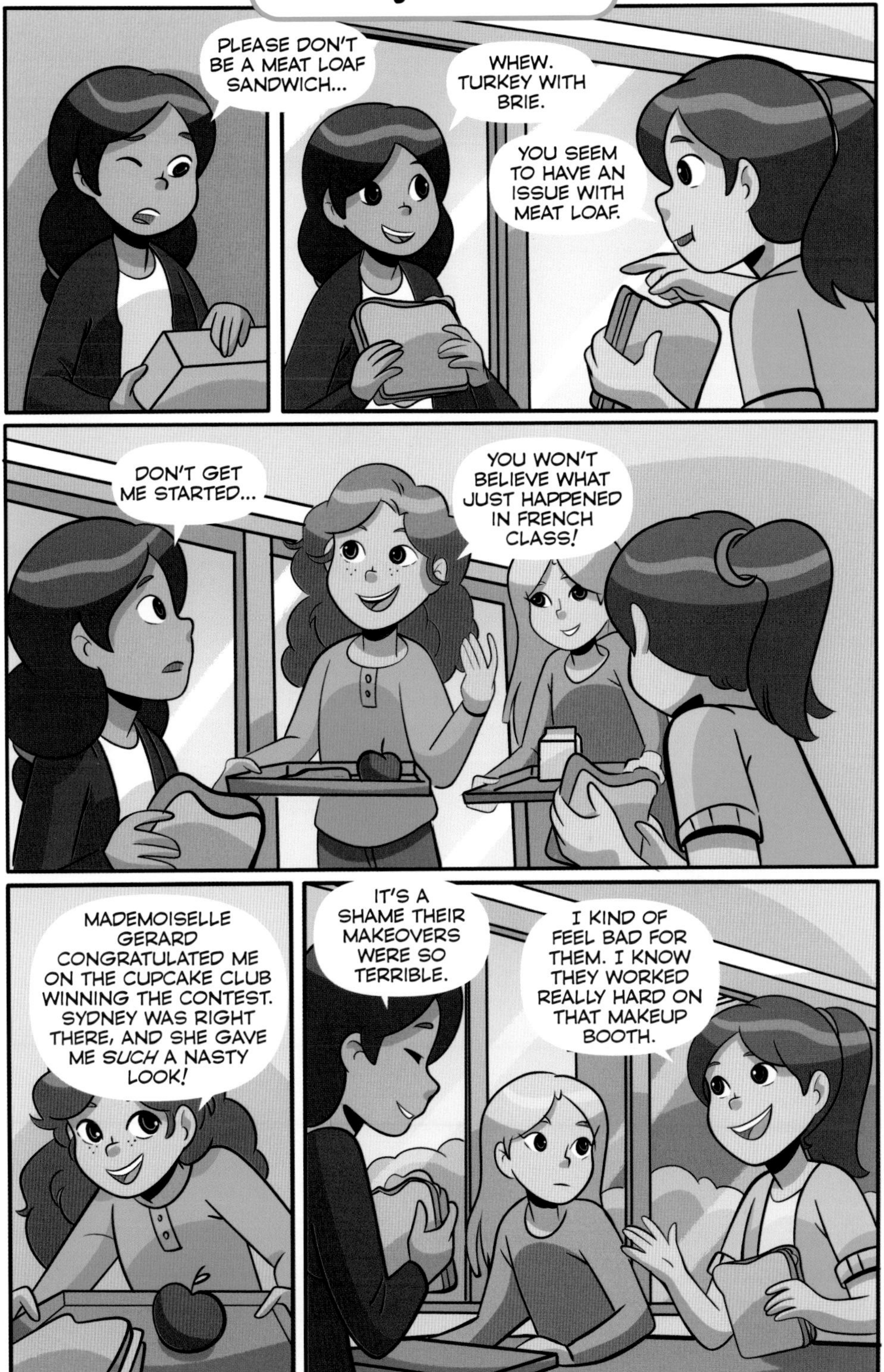

PLEASE DON'T BE A MEAT LOAF SANDWICH...
WHEW. TURKEY WITH BRIE.
YOU SEEM TO HAVE AN ISSUE WITH MEAT LOAF.
DON'T GET ME STARTED...
YOU WON'T BELIEVE WHAT JUST HAPPENED IN FRENCH CLASS!
MADEMOISELLE GERARD CONGRATULATED ME ON THE CUPCAKE CLUB WINNING THE CONTEST. SYDNEY WAS RIGHT THERE, AND SHE GAVE ME *SUCH* A NASTY LOOK!
IT'S A SHAME THEIR MAKEOVERS WERE SO TERRIBLE.
I KIND OF FEEL BAD FOR THEM. I KNOW THEY WORKED REALLY HARD ON THAT MAKEUP BOOTH.

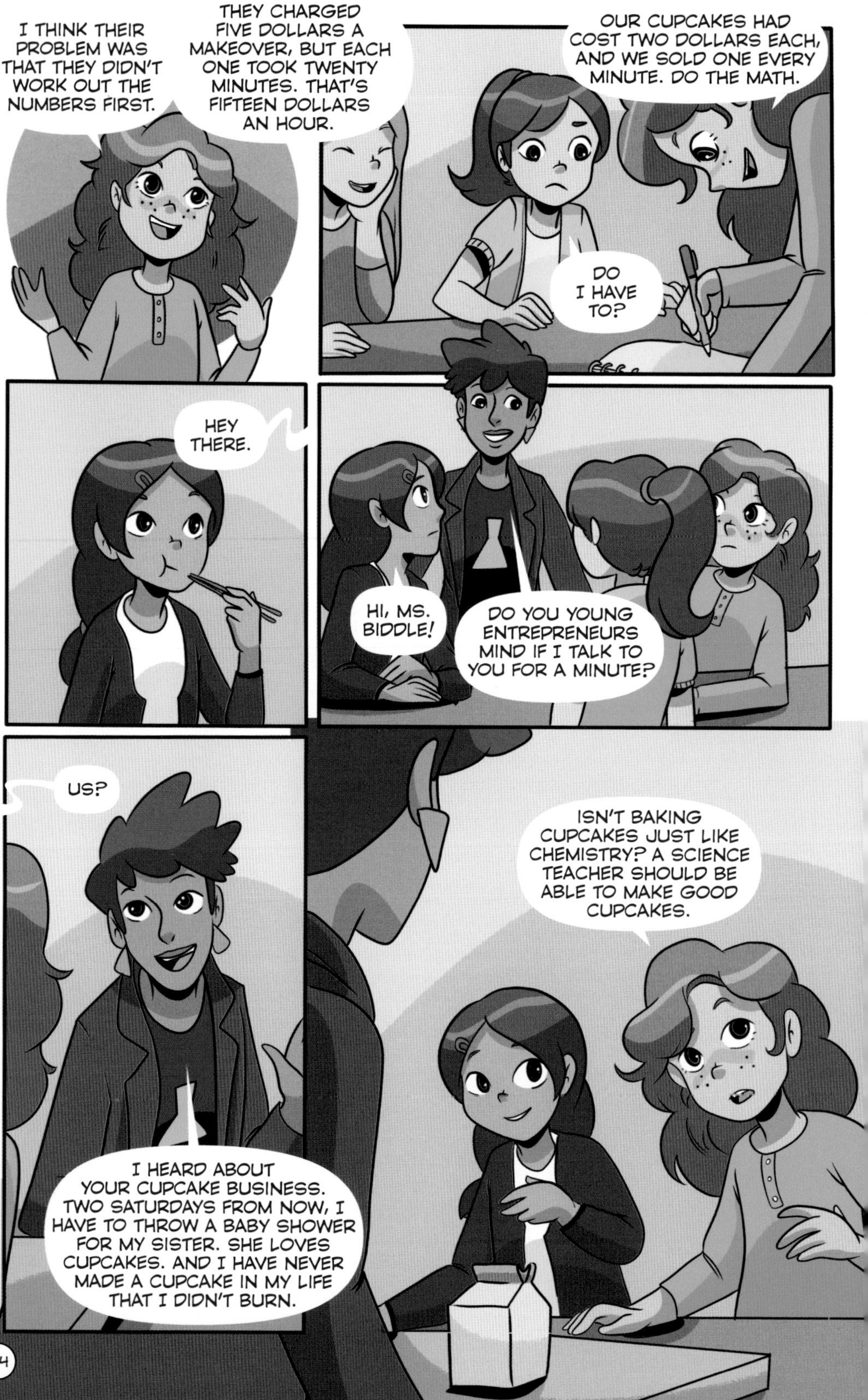
I THINK THEIR PROBLEM WAS THAT THEY DIDN'T WORK OUT THE NUMBERS FIRST.
THEY CHARGED FIVE DOLLARS A MAKEOVER, BUT EACH ONE TOOK TWENTY MINUTES. THAT'S FIFTEEN DOLLARS AN HOUR.
OUR CUPCAKES HAD COST TWO DOLLARS EACH, AND WE SOLD ONE EVERY MINUTE. DO THE MATH.
DO I HAVE TO?
HEY THERE.
HI, MS. BIDDLE!
DO YOU YOUNG ENTREPRENEURS MIND IF I TALK TO YOU FOR A MINUTE?
US?
I HEARD ABOUT YOUR CUPCAKE BUSINESS. TWO SATURDAYS FROM NOW, I HAVE TO THROW A BABY SHOWER FOR MY SISTER. SHE LOVES CUPCAKES. AND I HAVE NEVER MADE A CUPCAKE IN MY LIFE THAT I DIDN'T BURN.
ISN'T BAKING CUPCAKES JUST LIKE CHEMISTRY? A SCIENCE TEACHER SHOULD BE ABLE TO MAKE GOOD CUPCAKES.

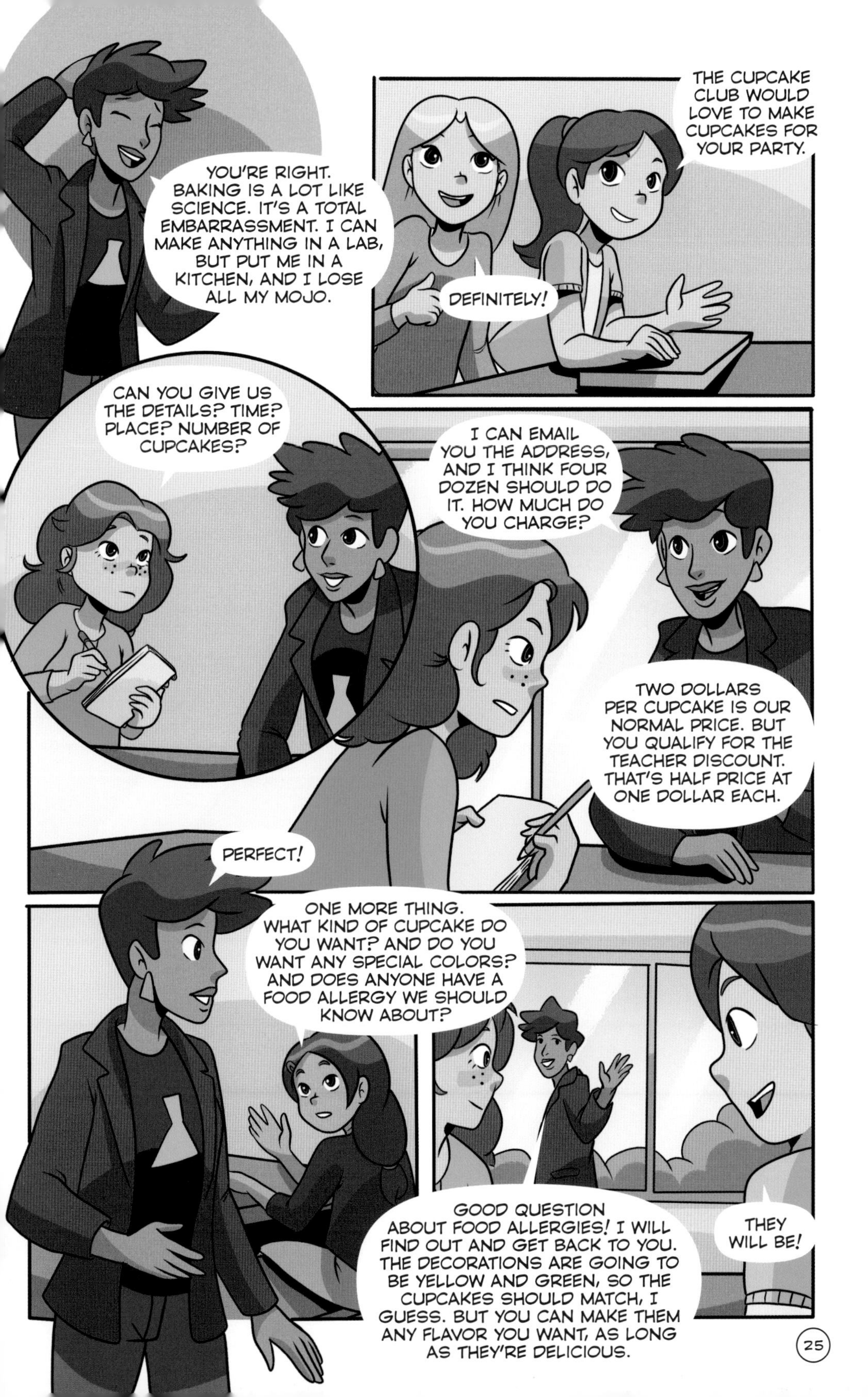
YOU'RE RIGHT. BAKING IS A LOT LIKE SCIENCE. IT'S A TOTAL EMBARRASSMENT. I CAN MAKE ANYTHING IN A LAB, BUT PUT ME IN A KITCHEN, AND I LOSE ALL MY MOJO.
THE CUPCAKE CLUB WOULD LOVE TO MAKE CUPCAKES FOR YOUR PARTY.
DEFINITELY!
CAN YOU GIVE US THE DETAILS? TIME? PLACE? NUMBER OF CUPCAKES?
I CAN EMAIL YOU THE ADDRESS, AND I THINK FOUR DOZEN SHOULD DO IT. HOW MUCH DO YOU CHARGE?
TWO DOLLARS PER CUPCAKE IS OUR NORMAL PRICE. BUT YOU QUALIFY FOR THE TEACHER DISCOUNT. THAT'S HALF PRICE AT ONE DOLLAR EACH.
PERFECT!
ONE MORE THING. WHAT KIND OF CUPCAKE DO YOU WANT? AND DO YOU WANT ANY SPECIAL COLORS? AND DOES ANYONE HAVE A FOOD ALLERGY WE SHOULD KNOW ABOUT?
GOOD QUESTION ABOUT FOOD ALLERGIES! I WILL FIND OUT AND GET BACK TO YOU. THE DECORATIONS ARE GOING TO BE YELLOW AND GREEN, SO THE CUPCAKES SHOULD MATCH, I GUESS. BUT YOU CAN MAKE THEM ANY FLAVOR YOU WANT, AS LONG AS THEY'RE DELICIOUS.
THEY WILL BE!

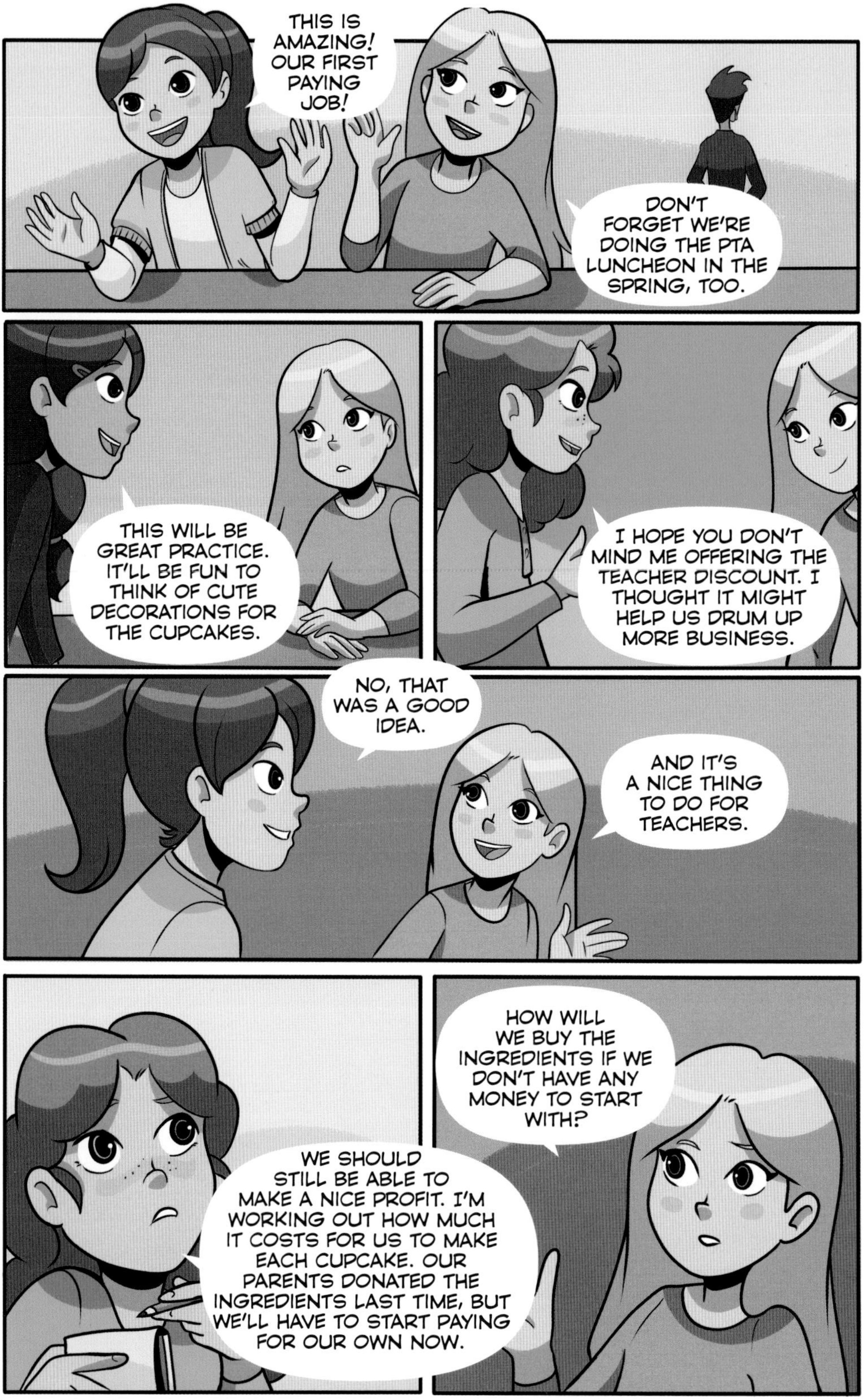
THIS IS AMAZING! OUR FIRST PAYING JOB!
DON'T FORGET WE'RE DOING THE PTA LUNCHEON IN THE SPRING, TOO.
THIS WILL BE GREAT PRACTICE. IT'LL BE FUN TO THINK OF CUTE DECORATIONS FOR THE CUPCAKES.
I HOPE YOU DON'T MIND ME OFFERING THE TEACHER DISCOUNT. I THOUGHT IT MIGHT HELP US DRUM UP MORE BUSINESS.
NO, THAT WAS A GOOD IDEA.
AND IT'S A NICE THING TO DO FOR TEACHERS.
HOW WILL WE BUY THE INGREDIENTS IF WE DON'T HAVE ANY MONEY TO START WITH?
WE SHOULD STILL BE ABLE TO MAKE A NICE PROFIT. I'M WORKING OUT HOW MUCH IT COSTS FOR US TO MAKE EACH CUPCAKE. OUR PARENTS DONATED THE INGREDIENTS LAST TIME, BUT WE'LL HAVE TO START PAYING FOR OUR OWN NOW.

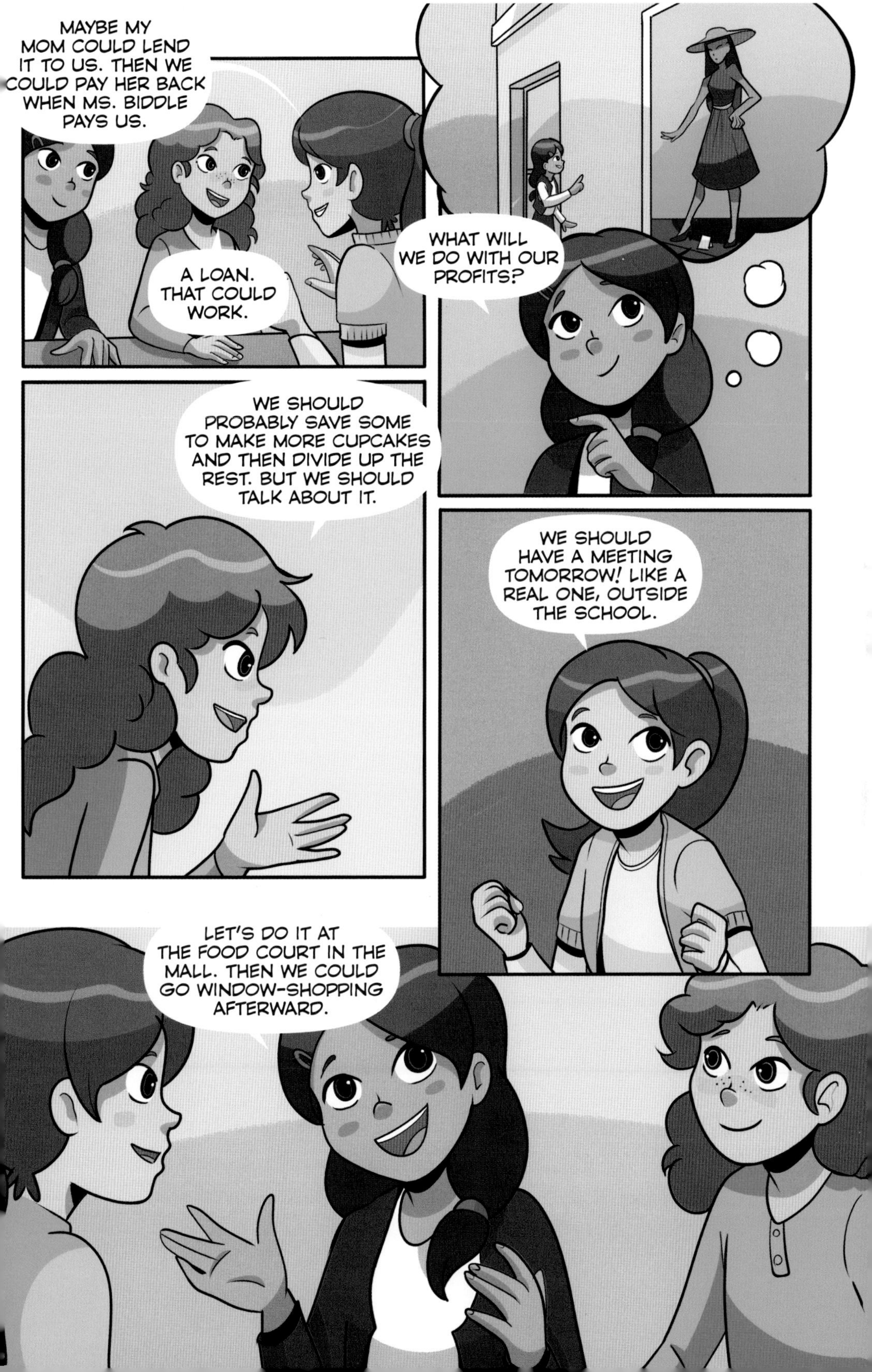
MAYBE MY MOM COULD LEND IT TO US. THEN WE COULD PAY HER BACK WHEN MS. BIDDLE PAYS US.
A LOAN. THAT COULD WORK.
WHAT WILL WE DO WITH OUR PROFITS?
WE SHOULD PROBABLY SAVE SOME TO MAKE MORE CUPCAKES AND THEN DIVIDE UP THE REST. BUT WE SHOULD TALK ABOUT IT.
WE SHOULD HAVE A MEETING TOMORROW! LIKE A REAL ONE, OUTSIDE THE SCHOOL.
LET'S DO IT AT THE FOOD COURT IN THE MALL. THEN WE COULD GO WINDOW-SHOPPING AFTERWARD.

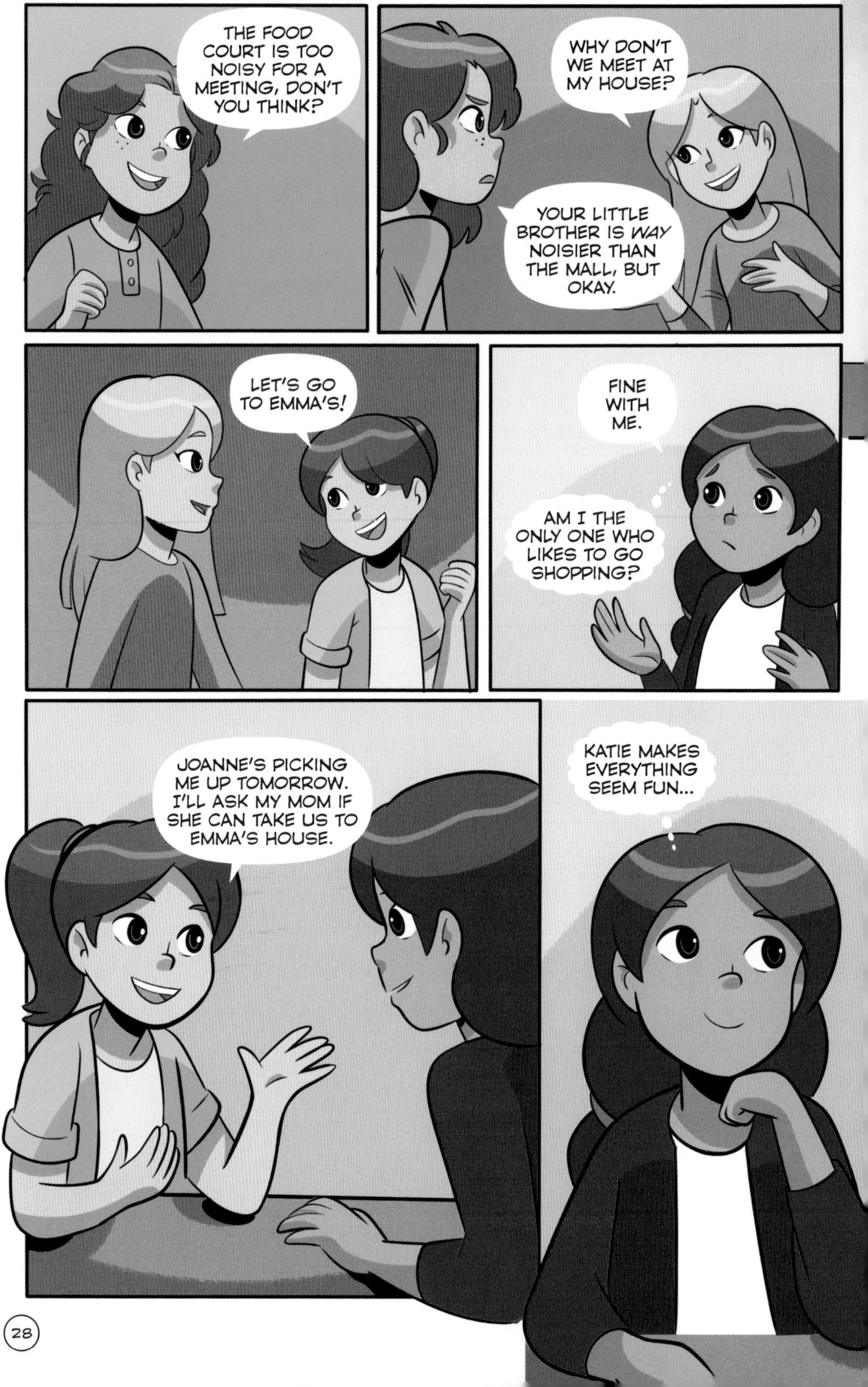
THE FOOD COURT IS TOO NOISY FOR A MEETING, DON'T YOU THINK?
WHY DON'T WE MEET AT MY HOUSE?
YOUR LITTLE BROTHER IS *WAY* NOISIER THAN THE MALL, BUT OKAY.
LET'S GO TO EMMA'S!
FINE WITH ME.
AM I THE ONLY ONE WHO LIKES TO GO SHOPPING?
JOANNE'S PICKING ME UP TOMORROW. I'LL ASK MY MOM IF SHE CAN TAKE US TO EMMA'S HOUSE.
KATIE MAKES EVERYTHING SEEM FUN...

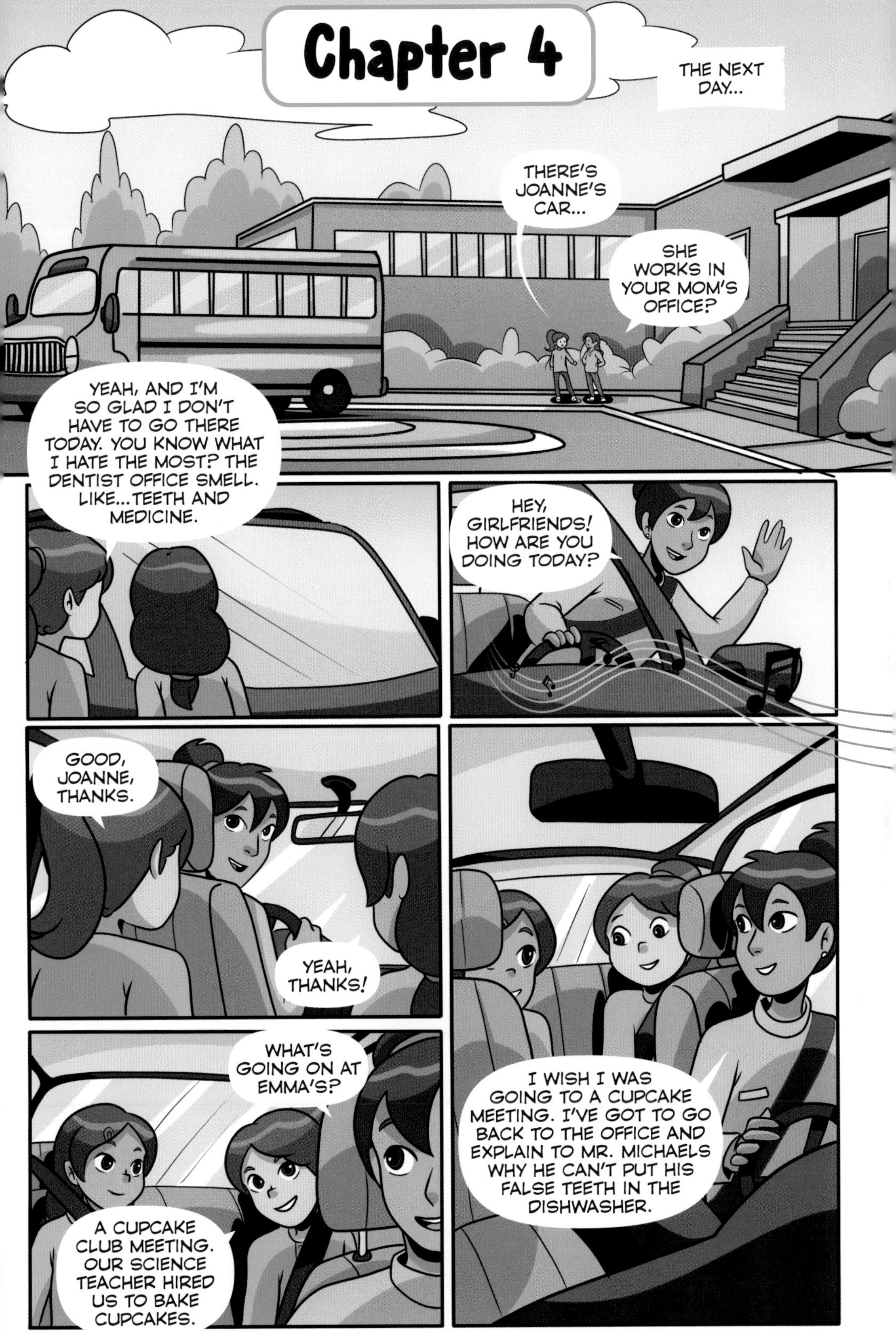
Chapter 4
THE NEXT DAY...
THERE'S JOANNE'S CAR...
SHE WORKS IN YOUR MOM'S OFFICE?
YEAH, AND I'M SO GLAD I DON'T HAVE TO GO THERE TODAY. YOU KNOW WHAT I HATE THE MOST? THE DENTIST OFFICE SMELL. LIKE...TEETH AND MEDICINE.
HEY, GIRLFRIENDS! HOW ARE YOU DOING TODAY?
GOOD, JOANNE, THANKS.
YEAH, THANKS!
WHAT'S GOING ON AT EMMA'S?
A CUPCAKE CLUB MEETING. OUR SCIENCE TEACHER HIRED US TO BAKE CUPCAKES.
I WISH I WAS GOING TO A CUPCAKE MEETING. I'VE GOT TO GO BACK TO THE OFFICE AND EXPLAIN TO MR. MICHAELS WHY HE CAN'T PUT HIS FALSE TEETH IN THE DISHWASHER.

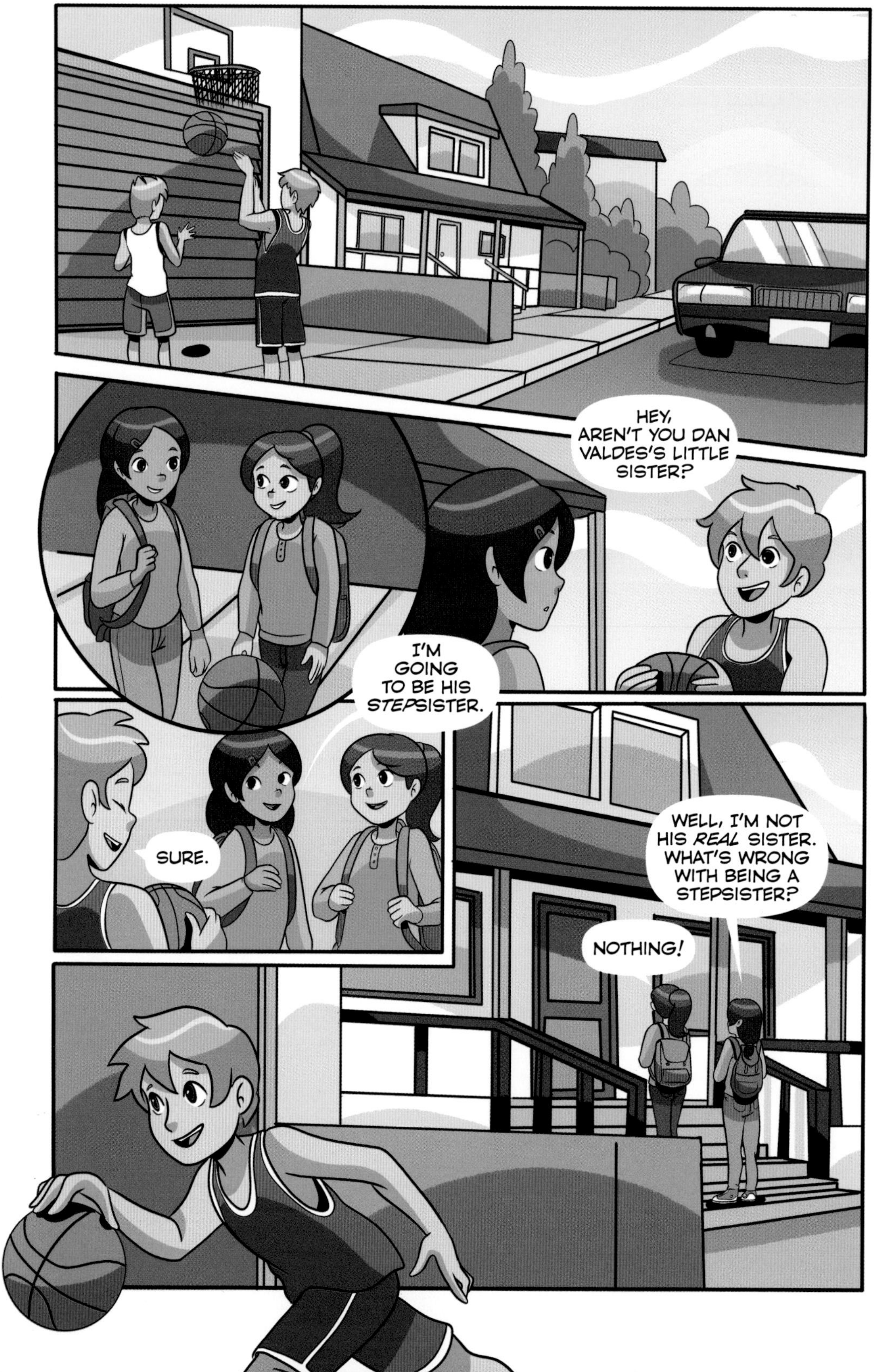
HEY, AREN'T YOU DAN VALDES'S LITTLE SISTER?
I'M GOING TO BE HIS STEPSISTER.
SURE.
WELL, I'M NOT HIS REAL SISTER. WHAT'S WRONG WITH BEING A STEPSISTER?
NOTHING!

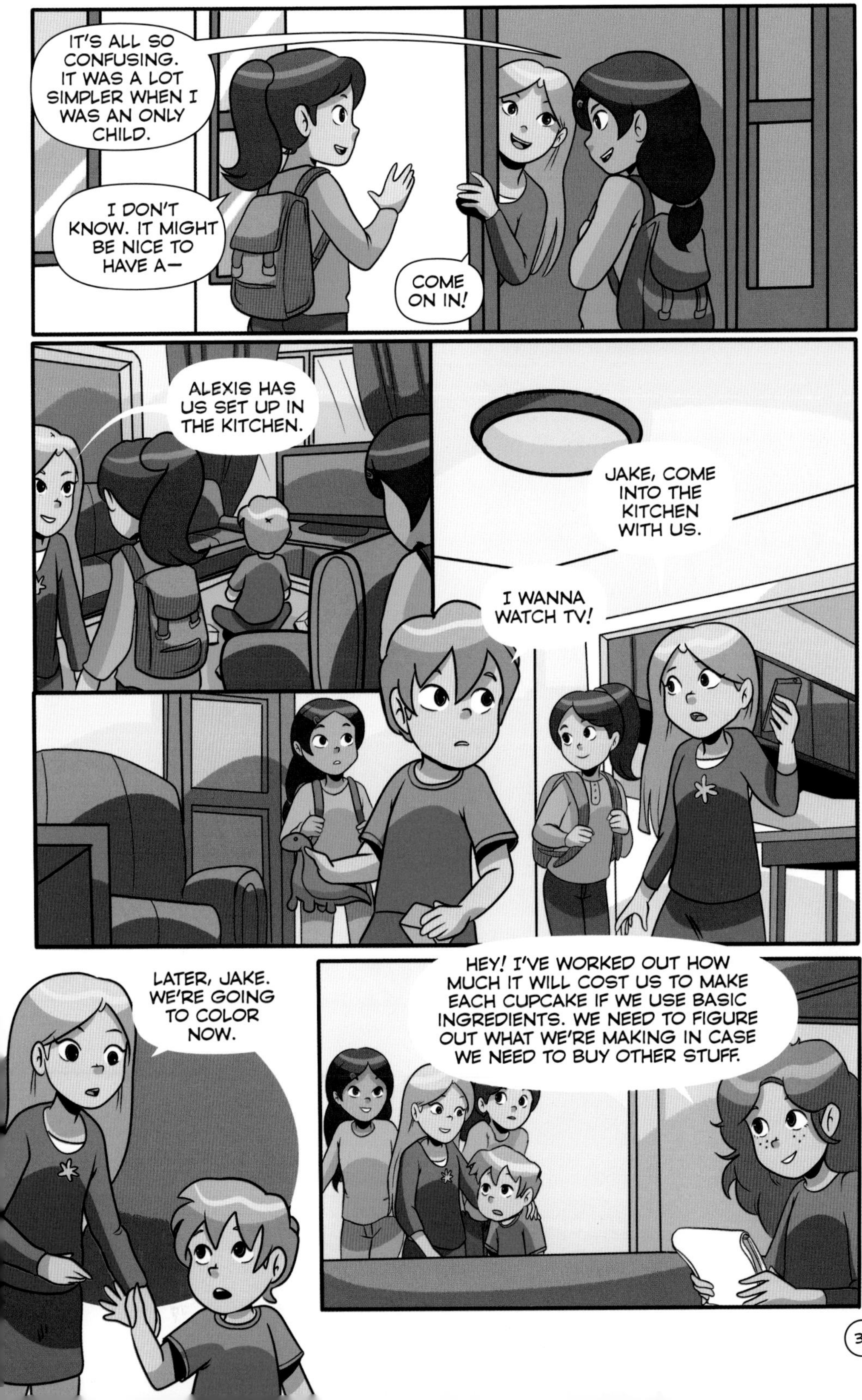
IT'S ALL SO CONFUSING. IT WAS A LOT SIMPLER WHEN I WAS AN ONLY CHILD.
I DON'T KNOW. IT MIGHT BE NICE TO HAVE A—
COME ON IN!
ALEXIS HAS US SET UP IN THE KITCHEN.
JAKE, COME INTO THE KITCHEN WITH US.
I WANNA WATCH TV!
LATER, JAKE. WE'RE GOING TO COLOR NOW.
HEY! I'VE WORKED OUT HOW MUCH IT WILL COST US TO MAKE EACH CUPCAKE IF WE USE BASIC INGREDIENTS. WE NEED TO FIGURE OUT WHAT WE'RE MAKING IN CASE WE NEED TO BUY OTHER STUFF.

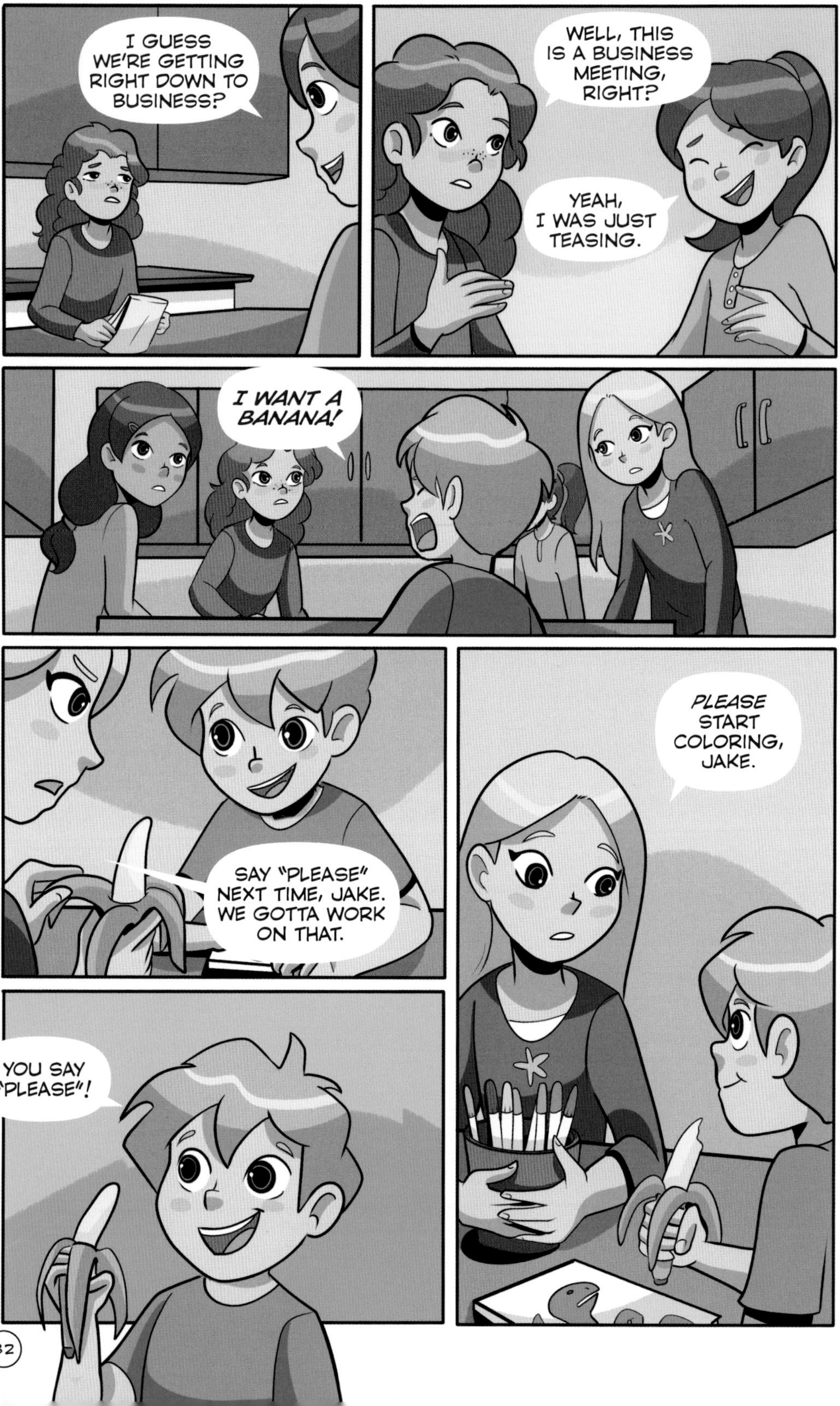
I GUESS WE'RE GETTING RIGHT DOWN TO BUSINESS?
WELL, THIS IS A BUSINESS MEETING, RIGHT?
YEAH, I WAS JUST TEASING.
I WANT A BANANA!
SAY "PLEASE" NEXT TIME, JAKE. WE GOTTA WORK ON THAT.
YOU SAY "PLEASE"!
PLEASE START COLORING, JAKE.

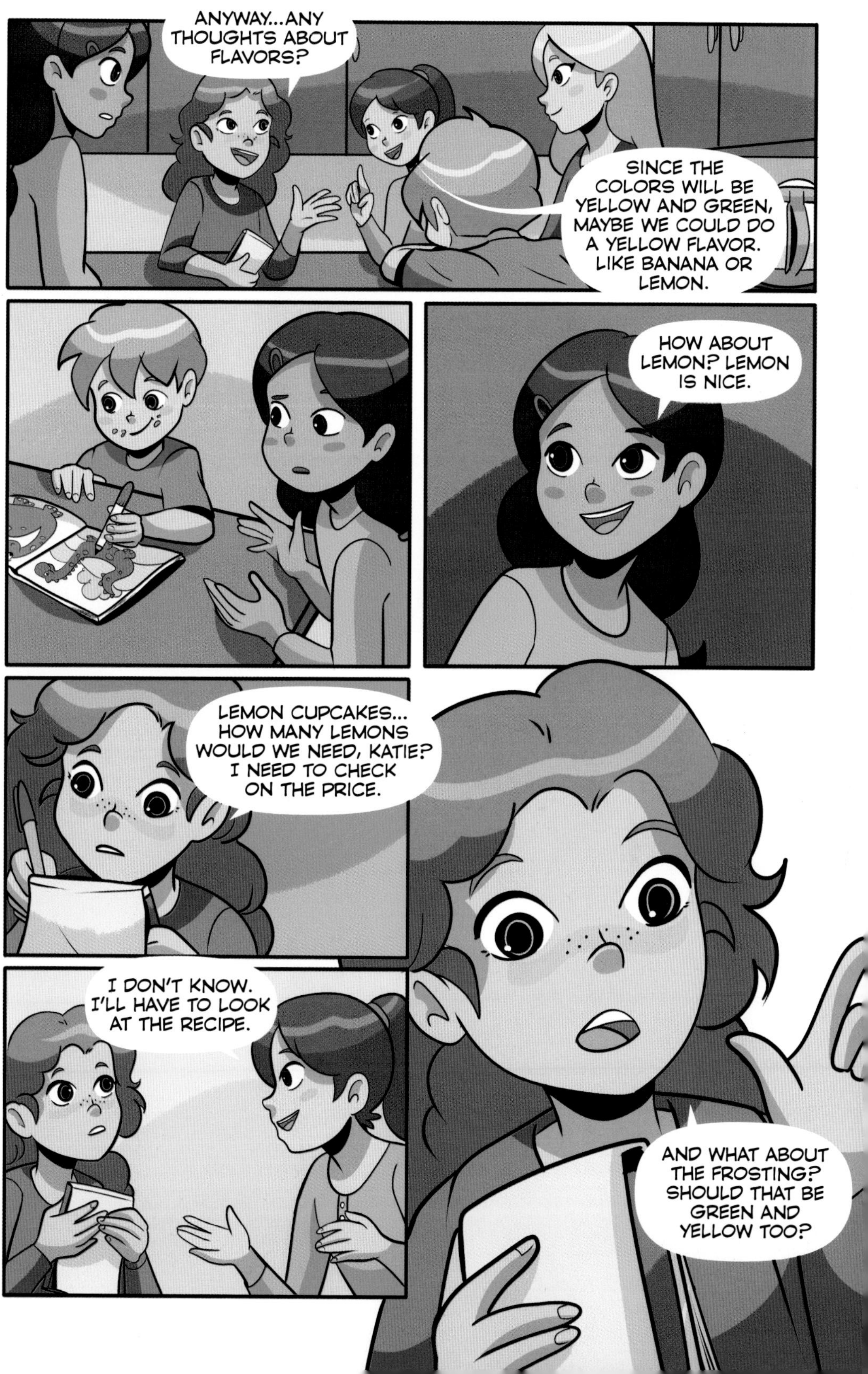
ANYWAY...ANY THOUGHTS ABOUT FLAVORS?
SINCE THE COLORS WILL BE YELLOW AND GREEN, MAYBE WE COULD DO A YELLOW FLAVOR. LIKE BANANA OR LEMON.
HOW ABOUT LEMON? LEMON IS NICE.
LEMON CUPCAKES... HOW MANY LEMONS WOULD WE NEED, KATIE? I NEED TO CHECK ON THE PRICE.
I DON'T KNOW. I'LL HAVE TO LOOK AT THE RECIPE.
AND WHAT ABOUT THE FROSTING? SHOULD THAT BE GREEN AND YELLOW TOO?

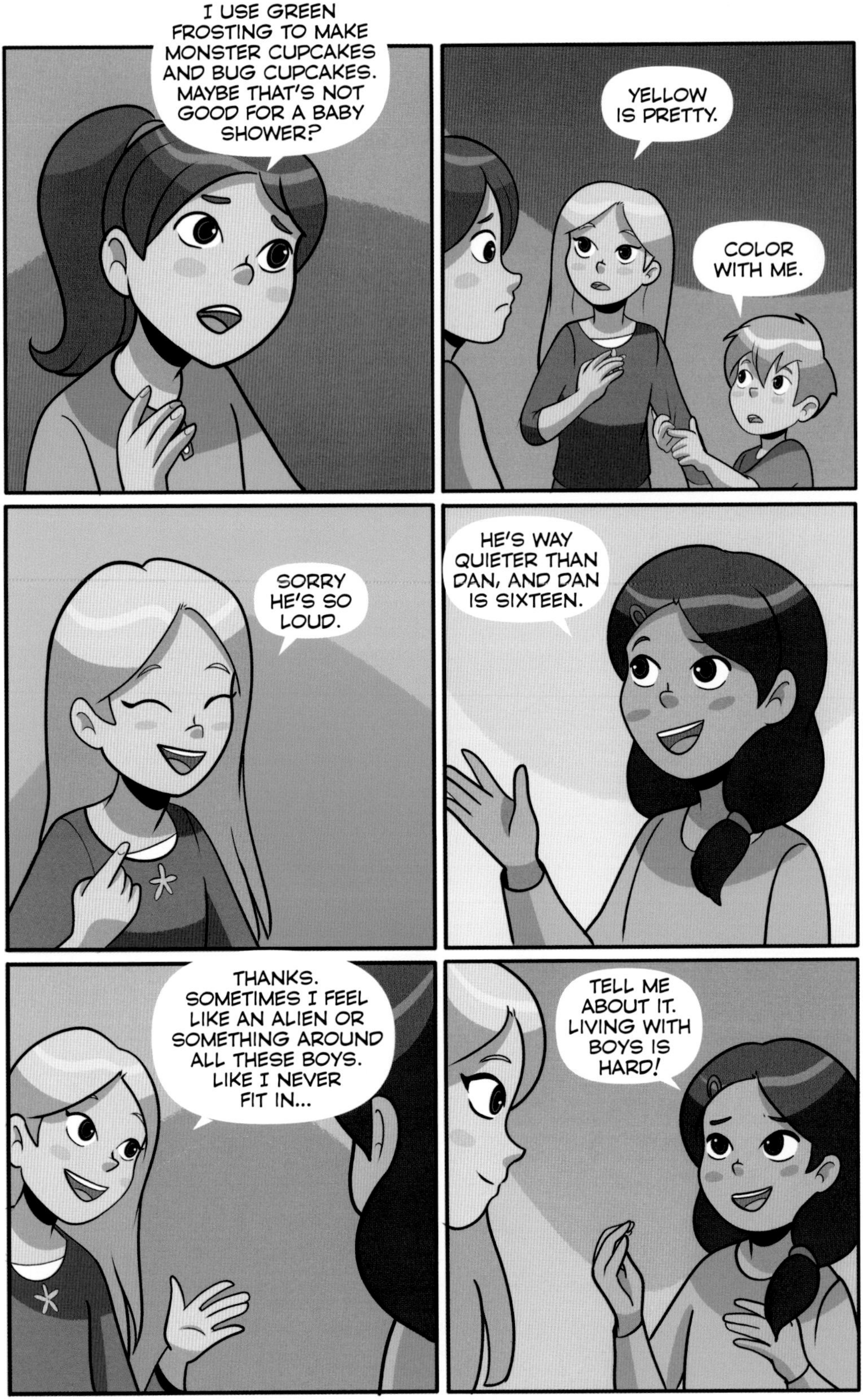
I USE GREEN FROSTING TO MAKE MONSTER CUPCAKES AND BUG CUPCAKES. MAYBE THAT'S NOT GOOD FOR A BABY SHOWER?
YELLOW IS PRETTY.
COLOR WITH ME.
SORRY HE'S SO LOUD.
HE'S WAY QUIETER THAN DAN, AND DAN IS SIXTEEN.
THANKS. SOMETIMES I FEEL LIKE AN ALIEN OR SOMETHING AROUND ALL THESE BOYS. LIKE I NEVER FIT IN...
TELL ME ABOUT IT. LIVING WITH BOYS IS HARD!

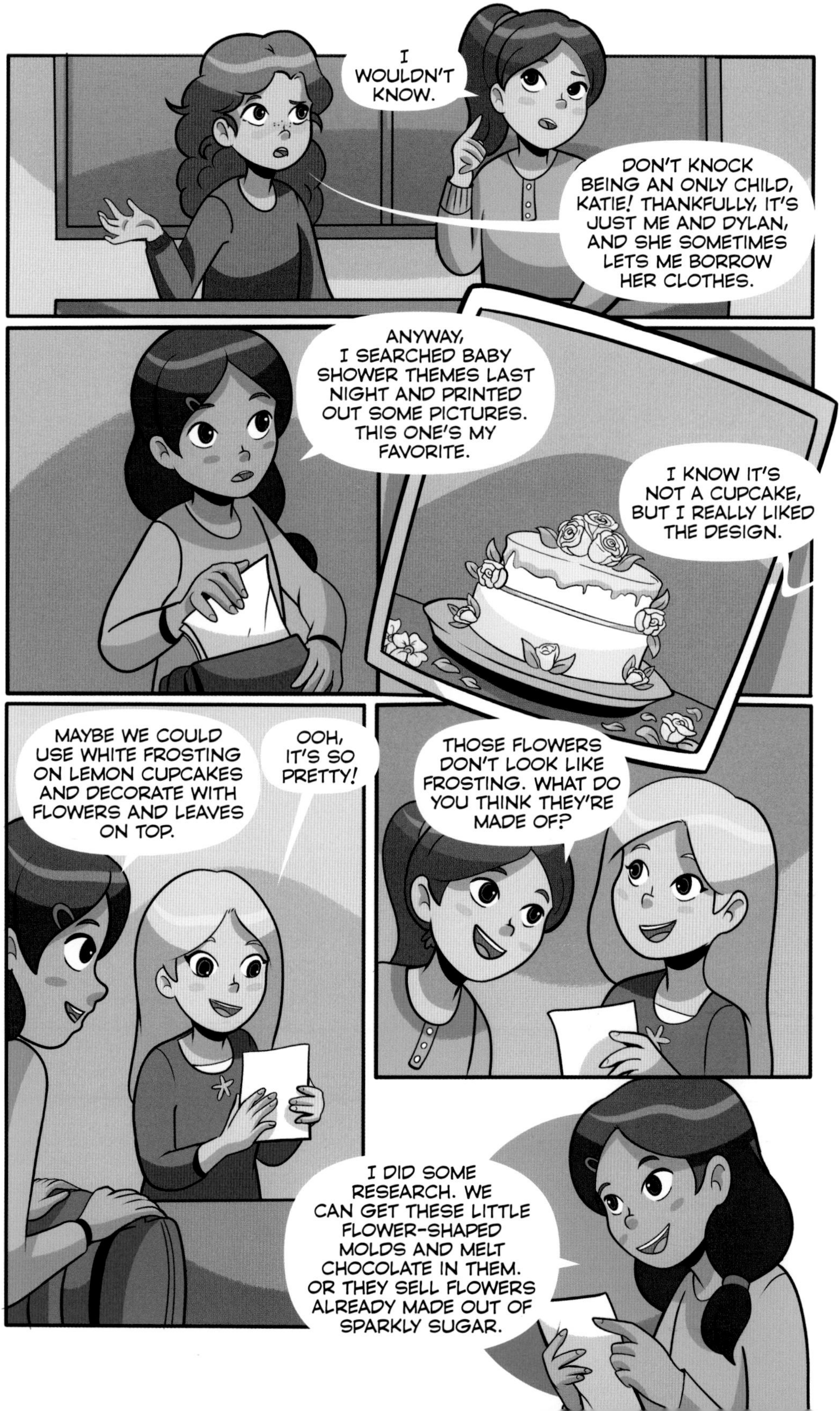
I WOULDN'T KNOW.
DON'T KNOCK BEING AN ONLY CHILD, KATIE! THANKFULLY, IT'S JUST ME AND DYLAN, AND SHE SOMETIMES LETS ME BORROW HER CLOTHES.
ANYWAY, I SEARCHED BABY SHOWER THEMES LAST NIGHT AND PRINTED OUT SOME PICTURES. THIS ONE'S MY FAVORITE.
I KNOW IT'S NOT A CUPCAKE, BUT I REALLY LIKED THE DESIGN.
MAYBE WE COULD USE WHITE FROSTING ON LEMON CUPCAKES AND DECORATE WITH FLOWERS AND LEAVES ON TOP.
OOH, IT'S SO PRETTY!
THOSE FLOWERS DON'T LOOK LIKE FROSTING. WHAT DO YOU THINK THEY'RE MADE OF?
I DID SOME RESEARCH. WE CAN GET THESE LITTLE FLOWER-SHAPED MOLDS AND MELT CHOCOLATE IN THEM. OR THEY SELL FLOWERS ALREADY MADE OUT OF SPARKLY SUGAR.

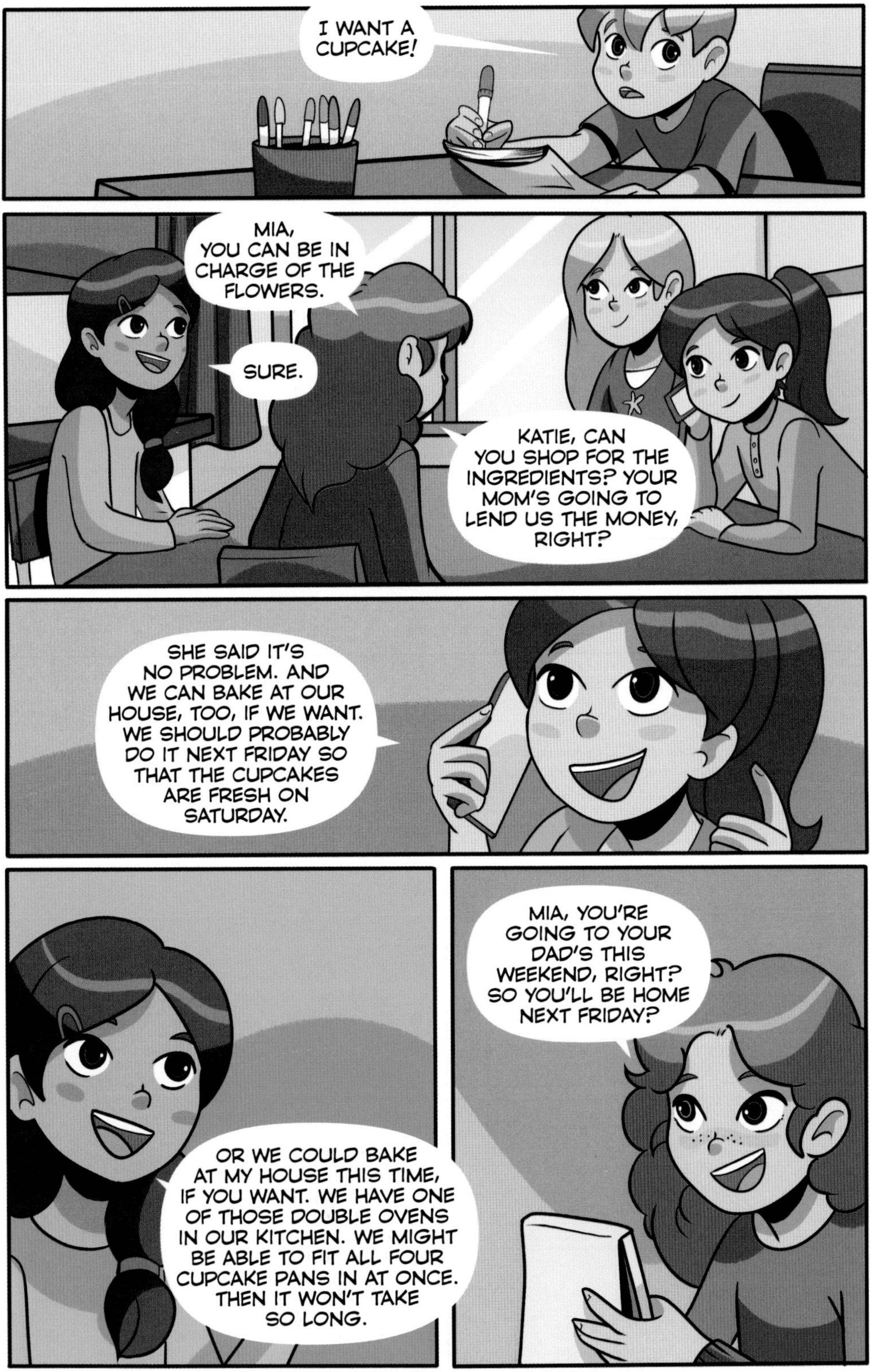

I WANT A CUPCAKE!
MIA, YOU CAN BE IN CHARGE OF THE FLOWERS.
SURE.
KATIE, CAN YOU SHOP FOR THE INGREDIENTS? YOUR MOM'S GOING TO LEND US THE MONEY, RIGHT?
SHE SAID IT'S NO PROBLEM. AND WE CAN BAKE AT OUR HOUSE, TOO, IF WE WANT. WE SHOULD PROBABLY DO IT NEXT FRIDAY SO THAT THE CUPCAKES ARE FRESH ON SATURDAY.
OR WE COULD BAKE AT MY HOUSE THIS TIME, IF YOU WANT. WE HAVE ONE OF THOSE DOUBLE OVENS IN OUR KITCHEN. WE MIGHT BE ABLE TO FIT ALL FOUR CUPCAKE PANS IN AT ONCE. THEN IT WON'T TAKE SO LONG.
MIA, YOU'RE GOING TO YOUR DAD'S THIS WEEKEND, RIGHT? SO YOU'LL BE HOME NEXT FRIDAY?

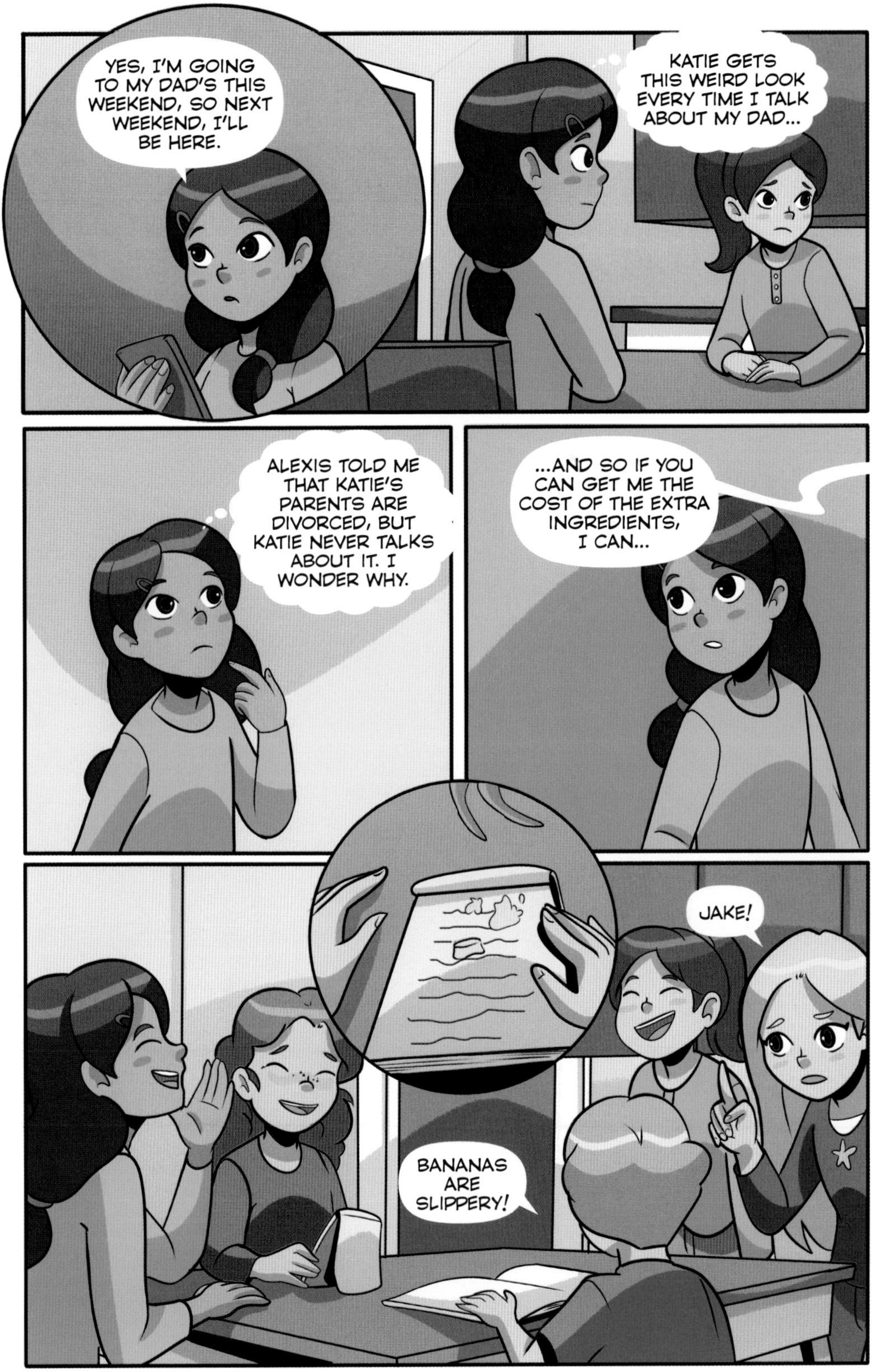
YES, I'M GOING TO MY DAD'S THIS WEEKEND, SO NEXT WEEKEND, I'LL BE HERE.
KATIE GETS THIS WEIRD LOOK EVERY TIME I TALK ABOUT MY DAD...
ALEXIS TOLD ME THAT KATIE'S PARENTS ARE DIVORCED, BUT KATIE NEVER TALKS ABOUT IT. I WONDER WHY.
...AND SO IF YOU CAN GET ME THE COST OF THE EXTRA INGREDIENTS, I CAN...
JAKE!
BANANAS ARE SLIPPERY!

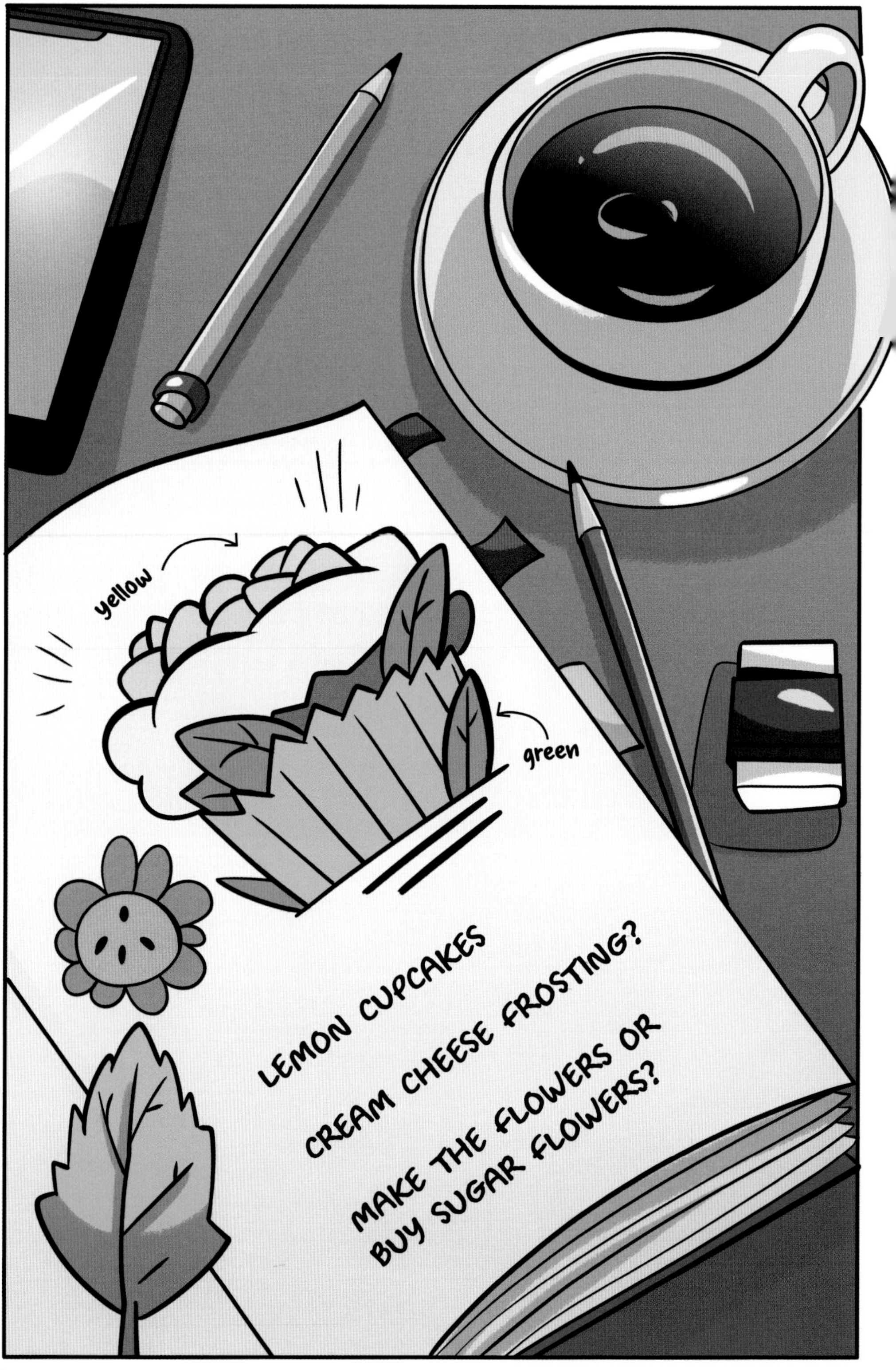

yellow
green
LEMON CUPCAKES
CREAM CHEESE FROSTING?
MAKE THE FLOWERS OR BUY SUGAR FLOWERS?

Chapter 5

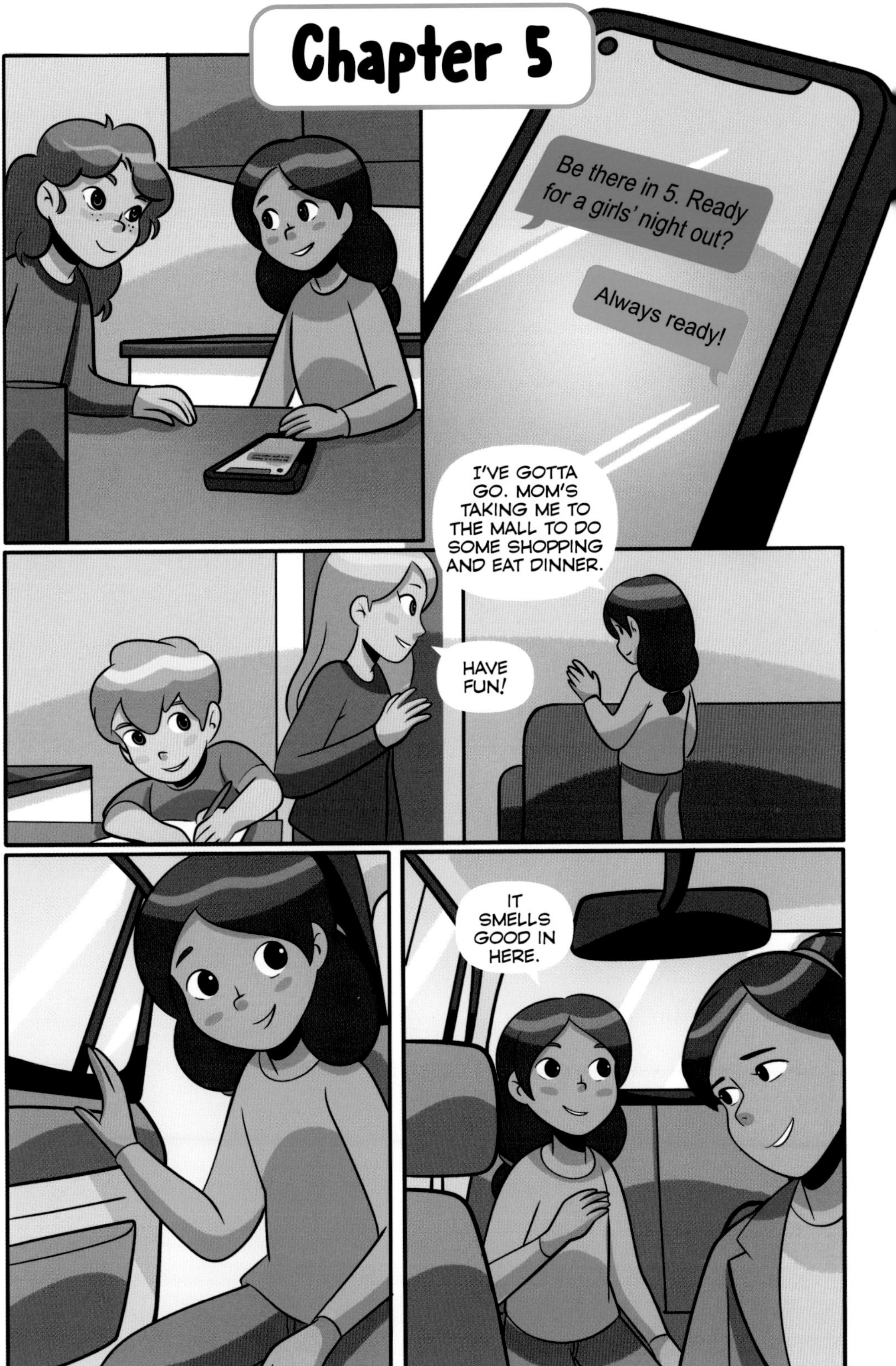

Be there in 5. Ready for a girls' night out?
Always ready!
I'VE GOTTA GO. MOM'S TAKING ME TO THE MALL TO DO SOME SHOPPING AND EAT DINNER.
HAVE FUN!
IT SMELLS GOOD IN HERE.

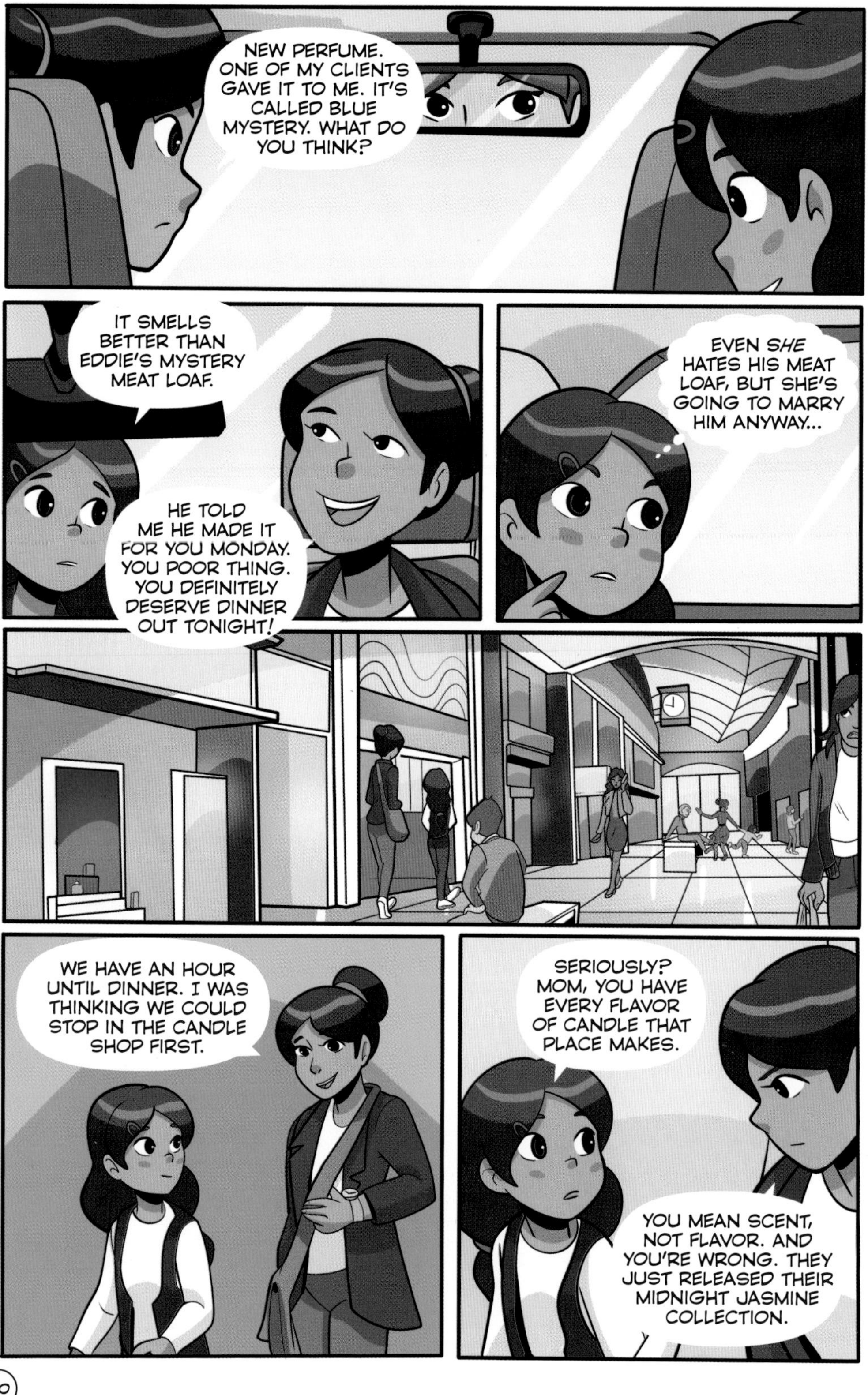
NEW PERFUME. ONE OF MY CLIENTS GAVE IT TO ME. IT'S CALLED BLUE MYSTERY. WHAT DO YOU THINK?
IT SMELLS BETTER THAN EDDIE'S MYSTERY MEAT LOAF.
HE TOLD ME HE MADE IT FOR YOU MONDAY. YOU POOR THING. YOU DEFINITELY DESERVE DINNER OUT TONIGHT!
EVEN *SHE* HATES HIS MEAT LOAF, BUT SHE'S GOING TO MARRY HIM ANYWAY...
WE HAVE AN HOUR UNTIL DINNER. I WAS THINKING WE COULD STOP IN THE CANDLE SHOP FIRST.
SERIOUSLY? MOM, YOU HAVE EVERY FLAVOR OF CANDLE THAT PLACE MAKES.
YOU MEAN SCENT, NOT FLAVOR. AND YOU'RE WRONG. THEY JUST RELEASED THEIR MIDNIGHT JASMINE COLLECTION.

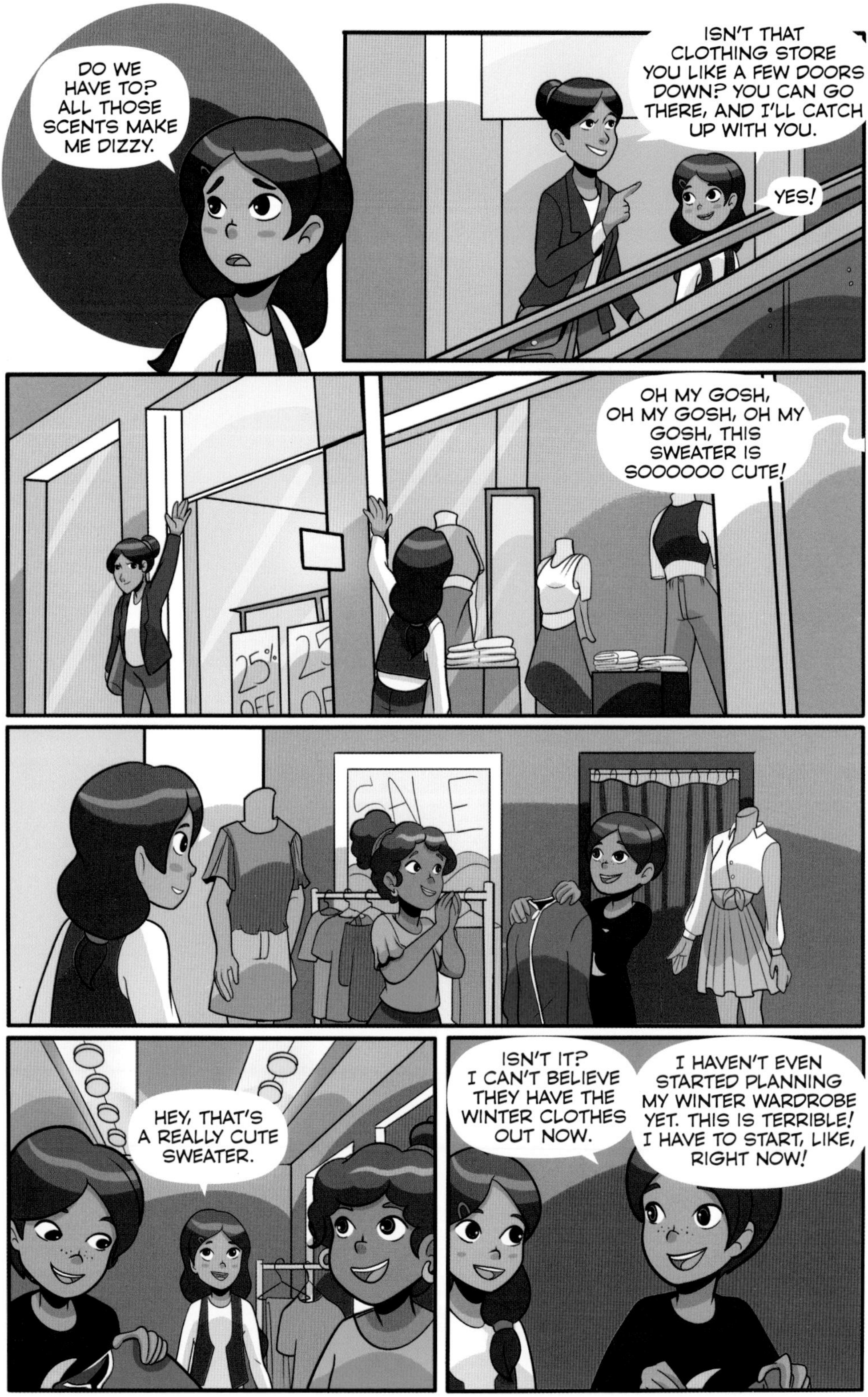
DO WE HAVE TO? ALL THOSE SCENTS MAKE ME DIZZY.
ISN'T THAT CLOTHING STORE YOU LIKE A FEW DOORS DOWN? YOU CAN GO THERE, AND I'LL CATCH UP WITH YOU.
YES!
OH MY GOSH, OH MY GOSH, OH MY GOSH, THIS SWEATER IS SOOOOOO CUTE!
25% OFF
SALE
HEY, THAT'S A REALLY CUTE SWEATER.
ISN'T IT? I CAN'T BELIEVE THEY HAVE THE WINTER CLOTHES OUT NOW.
I HAVEN'T EVEN STARTED PLANNING MY WINTER WARDROBE YET. THIS IS TERRIBLE! I HAVE TO START, LIKE, RIGHT NOW!

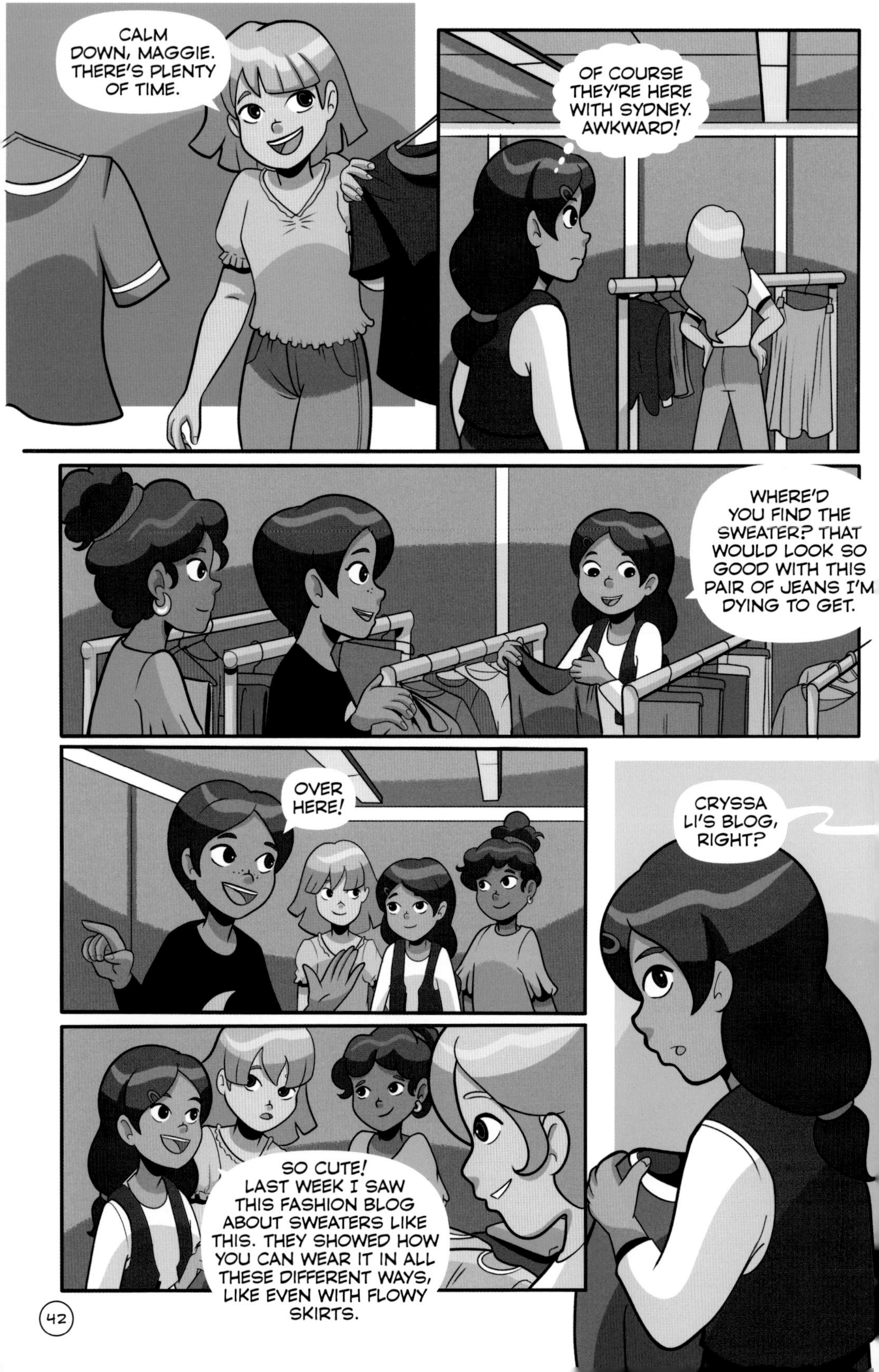

CALM DOWN, MAGGIE. THERE'S PLENTY OF TIME.
OF COURSE THEY'RE HERE WITH SYDNEY. AWKWARD!
WHERE'D YOU FIND THE SWEATER? THAT WOULD LOOK SO GOOD WITH THIS PAIR OF JEANS I'M DYING TO GET.
OVER HERE!
SO CUTE! LAST WEEK I SAW THIS FASHION BLOG ABOUT SWEATERS LIKE THIS. THEY SHOWED HOW YOU CAN WEAR IT IN ALL THESE DIFFERENT WAYS, LIKE EVEN WITH FLOWY SKIRTS.
CRYSSA LI'S BLOG, RIGHT?

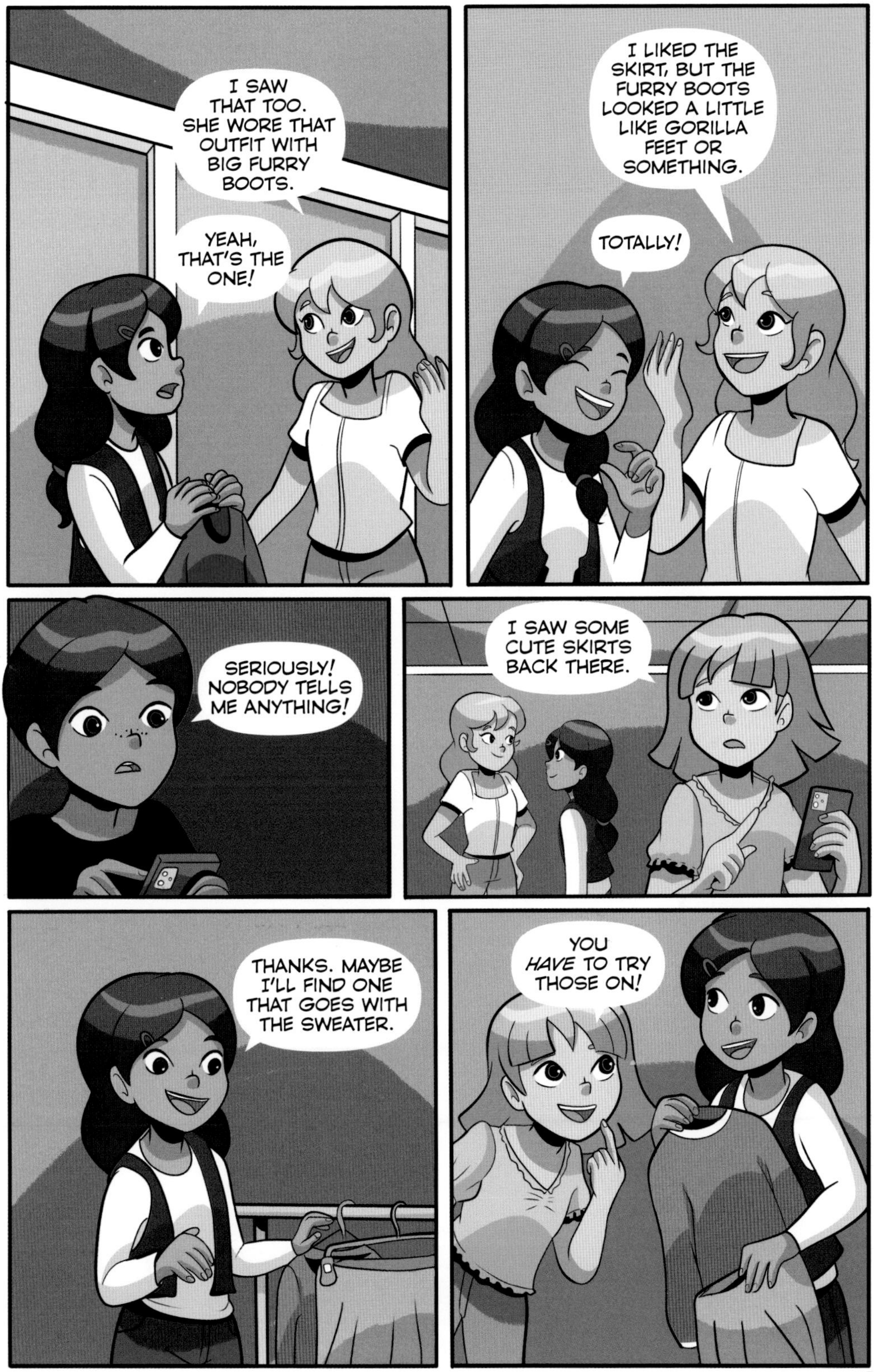
I SAW THAT TOO. SHE WORE THAT OUTFIT WITH BIG FURRY BOOTS.
YEAH, THAT'S THE ONE!
I LIKED THE SKIRT, BUT THE FURRY BOOTS LOOKED A LITTLE LIKE GORILLA FEET OR SOMETHING.
TOTALLY!
SERIOUSLY! NOBODY TELLS ME ANYTHING!
I SAW SOME CUTE SKIRTS BACK THERE.
THANKS. MAYBE I'LL FIND ONE THAT GOES WITH THE SWEATER.
YOU *HAVE* TO TRY THOSE ON!

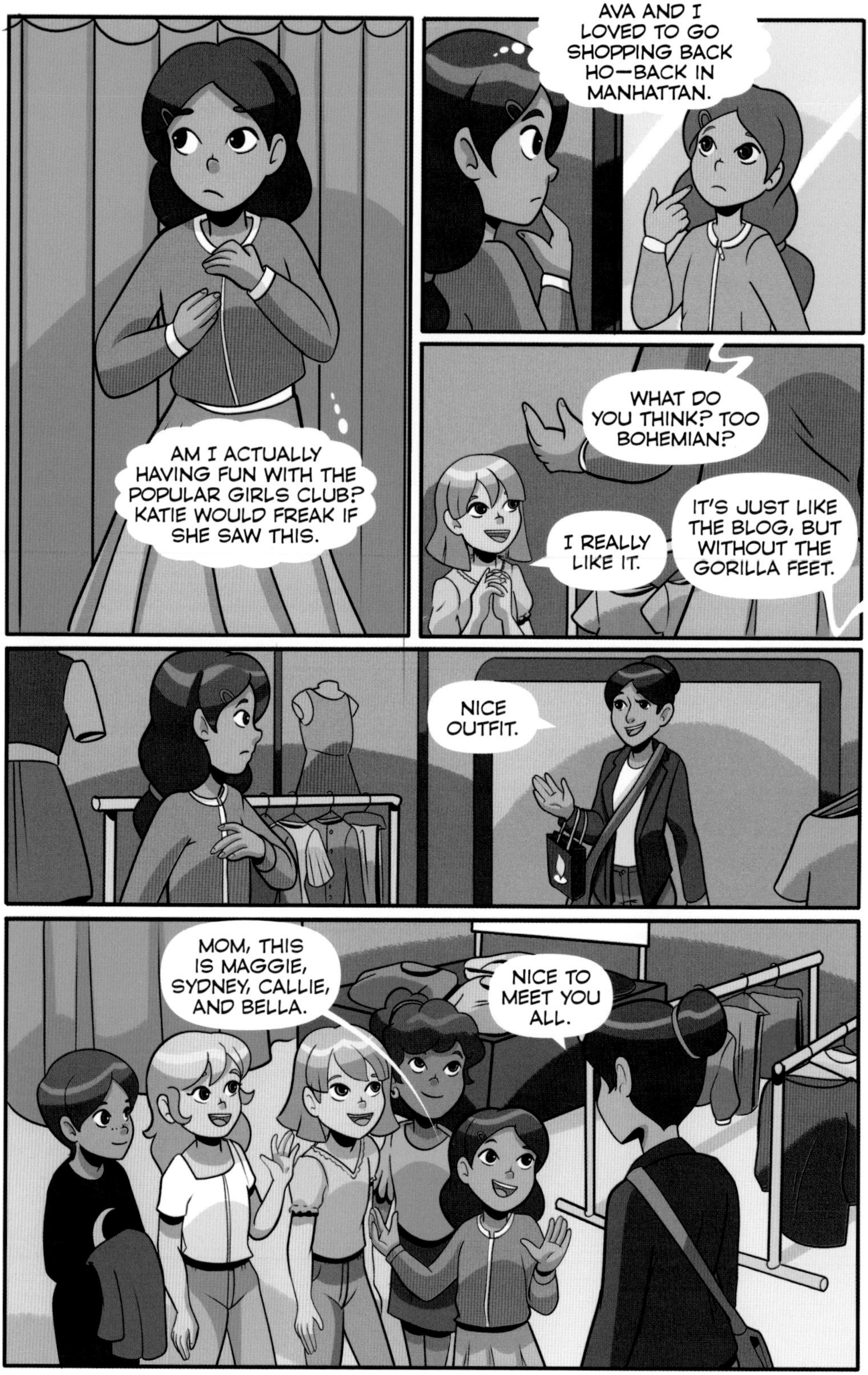
AM I ACTUALLY HAVING FUN WITH THE POPULAR GIRLS CLUB? KATIE WOULD FREAK IF SHE SAW THIS.
AVA AND I LOVED TO GO SHOPPING BACK HO—BACK IN MANHATTAN.
WHAT DO YOU THINK? TOO BOHEMIAN?
I REALLY LIKE IT.
IT'S JUST LIKE THE BLOG, BUT WITHOUT THE GORILLA FEET.
NICE OUTFIT.
MOM, THIS IS MAGGIE, SYDNEY, CALLIE, AND BELLA.
NICE TO MEET YOU ALL.

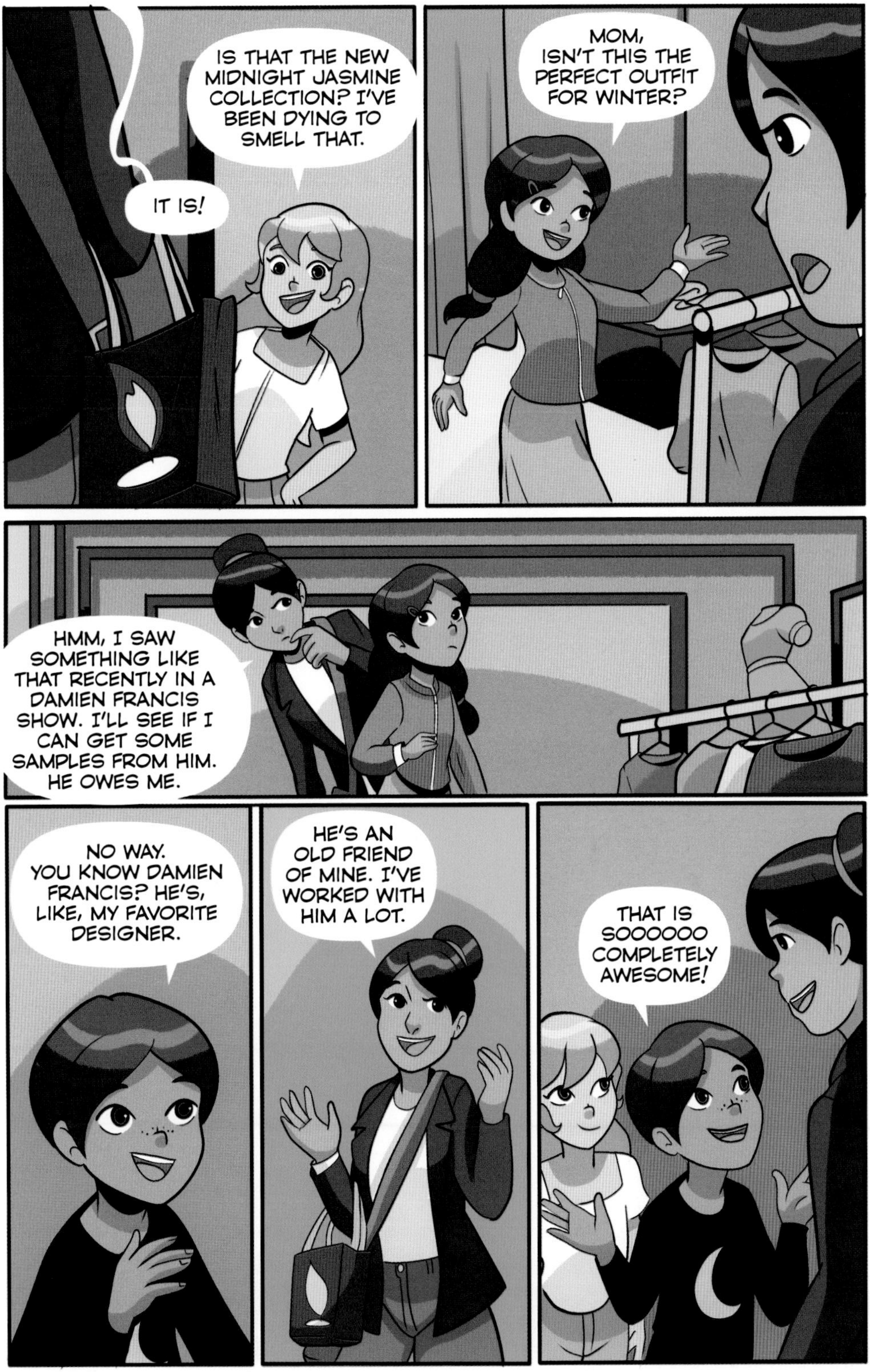
IS THAT THE NEW MIDNIGHT JASMINE COLLECTION? I'VE BEEN DYING TO SMELL THAT.
IT IS!
MOM, ISN'T THIS THE PERFECT OUTFIT FOR WINTER?
HMM, I SAW SOMETHING LIKE THAT RECENTLY IN A DAMIEN FRANCIS SHOW. I'LL SEE IF I CAN GET SOME SAMPLES FROM HIM. HE OWES ME.
NO WAY. YOU KNOW DAMIEN FRANCIS? HE'S, LIKE, MY FAVORITE DESIGNER.
HE'S AN OLD FRIEND OF MINE. I'VE WORKED WITH HIM A LOT.
THAT IS SOOOOOO COMPLETELY AWESOME!

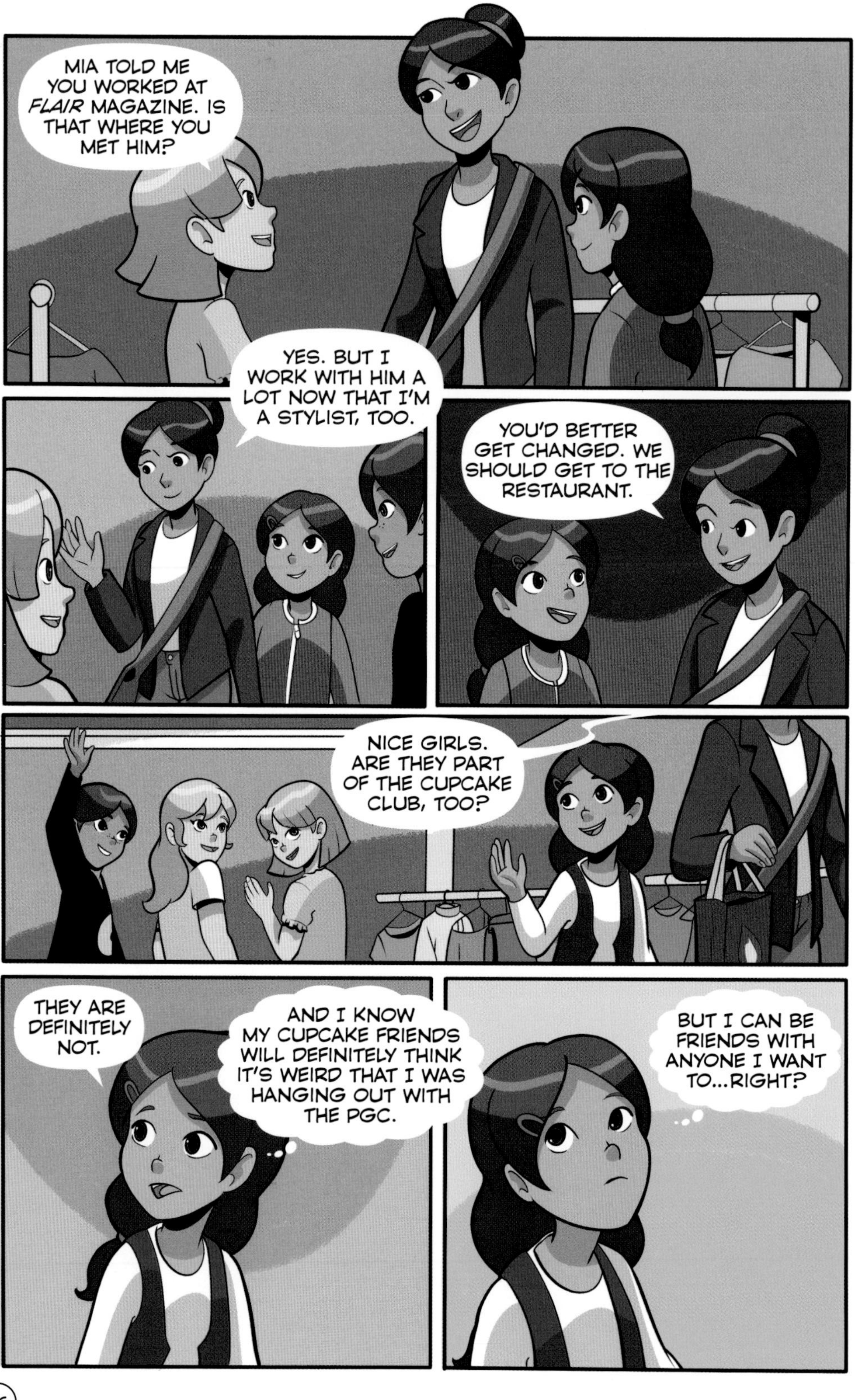

MIA TOLD ME YOU WORKED AT *FLAIR* MAGAZINE. IS THAT WHERE YOU MET HIM?
YES. BUT I WORK WITH HIM A LOT NOW THAT I'M A STYLIST, TOO.
YOU'D BETTER GET CHANGED. WE SHOULD GET TO THE RESTAURANT.
NICE GIRLS. ARE THEY PART OF THE CUPCAKE CLUB, TOO?
THEY ARE DEFINITELY NOT.
AND I KNOW MY CUPCAKE FRIENDS WILL DEFINITELY THINK IT'S WEIRD THAT I WAS HANGING OUT WITH THE PGC.
BUT I CAN BE FRIENDS WITH ANYONE I WANT TO...RIGHT?

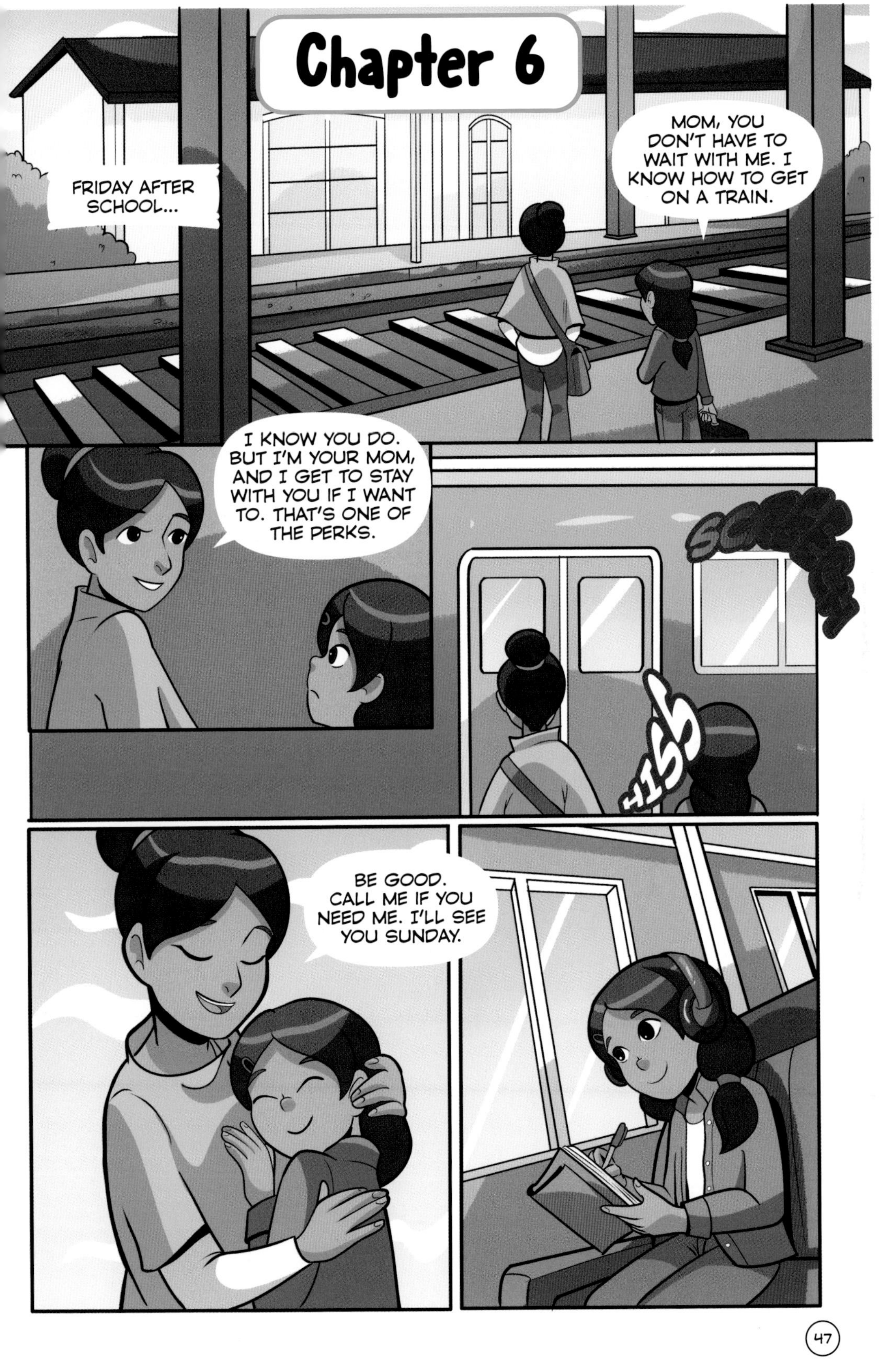
Chapter 6
FRIDAY AFTER SCHOOL...
MOM, YOU DON'T HAVE TO WAIT WITH ME. I KNOW HOW TO GET ON A TRAIN.
I KNOW YOU DO. BUT I'M YOUR MOM, AND I GET TO STAY WITH YOU IF I WANT TO. THAT'S ONE OF THE PERKS.
HISS
BE GOOD. CALL ME IF YOU NEED ME. I'LL SEE YOU SUNDAY.

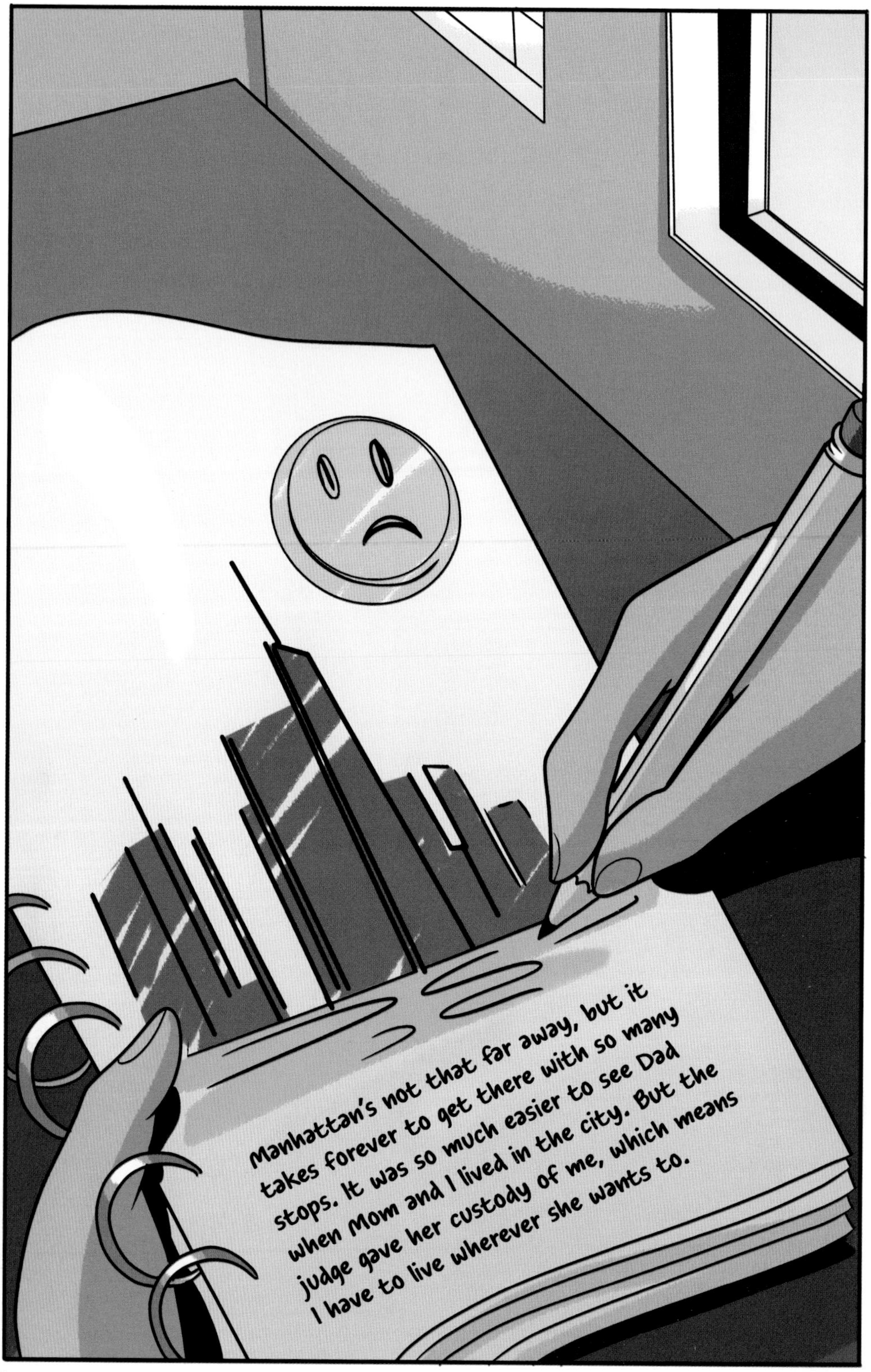
Manhattan's not that far away, but it takes forever to get there with so many stops. It was so much easier to see Dad when Mom and I lived in the city. But the judge gave her custody of me, which means I have to live wherever she wants to.

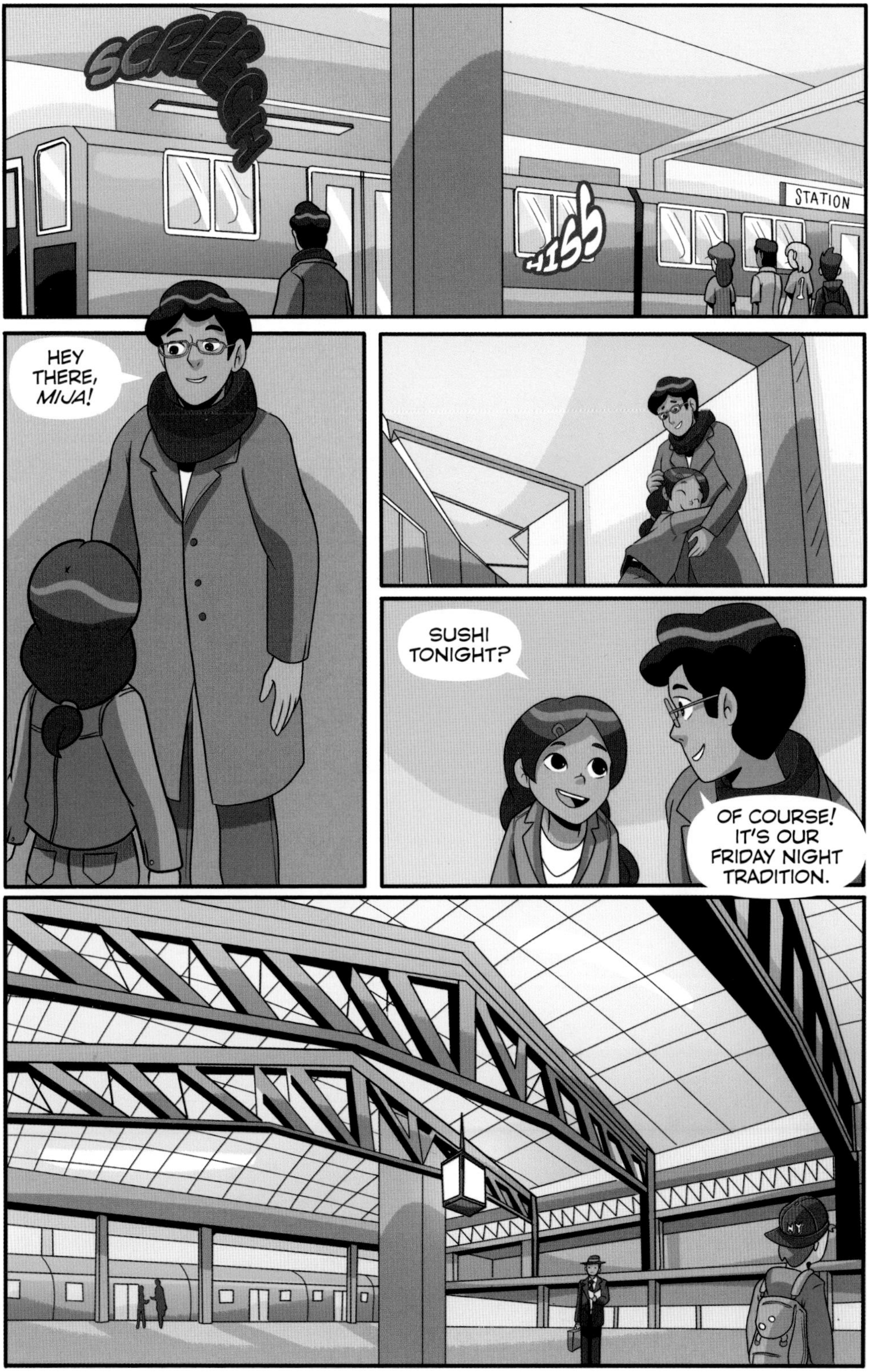
SCREECH
STATION
HISS
HEY THERE, MIJA!
SUSHI TONIGHT?
OF COURSE! IT'S OUR FRIDAY NIGHT TRADITION.
NY

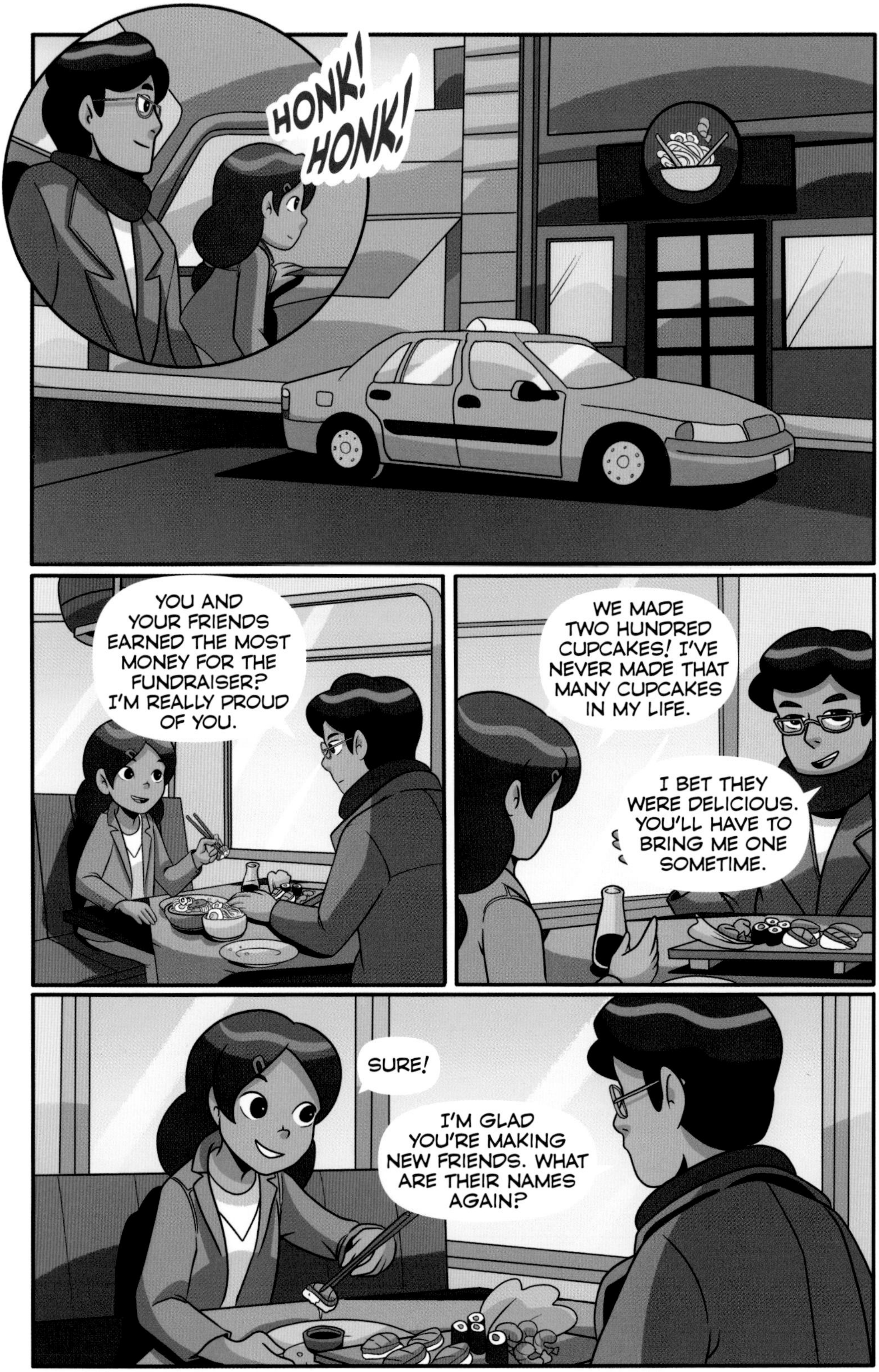
HONK! HONK!
YOU AND YOUR FRIENDS EARNED THE MOST MONEY FOR THE FUNDRAISER? I'M REALLY PROUD OF YOU.
WE MADE TWO HUNDRED CUPCAKES! I'VE NEVER MADE THAT MANY CUPCAKES IN MY LIFE.
I BET THEY WERE DELICIOUS. YOU'LL HAVE TO BRING ME ONE SOMETIME.
SURE!
I'M GLAD YOU'RE MAKING NEW FRIENDS. WHAT ARE THEIR NAMES AGAIN?

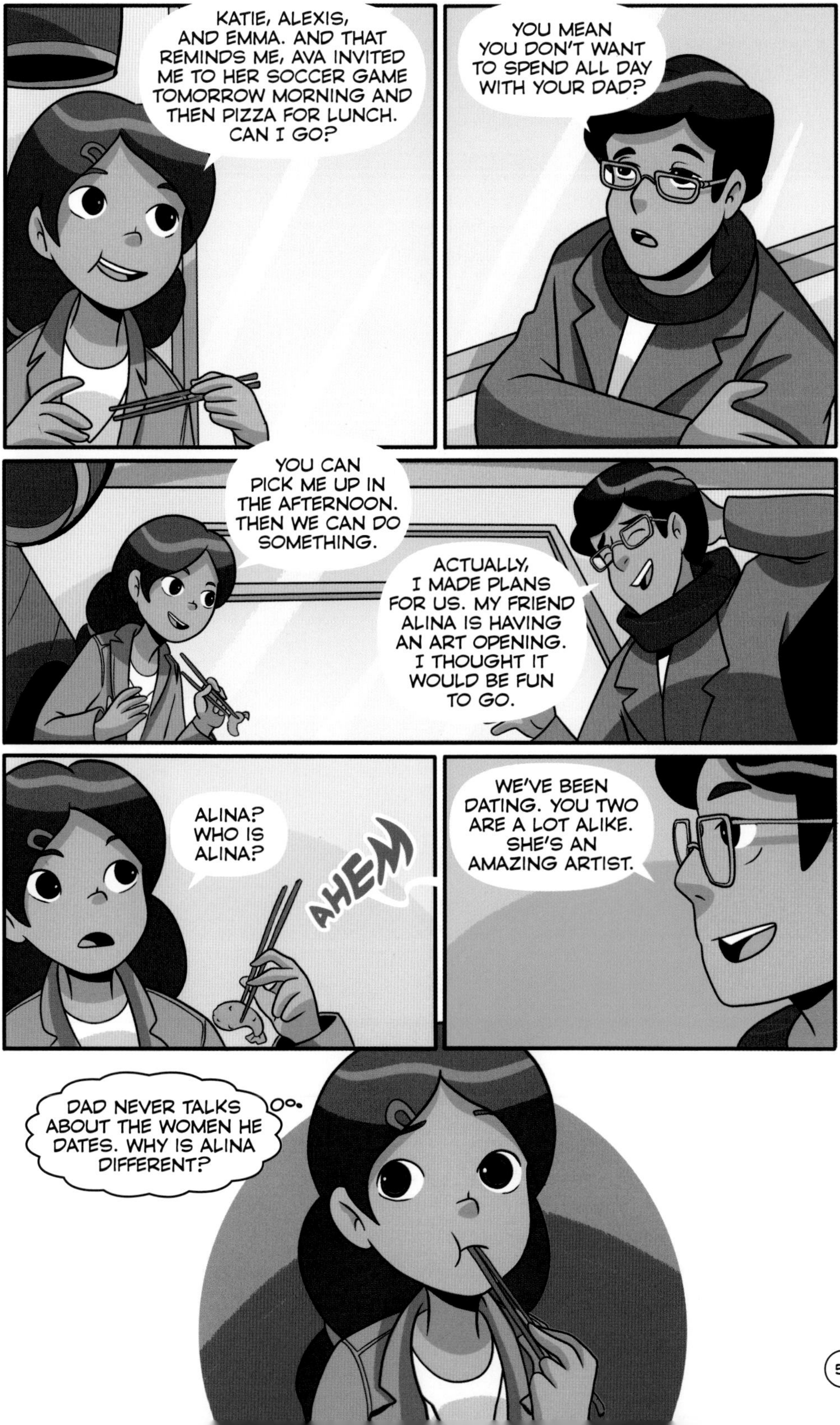
KATIE, ALEXIS, AND EMMA. AND THAT REMINDS ME, AVA INVITED ME TO HER SOCCER GAME TOMORROW MORNING AND THEN PIZZA FOR LUNCH. CAN I GO?
YOU MEAN YOU DON'T WANT TO SPEND ALL DAY WITH YOUR DAD?
YOU CAN PICK ME UP IN THE AFTERNOON. THEN WE CAN DO SOMETHING.
ACTUALLY, I MADE PLANS FOR US. MY FRIEND ALINA IS HAVING AN ART OPENING. I THOUGHT IT WOULD BE FUN TO GO.
ALINA? WHO IS ALINA?
AHEM
WE'VE BEEN DATING. YOU TWO ARE A LOT ALIKE. SHE'S AN AMAZING ARTIST.
DAD NEVER TALKS ABOUT THE WOMEN HE DATES. WHY IS ALINA DIFFERENT?

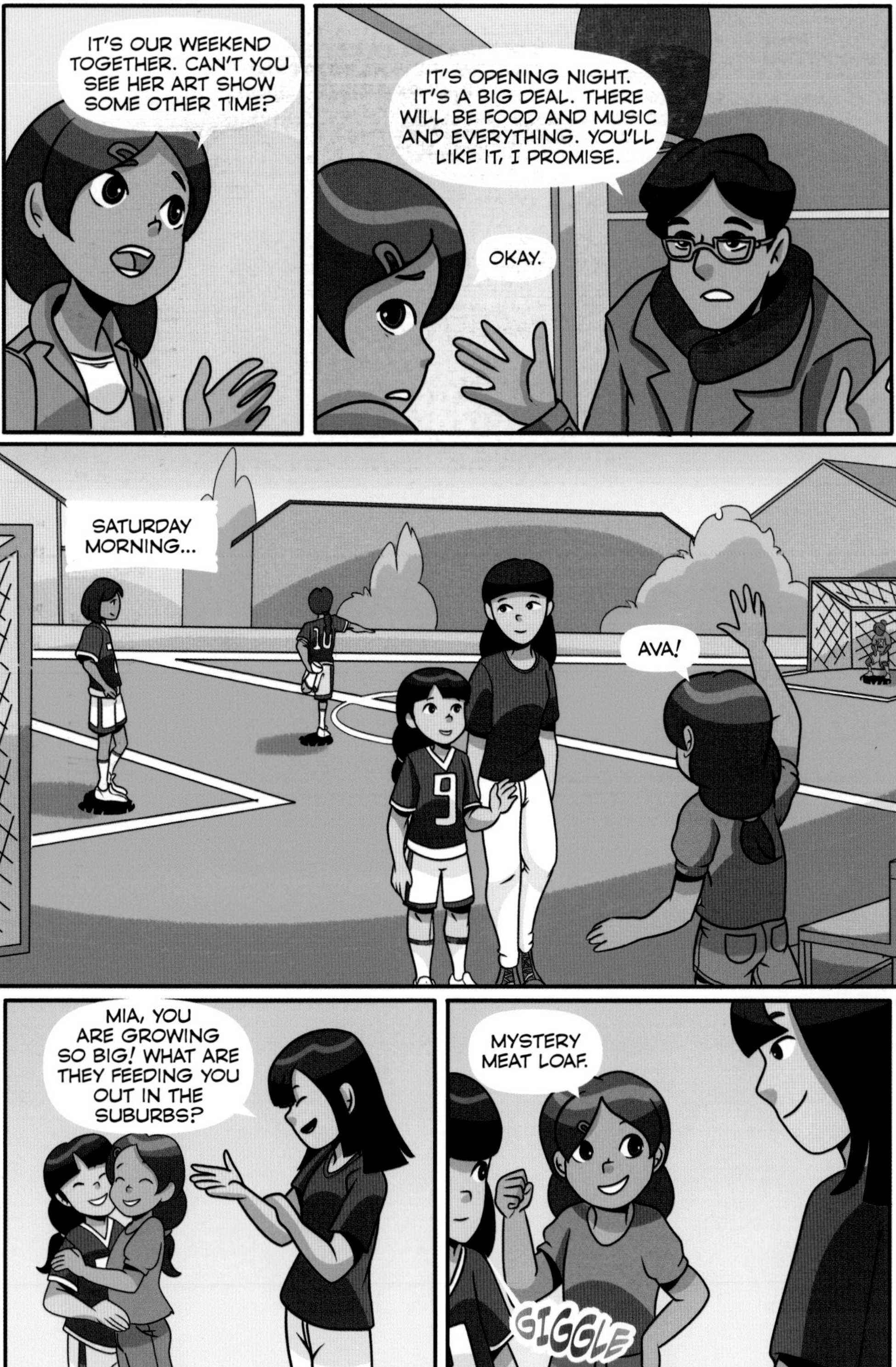
IT'S OUR WEEKEND TOGETHER. CAN'T YOU SEE HER ART SHOW SOME OTHER TIME?
IT'S OPENING NIGHT. IT'S A BIG DEAL. THERE WILL BE FOOD AND MUSIC AND EVERYTHING. YOU'LL LIKE IT, I PROMISE.
OKAY.
SATURDAY MORNING...
AVA!
MIA, YOU ARE GROWING SO BIG! WHAT ARE THEY FEEDING YOU OUT IN THE SUBURBS?
MYSTERY MEAT LOAF.
GIGGLE

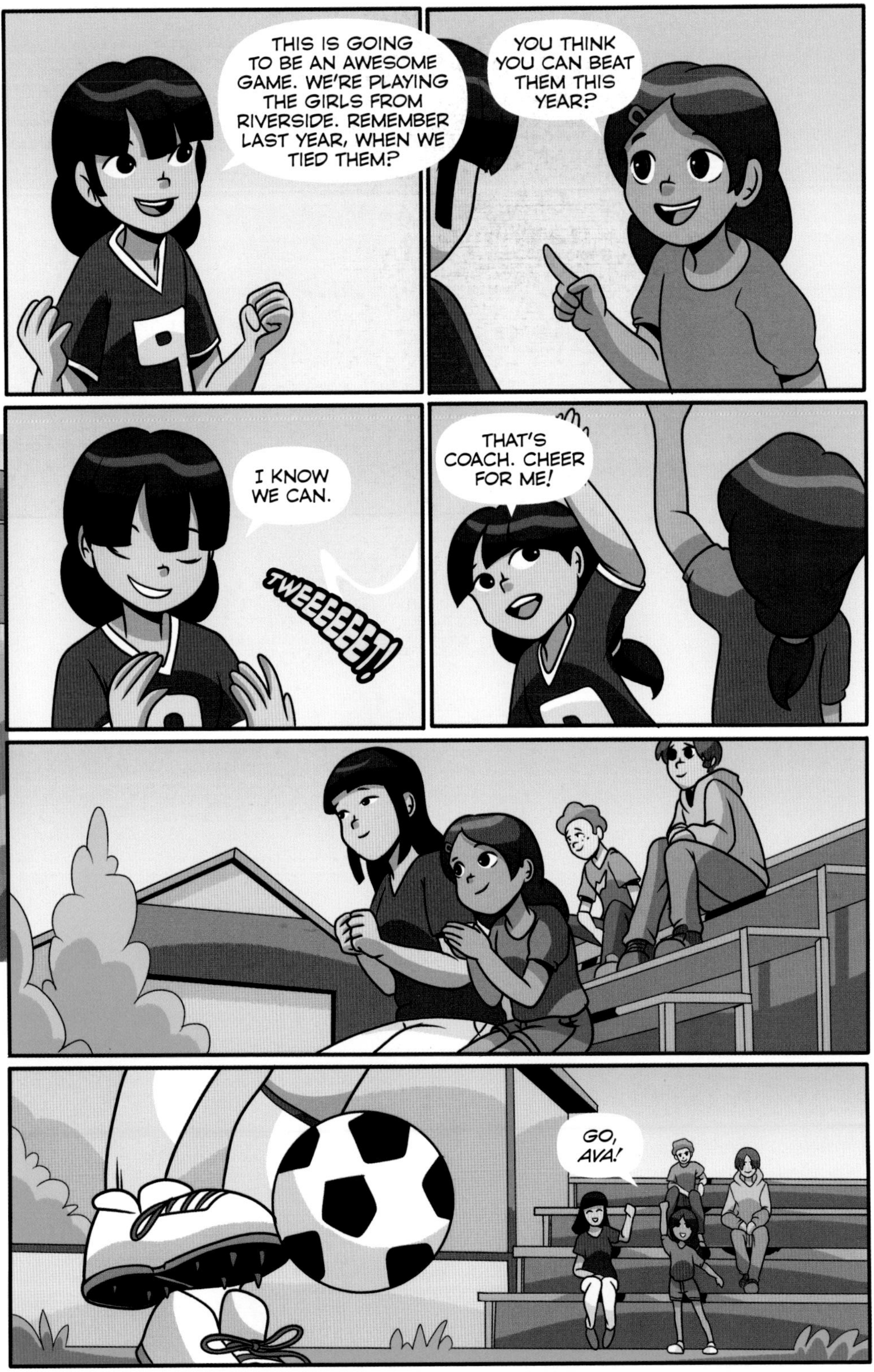
THIS IS GOING TO BE AN AWESOME GAME. WE'RE PLAYING THE GIRLS FROM RIVERSIDE. REMEMBER LAST YEAR, WHEN WE TIED THEM?
YOU THINK YOU CAN BEAT THEM THIS YEAR?
I KNOW WE CAN.
TWEEEEEEET!
THAT'S COACH. CHEER FOR ME!
GO, AVA!

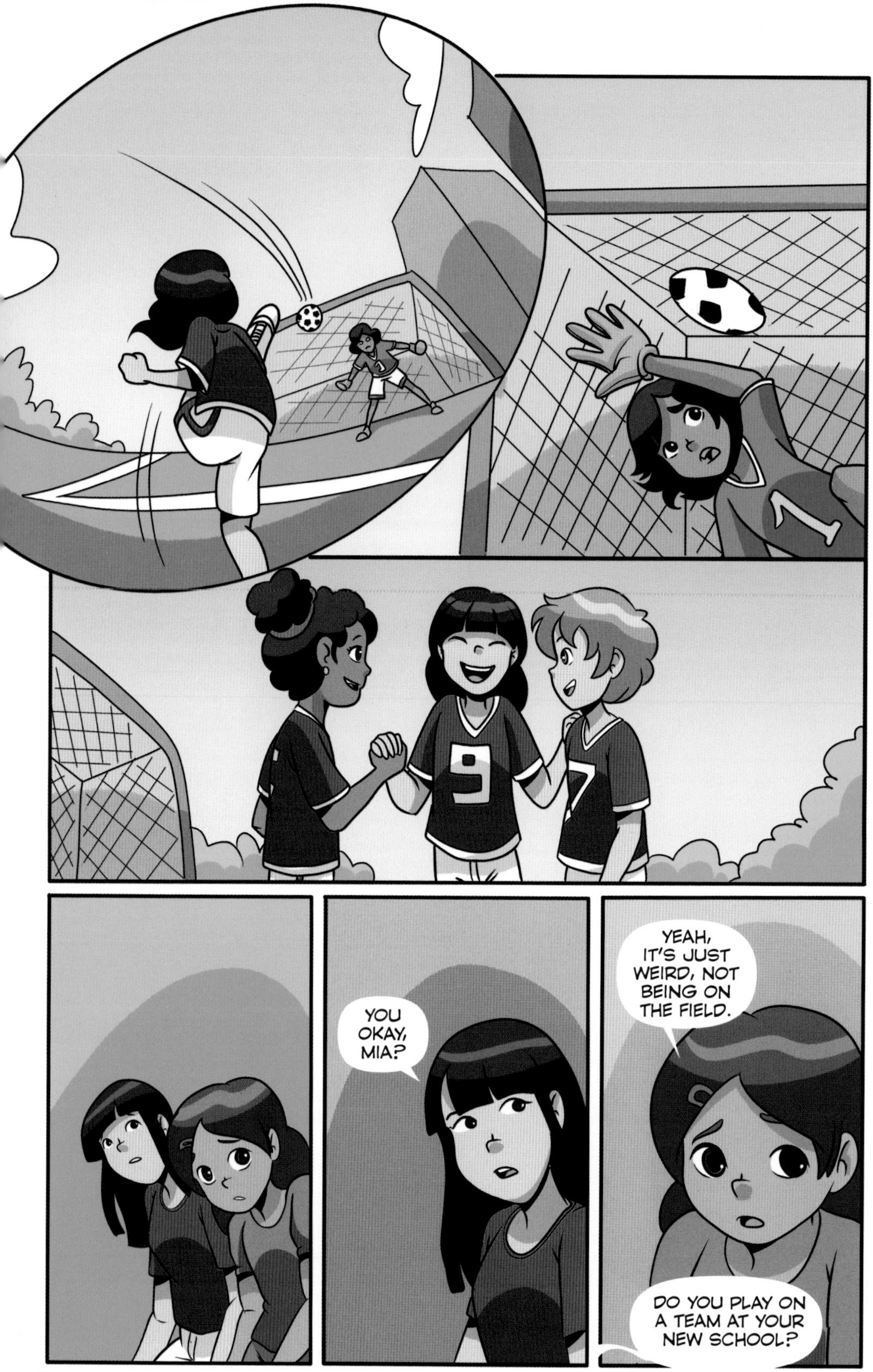
YOU OKAY, MIA?
YEAH, IT'S JUST WEIRD, NOT BEING ON THE FIELD.
DO YOU PLAY ON A TEAM AT YOUR NEW SCHOOL?

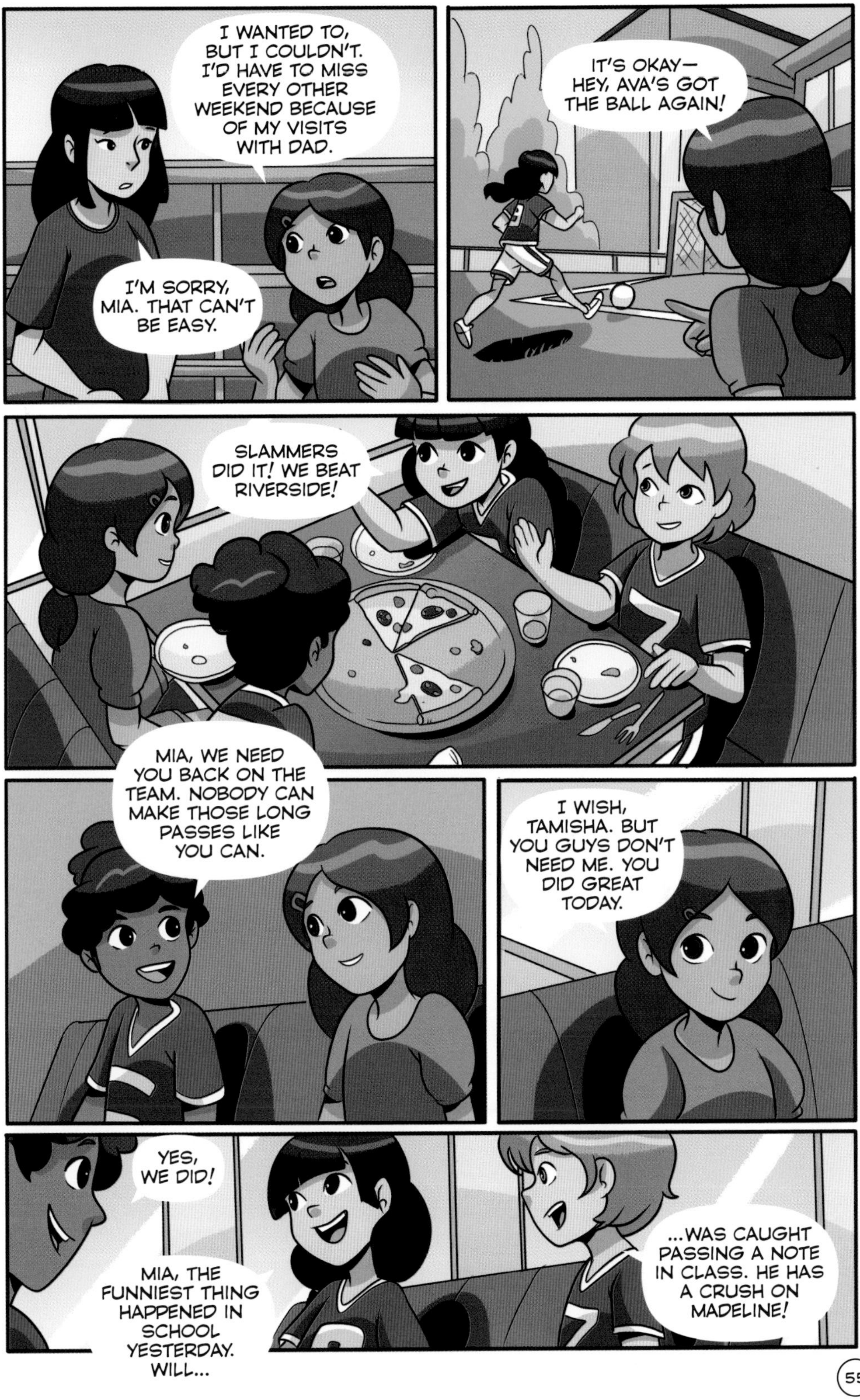
I WANTED TO, BUT I COULDN'T. I'D HAVE TO MISS EVERY OTHER WEEKEND BECAUSE OF MY VISITS WITH DAD.
I'M SORRY, MIA. THAT CAN'T BE EASY.
IT'S OKAY— HEY, AVA'S GOT THE BALL AGAIN!
SLAMMERS DID IT! WE BEAT RIVERSIDE!
MIA, WE NEED YOU BACK ON THE TEAM. NOBODY CAN MAKE THOSE LONG PASSES LIKE YOU CAN.
I WISH, TAMISHA. BUT YOU GUYS DON'T NEED ME. YOU DID GREAT TODAY.
YES, WE DID!
MIA, THE FUNNIEST THING HAPPENED IN SCHOOL YESTERDAY. WILL...
...WAS CAUGHT PASSING A NOTE IN CLASS. HE HAS A CRUSH ON MADELINE!

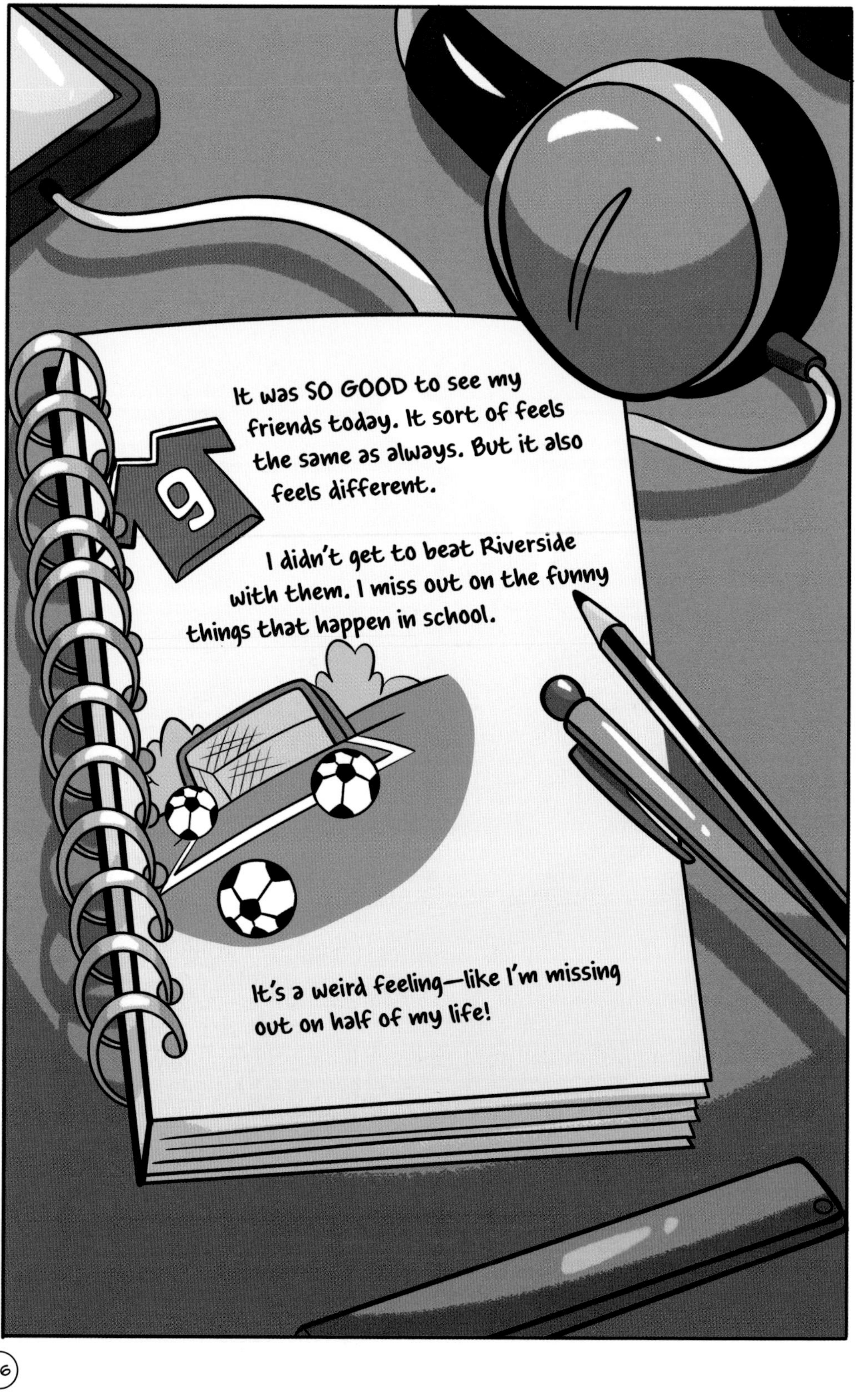
It was SO GOOD to see my friends today. It sort of feels the same as always. But it also feels different.
I didn't get to beat Riverside with them. I miss out on the funny things that happen in school.
It's a weird feeling—like I'm missing out on half of my life!

Chapter 7

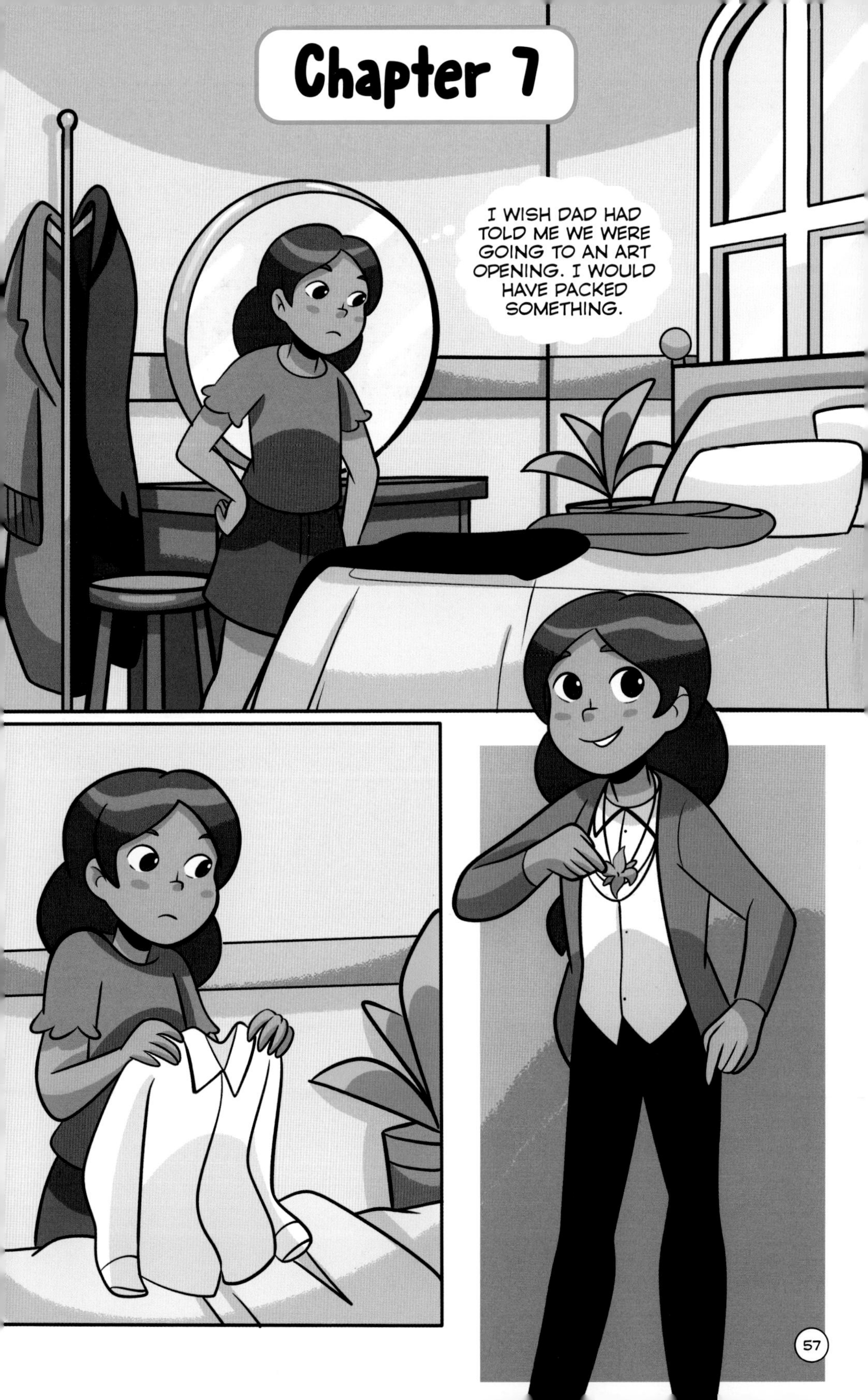
I WISH DAD HAD TOLD ME WE WERE GOING TO AN ART OPENING. I WOULD HAVE PACKED SOMETHING.

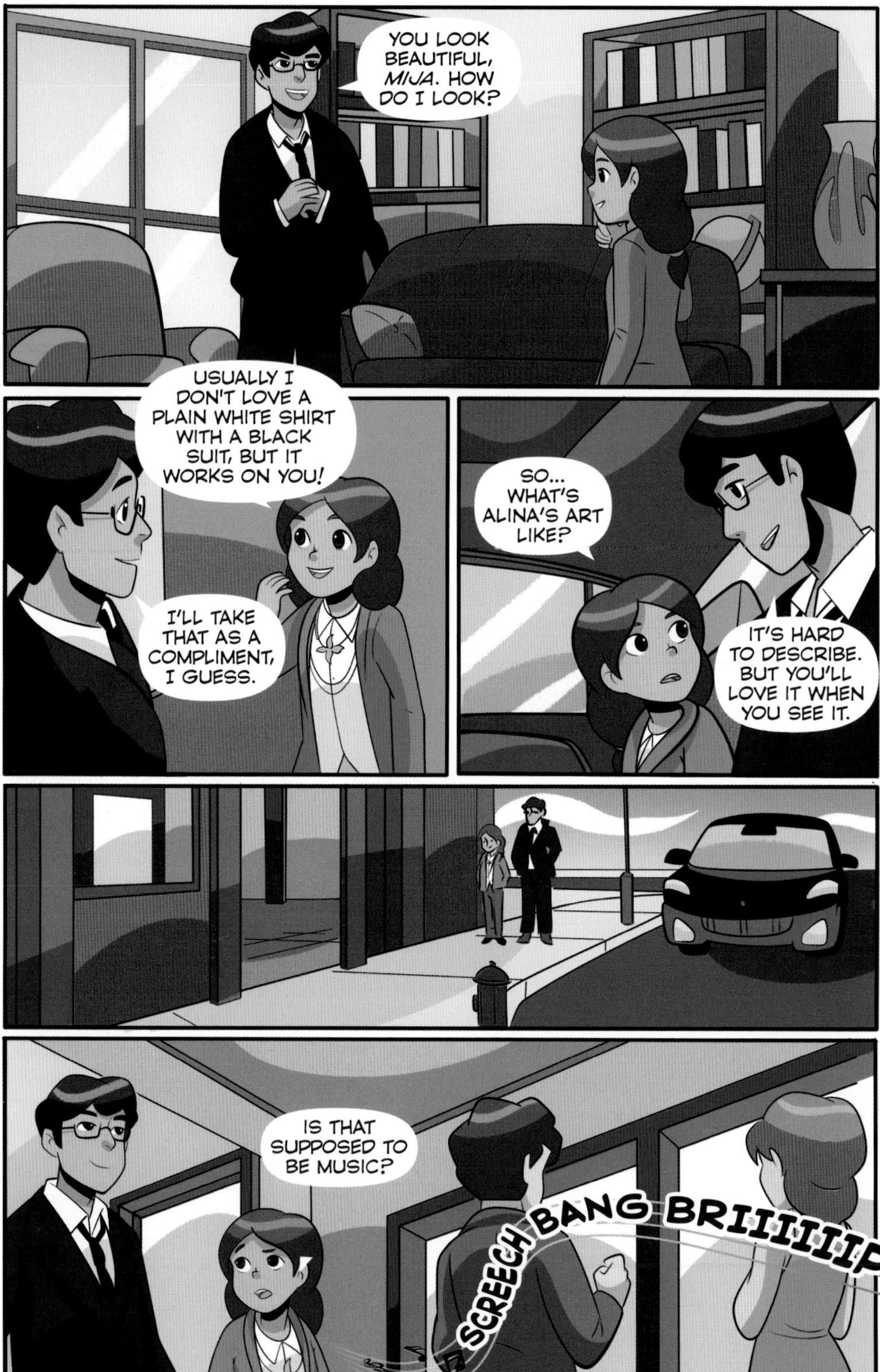
YOU LOOK BEAUTIFUL, *MIJA*. HOW DO I LOOK?
USUALLY I DON'T LOVE A PLAIN WHITE SHIRT WITH A BLACK SUIT, BUT IT WORKS ON YOU!
I'LL TAKE THAT AS A COMPLIMENT, I GUESS.
SO... WHAT'S ALINA'S ART LIKE?
IT'S HARD TO DESCRIBE. BUT YOU'LL LOVE IT WHEN YOU SEE IT.
IS THAT SUPPOSED TO BE MUSIC?
SCREECH BANG BRIIIIIIP

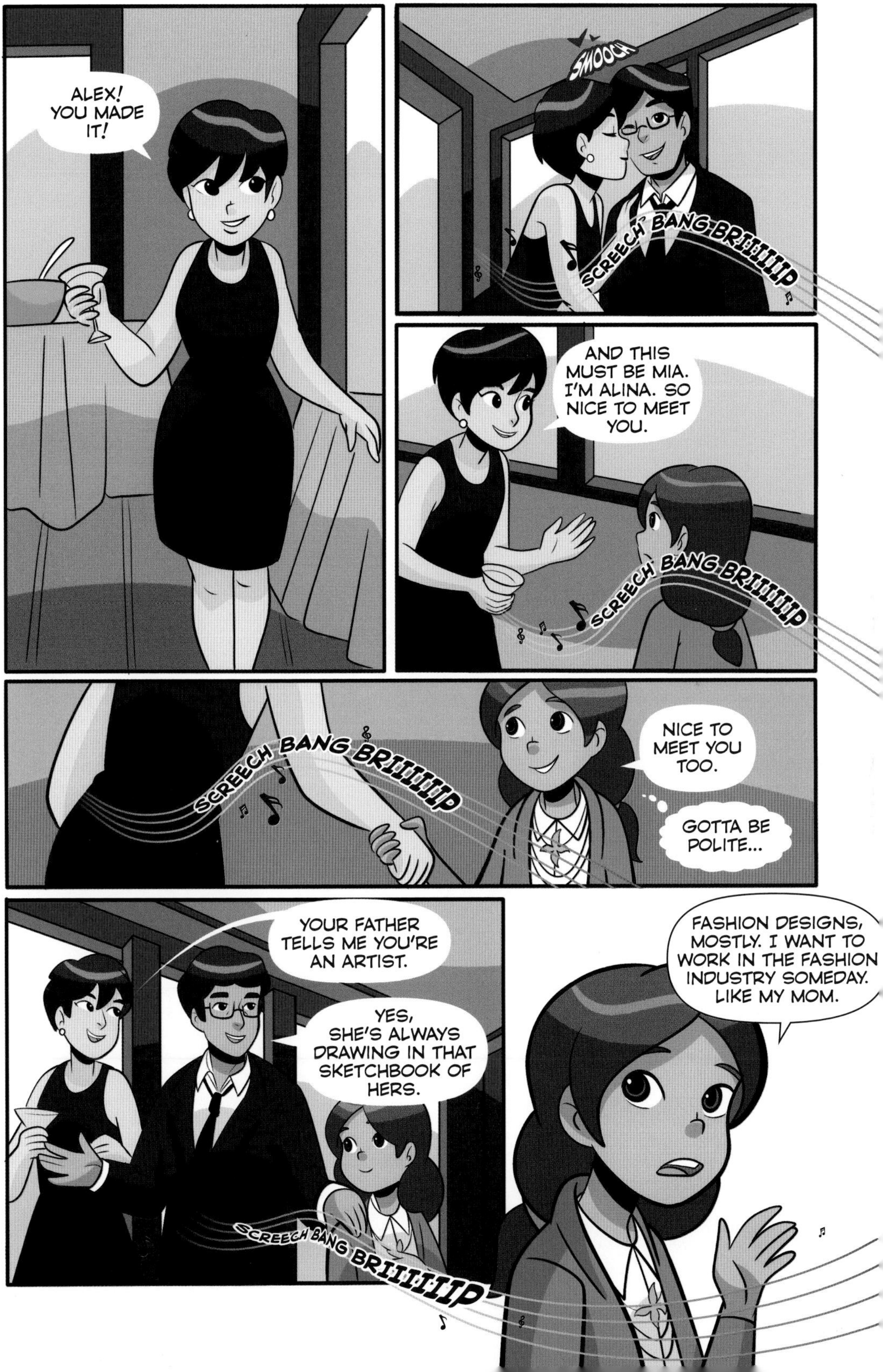
ALEX! YOU MADE IT!
SMOOCH
SCREECH BANG BRIIIIIIP
AND THIS MUST BE MIA. I'M ALINA. SO NICE TO MEET YOU.
SCREECH BANG BRIIIIIIP
SCREECH BANG BRIIIIIIP
NICE TO MEET YOU TOO.
GOTTA BE POLITE...
YOUR FATHER TELLS ME YOU'RE AN ARTIST.
YES, SHE'S ALWAYS DRAWING IN THAT SKETCHBOOK OF HERS.
SCREECH BANG BRIIIIIIP
FASHION DESIGNS, MOSTLY. I WANT TO WORK IN THE FASHION INDUSTRY SOMEDAY. LIKE MY MOM.

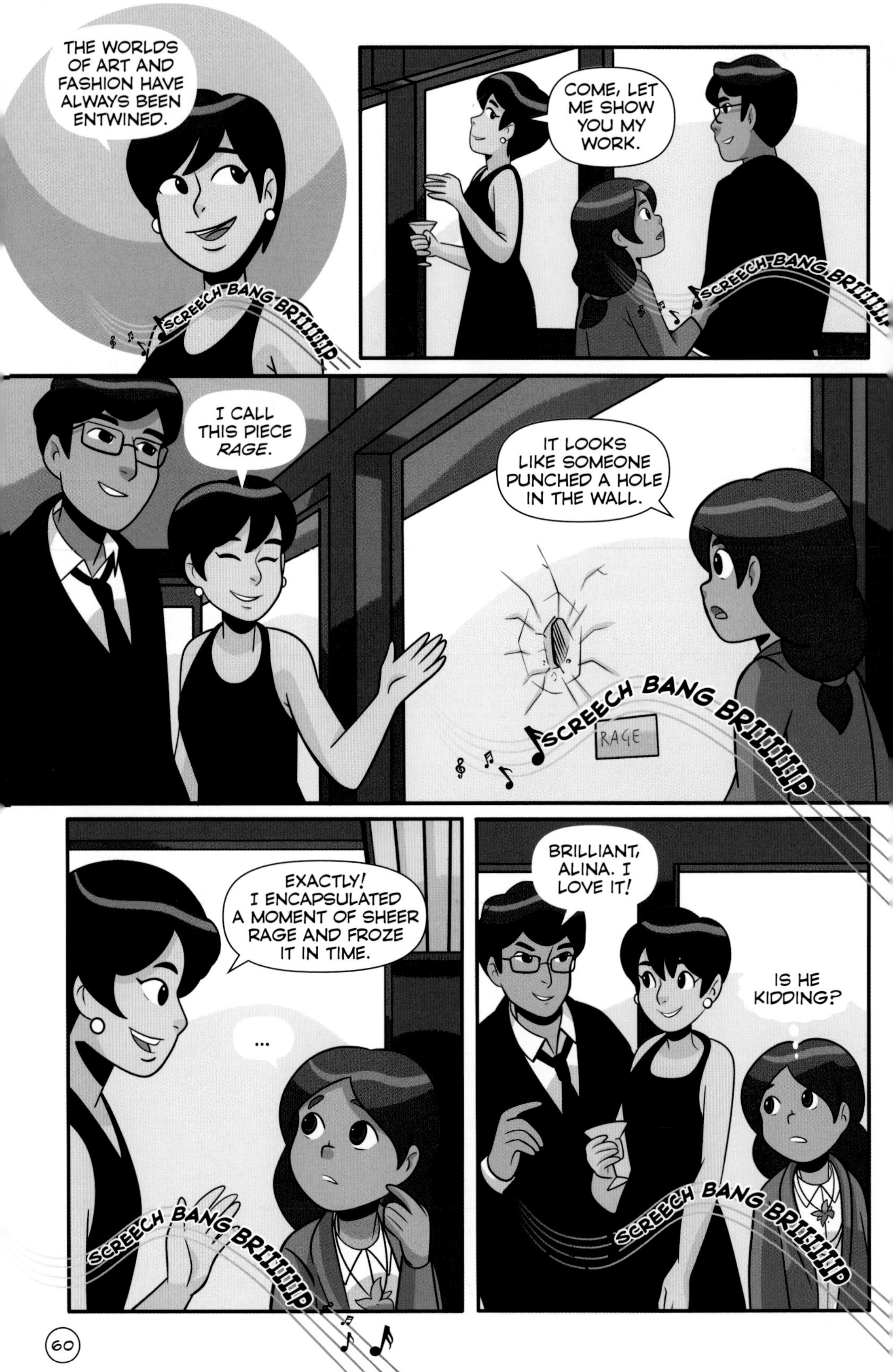
THE WORLDS OF ART AND FASHION HAVE ALWAYS BEEN ENTWINED.
SCREECH BANG BRIIIIIIP
COME, LET ME SHOW YOU MY WORK.
SCREECH BANG BRIIIIIIP
I CALL THIS PIECE *RAGE*.
IT LOOKS LIKE SOMEONE PUNCHED A HOLE IN THE WALL.
RAGE
SCREECH BANG BRIIIIIIP
EXACTLY! I ENCAPSULATED A MOMENT OF SHEER RAGE AND FROZE IT IN TIME.
...
SCREECH BANG BRIIIIIIP
BRILLIANT, ALINA. I LOVE IT!
IS HE KIDDING?
SCREECH BANG BRIIIIIIP

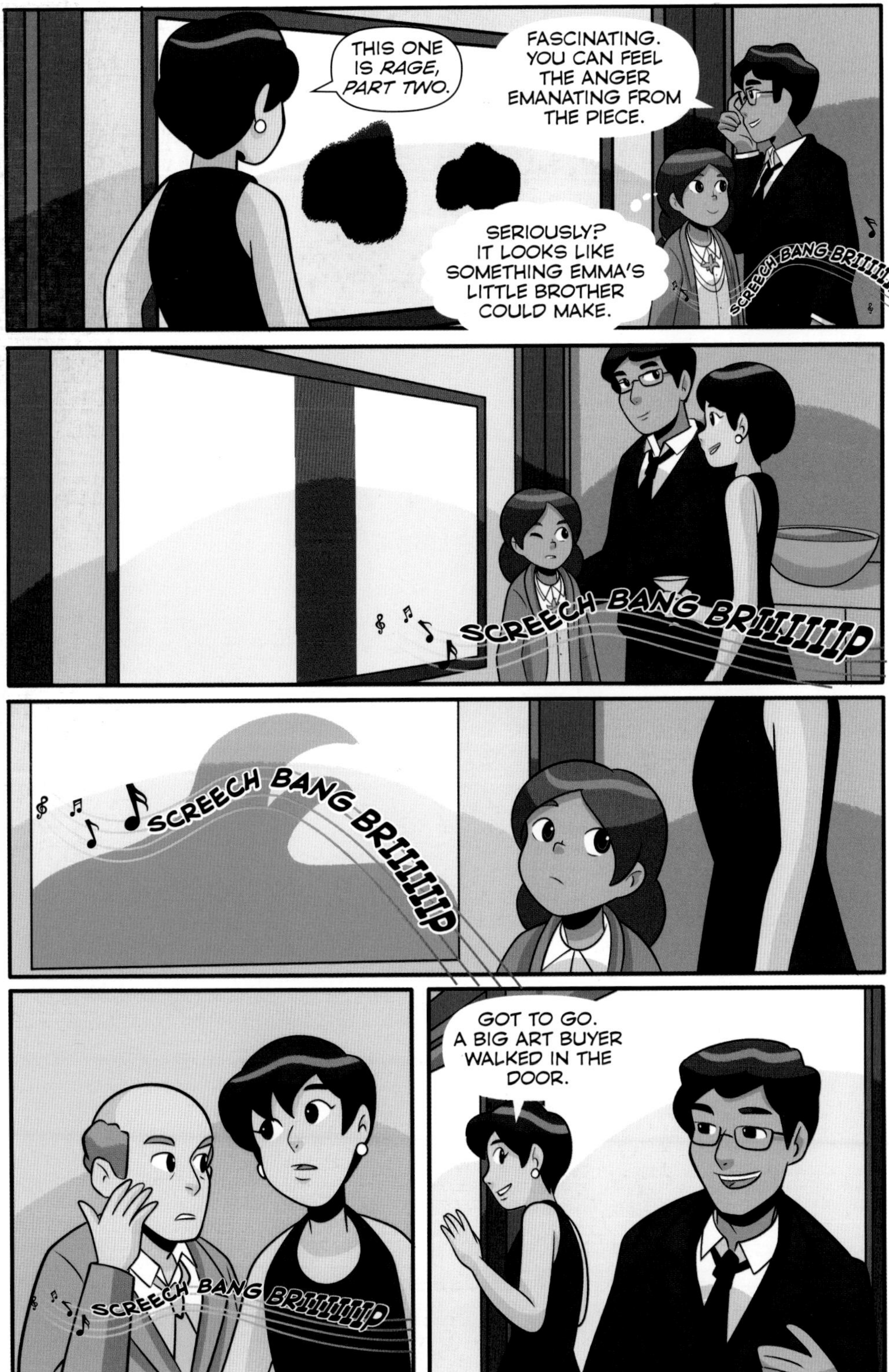
THIS ONE IS *RAGE, PART TWO.*
FASCINATING. YOU CAN FEEL THE ANGER EMANATING FROM THE PIECE.
SERIOUSLY? IT LOOKS LIKE SOMETHING EMMA'S LITTLE BROTHER COULD MAKE.
SCREECH BANG BRIIIIIIP
SCREECH BANG BRIIIIIIP
SCREECH BANG BRIIIIIIP
SCREECH BANG BRIIIIIIP
GOT TO GO. A BIG ART BUYER WALKED IN THE DOOR.

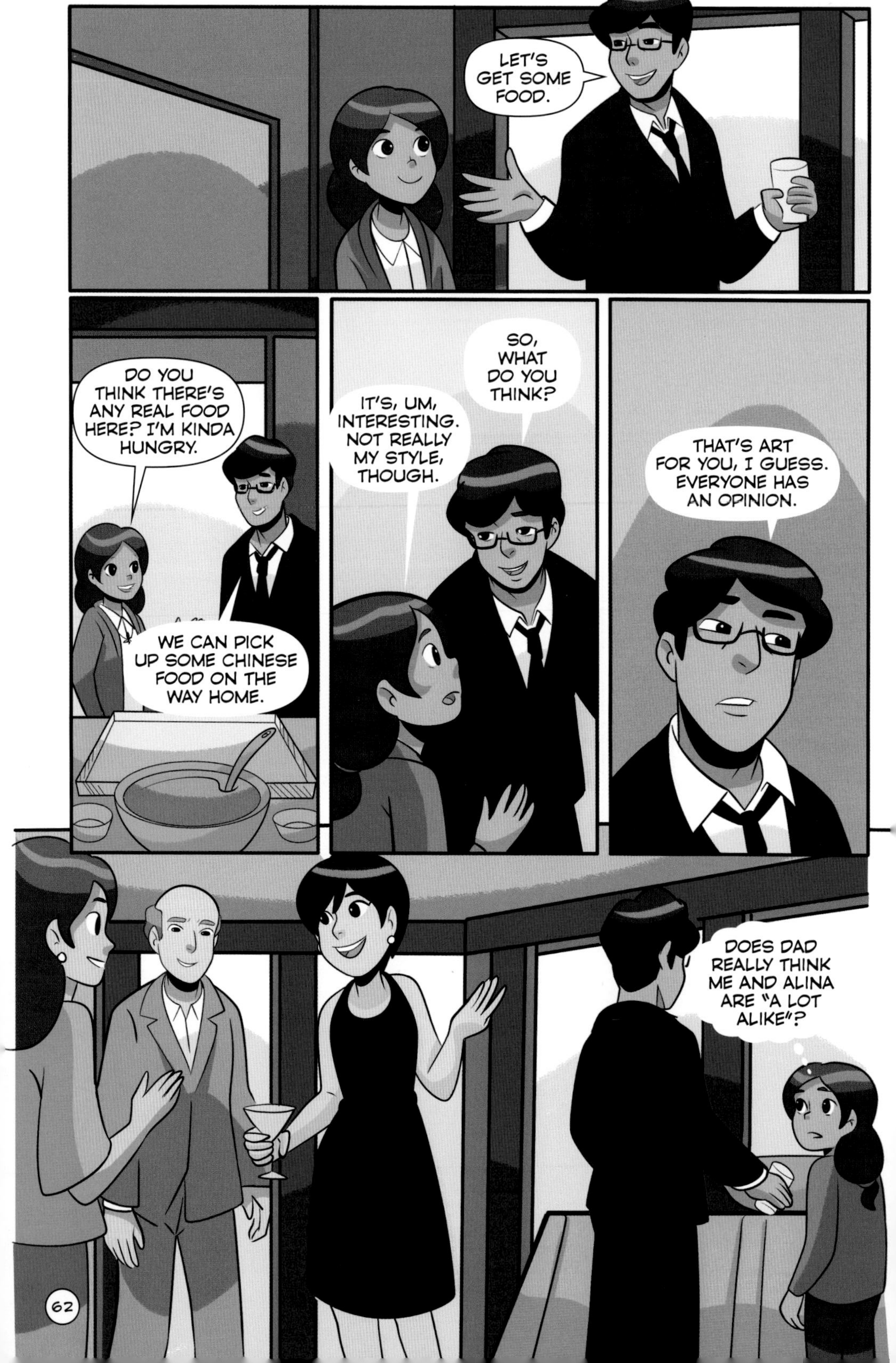

LET'S GET SOME FOOD.
DO YOU THINK THERE'S ANY REAL FOOD HERE? I'M KINDA HUNGRY.
WE CAN PICK UP SOME CHINESE FOOD ON THE WAY HOME.
SO, WHAT DO YOU THINK?
IT'S, UM, INTERESTING. NOT REALLY MY STYLE, THOUGH.
THAT'S ART FOR YOU, I GUESS. EVERYONE HAS AN OPINION.
DOES DAD REALLY THINK ME AND ALINA ARE "A LOT ALIKE"?

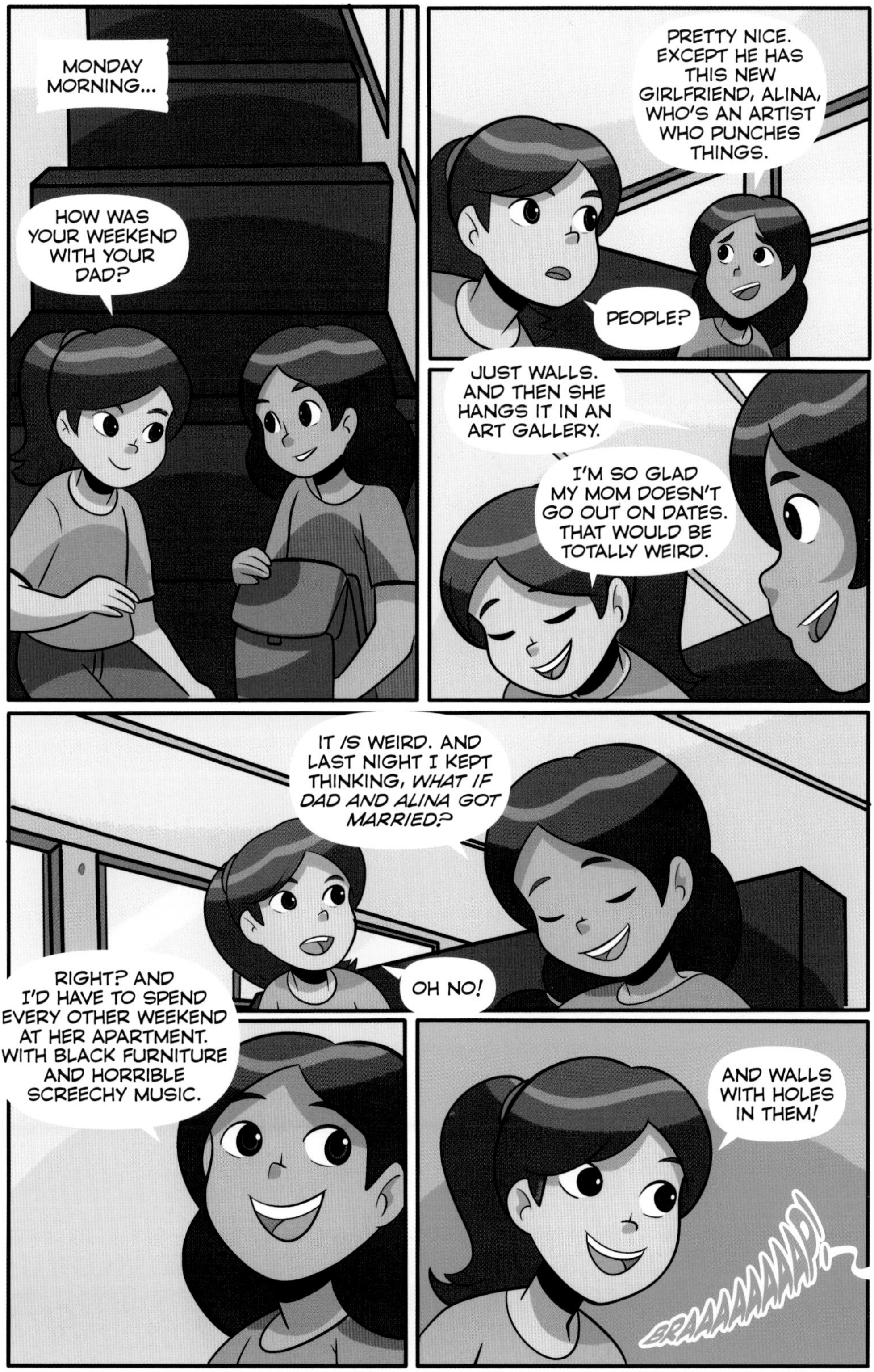
MONDAY MORNING...
HOW WAS YOUR WEEKEND WITH YOUR DAD?
PRETTY NICE. EXCEPT HE HAS THIS NEW GIRLFRIEND, ALINA, WHO'S AN ARTIST WHO PUNCHES THINGS.
PEOPLE?
JUST WALLS. AND THEN SHE HANGS IT IN AN ART GALLERY.
I'M SO GLAD MY MOM DOESN'T GO OUT ON DATES. THAT WOULD BE TOTALLY WEIRD.
IT *IS* WEIRD. AND LAST NIGHT I KEPT THINKING, *WHAT IF DAD AND ALINA GOT MARRIED?*
OH NO!
RIGHT? AND I'D HAVE TO SPEND EVERY OTHER WEEKEND AT HER APARTMENT. WITH BLACK FURNITURE AND HORRIBLE SCREECHY MUSIC.
AND WALLS WITH HOLES IN THEM!
BRAAAAAAAAP!

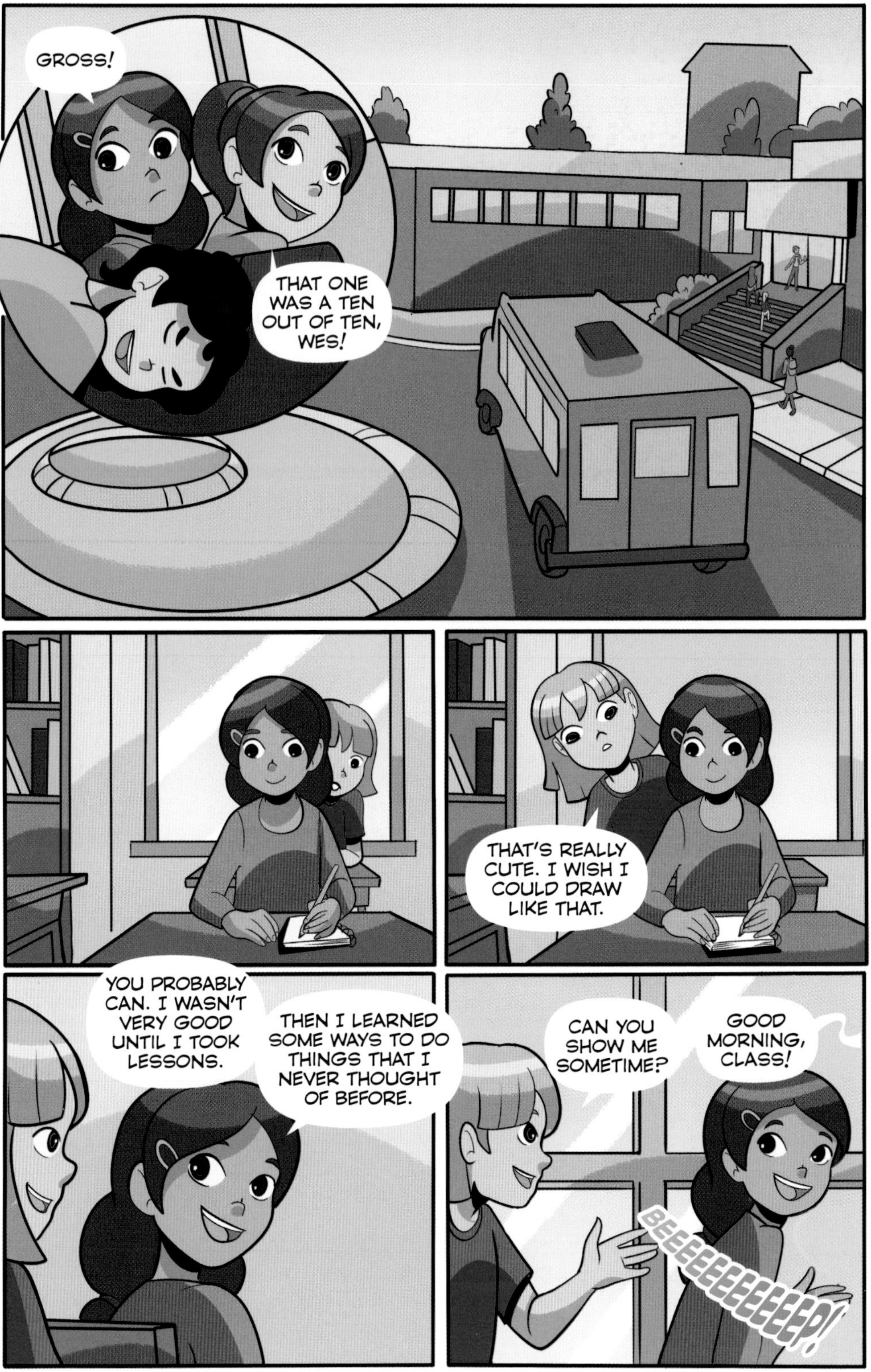
GROSS!
THAT ONE WAS A TEN OUT OF TEN, WES!
THAT'S REALLY CUTE. I WISH I COULD DRAW LIKE THAT.
YOU PROBABLY CAN. I WASN'T VERY GOOD UNTIL I TOOK LESSONS.
THEN I LEARNED SOME WAYS TO DO THINGS THAT I NEVER THOUGHT OF BEFORE.
CAN YOU SHOW ME SOMETIME?
GOOD MORNING, CLASS!
BEEEEEEEEEEEEP!

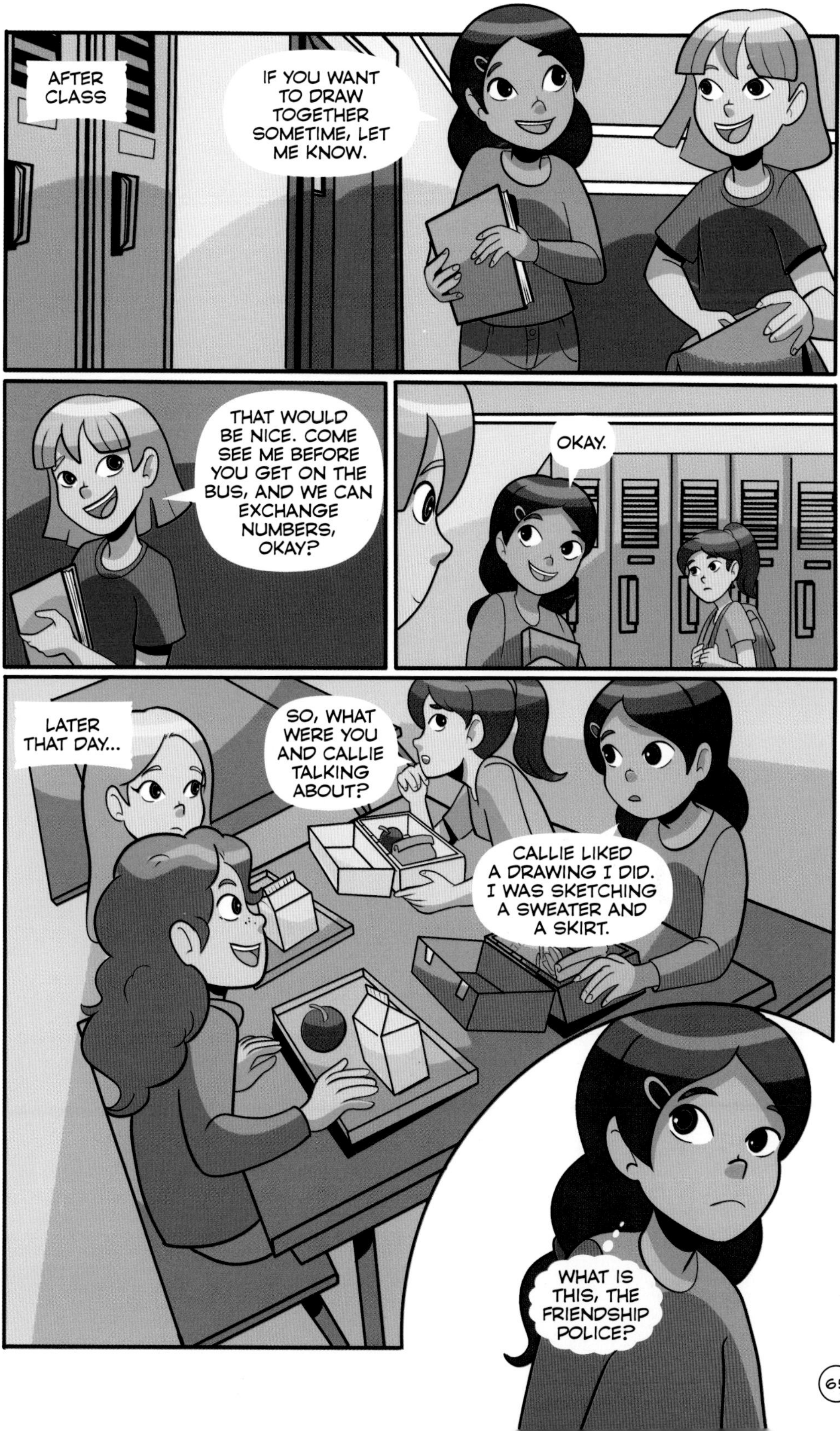
AFTER CLASS
IF YOU WANT TO DRAW TOGETHER SOMETIME, LET ME KNOW.
THAT WOULD BE NICE. COME SEE ME BEFORE YOU GET ON THE BUS, AND WE CAN EXCHANGE NUMBERS, OKAY?
OKAY.
LATER THAT DAY...
SO, WHAT WERE YOU AND CALLIE TALKING ABOUT?
CALLIE LIKED A DRAWING I DID. I WAS SKETCHING A SWEATER AND A SKIRT.
WHAT IS THIS, THE FRIENDSHIP POLICE?

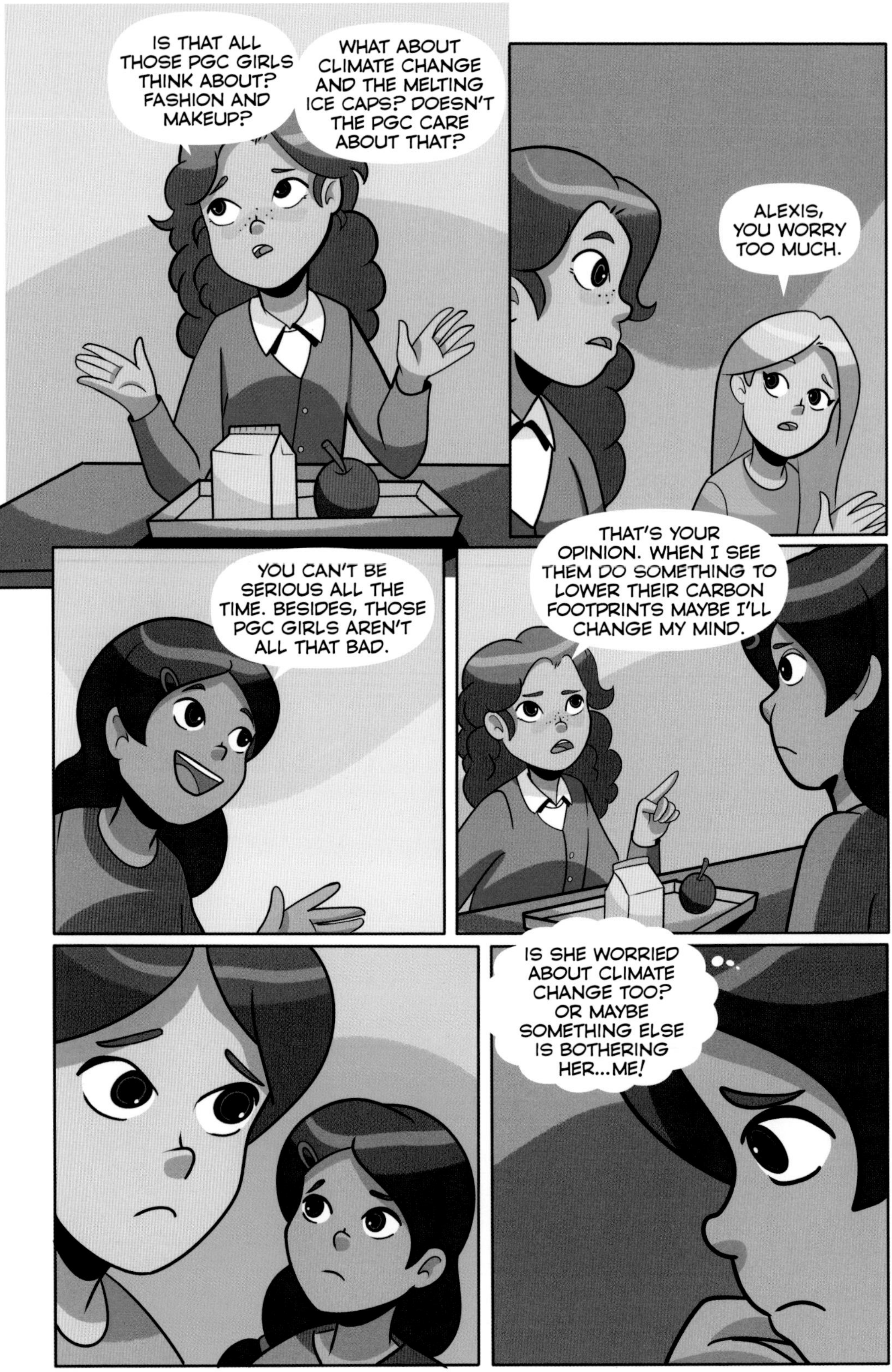
IS THAT ALL THOSE PGC GIRLS THINK ABOUT? FASHION AND MAKEUP?
WHAT ABOUT CLIMATE CHANGE AND THE MELTING ICE CAPS? DOESN'T THE PGC CARE ABOUT THAT?
ALEXIS, YOU WORRY TOO MUCH.
YOU CAN'T BE SERIOUS ALL THE TIME. BESIDES, THOSE PGC GIRLS AREN'T ALL THAT BAD.
THAT'S YOUR OPINION. WHEN I SEE THEM DO SOMETHING TO LOWER THEIR CARBON FOOTPRINTS MAYBE I'LL CHANGE MY MIND.
IS SHE WORRIED ABOUT CLIMATE CHANGE TOO? OR MAYBE SOMETHING ELSE IS BOTHERING HER...ME!

Chapter 8

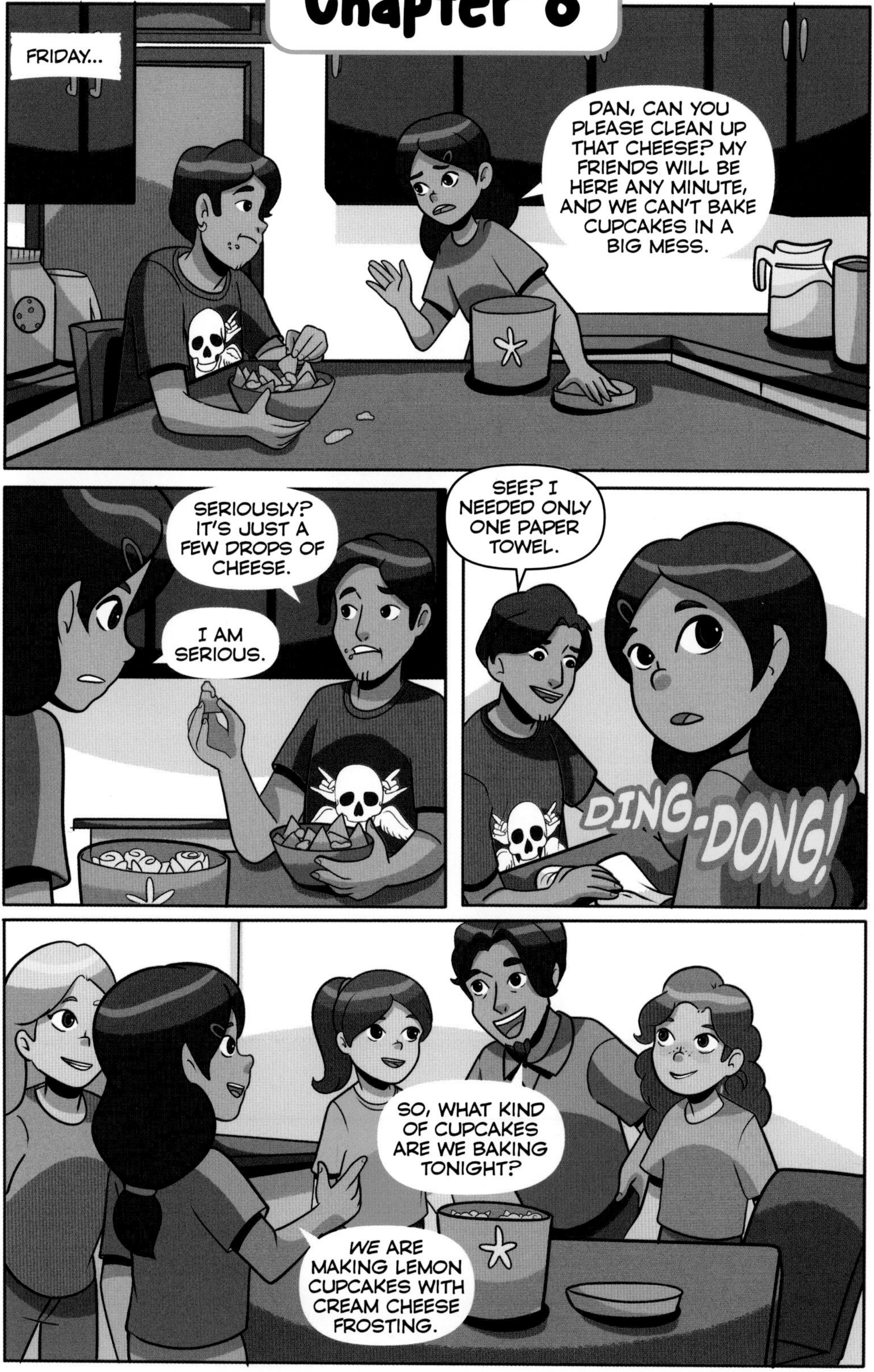
FRIDAY...
DAN, CAN YOU PLEASE CLEAN UP THAT CHEESE? MY FRIENDS WILL BE HERE ANY MINUTE, AND WE CAN'T BAKE CUPCAKES IN A BIG MESS.
SERIOUSLY? IT'S JUST A FEW DROPS OF CHEESE.
I AM SERIOUS.
SEE? I NEEDED ONLY ONE PAPER TOWEL.
DING-DONG!
SO, WHAT KIND OF CUPCAKES ARE WE BAKING TONIGHT?
WE ARE MAKING LEMON CUPCAKES WITH CREAM CHEESE FROSTING.

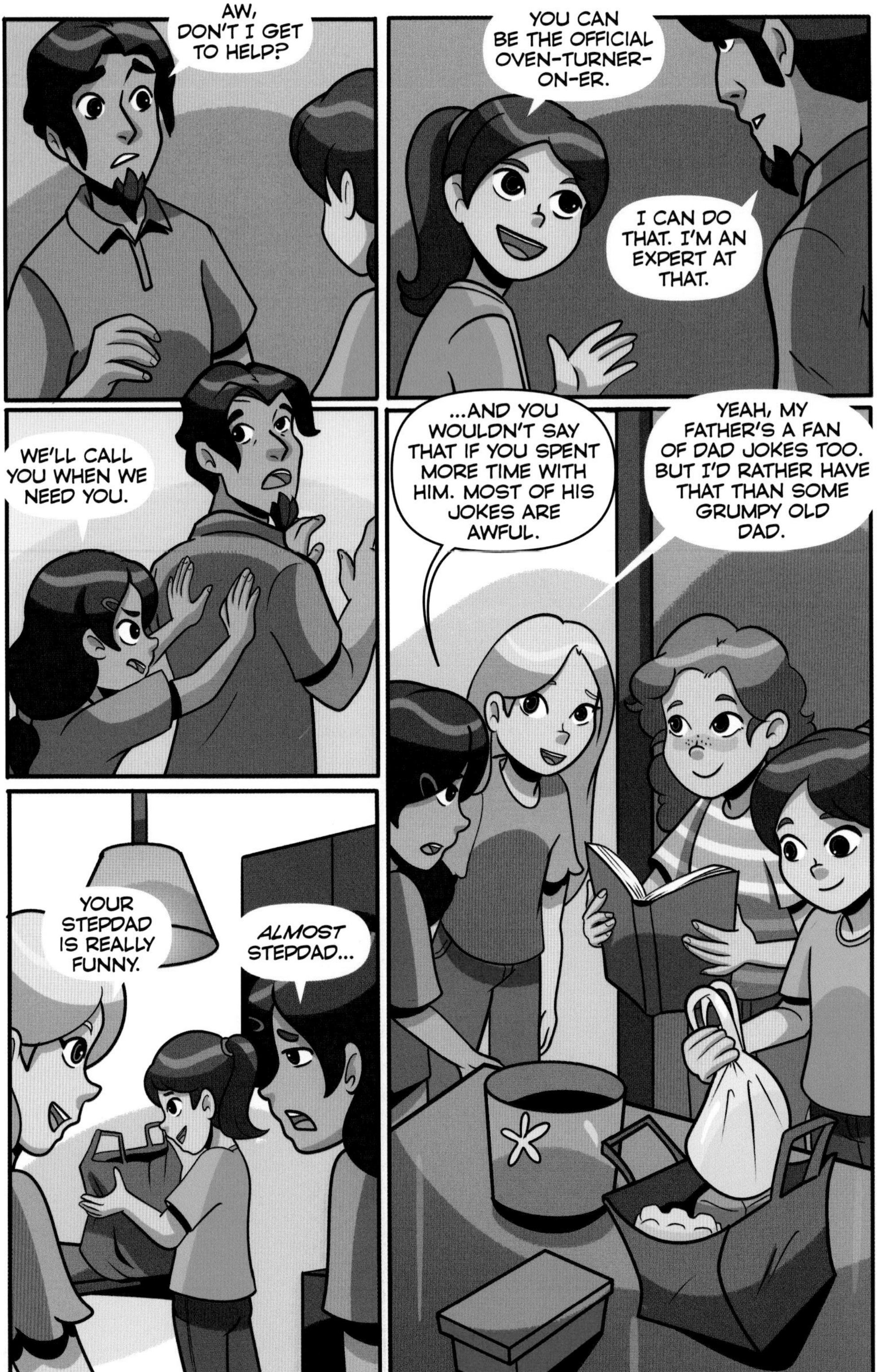
AW, DON'T I GET TO HELP?
YOU CAN BE THE OFFICIAL OVEN-TURNER-ON-ER.
I CAN DO THAT. I'M AN EXPERT AT THAT.
WE'LL CALL YOU WHEN WE NEED YOU.
YOUR STEPDAD IS REALLY FUNNY.
ALMOST STEPDAD...
...AND YOU WOULDN'T SAY THAT IF YOU SPENT MORE TIME WITH HIM. MOST OF HIS JOKES ARE AWFUL.
YEAH, MY FATHER'S A FAN OF DAD JOKES TOO. BUT I'D RATHER HAVE THAT THAN SOME GRUMPY OLD DAD.

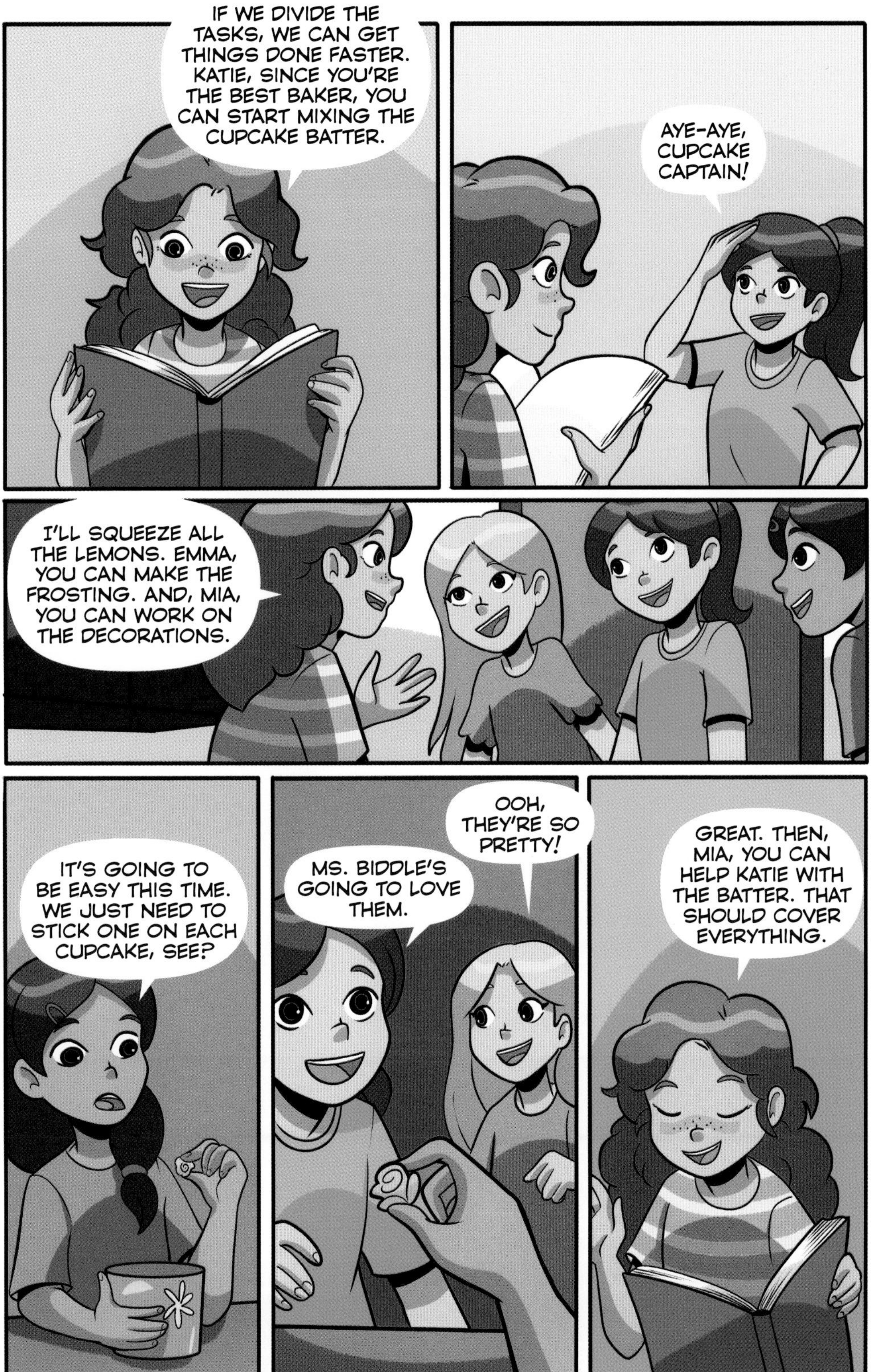
IF WE DIVIDE THE TASKS, WE CAN GET THINGS DONE FASTER. KATIE, SINCE YOU'RE THE BEST BAKER, YOU CAN START MIXING THE CUPCAKE BATTER.
AYE-AYE, CUPCAKE CAPTAIN!
I'LL SQUEEZE ALL THE LEMONS. EMMA, YOU CAN MAKE THE FROSTING. AND, MIA, YOU CAN WORK ON THE DECORATIONS.
IT'S GOING TO BE EASY THIS TIME. WE JUST NEED TO STICK ONE ON EACH CUPCAKE, SEE?
MS. BIDDLE'S GOING TO LOVE THEM.
OOH, THEY'RE SO PRETTY!
GREAT. THEN, MIA, YOU CAN HELP KATIE WITH THE BATTER. THAT SHOULD COVER EVERYTHING.

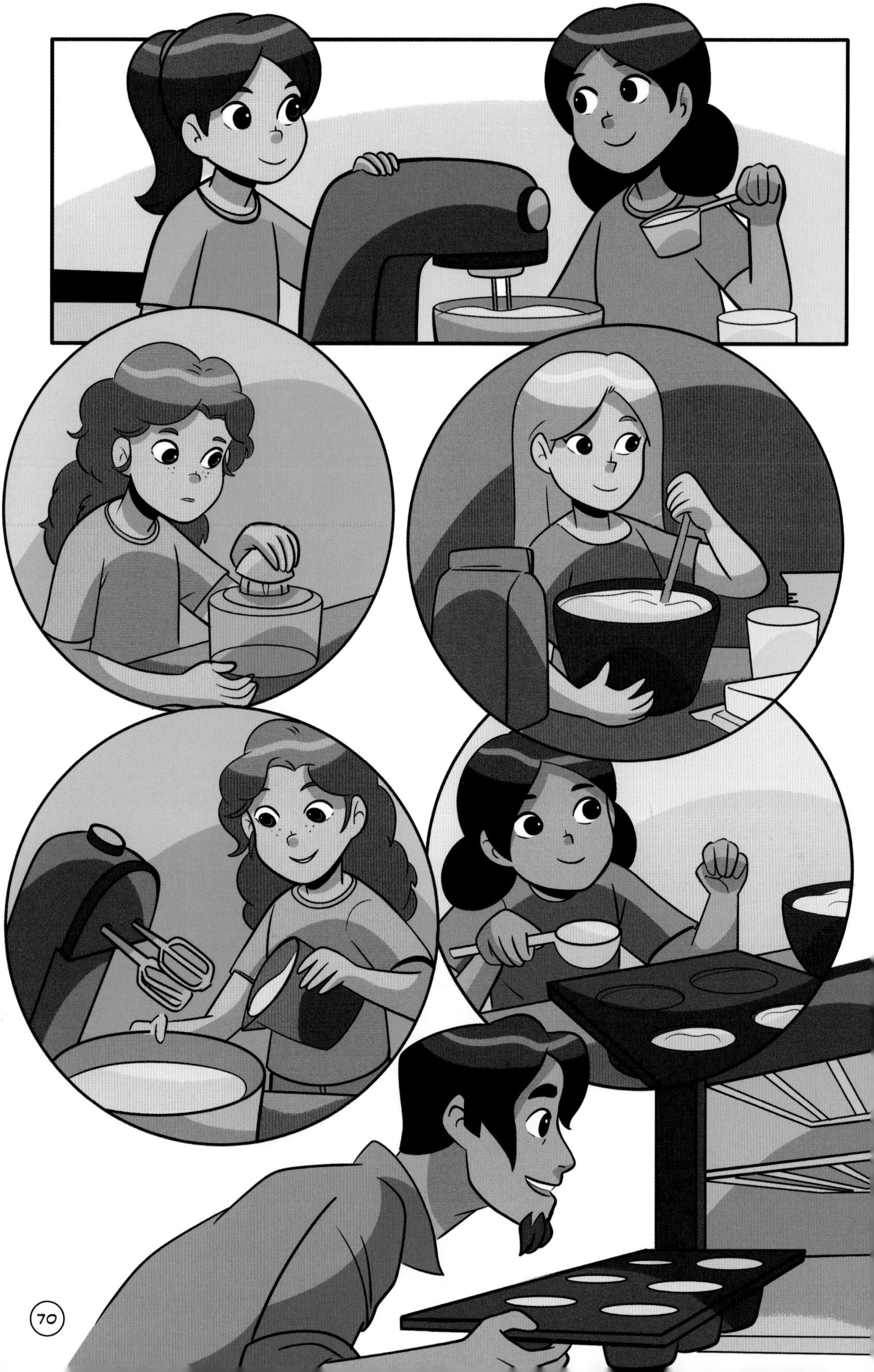

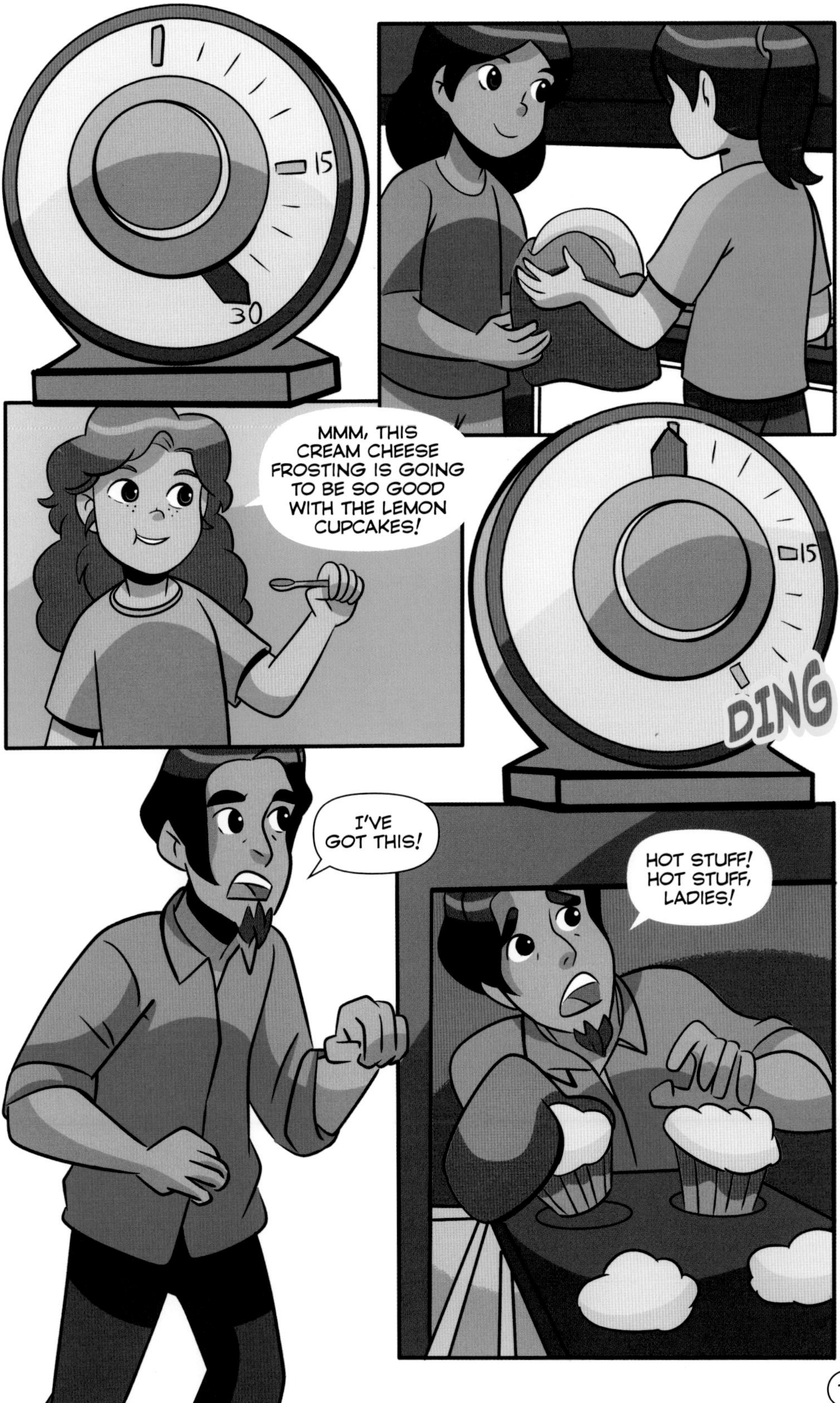
15
30
MMM, THIS CREAM CHEESE FROSTING IS GOING TO BE SO GOOD WITH THE LEMON CUPCAKES!
15
DING
I'VE GOT THIS!
HOT STUFF! HOT STUFF, LADIES!

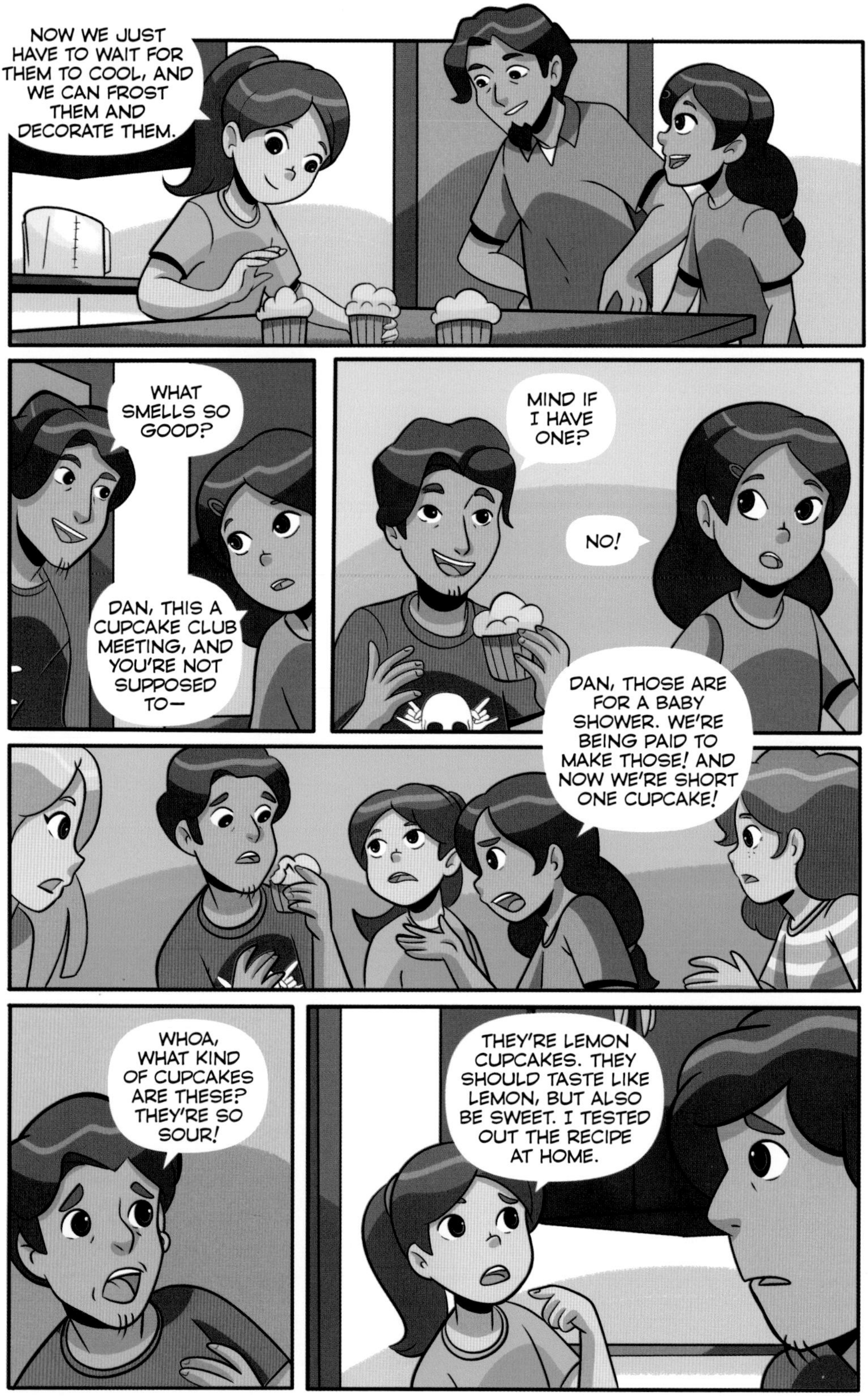
NOW WE JUST HAVE TO WAIT FOR THEM TO COOL, AND WE CAN FROST THEM AND DECORATE THEM.
WHAT SMELLS SO GOOD?
DAN, THIS A CUPCAKE CLUB MEETING, AND YOU'RE NOT SUPPOSED TO—
MIND IF I HAVE ONE?
NO!
DAN, THOSE ARE FOR A BABY SHOWER. WE'RE BEING PAID TO MAKE THOSE! AND NOW WE'RE SHORT ONE CUPCAKE!
WHOA, WHAT KIND OF CUPCAKES ARE THESE? THEY'RE SO SOUR!
THEY'RE LEMON CUPCAKES. THEY SHOULD TASTE LIKE LEMON, BUT ALSO BE SWEET. I TESTED OUT THE RECIPE AT HOME.

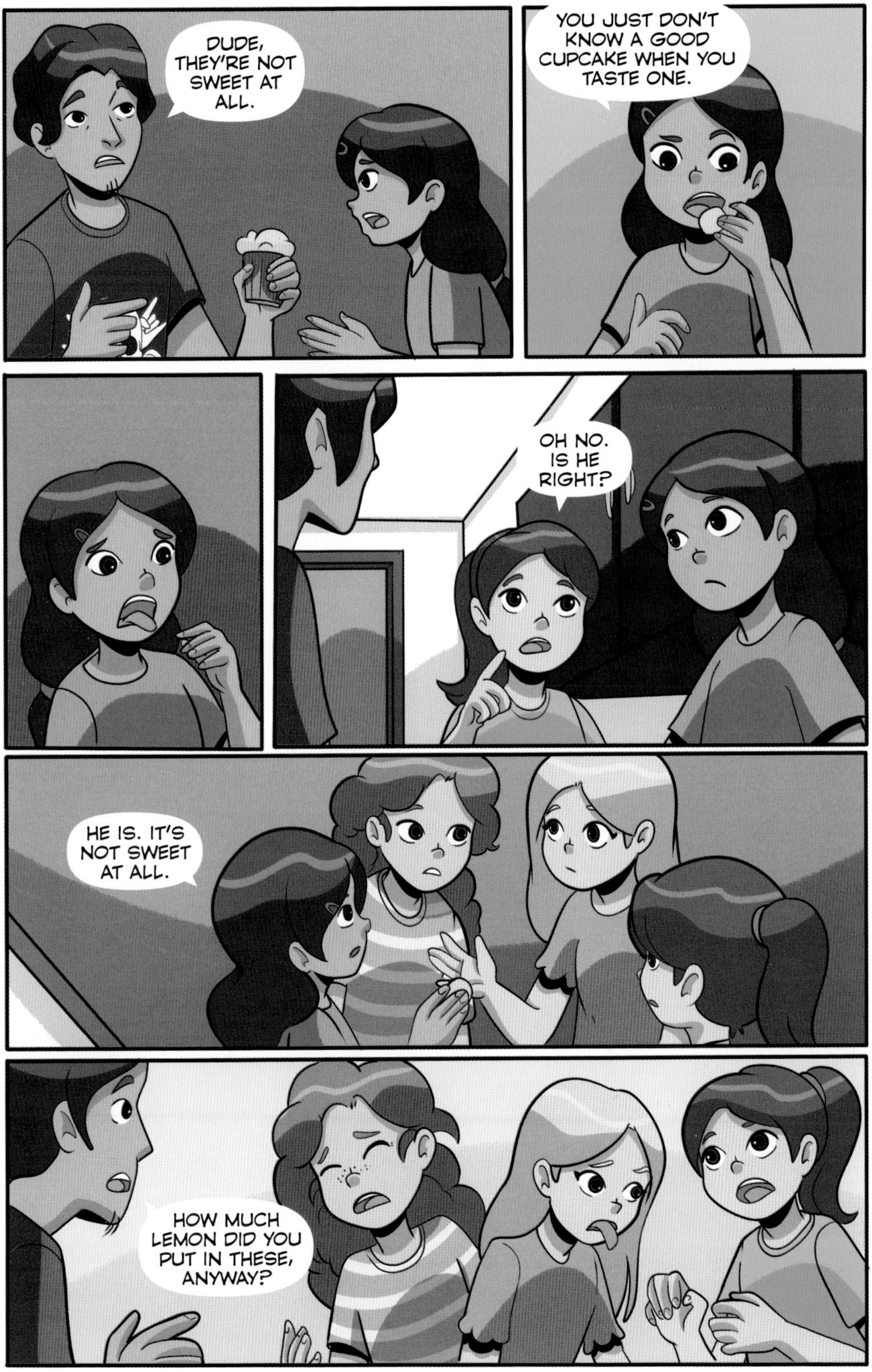
DUDE, THEY'RE NOT SWEET AT ALL.
YOU JUST DON'T KNOW A GOOD CUPCAKE WHEN YOU TASTE ONE.
OH NO. IS HE RIGHT?
HE IS. IT'S NOT SWEET AT ALL.
HOW MUCH LEMON DID YOU PUT IN THESE, ANYWAY?

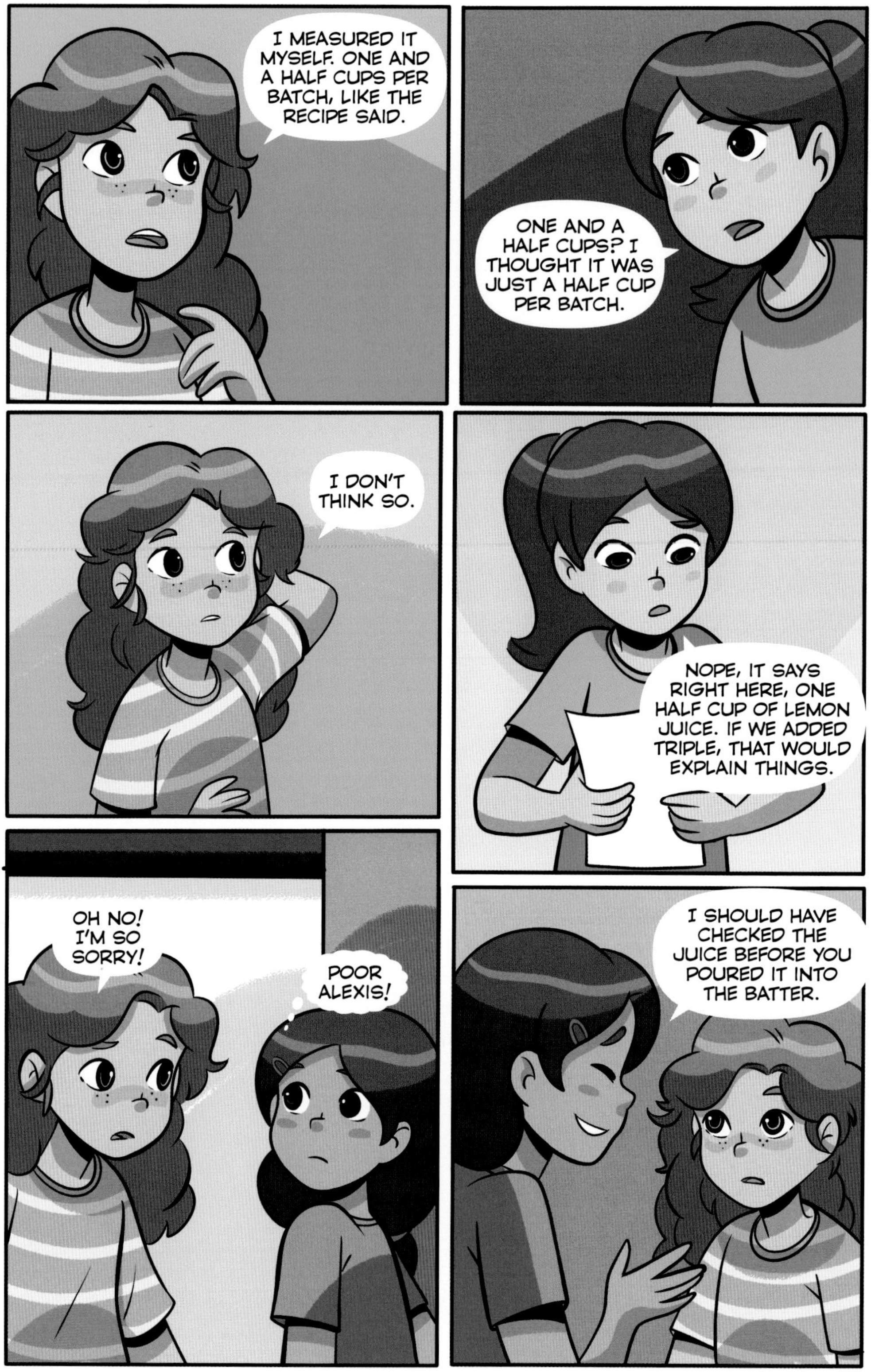
I MEASURED IT MYSELF. ONE AND A HALF CUPS PER BATCH, LIKE THE RECIPE SAID.
ONE AND A HALF CUPS? I THOUGHT IT WAS JUST A HALF CUP PER BATCH.
I DON'T THINK SO.
NOPE, IT SAYS RIGHT HERE, ONE HALF CUP OF LEMON JUICE. IF WE ADDED TRIPLE, THAT WOULD EXPLAIN THINGS.
OH NO! I'M SO SORRY!
POOR ALEXIS!
I SHOULD HAVE CHECKED THE JUICE BEFORE YOU POURED IT INTO THE BATTER.

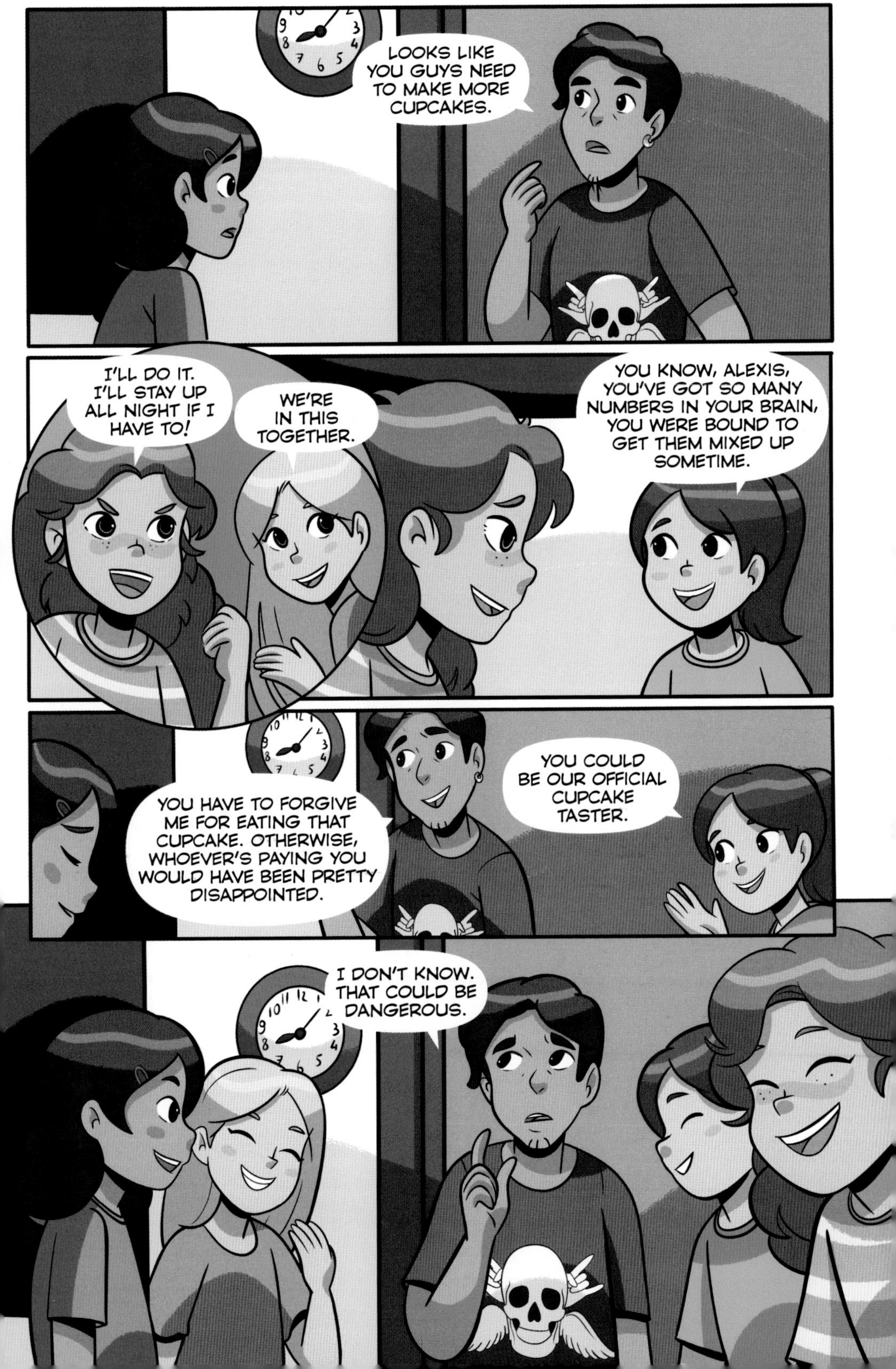
LOOKS LIKE YOU GUYS NEED TO MAKE MORE CUPCAKES.
I'LL DO IT. I'LL STAY UP ALL NIGHT IF I HAVE TO!
WE'RE IN THIS TOGETHER.
YOU KNOW, ALEXIS, YOU'VE GOT SO MANY NUMBERS IN YOUR BRAIN, YOU WERE BOUND TO GET THEM MIXED UP SOMETIME.
YOU HAVE TO FORGIVE ME FOR EATING THAT CUPCAKE. OTHERWISE, WHOEVER'S PAYING YOU WOULD HAVE BEEN PRETTY DISAPPOINTED.
YOU COULD BE OUR OFFICIAL CUPCAKE TASTER.
I DON'T KNOW. THAT COULD BE DANGEROUS.

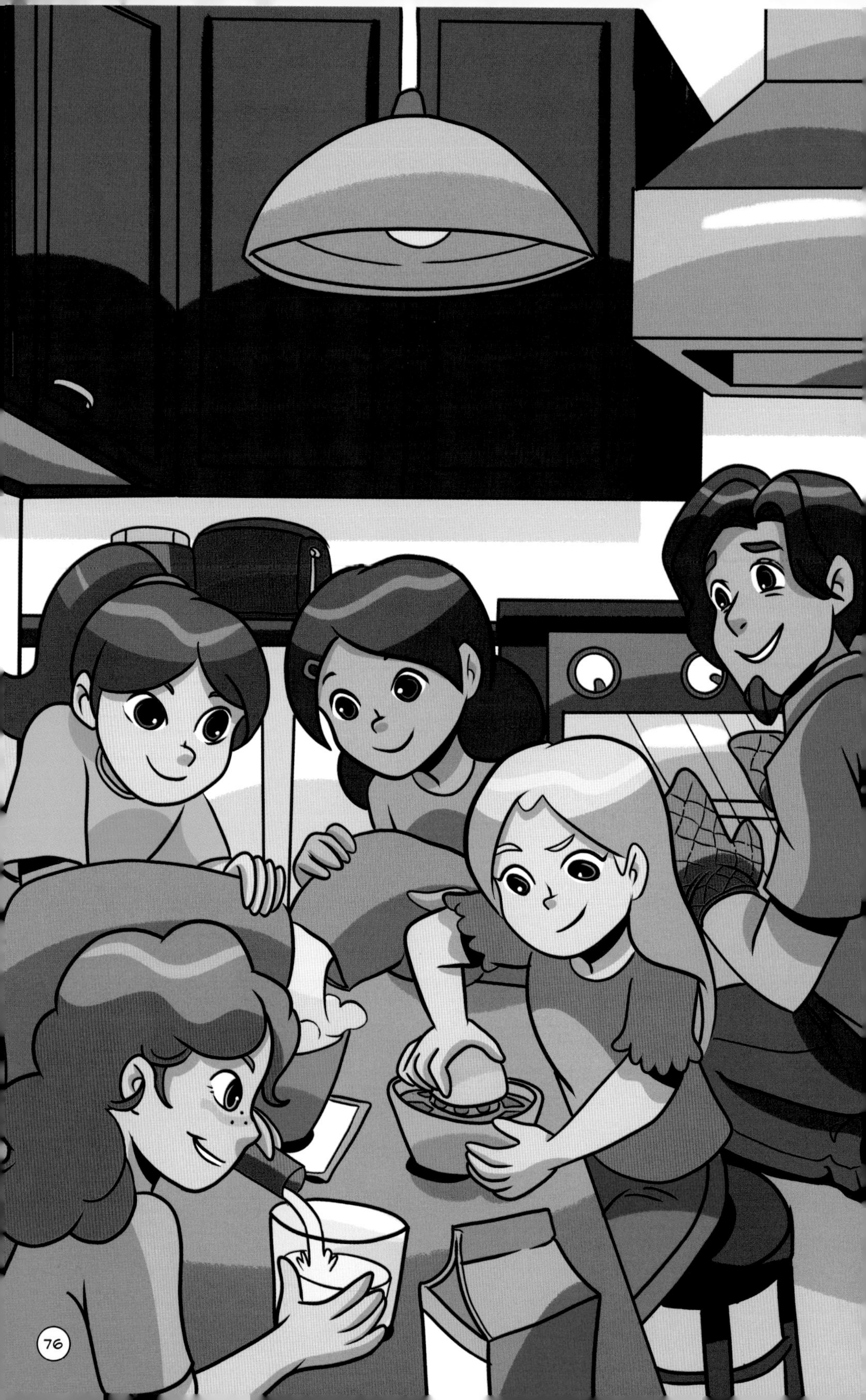

Chapter 9

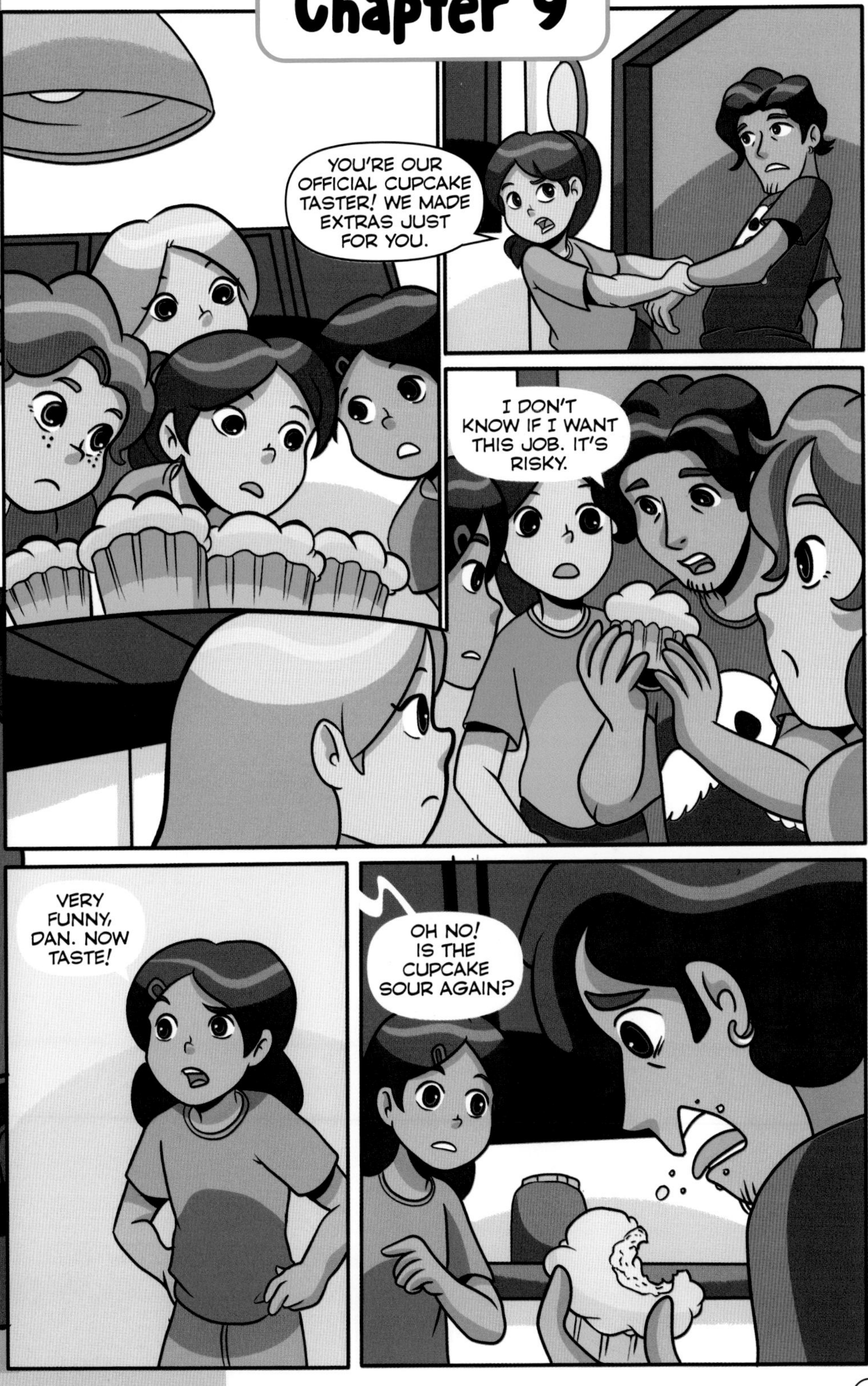
YOU'RE OUR OFFICIAL CUPCAKE TASTER! WE MADE EXTRAS JUST FOR YOU.
I DON'T KNOW IF I WANT THIS JOB. IT'S RISKY.
VERY FUNNY, DAN. NOW TASTE!
OH NO! IS THE CUPCAKE SOUR AGAIN?

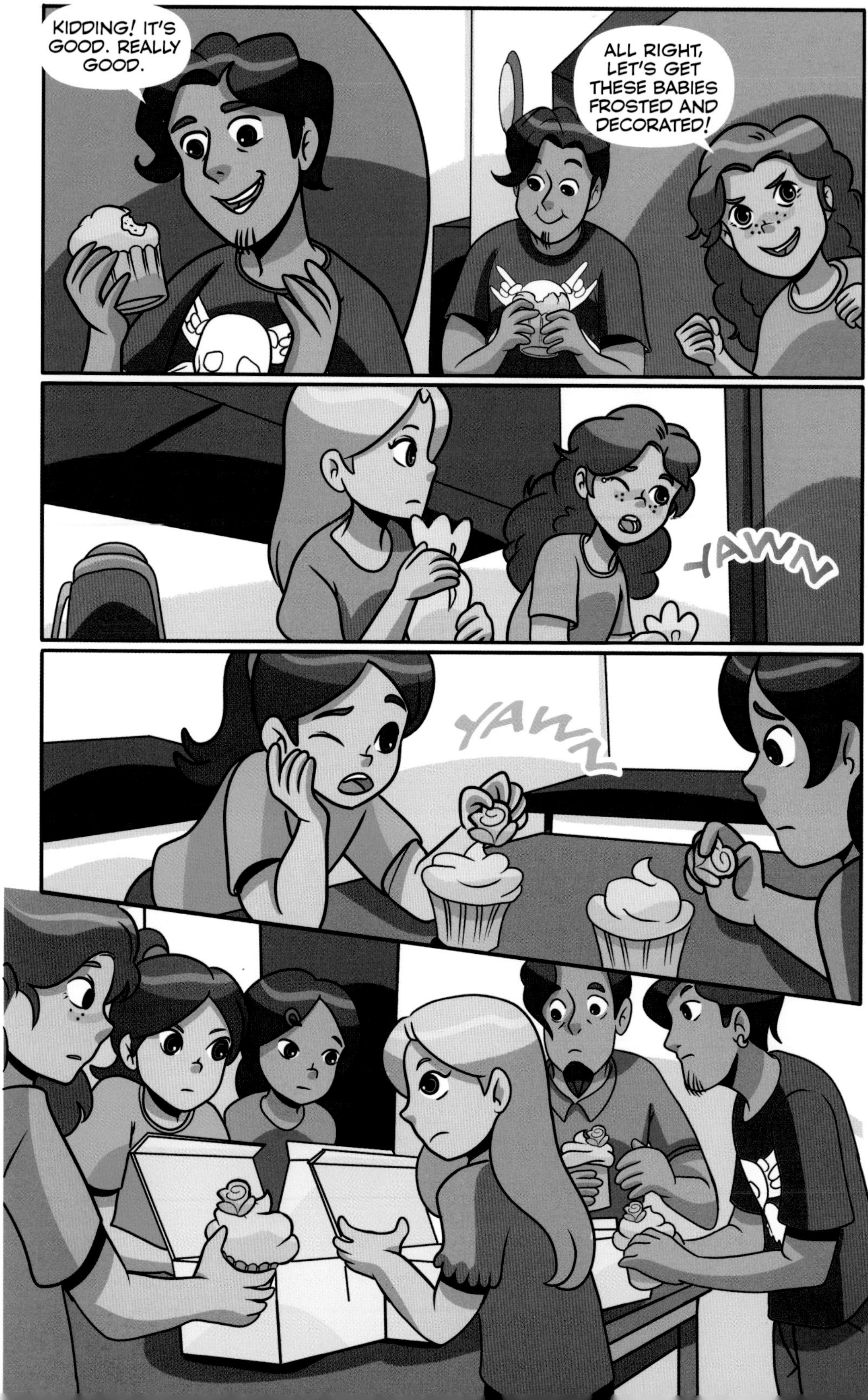
KIDDING! IT'S GOOD. REALLY GOOD.
ALL RIGHT, LET'S GET THESE BABIES FROSTED AND DECORATED!
YAWN
YAWN

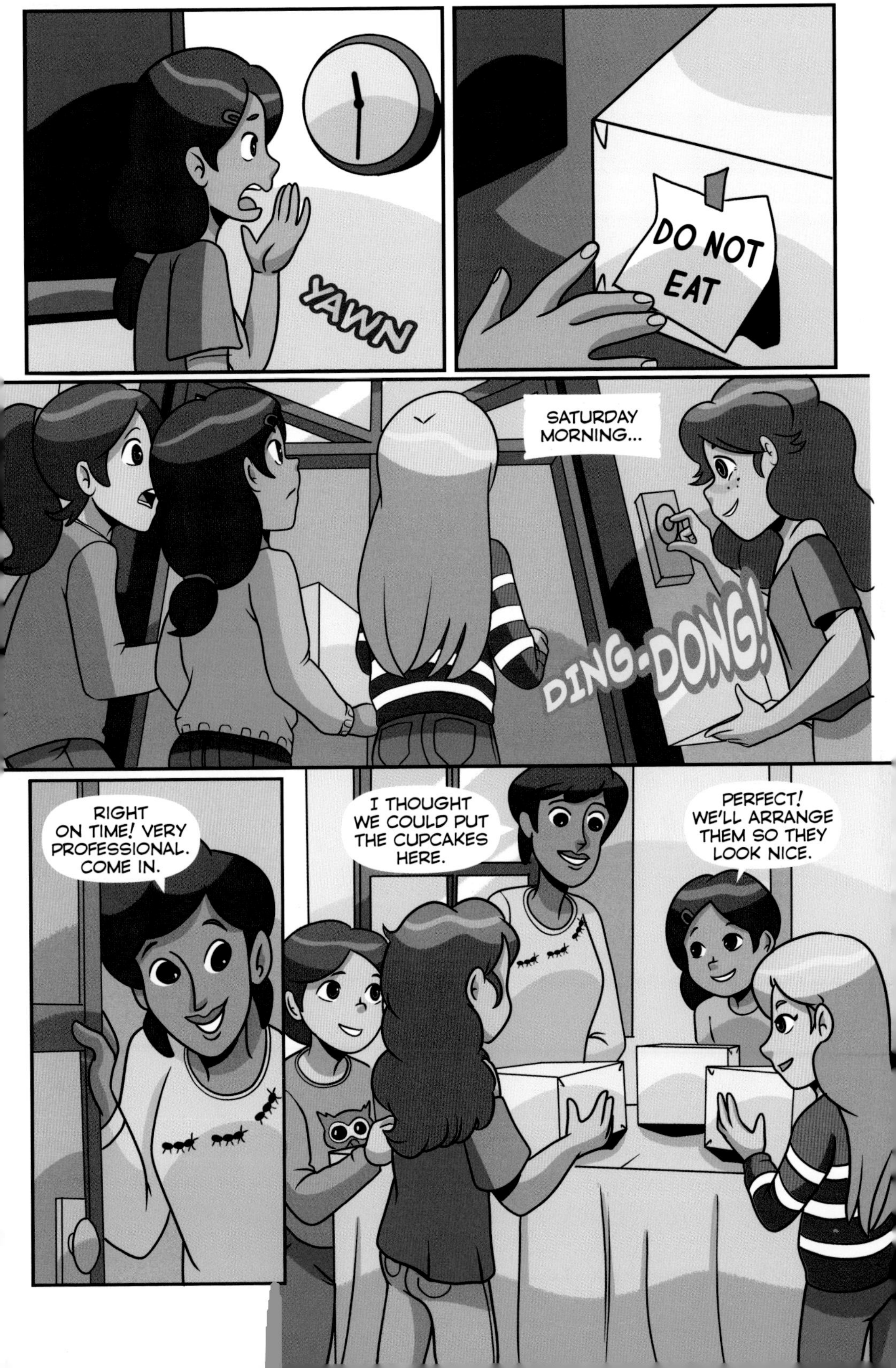
YAWN
DO NOT EAT
SATURDAY MORNING...
DING-DONG!
RIGHT ON TIME! VERY PROFESSIONAL. COME IN.
I THOUGHT WE COULD PUT THE CUPCAKES HERE.
PERFECT! WE'LL ARRANGE THEM SO THEY LOOK NICE.

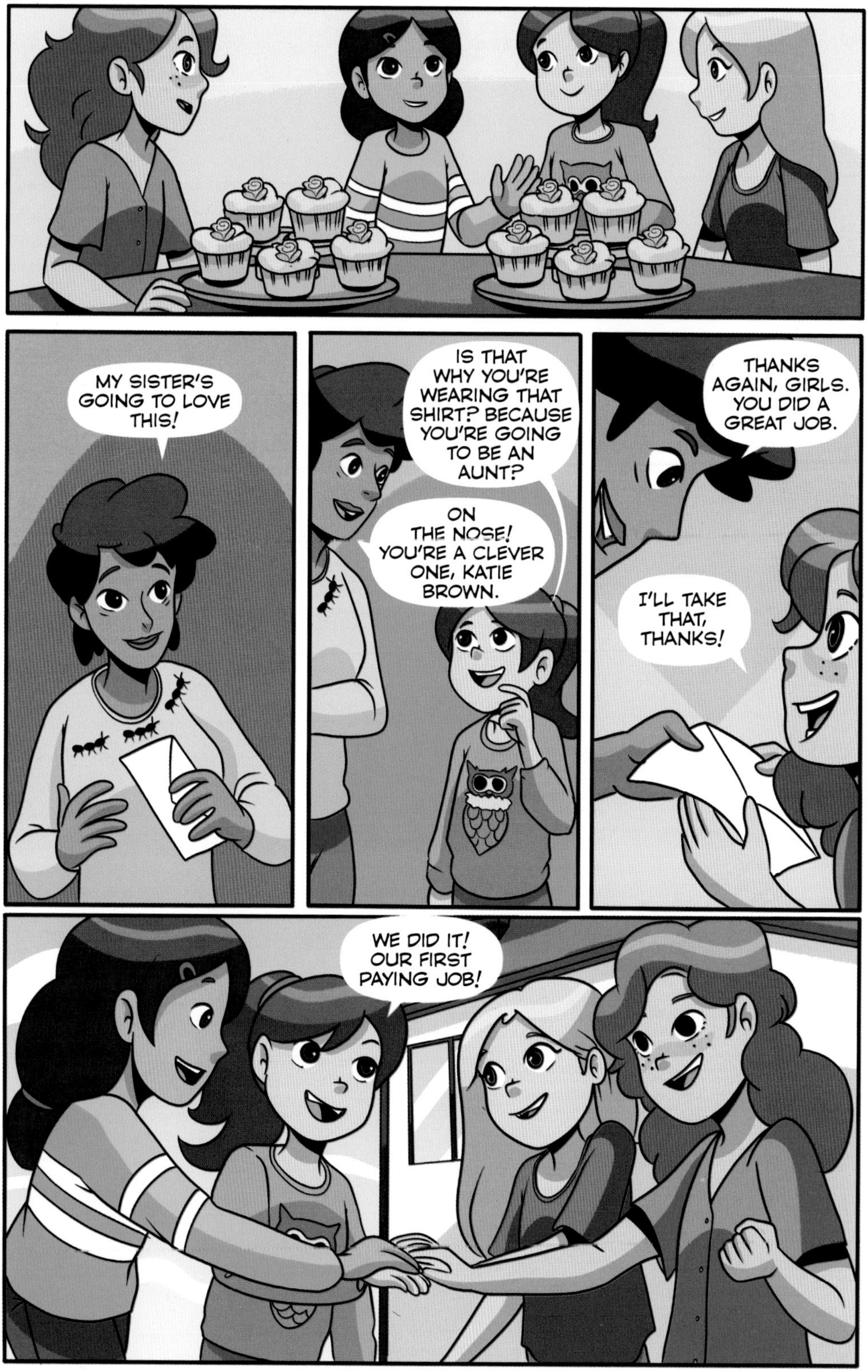
MY SISTER'S GOING TO LOVE THIS!
IS THAT WHY YOU'RE WEARING THAT SHIRT? BECAUSE YOU'RE GOING TO BE AN AUNT?
ON THE NOSE! YOU'RE A CLEVER ONE, KATIE BROWN.
THANKS AGAIN, GIRLS. YOU DID A GREAT JOB.
I'LL TAKE THAT, THANKS!
WE DID IT! OUR FIRST PAYING JOB!

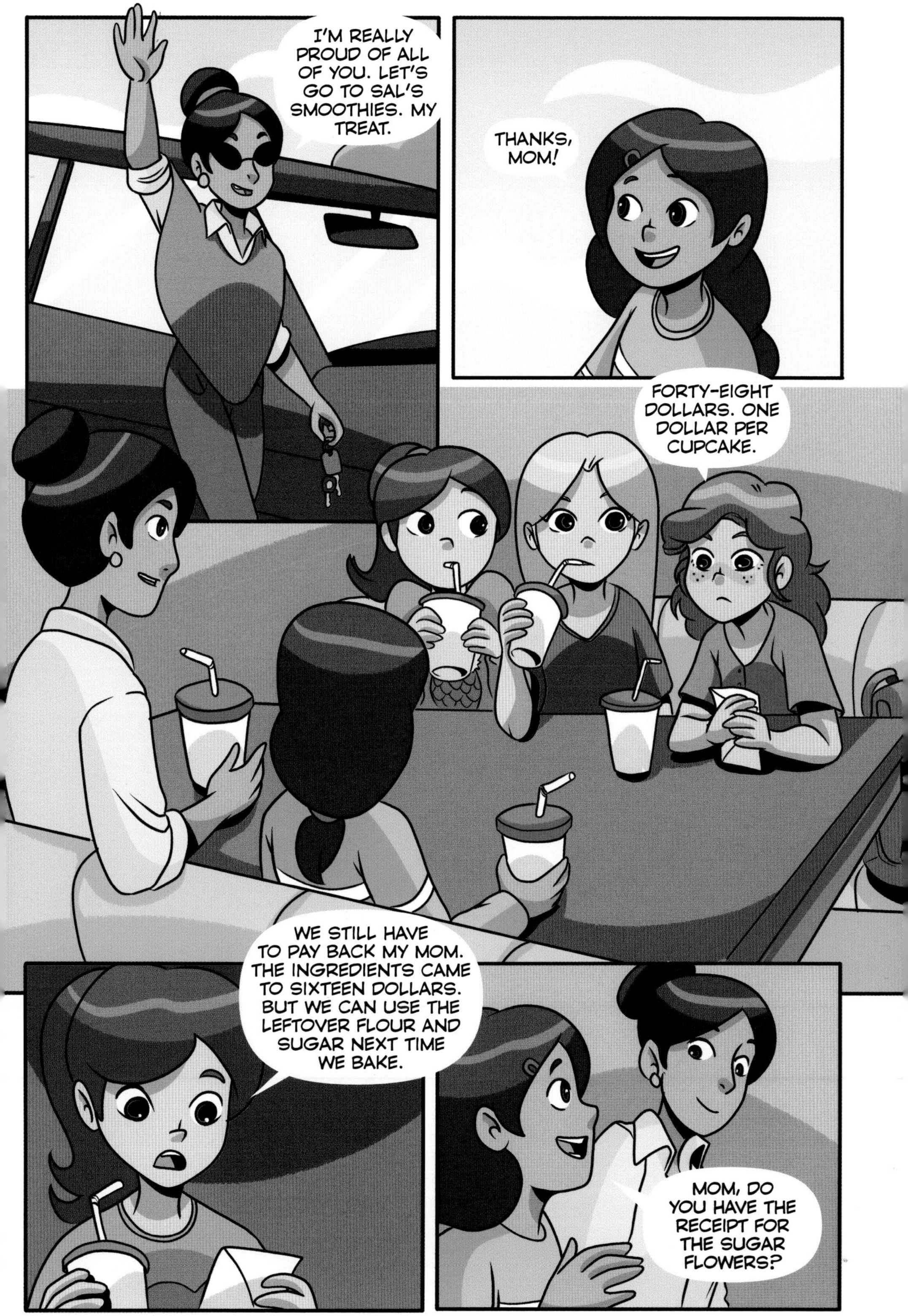
I'M REALLY PROUD OF ALL OF YOU. LET'S GO TO SAL'S SMOOTHIES. MY TREAT.
THANKS, MOM!
FORTY-EIGHT DOLLARS. ONE DOLLAR PER CUPCAKE.
WE STILL HAVE TO PAY BACK MY MOM. THE INGREDIENTS CAME TO SIXTEEN DOLLARS. BUT WE CAN USE THE LEFTOVER FLOUR AND SUGAR NEXT TIME WE BAKE.
MOM, DO YOU HAVE THE RECEIPT FOR THE SUGAR FLOWERS?

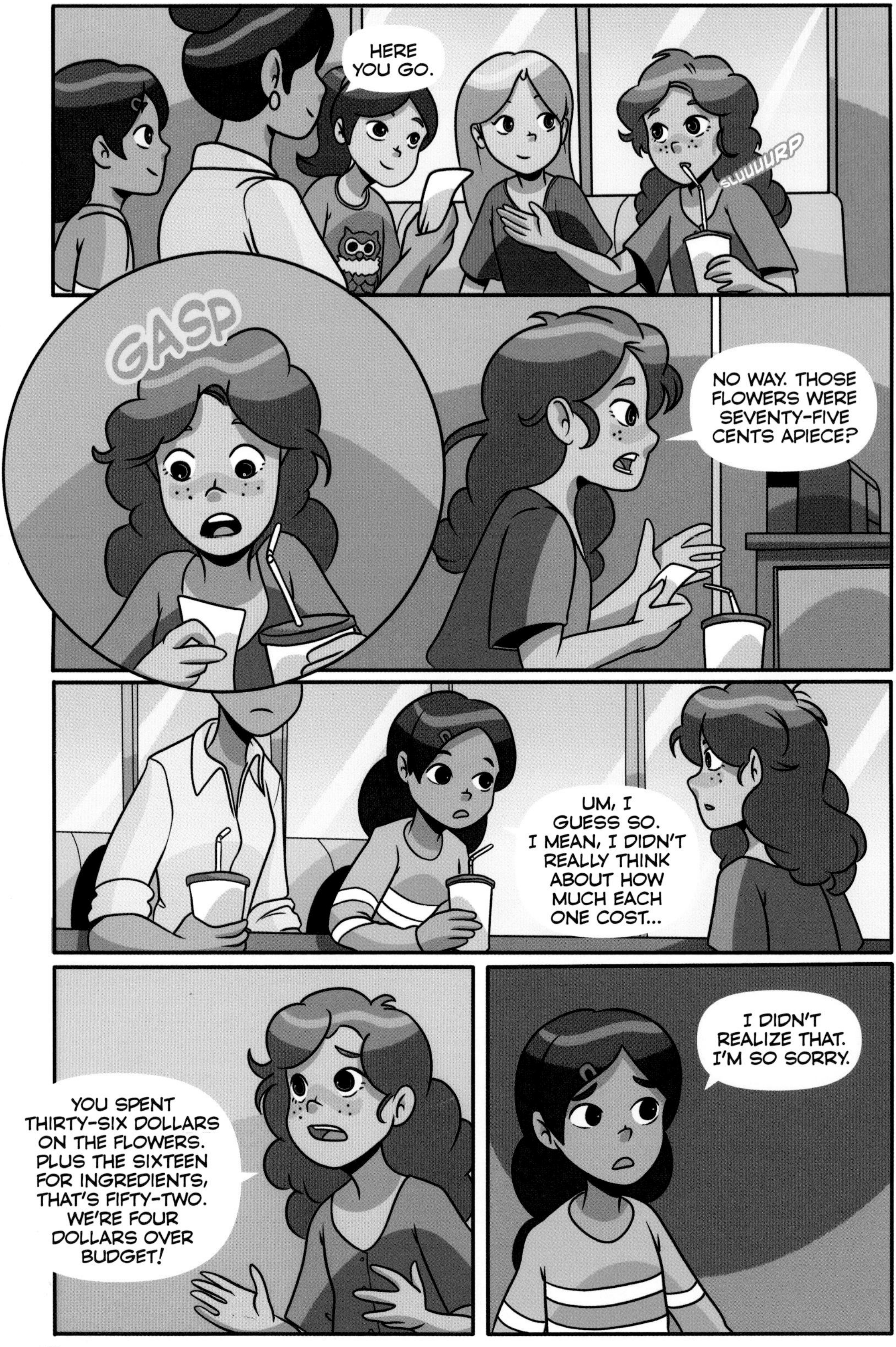
HERE YOU GO.
SWUUUURP
GASP
NO WAY. THOSE FLOWERS WERE SEVENTY-FIVE CENTS APIECE?
UM, I GUESS SO. I MEAN, I DIDN'T REALLY THINK ABOUT HOW MUCH EACH ONE COST...
YOU SPENT THIRTY-SIX DOLLARS ON THE FLOWERS. PLUS THE SIXTEEN FOR INGREDIENTS, THAT'S FIFTY-TWO. WE'RE FOUR DOLLARS OVER BUDGET!
I DIDN'T REALIZE THAT. I'M SO SORRY.

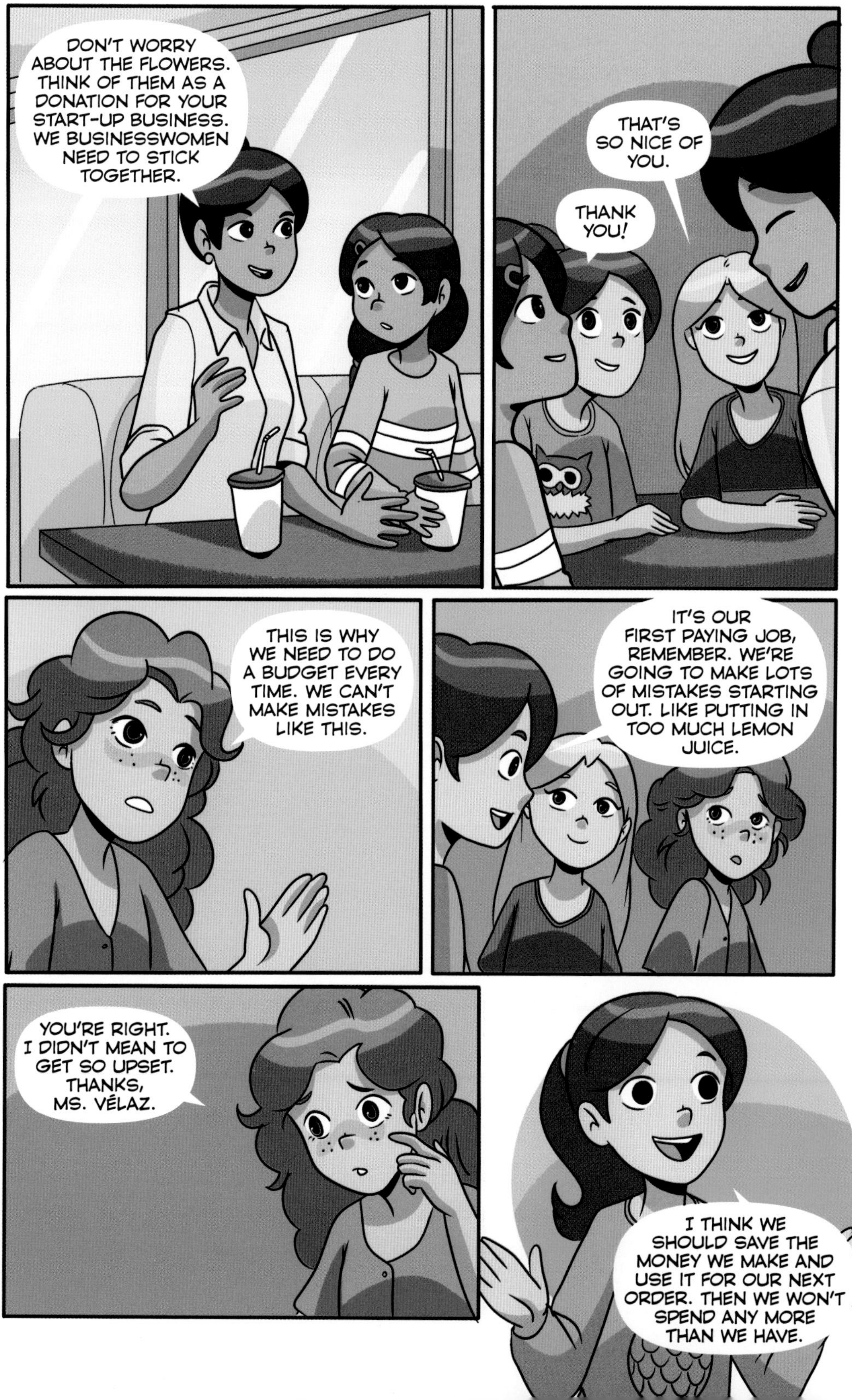
DON'T WORRY ABOUT THE FLOWERS. THINK OF THEM AS A DONATION FOR YOUR START-UP BUSINESS. WE BUSINESSWOMEN NEED TO STICK TOGETHER.
THAT'S SO NICE OF YOU.
THANK YOU!
THIS IS WHY WE NEED TO DO A BUDGET EVERY TIME. WE CAN'T MAKE MISTAKES LIKE THIS.
IT'S OUR FIRST PAYING JOB, REMEMBER. WE'RE GOING TO MAKE LOTS OF MISTAKES STARTING OUT. LIKE PUTTING IN TOO MUCH LEMON JUICE.
YOU'RE RIGHT. I DIDN'T MEAN TO GET SO UPSET. THANKS, MS. VÉLAZ.
I THINK WE SHOULD SAVE THE MONEY WE MAKE AND USE IT FOR OUR NEXT ORDER. THEN WE WON'T SPEND ANY MORE THAN WE HAVE.

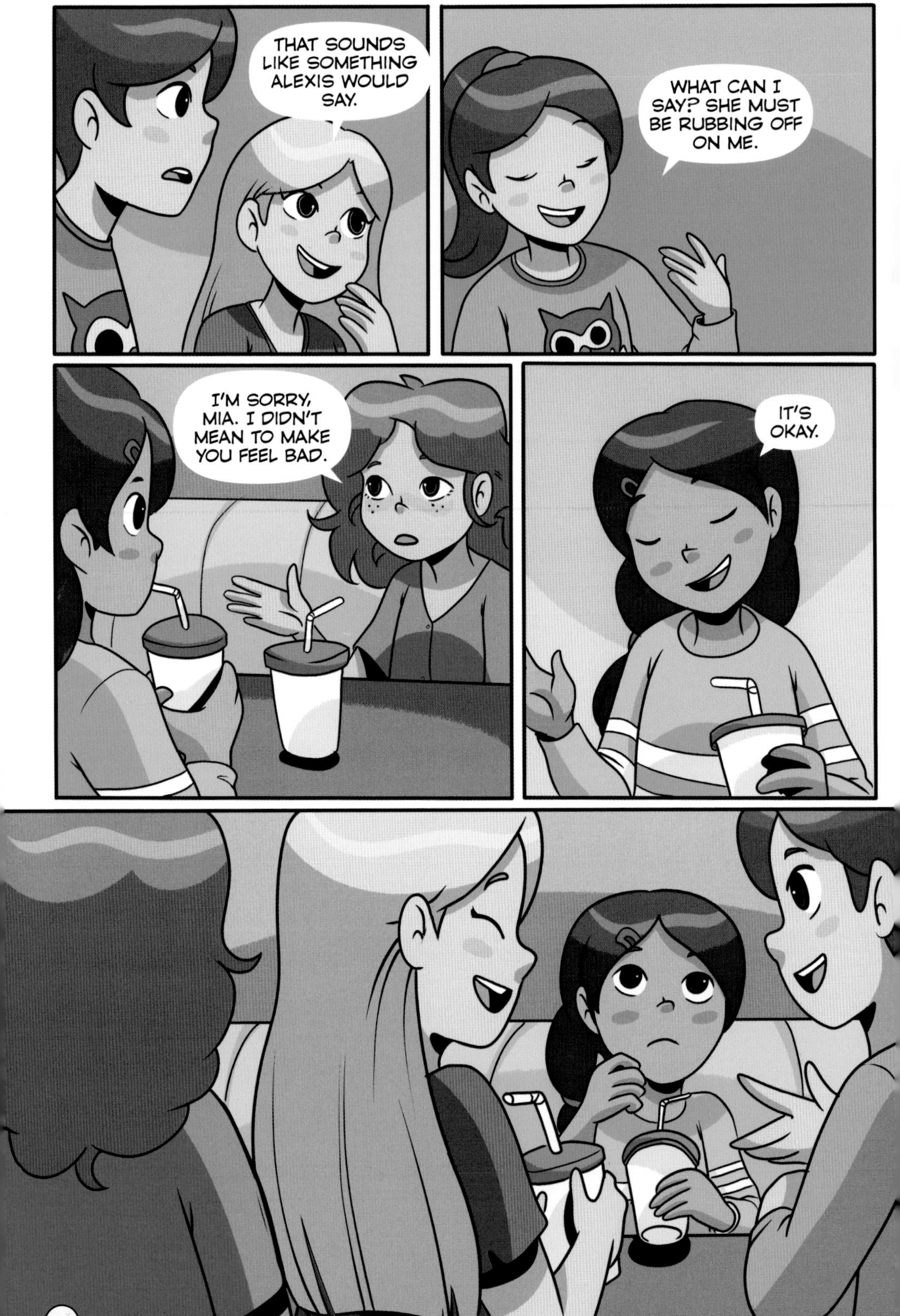
THAT SOUNDS LIKE SOMETHING ALEXIS WOULD SAY.
WHAT CAN I SAY? SHE MUST BE RUBBING OFF ON ME.
I'M SORRY, MIA. I DIDN'T MEAN TO MAKE YOU FEEL BAD.
IT'S OKAY.

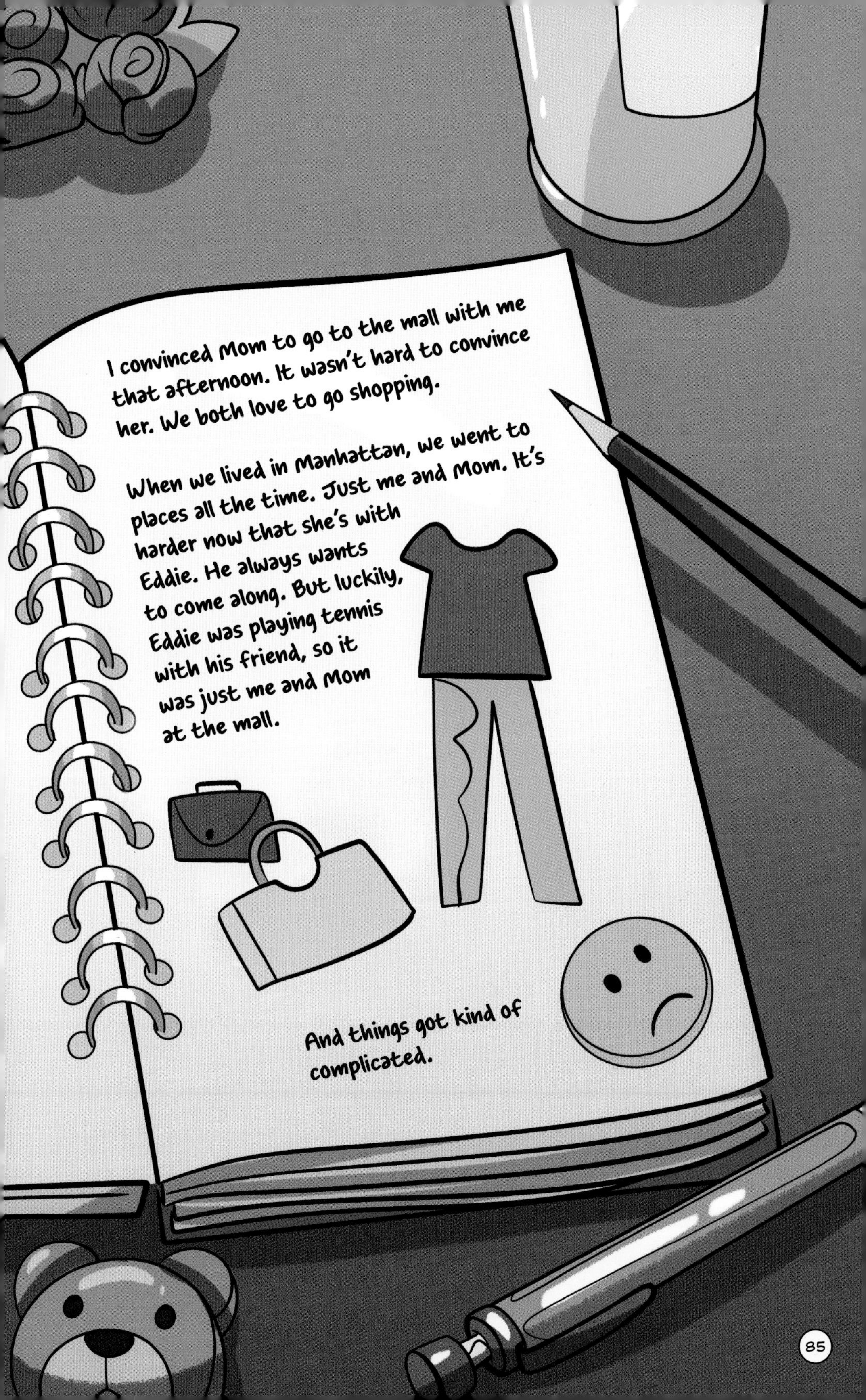
I convinced Mom to go to the mall with me that afternoon. It wasn't hard to convince her. We both love to go shopping.
When we lived in Manhattan, we went to places all the time. Just me and Mom. It's harder now that she's with Eddie. He always wants to come along. But luckily, Eddie was playing tennis with his friend, so it was just me and Mom at the mall.
And things got kind of complicated.

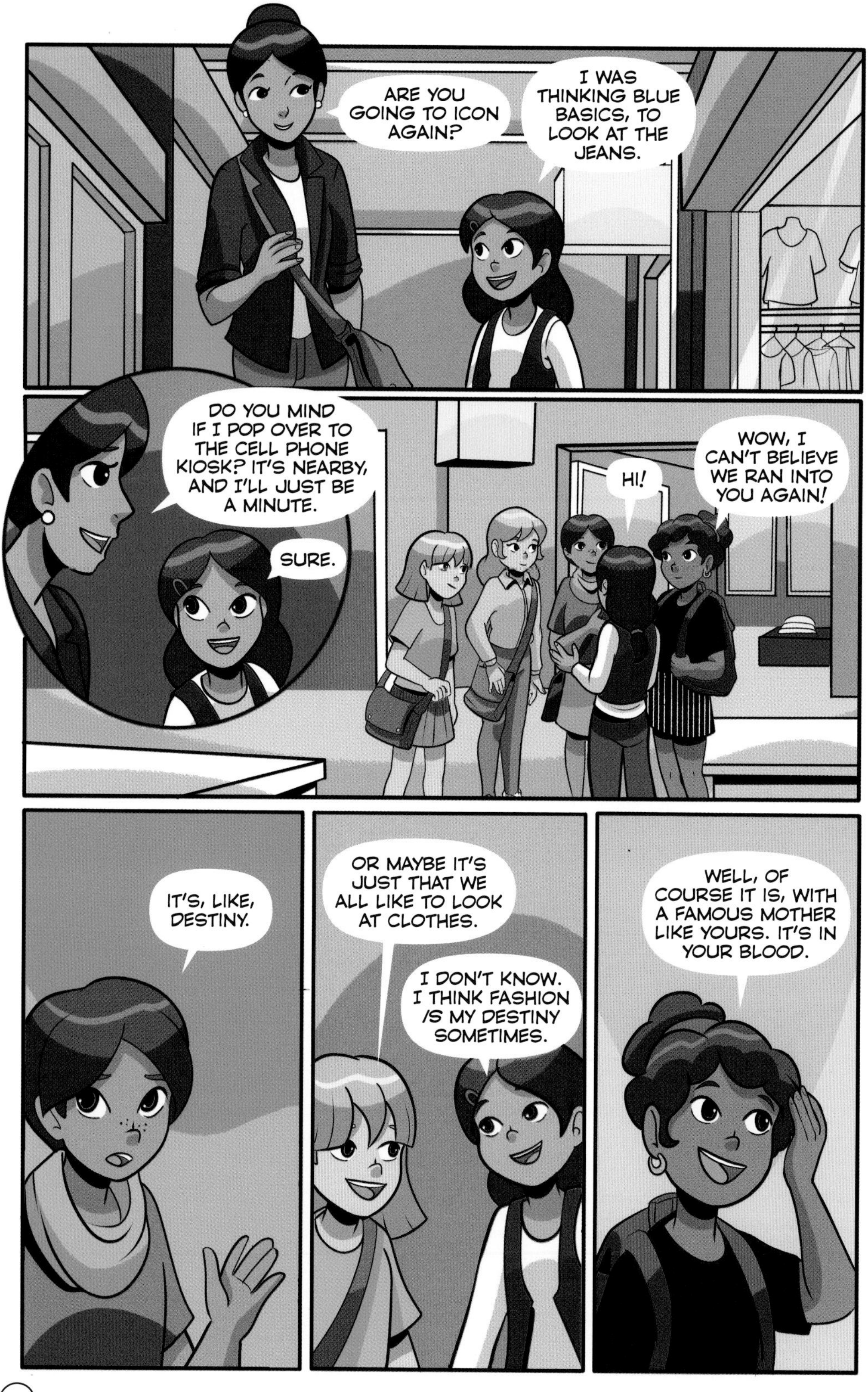
ARE YOU GOING TO ICON AGAIN?
I WAS THINKING BLUE BASICS, TO LOOK AT THE JEANS.
DO YOU MIND IF I POP OVER TO THE CELL PHONE KIOSK? IT'S NEARBY, AND I'LL JUST BE A MINUTE.
SURE.
HI!
WOW, I CAN'T BELIEVE WE RAN INTO YOU AGAIN!
IT'S, LIKE, DESTINY.
OR MAYBE IT'S JUST THAT WE ALL LIKE TO LOOK AT CLOTHES.
I DON'T KNOW. I THINK FASHION *IS* MY DESTINY SOMETIMES.
WELL, OF COURSE IT IS, WITH A FAMOUS MOTHER LIKE YOURS. IT'S IN YOUR BLOOD.

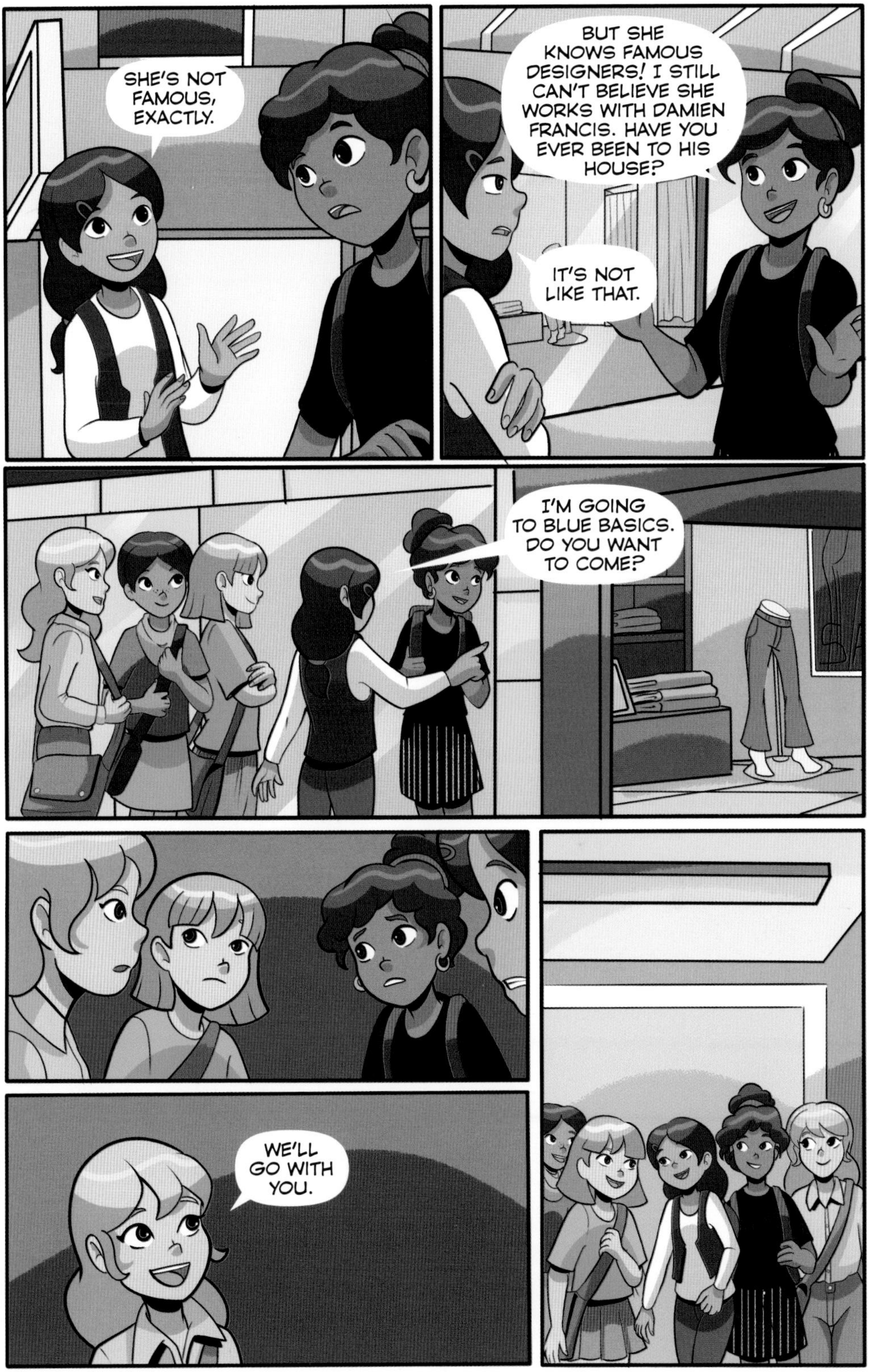
SHE'S NOT FAMOUS, EXACTLY.
BUT SHE KNOWS FAMOUS DESIGNERS! I STILL CAN'T BELIEVE SHE WORKS WITH DAMIEN FRANCIS. HAVE YOU EVER BEEN TO HIS HOUSE?
IT'S NOT LIKE THAT.
I'M GOING TO BLUE BASICS. DO YOU WANT TO COME?
WE'LL GO WITH YOU.

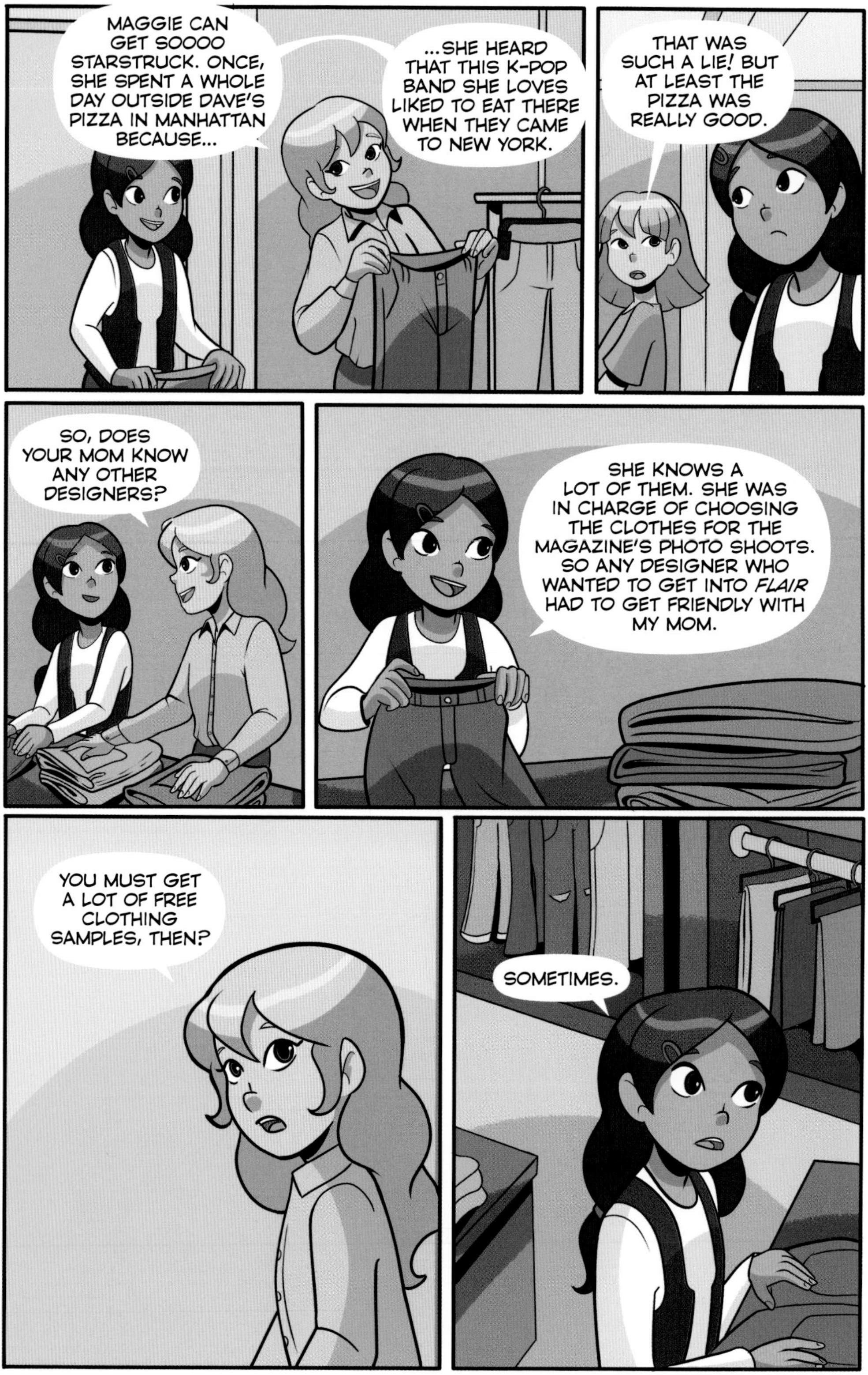
MAGGIE CAN GET SOOOO STARSTRUCK. ONCE, SHE SPENT A WHOLE DAY OUTSIDE DAVE'S PIZZA IN MANHATTAN BECAUSE...
...SHE HEARD THAT THIS K-POP BAND SHE LOVES LIKED TO EAT THERE WHEN THEY CAME TO NEW YORK.
THAT WAS SUCH A LIE! BUT AT LEAST THE PIZZA WAS REALLY GOOD.
SO, DOES YOUR MOM KNOW ANY OTHER DESIGNERS?
SHE KNOWS A LOT OF THEM. SHE WAS IN CHARGE OF CHOOSING THE CLOTHES FOR THE MAGAZINE'S PHOTO SHOOTS. SO ANY DESIGNER WHO WANTED TO GET INTO *FLAIR* HAD TO GET FRIENDLY WITH MY MOM.
YOU MUST GET A LOT OF FREE CLOTHING SAMPLES, THEN?
SOMETIMES.

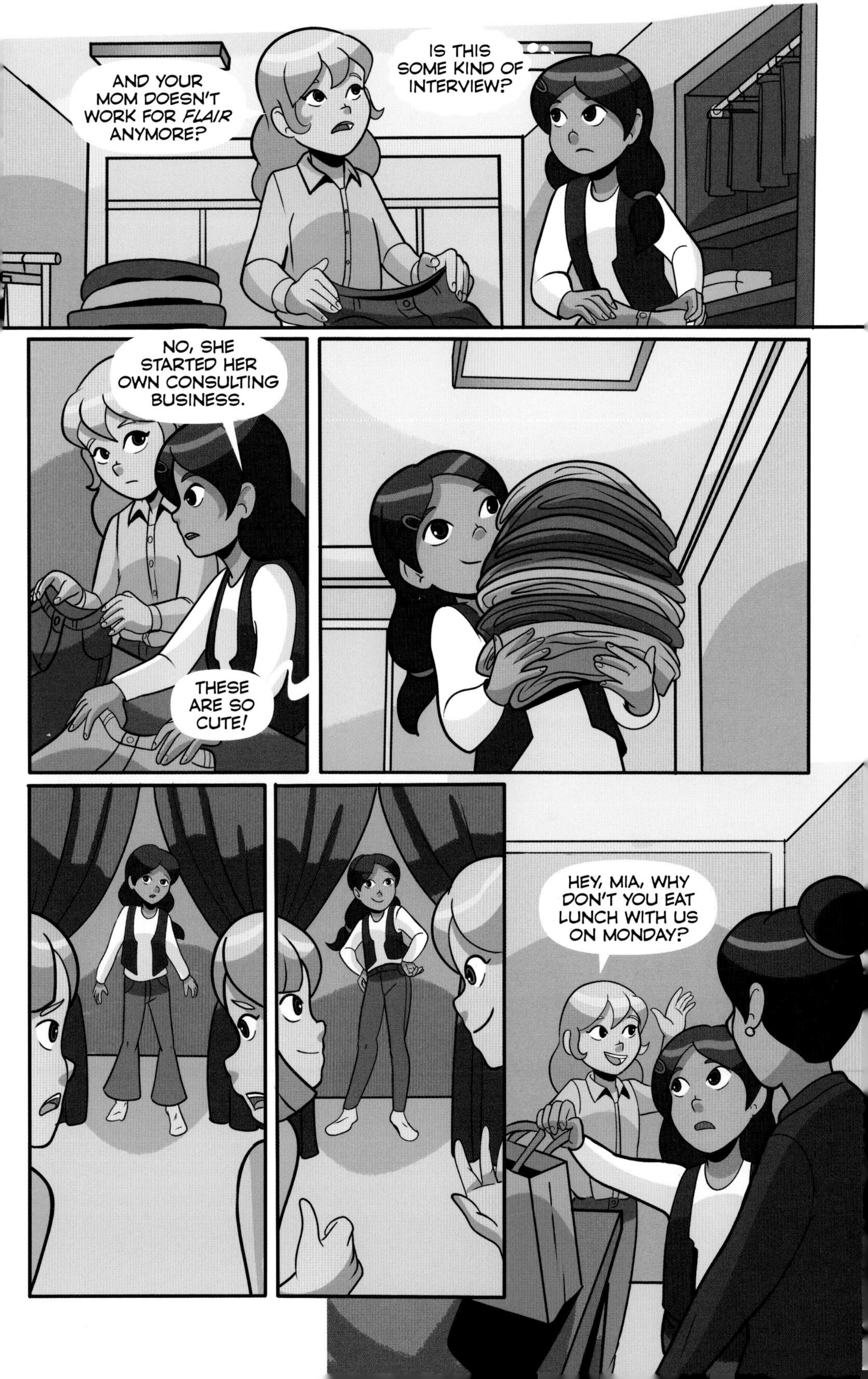
AND YOUR MOM DOESN'T WORK FOR *FLAIR* ANYMORE?
IS THIS SOME KIND OF INTERVIEW?
NO, SHE STARTED HER OWN CONSULTING BUSINESS.
THESE ARE SO CUTE!
HEY, MIA, WHY DON'T YOU EAT LUNCH WITH US ON MONDAY?

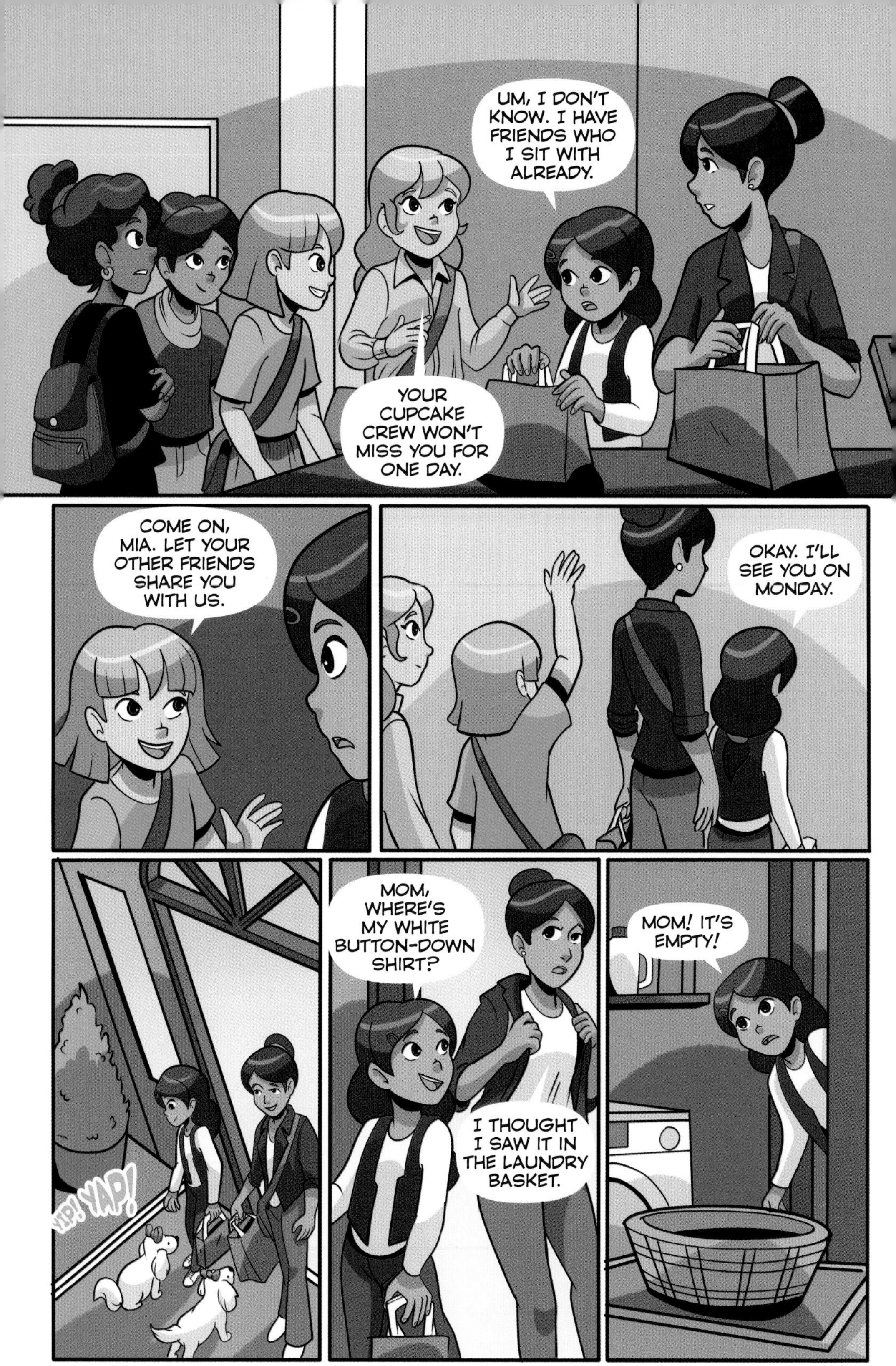
UM, I DON'T KNOW. I HAVE FRIENDS WHO I SIT WITH ALREADY.
YOUR CUPCAKE CREW WON'T MISS YOU FOR ONE DAY.
COME ON, MIA. LET YOUR OTHER FRIENDS SHARE YOU WITH US.
OKAY. I'LL SEE YOU ON MONDAY.
YIP! YAP!
MOM, WHERE'S MY WHITE BUTTON-DOWN SHIRT?
I THOUGHT I SAW IT IN THE LAUNDRY BASKET.
MOM! IT'S EMPTY!

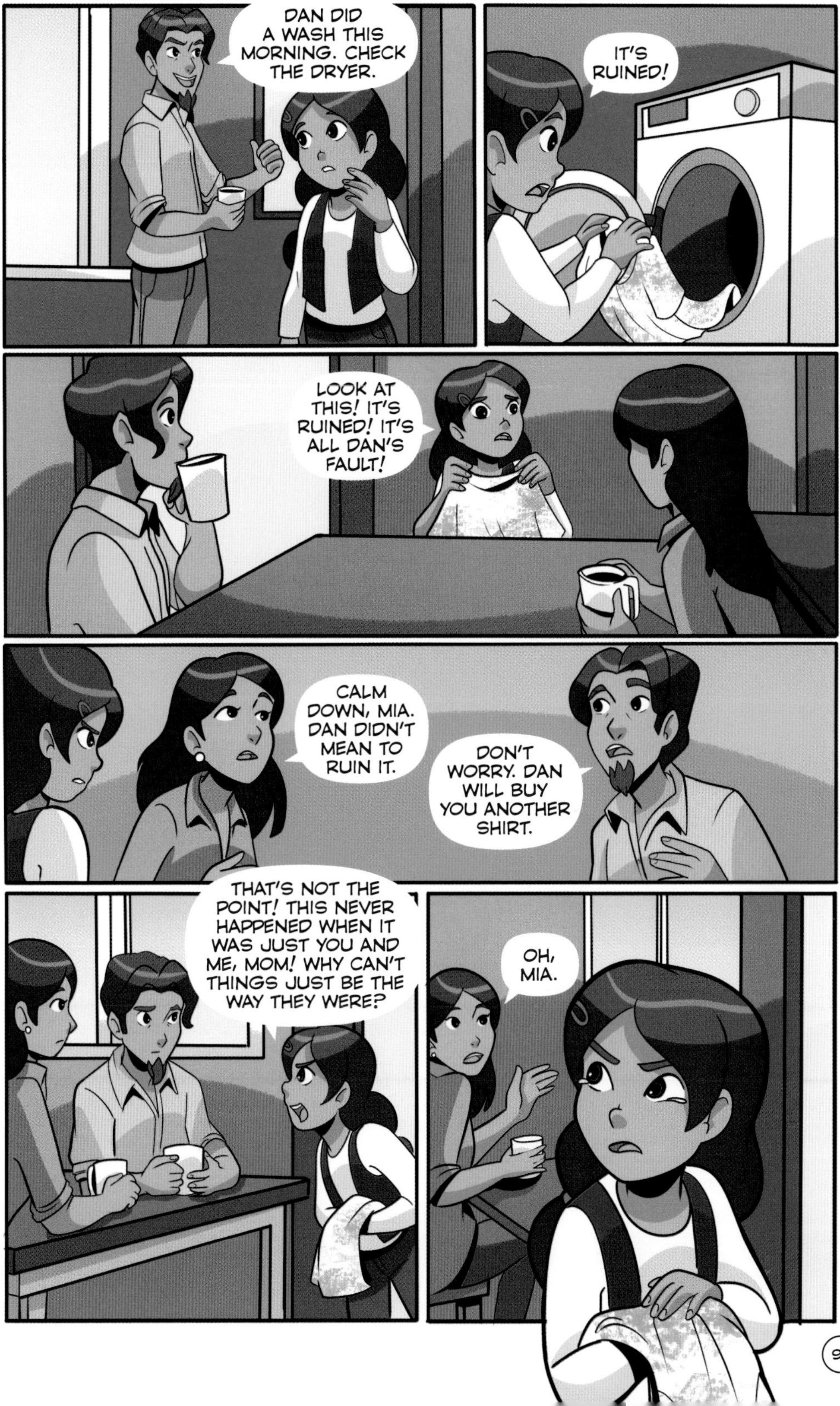
DAN DID A WASH THIS MORNING. CHECK THE DRYER.
IT'S RUINED!
LOOK AT THIS! IT'S RUINED! IT'S ALL DAN'S FAULT!
CALM DOWN, MIA. DAN DIDN'T MEAN TO RUIN IT.
DON'T WORRY. DAN WILL BUY YOU ANOTHER SHIRT.
THAT'S NOT THE POINT! THIS NEVER HAPPENED WHEN IT WAS JUST YOU AND ME, MOM! WHY CAN'T THINGS JUST BE THE WAY THEY WERE?
OH, MIA.

Chapter 10

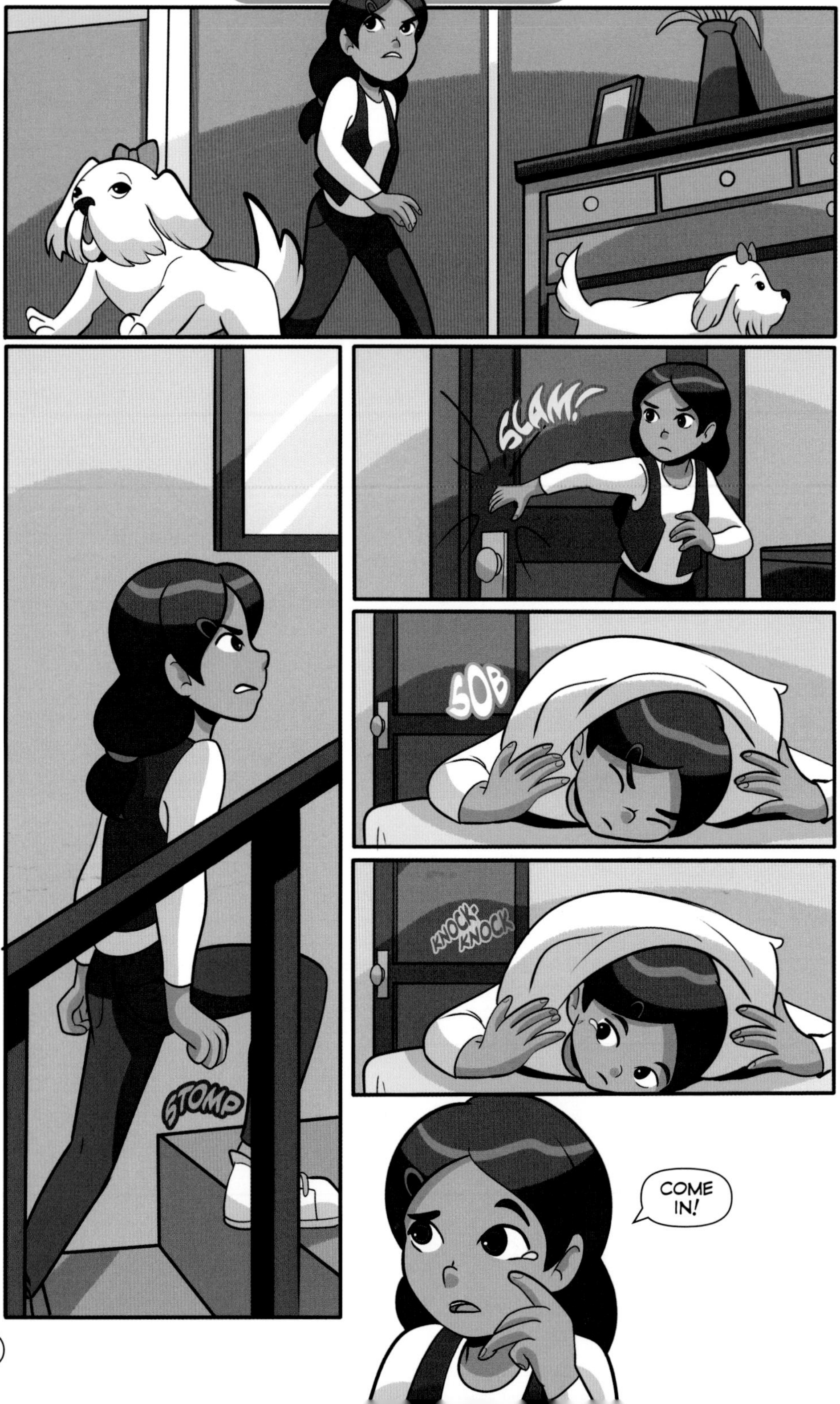
SLAM!
STOMP
SOB
KNOCK-KNOCK
COME IN!

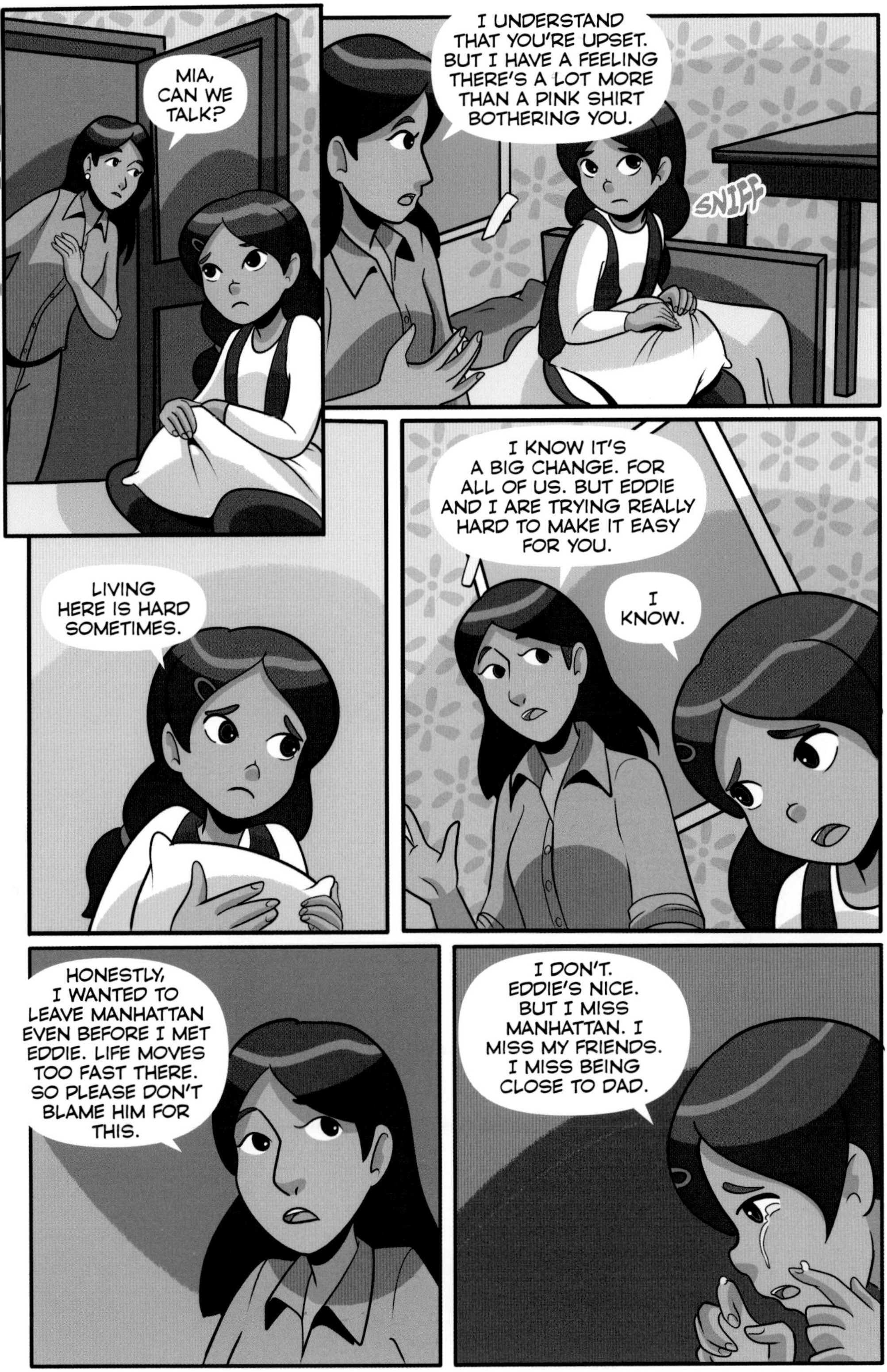
MIA, CAN WE TALK?
I UNDERSTAND THAT YOU'RE UPSET. BUT I HAVE A FEELING THERE'S A LOT MORE THAN A PINK SHIRT BOTHERING YOU.
SNIFF
LIVING HERE IS HARD SOMETIMES.
I KNOW IT'S A BIG CHANGE. FOR ALL OF US. BUT EDDIE AND I ARE TRYING REALLY HARD TO MAKE IT EASY FOR YOU.
I KNOW.
HONESTLY, I WANTED TO LEAVE MANHATTAN EVEN BEFORE I MET EDDIE. LIFE MOVES TOO FAST THERE. SO PLEASE DON'T BLAME HIM FOR THIS.
I DON'T. EDDIE'S NICE. BUT I MISS MANHATTAN. I MISS MY FRIENDS. I MISS BEING CLOSE TO DAD.

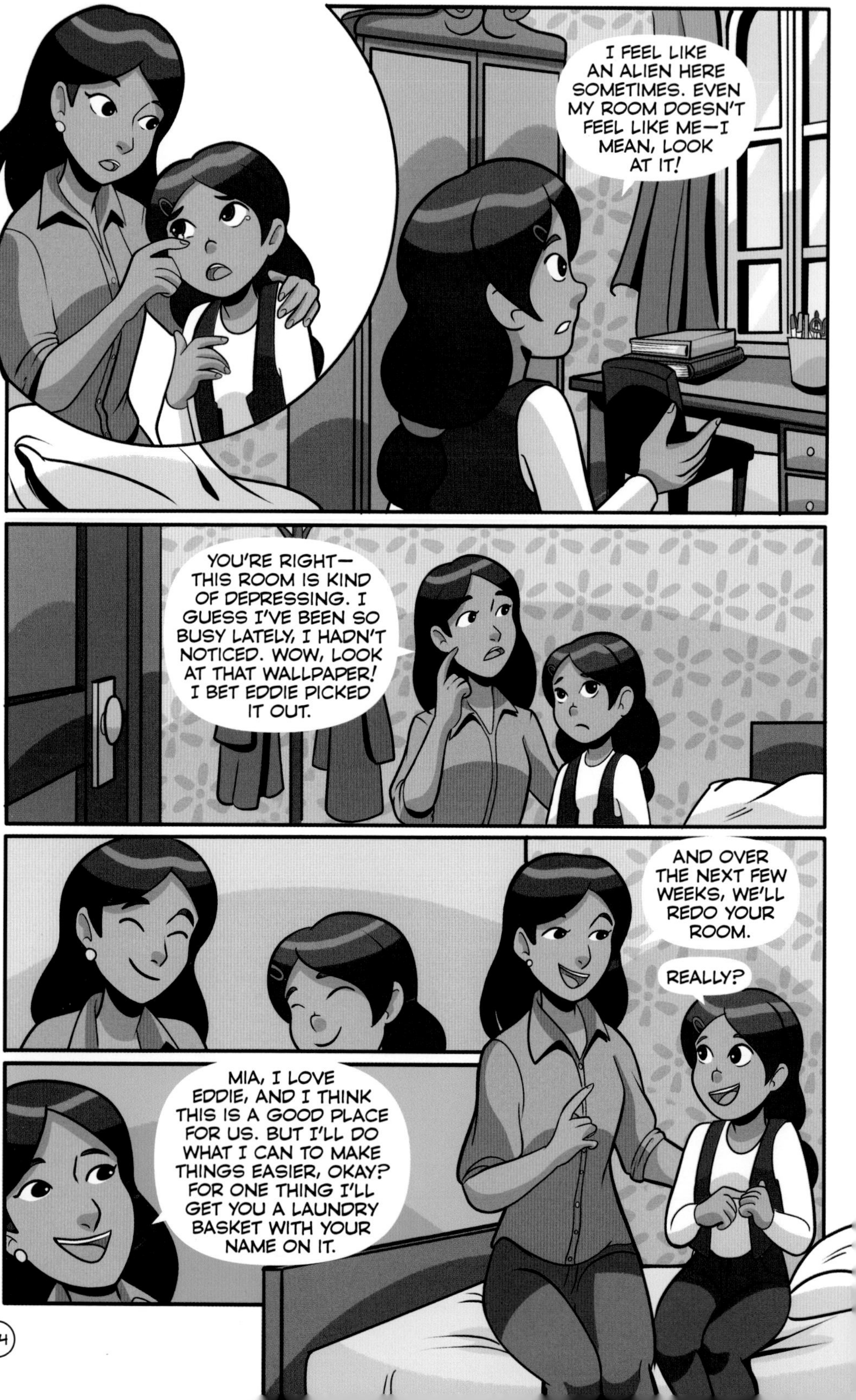
I FEEL LIKE AN ALIEN HERE SOMETIMES. EVEN MY ROOM DOESN'T FEEL LIKE ME—I MEAN, LOOK AT IT!
YOU'RE RIGHT—THIS ROOM IS KIND OF DEPRESSING. I GUESS I'VE BEEN SO BUSY LATELY, I HADN'T NOTICED. WOW, LOOK AT THAT WALLPAPER! I BET EDDIE PICKED IT OUT.
AND OVER THE NEXT FEW WEEKS, WE'LL REDO YOUR ROOM.
REALLY?
MIA, I LOVE EDDIE, AND I THINK THIS IS A GOOD PLACE FOR US. BUT I'LL DO WHAT I CAN TO MAKE THINGS EASIER, OKAY? FOR ONE THING I'LL GET YOU A LAUNDRY BASKET WITH YOUR NAME ON IT.

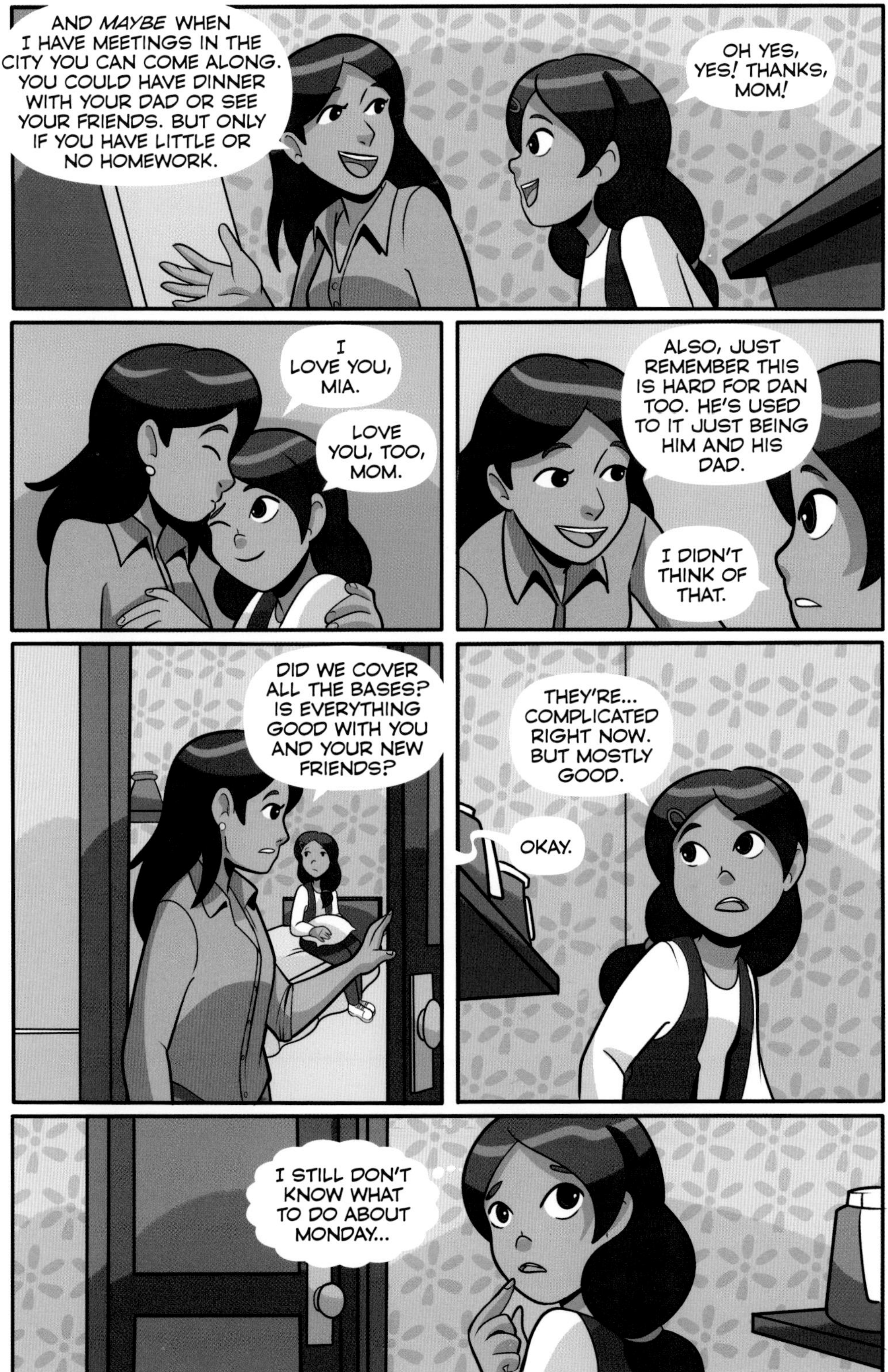
AND *MAYBE* WHEN I HAVE MEETINGS IN THE CITY YOU CAN COME ALONG. YOU COULD HAVE DINNER WITH YOUR DAD OR SEE YOUR FRIENDS. BUT ONLY IF YOU HAVE LITTLE OR NO HOMEWORK.
OH YES, YES! THANKS, MOM!
I LOVE YOU, MIA.
LOVE YOU, TOO, MOM.
ALSO, JUST REMEMBER THIS IS HARD FOR DAN TOO. HE'S USED TO IT JUST BEING HIM AND HIS DAD.
I DIDN'T THINK OF THAT.
DID WE COVER ALL THE BASES? IS EVERYTHING GOOD WITH YOU AND YOUR NEW FRIENDS?
THEY'RE... COMPLICATED RIGHT NOW. BUT MOSTLY GOOD.
OKAY.
I STILL DON'T KNOW WHAT TO DO ABOUT MONDAY...

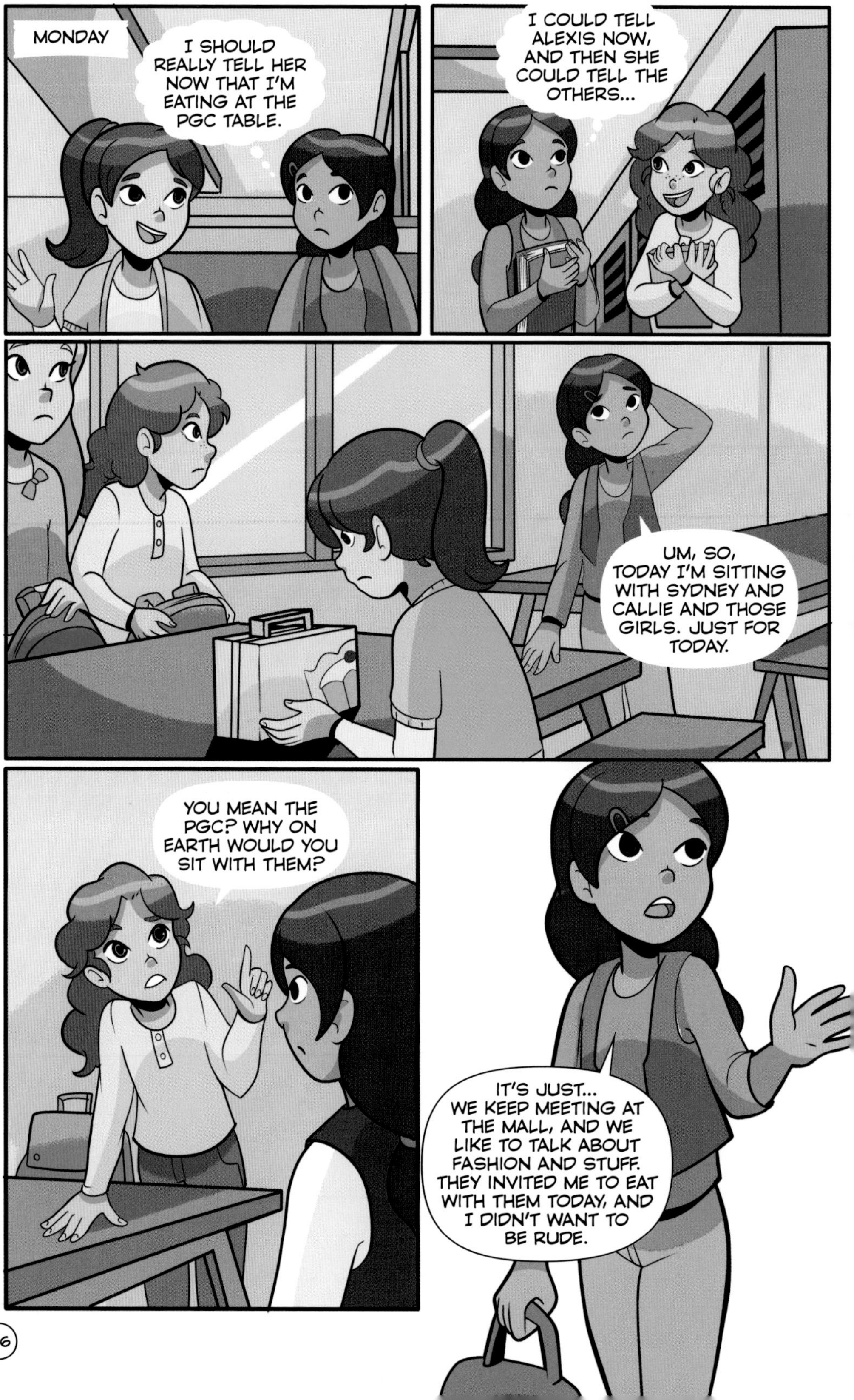
MONDAY
I SHOULD REALLY TELL HER NOW THAT I'M EATING AT THE PGC TABLE.
I COULD TELL ALEXIS NOW, AND THEN SHE COULD TELL THE OTHERS...
UM, SO, TODAY I'M SITTING WITH SYDNEY AND CALLIE AND THOSE GIRLS. JUST FOR TODAY.
YOU MEAN THE PGC? WHY ON EARTH WOULD YOU SIT WITH THEM?
IT'S JUST... WE KEEP MEETING AT THE MALL, AND WE LIKE TO TALK ABOUT FASHION AND STUFF. THEY INVITED ME TO EAT WITH THEM TODAY, AND I DIDN'T WANT TO BE RUDE.

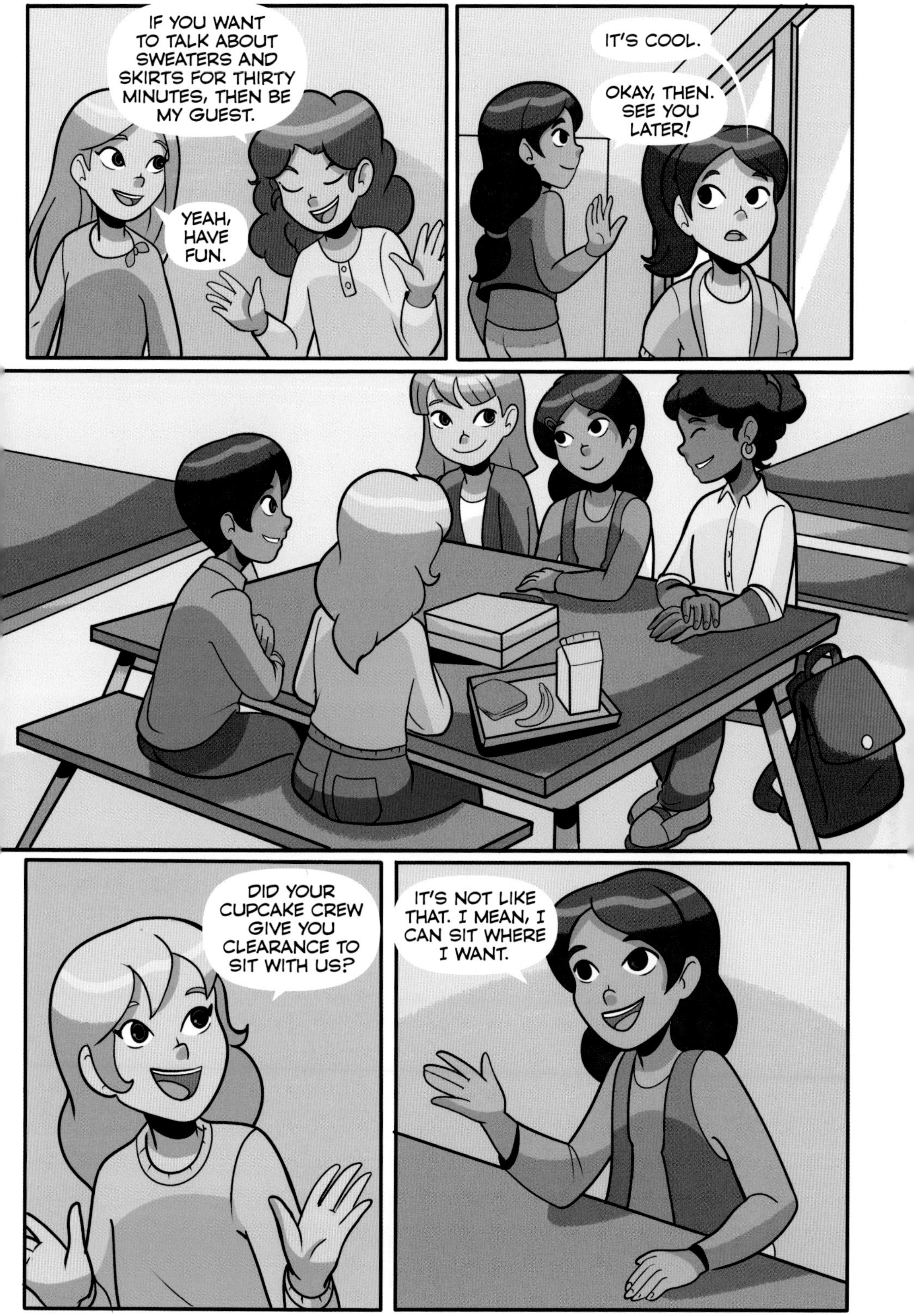
IF YOU WANT TO TALK ABOUT SWEATERS AND SKIRTS FOR THIRTY MINUTES, THEN BE MY GUEST.
YEAH, HAVE FUN.
IT'S COOL.
OKAY, THEN. SEE YOU LATER!
DID YOUR CUPCAKE CREW GIVE YOU CLEARANCE TO SIT WITH US?
IT'S NOT LIKE THAT. I MEAN, I CAN SIT WHERE I WANT.

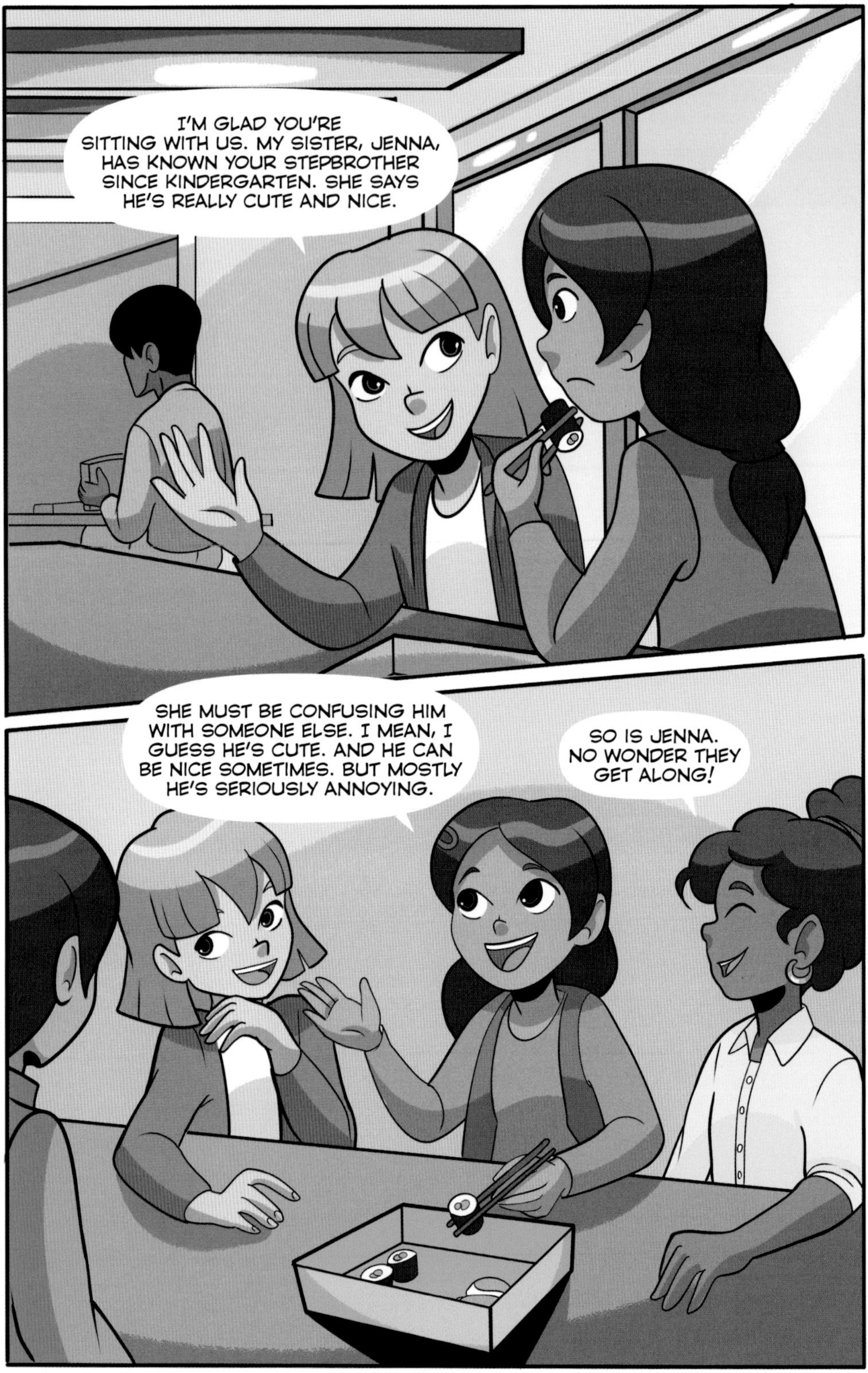
I'M GLAD YOU'RE SITTING WITH US. MY SISTER, JENNA, HAS KNOWN YOUR STEPBROTHER SINCE KINDERGARTEN. SHE SAYS HE'S REALLY CUTE AND NICE.
SHE MUST BE CONFUSING HIM WITH SOMEONE ELSE. I MEAN, I GUESS HE'S CUTE. AND HE CAN BE NICE SOMETIMES. BUT MOSTLY HE'S SERIOUSLY ANNOYING.
SO IS JENNA. NO WONDER THEY GET ALONG!

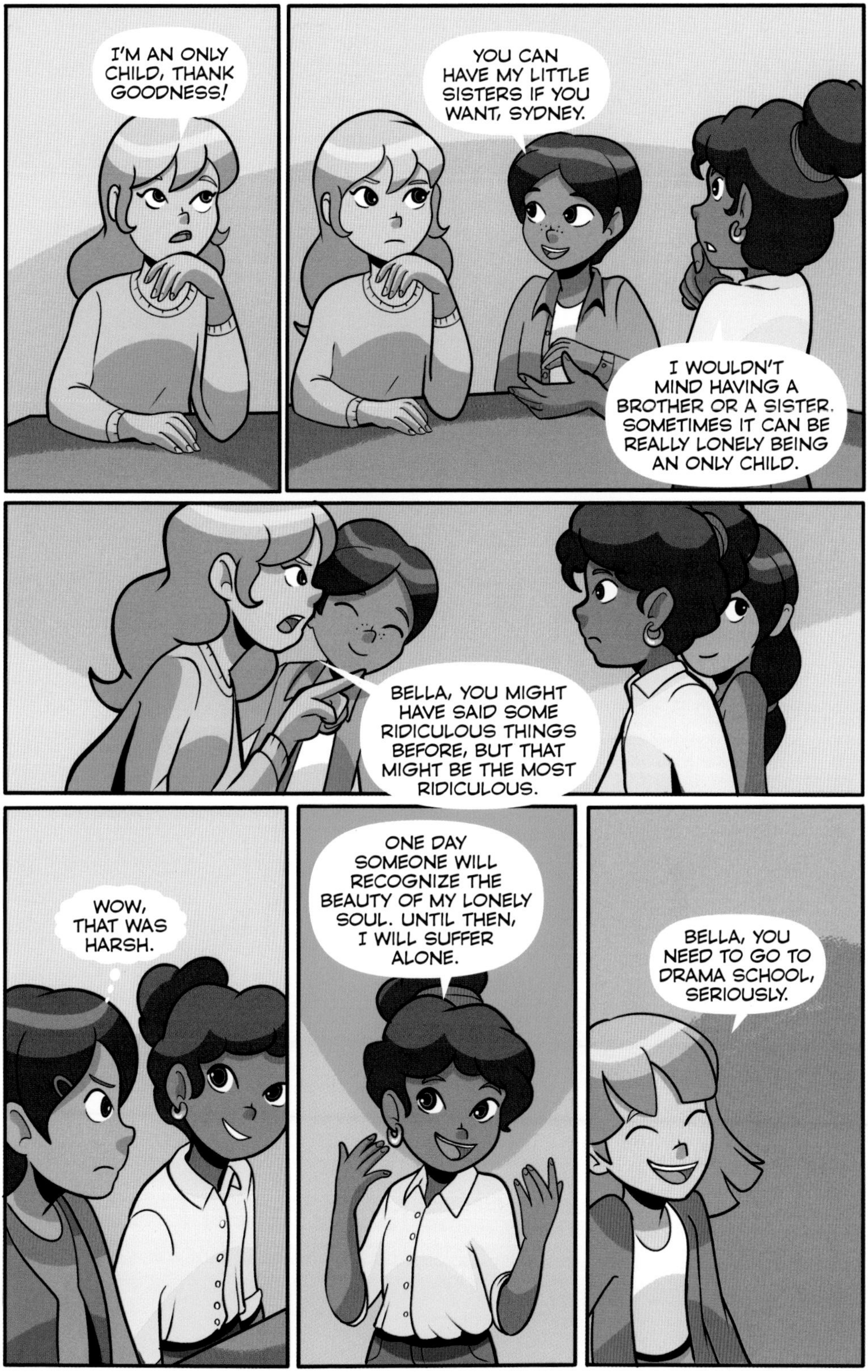
I'M AN ONLY CHILD, THANK GOODNESS!
YOU CAN HAVE MY LITTLE SISTERS IF YOU WANT, SYDNEY.
I WOULDN'T MIND HAVING A BROTHER OR A SISTER. SOMETIMES IT CAN BE REALLY LONELY BEING AN ONLY CHILD.
BELLA, YOU MIGHT HAVE SAID SOME RIDICULOUS THINGS BEFORE, BUT THAT MIGHT BE THE MOST RIDICULOUS.
WOW, THAT WAS HARSH.
ONE DAY SOMEONE WILL RECOGNIZE THE BEAUTY OF MY LONELY SOUL. UNTIL THEN, I WILL SUFFER ALONE.
BELLA, YOU NEED TO GO TO DRAMA SCHOOL, SERIOUSLY.

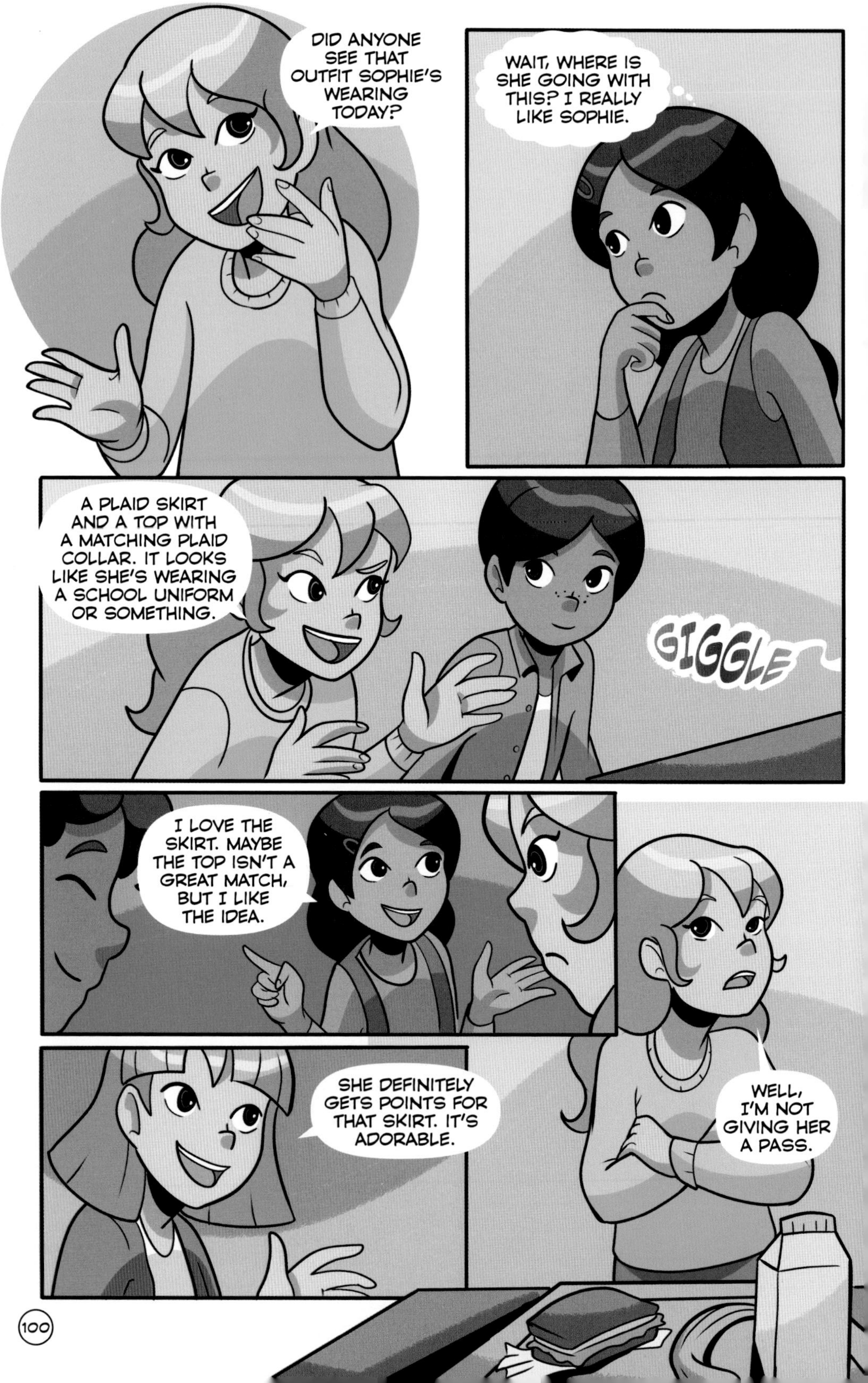

DID ANYONE SEE THAT OUTFIT SOPHIE'S WEARING TODAY?
WAIT, WHERE IS SHE GOING WITH THIS? I REALLY LIKE SOPHIE.
A PLAID SKIRT AND A TOP WITH A MATCHING PLAID COLLAR. IT LOOKS LIKE SHE'S WEARING A SCHOOL UNIFORM OR SOMETHING.
GIGGLE
I LOVE THE SKIRT. MAYBE THE TOP ISN'T A GREAT MATCH, BUT I LIKE THE IDEA.
SHE DEFINITELY GETS POINTS FOR THAT SKIRT. IT'S ADORABLE.
WELL, I'M NOT GIVING HER A PASS.

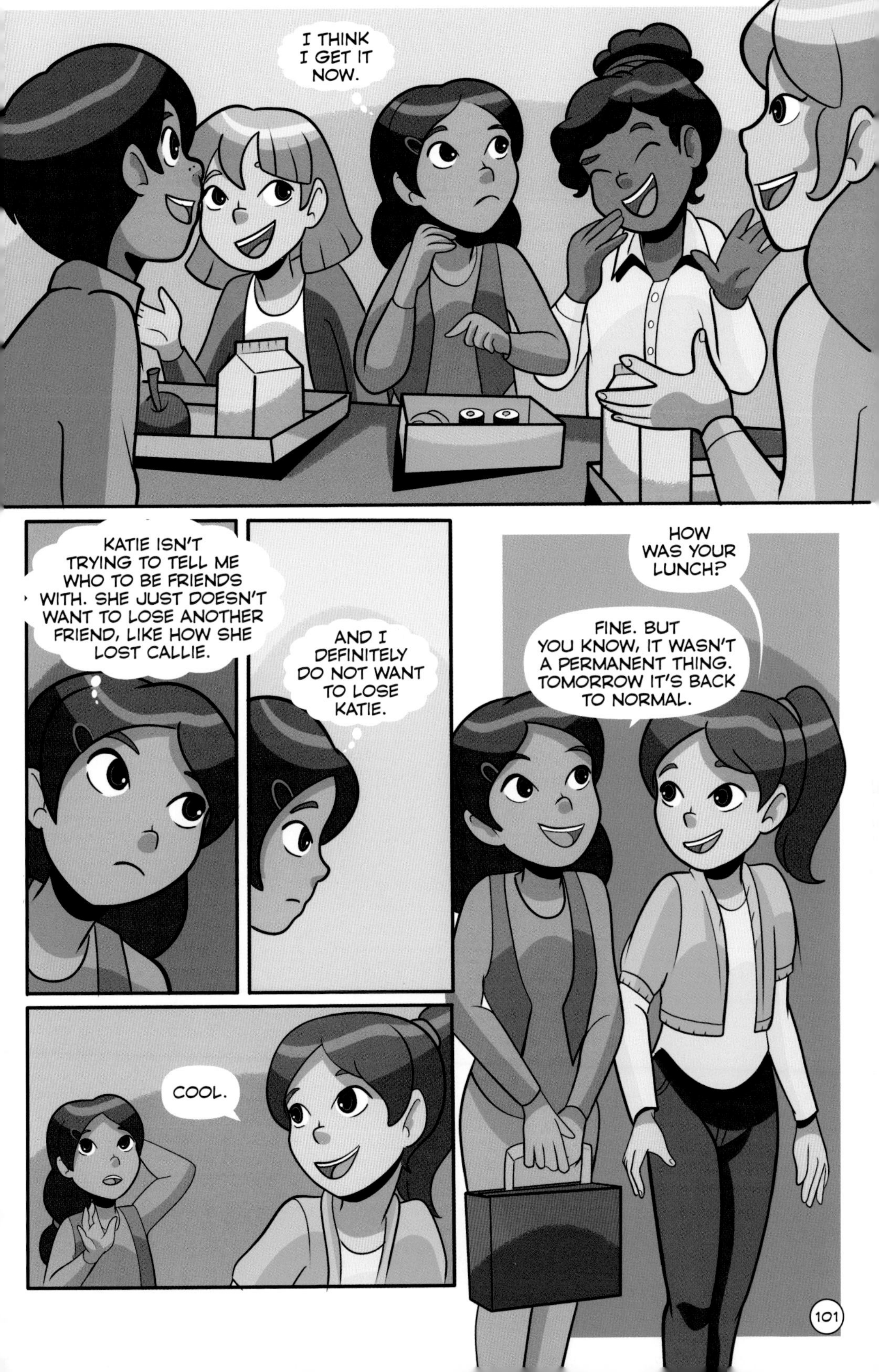
I THINK I GET IT NOW.
KATIE ISN'T TRYING TO TELL ME WHO TO BE FRIENDS WITH. SHE JUST DOESN'T WANT TO LOSE ANOTHER FRIEND, LIKE HOW SHE LOST CALLIE.
AND I DEFINITELY DO NOT WANT TO LOSE KATIE.
COOL.
HOW WAS YOUR LUNCH?
FINE. BUT YOU KNOW, IT WASN'T A PERMANENT THING. TOMORROW IT'S BACK TO NORMAL.

Chapter 11

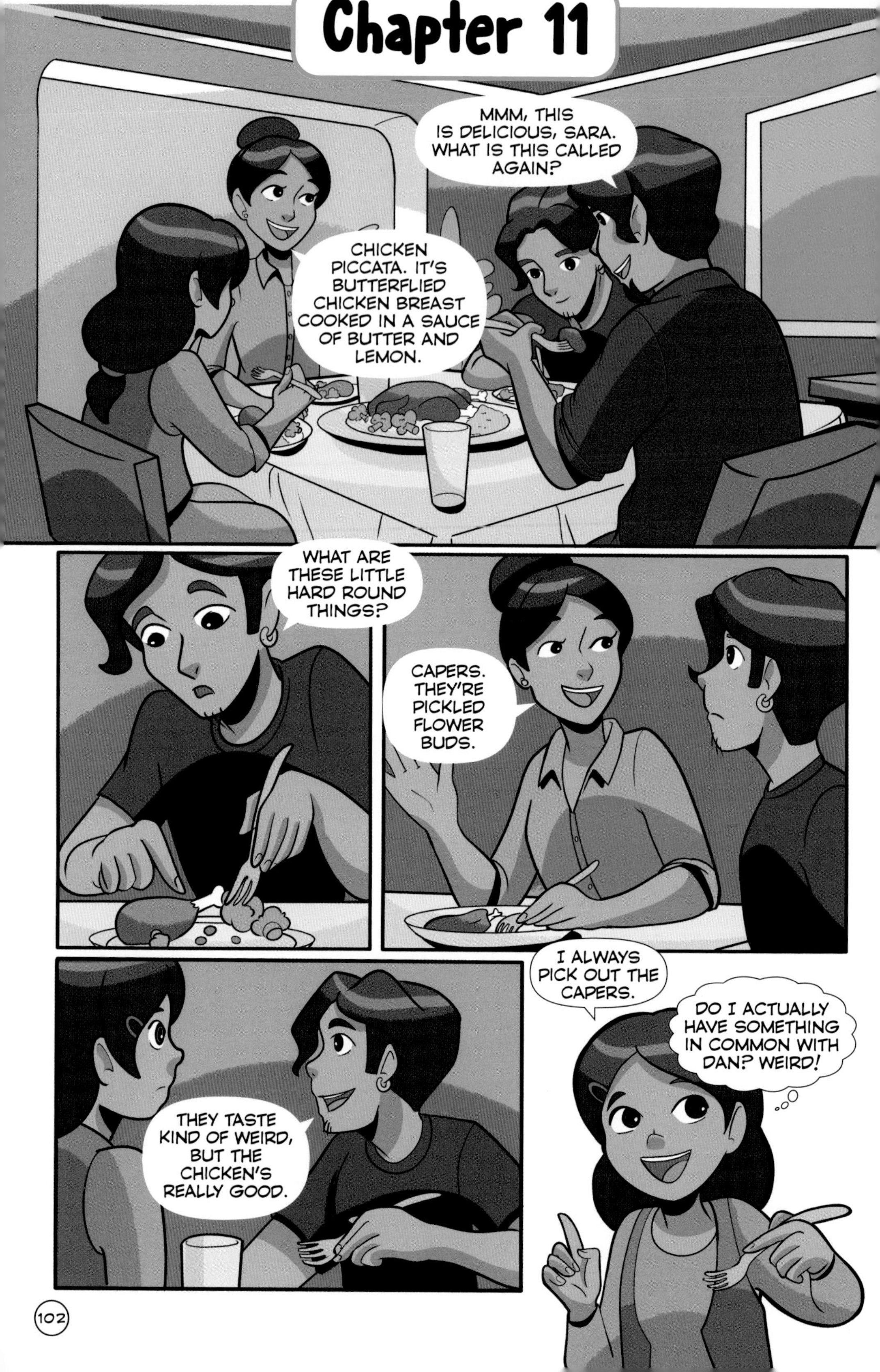
MMM, THIS IS DELICIOUS, SARA. WHAT IS THIS CALLED AGAIN?
CHICKEN PICCATA. IT'S BUTTERFLIED CHICKEN BREAST COOKED IN A SAUCE OF BUTTER AND LEMON.
WHAT ARE THESE LITTLE HARD ROUND THINGS?
CAPERS. THEY'RE PICKLED FLOWER BUDS.
THEY TASTE KIND OF WEIRD, BUT THE CHICKEN'S REALLY GOOD.
I ALWAYS PICK OUT THE CAPERS.
DO I ACTUALLY HAVE SOMETHING IN COMMON WITH DAN? WEIRD!

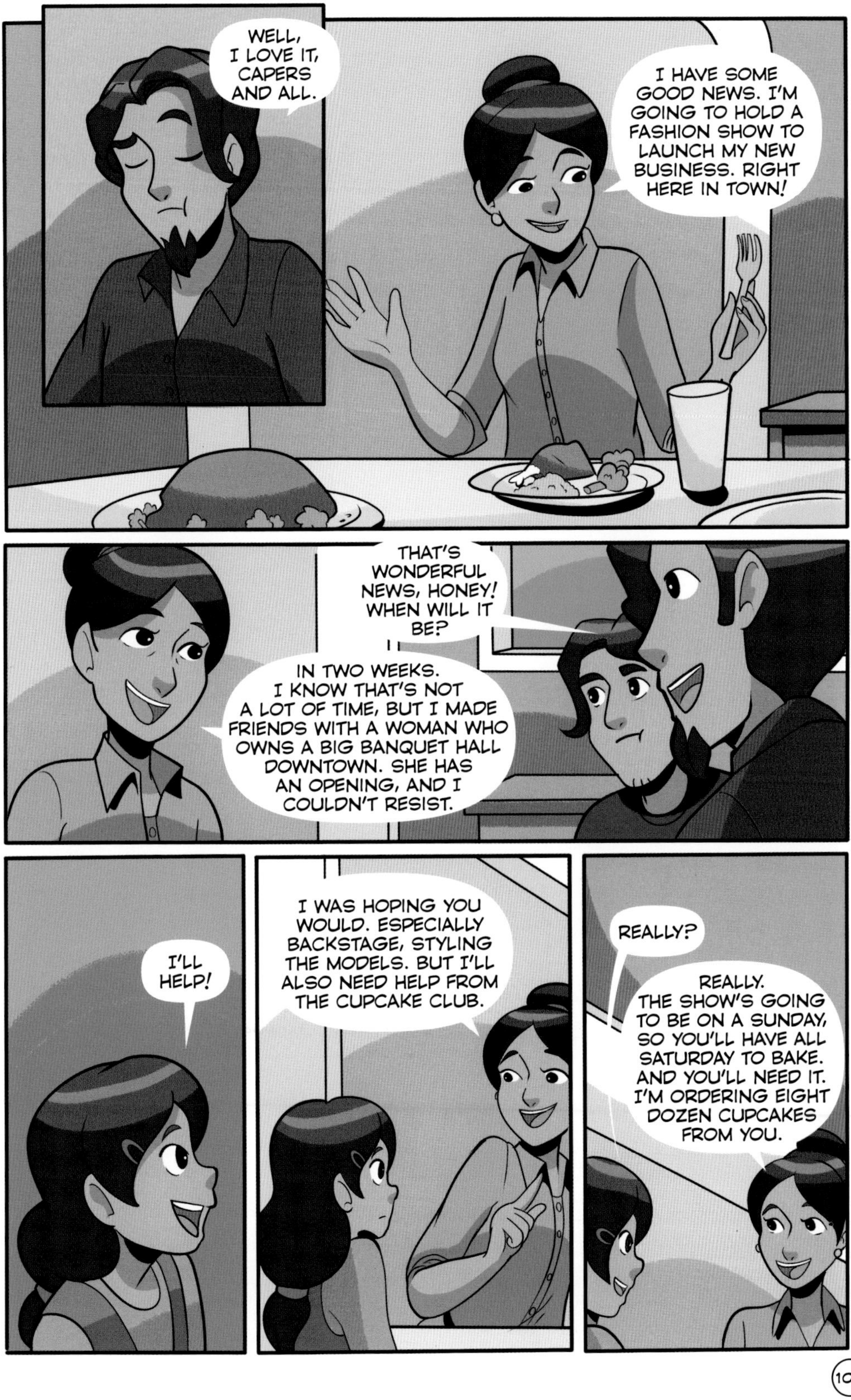
WELL, I LOVE IT, CAPERS AND ALL.
I HAVE SOME GOOD NEWS. I'M GOING TO HOLD A FASHION SHOW TO LAUNCH MY NEW BUSINESS. RIGHT HERE IN TOWN!
THAT'S WONDERFUL NEWS, HONEY! WHEN WILL IT BE?
IN TWO WEEKS. I KNOW THAT'S NOT A LOT OF TIME, BUT I MADE FRIENDS WITH A WOMAN WHO OWNS A BIG BANQUET HALL DOWNTOWN. SHE HAS AN OPENING, AND I COULDN'T RESIST.
I'LL HELP!
I WAS HOPING YOU WOULD. ESPECIALLY BACKSTAGE, STYLING THE MODELS. BUT I'LL ALSO NEED HELP FROM THE CUPCAKE CLUB.
REALLY?
REALLY. THE SHOW'S GOING TO BE ON A SUNDAY, SO YOU'LL HAVE ALL SATURDAY TO BAKE. AND YOU'LL NEED IT. I'M ORDERING EIGHT DOZEN CUPCAKES FROM YOU.

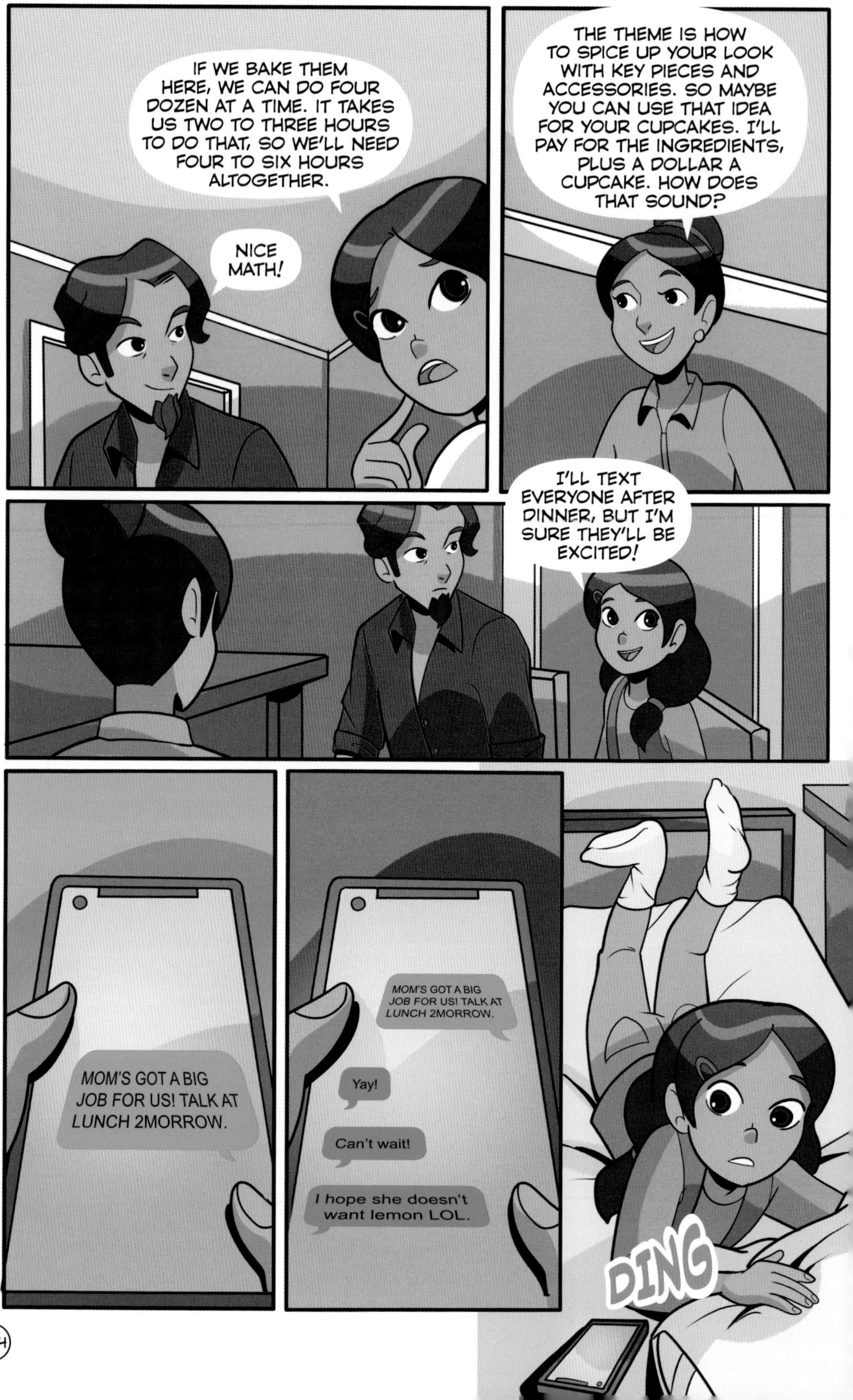
IF WE BAKE THEM HERE, WE CAN DO FOUR DOZEN AT A TIME. IT TAKES US TWO TO THREE HOURS TO DO THAT, SO WE'LL NEED FOUR TO SIX HOURS ALTOGETHER.
NICE MATH!
THE THEME IS HOW TO SPICE UP YOUR LOOK WITH KEY PIECES AND ACCESSORIES. SO MAYBE YOU CAN USE THAT IDEA FOR YOUR CUPCAKES. I'LL PAY FOR THE INGREDIENTS, PLUS A DOLLAR A CUPCAKE. HOW DOES THAT SOUND?
I'LL TEXT EVERYONE AFTER DINNER, BUT I'M SURE THEY'LL BE EXCITED!
MOM'S GOT A BIG JOB FOR US! TALK AT LUNCH 2MORROW.
MOM'S GOT A BIG JOB FOR US! TALK AT LUNCH 2MORROW.
Yay!
Can't wait!
I hope she doesn't want lemon LOL.
DING

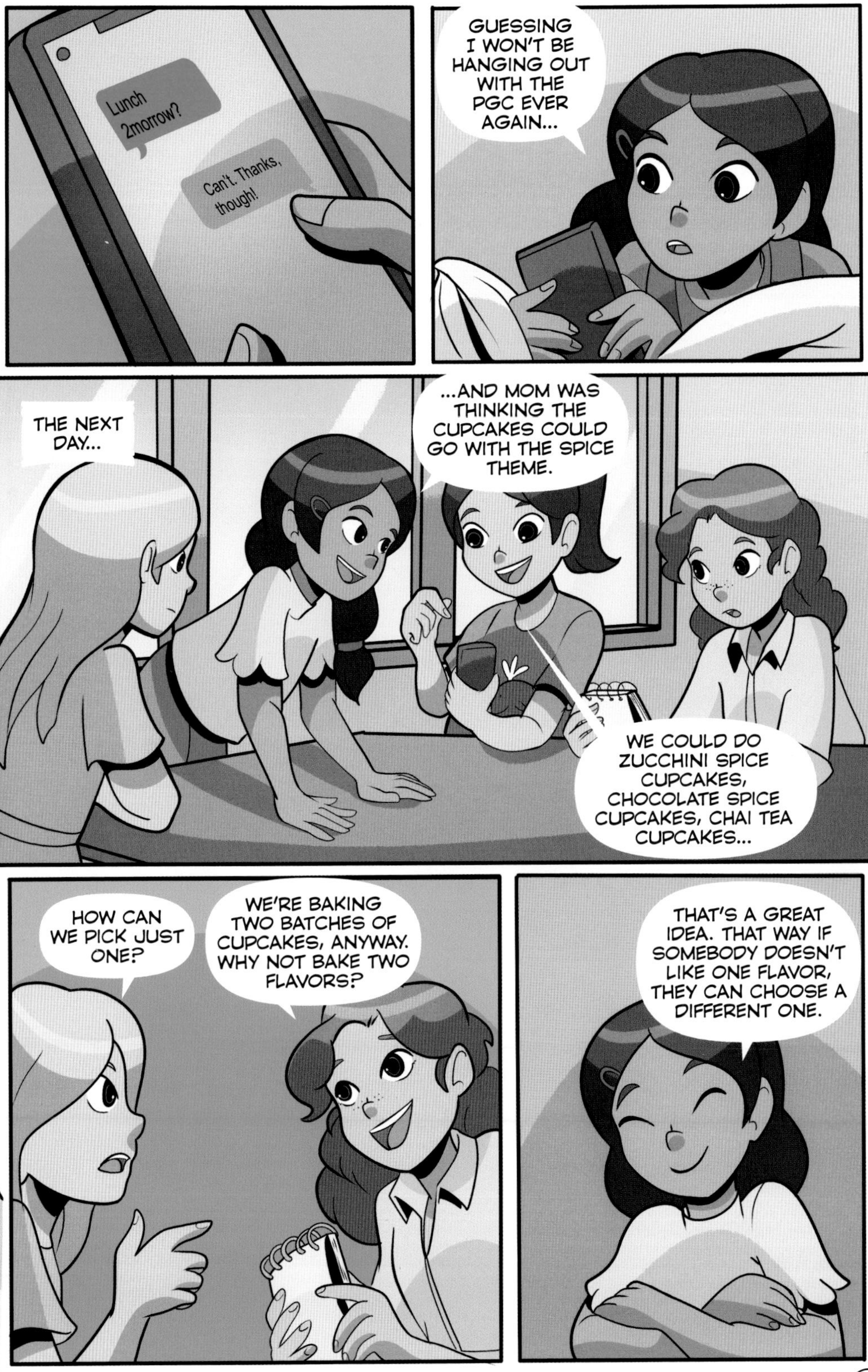
Lunch 2morrow?
Can't. Thanks, though!
GUESSING I WON'T BE HANGING OUT WITH THE PGC EVER AGAIN...
THE NEXT DAY...
...AND MOM WAS THINKING THE CUPCAKES COULD GO WITH THE SPICE THEME.
WE COULD DO ZUCCHINI SPICE CUPCAKES, CHOCOLATE SPICE CUPCAKES, CHAI TEA CUPCAKES...
HOW CAN WE PICK JUST ONE?
WE'RE BAKING TWO BATCHES OF CUPCAKES, ANYWAY. WHY NOT BAKE TWO FLAVORS?
THAT'S A GREAT IDEA. THAT WAY IF SOMEBODY DOESN'T LIKE ONE FLAVOR, THEY CAN CHOOSE A DIFFERENT ONE.

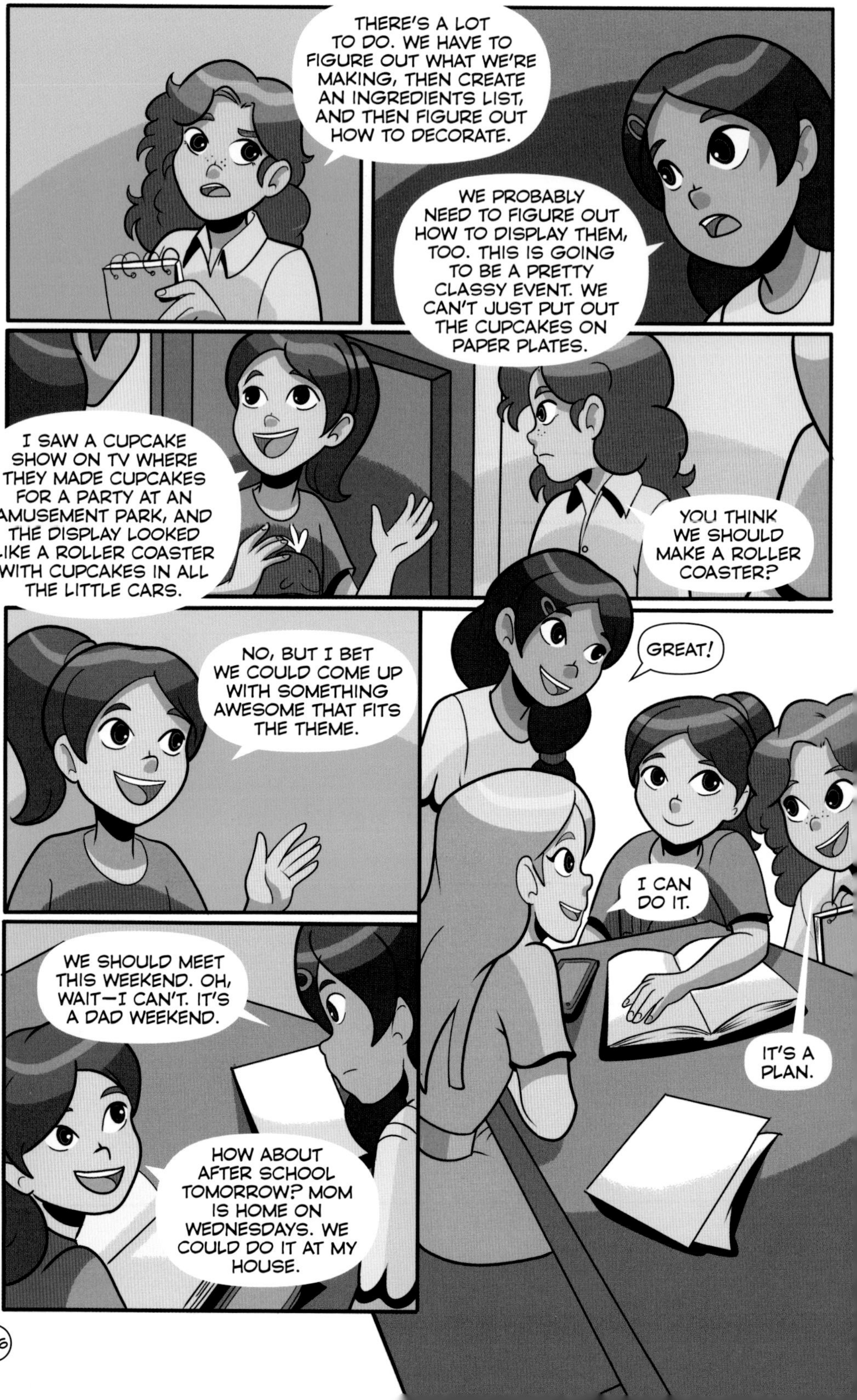
THERE'S A LOT TO DO. WE HAVE TO FIGURE OUT WHAT WE'RE MAKING, THEN CREATE AN INGREDIENTS LIST, AND THEN FIGURE OUT HOW TO DECORATE.
WE PROBABLY NEED TO FIGURE OUT HOW TO DISPLAY THEM, TOO. THIS IS GOING TO BE A PRETTY CLASSY EVENT. WE CAN'T JUST PUT OUT THE CUPCAKES ON PAPER PLATES.
I SAW A CUPCAKE SHOW ON TV WHERE THEY MADE CUPCAKES FOR A PARTY AT AN AMUSEMENT PARK, AND THE DISPLAY LOOKED LIKE A ROLLER COASTER WITH CUPCAKES IN ALL THE LITTLE CARS.
YOU THINK WE SHOULD MAKE A ROLLER COASTER?
NO, BUT I BET WE COULD COME UP WITH SOMETHING AWESOME THAT FITS THE THEME.
WE SHOULD MEET THIS WEEKEND. OH, WAIT—I CAN'T. IT'S A DAD WEEKEND.
HOW ABOUT AFTER SCHOOL TOMORROW? MOM IS HOME ON WEDNESDAYS. WE COULD DO IT AT MY HOUSE.
GREAT!
I CAN DO IT.
IT'S A PLAN.

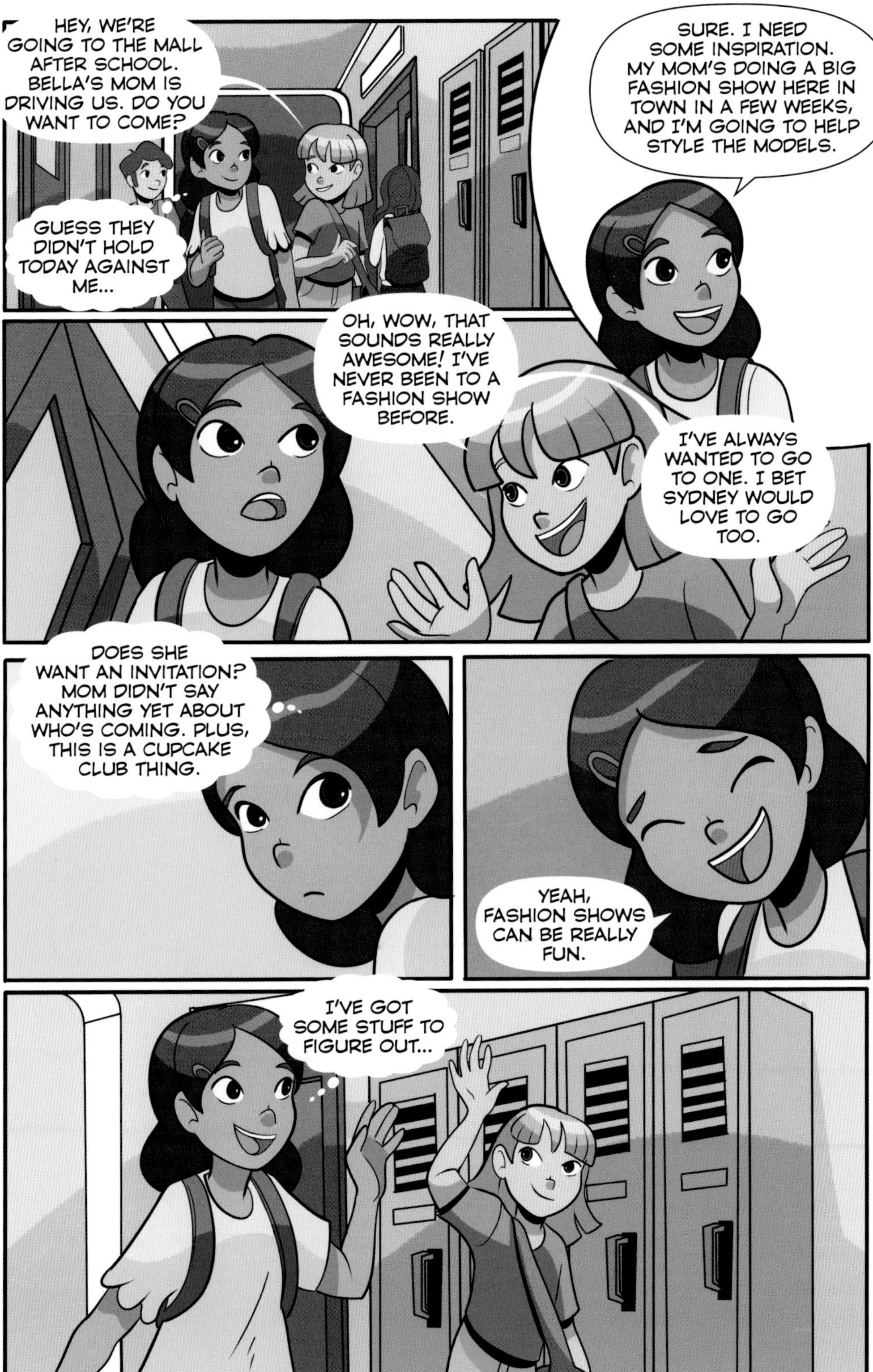
HEY, WE'RE GOING TO THE MALL AFTER SCHOOL. BELLA'S MOM IS DRIVING US. DO YOU WANT TO COME?
GUESS THEY DIDN'T HOLD TODAY AGAINST ME...
SURE. I NEED SOME INSPIRATION. MY MOM'S DOING A BIG FASHION SHOW HERE IN TOWN IN A FEW WEEKS, AND I'M GOING TO HELP STYLE THE MODELS.
OH, WOW, THAT SOUNDS REALLY AWESOME! I'VE NEVER BEEN TO A FASHION SHOW BEFORE.
I'VE ALWAYS WANTED TO GO TO ONE. I BET SYDNEY WOULD LOVE TO GO TOO.
DOES SHE WANT AN INVITATION? MOM DIDN'T SAY ANYTHING YET ABOUT WHO'S COMING. PLUS, THIS IS A CUPCAKE CLUB THING.
YEAH, FASHION SHOWS CAN BE REALLY FUN.
I'VE GOT SOME STUFF TO FIGURE OUT...

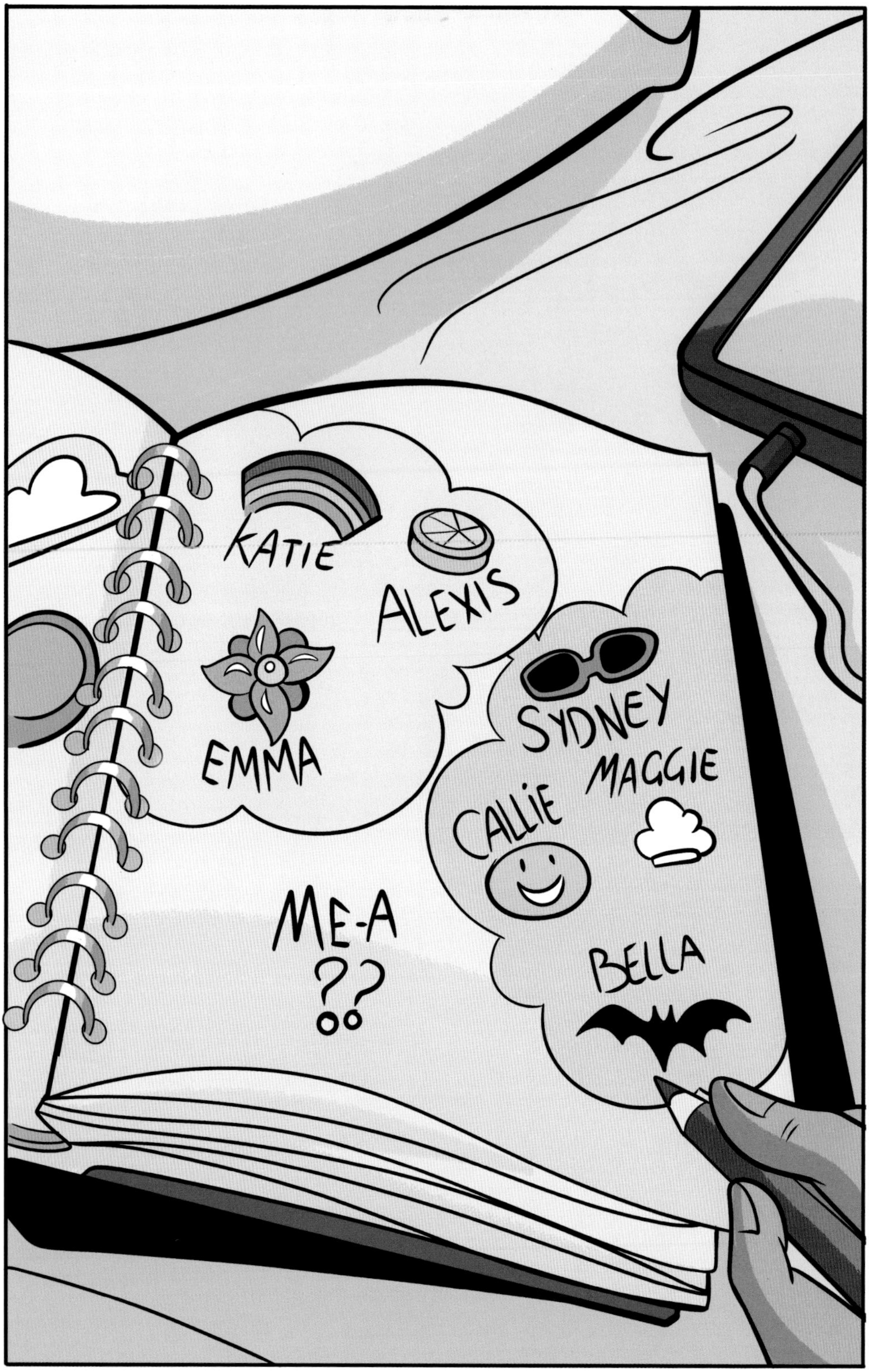
KATIE
ALEXIS
EMMA
SYDNEY
CALLIE
MAGGIE
ME-A
??
BELLA

Chapter 12

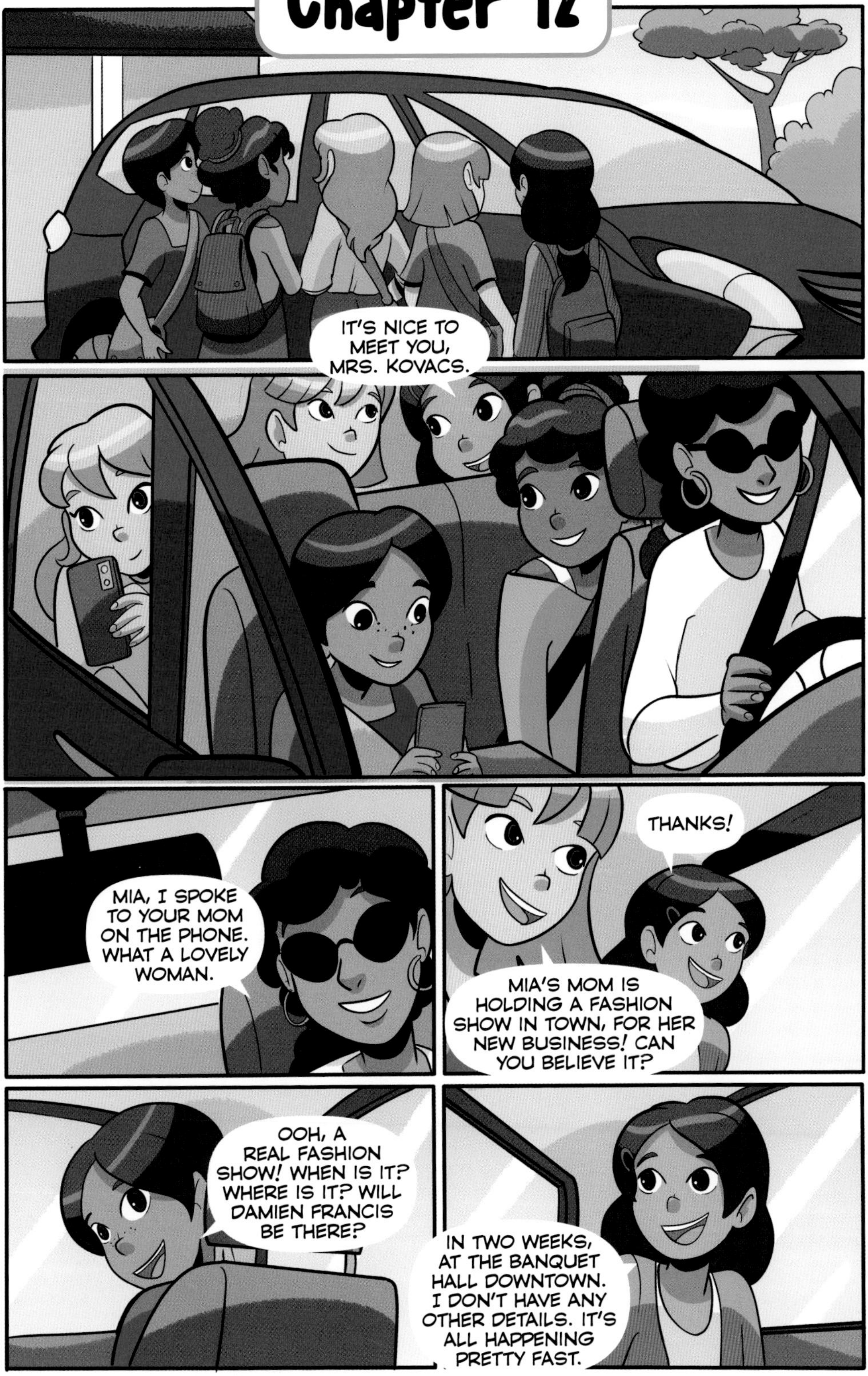

IT'S NICE TO MEET YOU, MRS. KOVACS.
MIA, I SPOKE TO YOUR MOM ON THE PHONE. WHAT A LOVELY WOMAN.
THANKS!
MIA'S MOM IS HOLDING A FASHION SHOW IN TOWN, FOR HER NEW BUSINESS! CAN YOU BELIEVE IT?
OOH, A REAL FASHION SHOW! WHEN IS IT? WHERE IS IT? WILL DAMIEN FRANCIS BE THERE?
IN TWO WEEKS, AT THE BANQUET HALL DOWNTOWN. I DON'T HAVE ANY OTHER DETAILS. IT'S ALL HAPPENING PRETTY FAST.

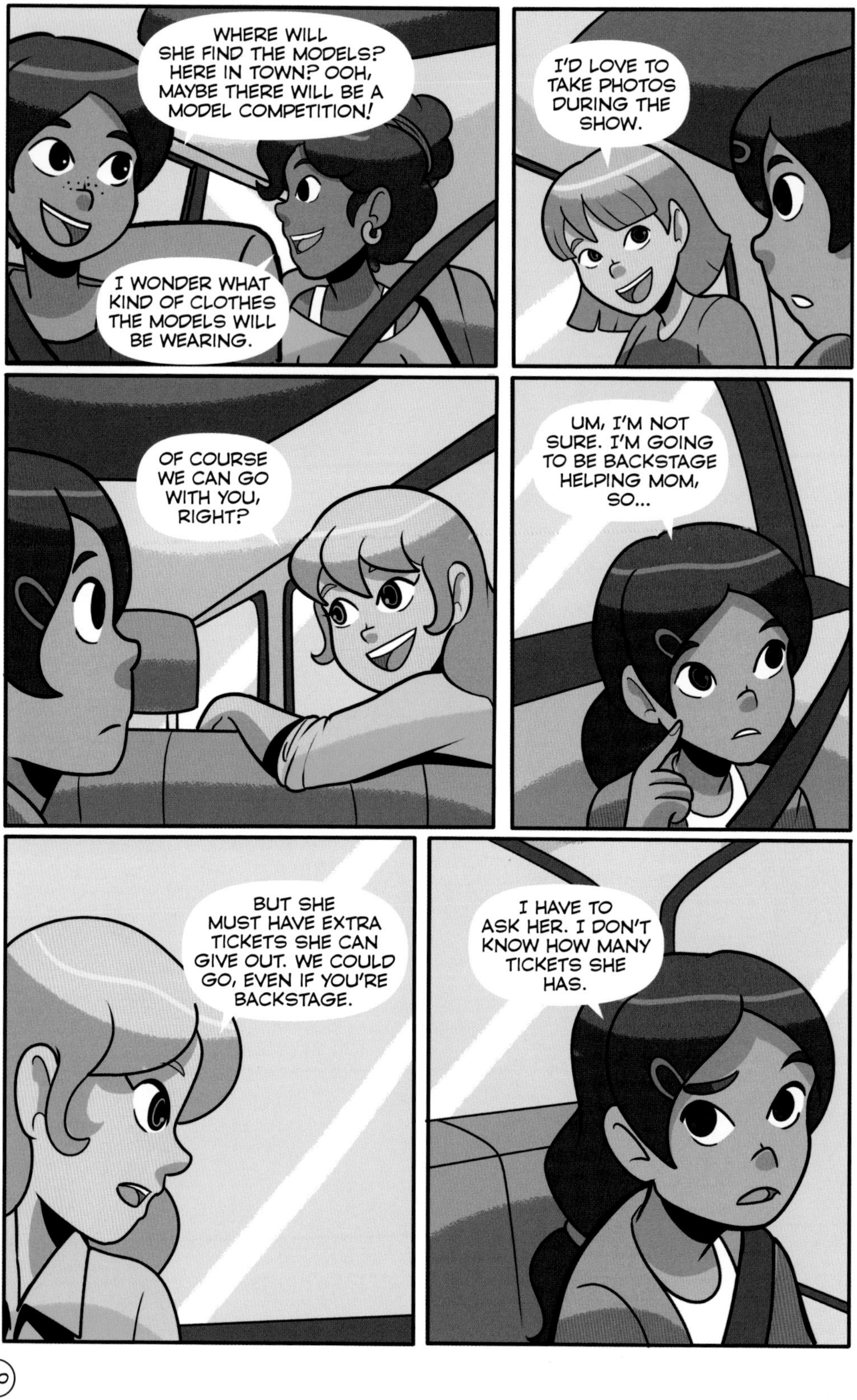
WHERE WILL SHE FIND THE MODELS? HERE IN TOWN? OOH, MAYBE THERE WILL BE A MODEL COMPETITION!
I WONDER WHAT KIND OF CLOTHES THE MODELS WILL BE WEARING.
I'D LOVE TO TAKE PHOTOS DURING THE SHOW.
OF COURSE WE CAN GO WITH YOU, RIGHT?
UM, I'M NOT SURE. I'M GOING TO BE BACKSTAGE HELPING MOM, SO...
BUT SHE MUST HAVE EXTRA TICKETS SHE CAN GIVE OUT. WE COULD GO, EVEN IF YOU'RE BACKSTAGE.
I HAVE TO ASK HER. I DON'T KNOW HOW MANY TICKETS SHE HAS.

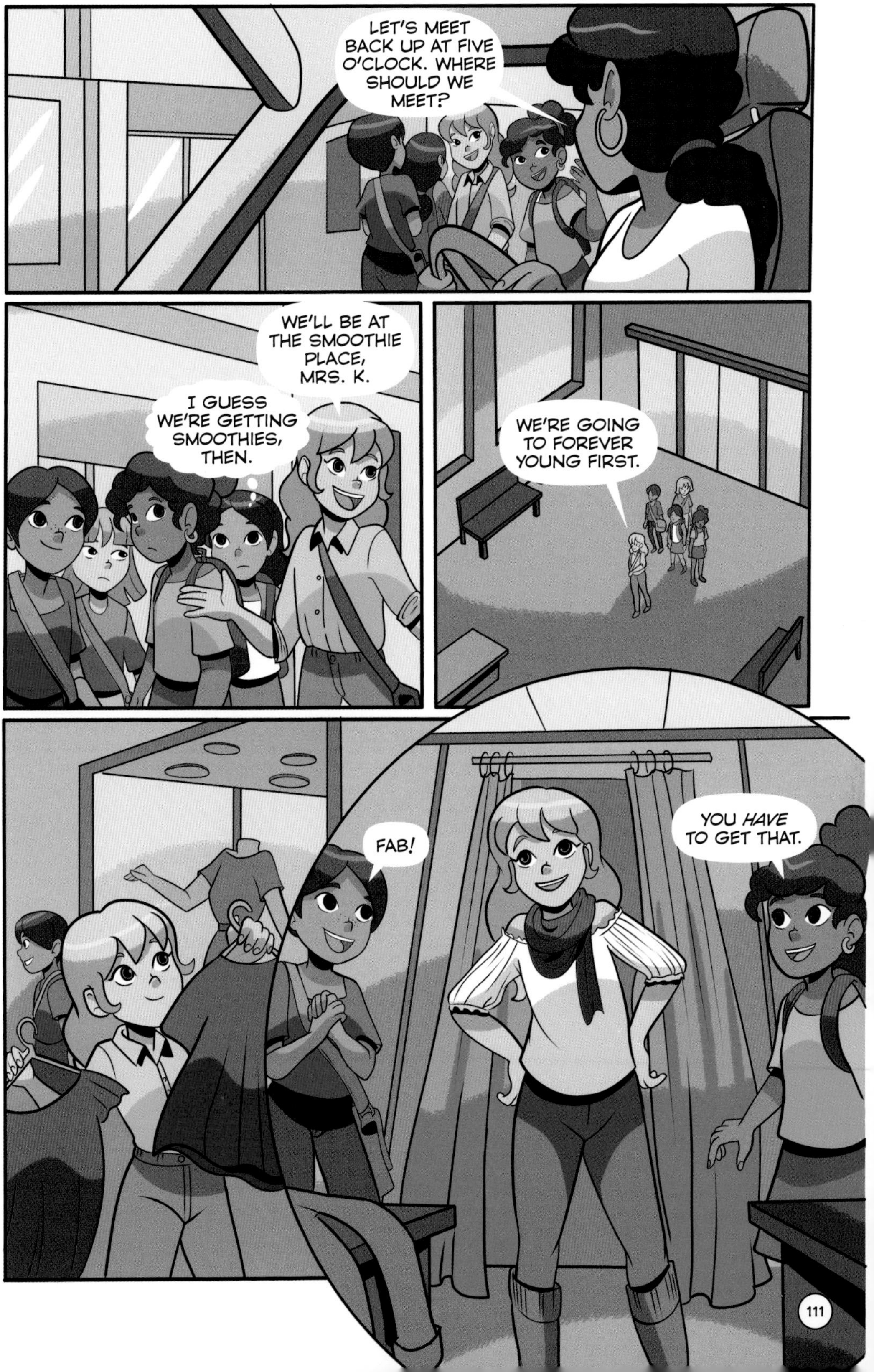
LET'S MEET BACK UP AT FIVE O'CLOCK. WHERE SHOULD WE MEET?
WE'LL BE AT THE SMOOTHIE PLACE, MRS. K.
I GUESS WE'RE GETTING SMOOTHIES, THEN.
WE'RE GOING TO FOREVER YOUNG FIRST.
FAB!
YOU *HAVE* TO GET THAT.

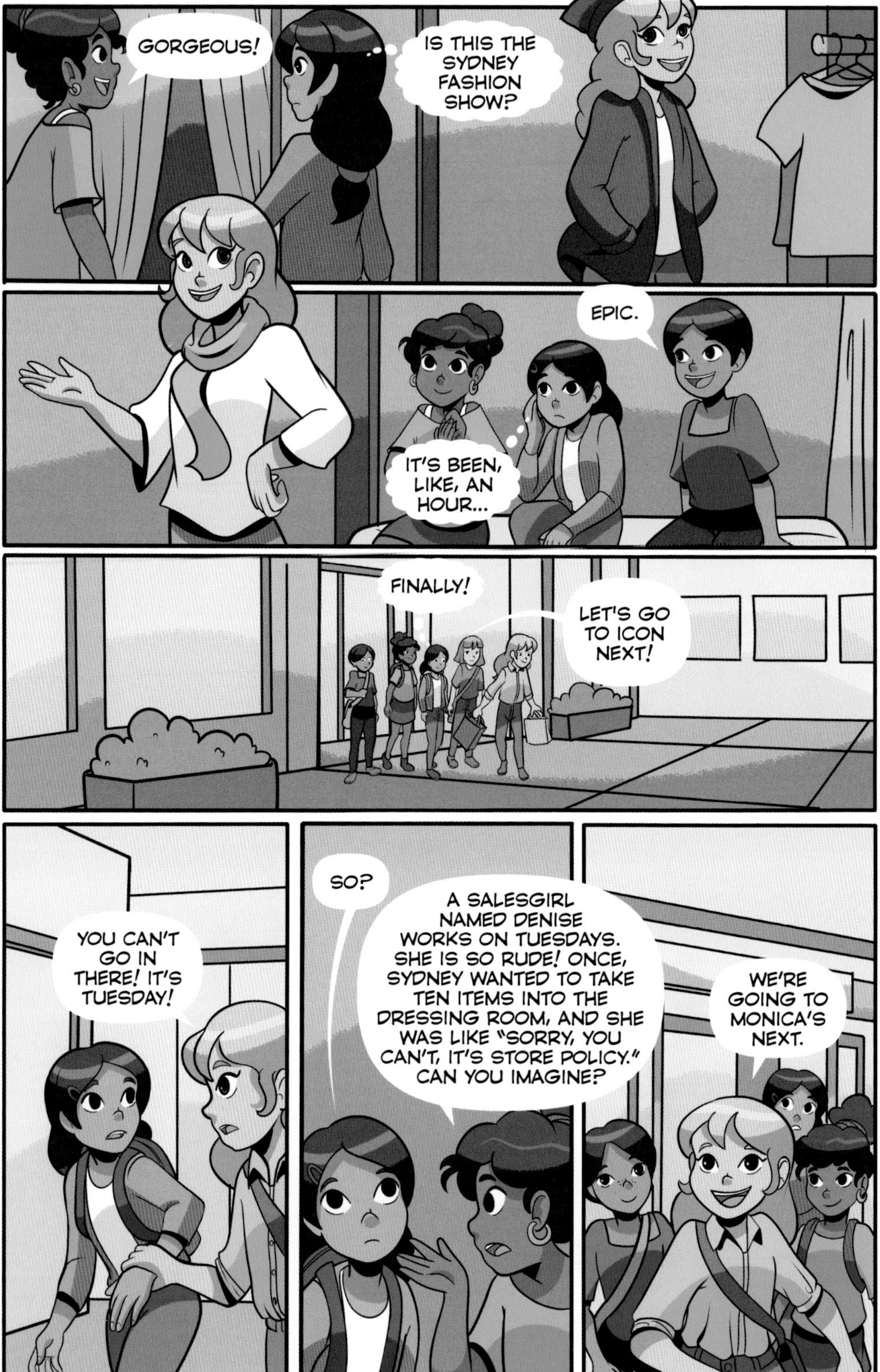
GORGEOUS!
IS THIS THE SYDNEY FASHION SHOW?
EPIC.
IT'S BEEN, LIKE, AN HOUR...
FINALLY!
LET'S GO TO ICON NEXT!
YOU CAN'T GO IN THERE! IT'S TUESDAY!
SO?
A SALESGIRL NAMED DENISE WORKS ON TUESDAYS. SHE IS SO RUDE! ONCE, SYDNEY WANTED TO TAKE TEN ITEMS INTO THE DRESSING ROOM, AND SHE WAS LIKE "SORRY, YOU CAN'T, IT'S STORE POLICY." CAN YOU IMAGINE?
WE'RE GOING TO MONICA'S NEXT.

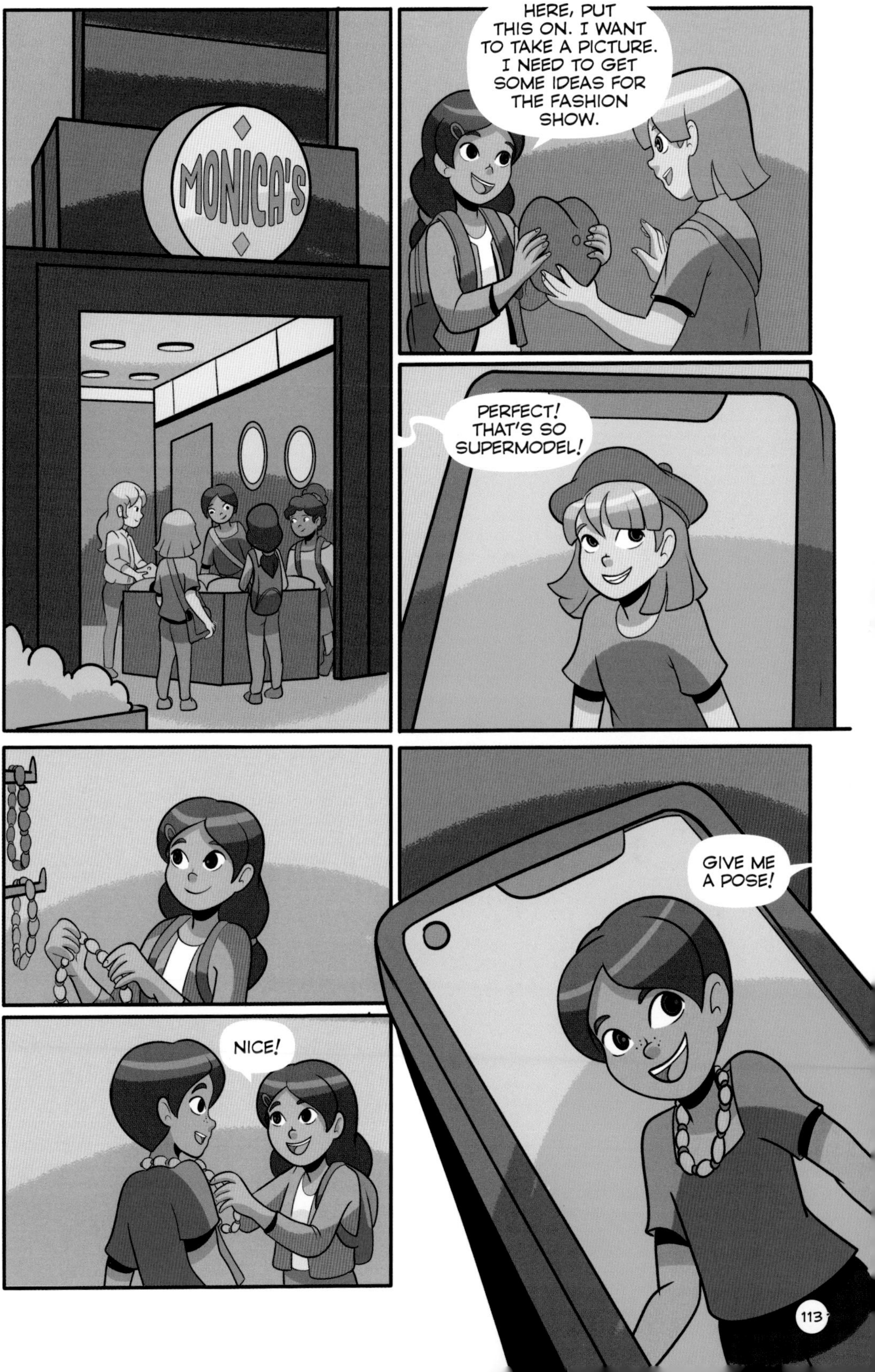

MONICA'S
HERE, PUT THIS ON. I WANT TO TAKE A PICTURE. I NEED TO GET SOME IDEAS FOR THE FASHION SHOW.
PERFECT! THAT'S SO SUPERMODEL!
GIVE ME A POSE!
NICE!

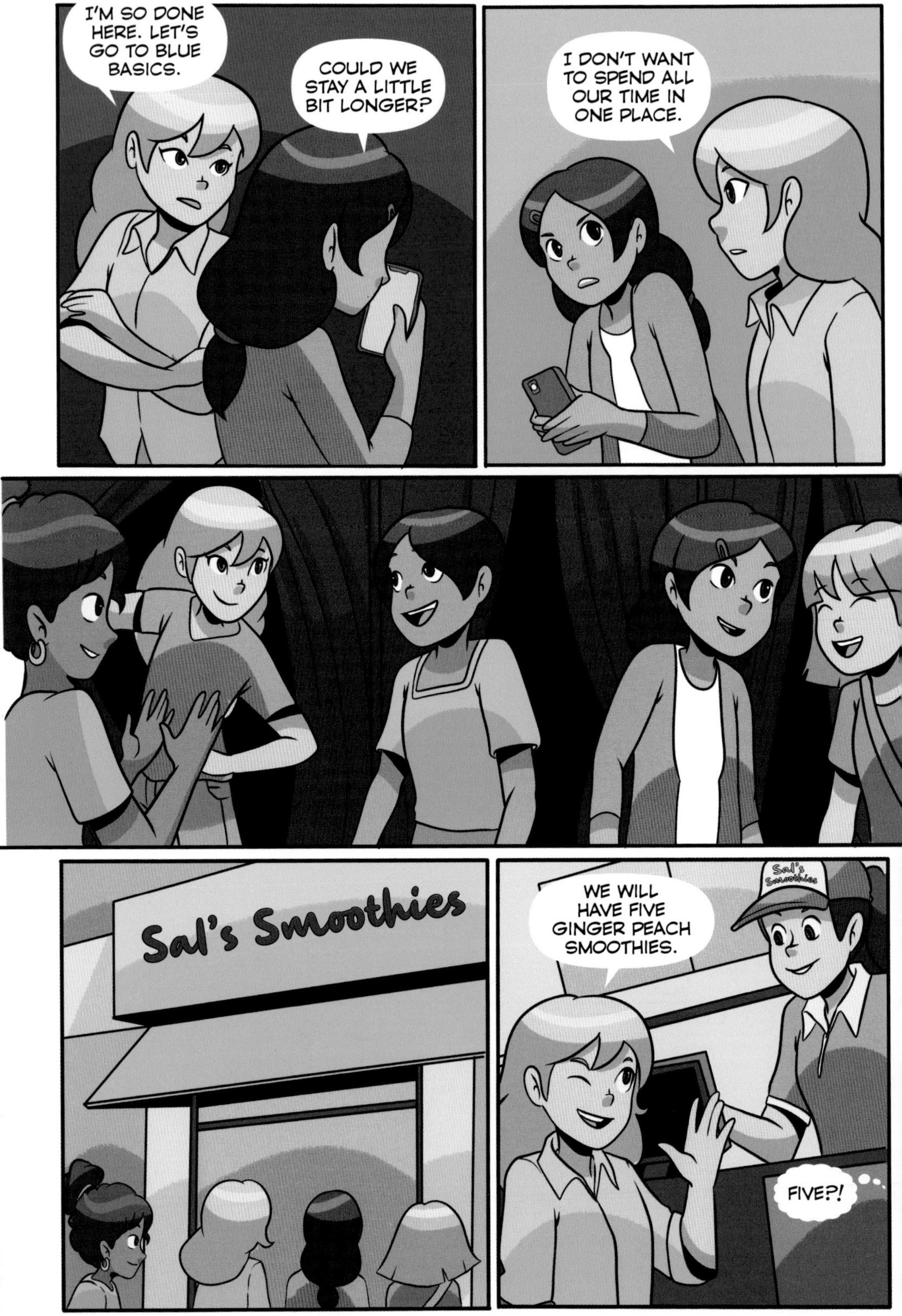
I'M SO DONE HERE. LET'S GO TO BLUE BASICS.
COULD WE STAY A LITTLE BIT LONGER?
I DON'T WANT TO SPEND ALL OUR TIME IN ONE PLACE.
Sal's Smoothies
Sal's Smoothies
WE WILL HAVE FIVE GINGER PEACH SMOOTHIES.
FIVE?!

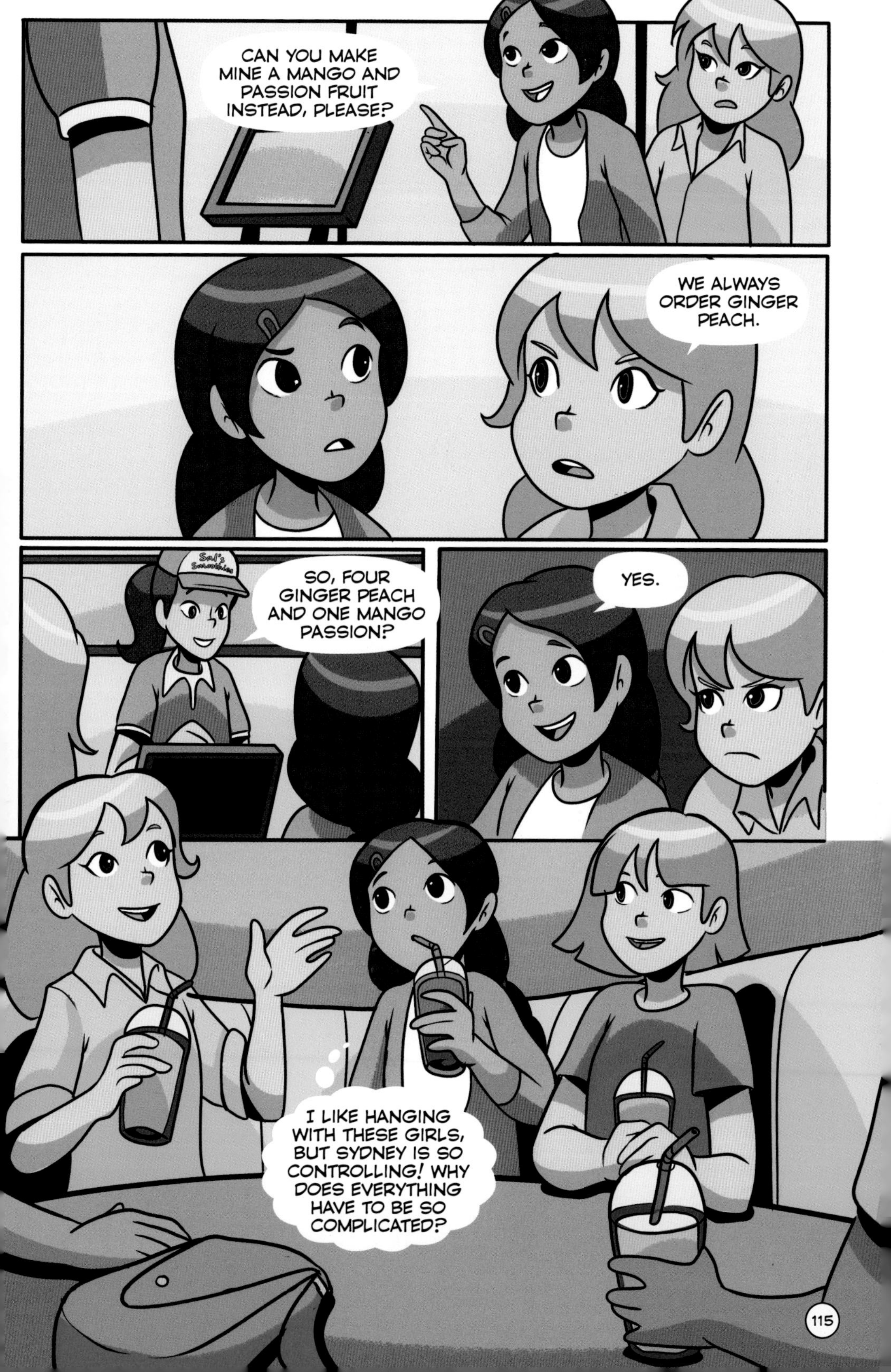
CAN YOU MAKE MINE A MANGO AND PASSION FRUIT INSTEAD, PLEASE?
WE ALWAYS ORDER GINGER PEACH.
Sal's Smoothies
SO, FOUR GINGER PEACH AND ONE MANGO PASSION?
YES.
I LIKE HANGING WITH THESE GIRLS, BUT SYDNEY IS SO CONTROLLING! WHY DOES EVERYTHING HAVE TO BE SO COMPLICATED?

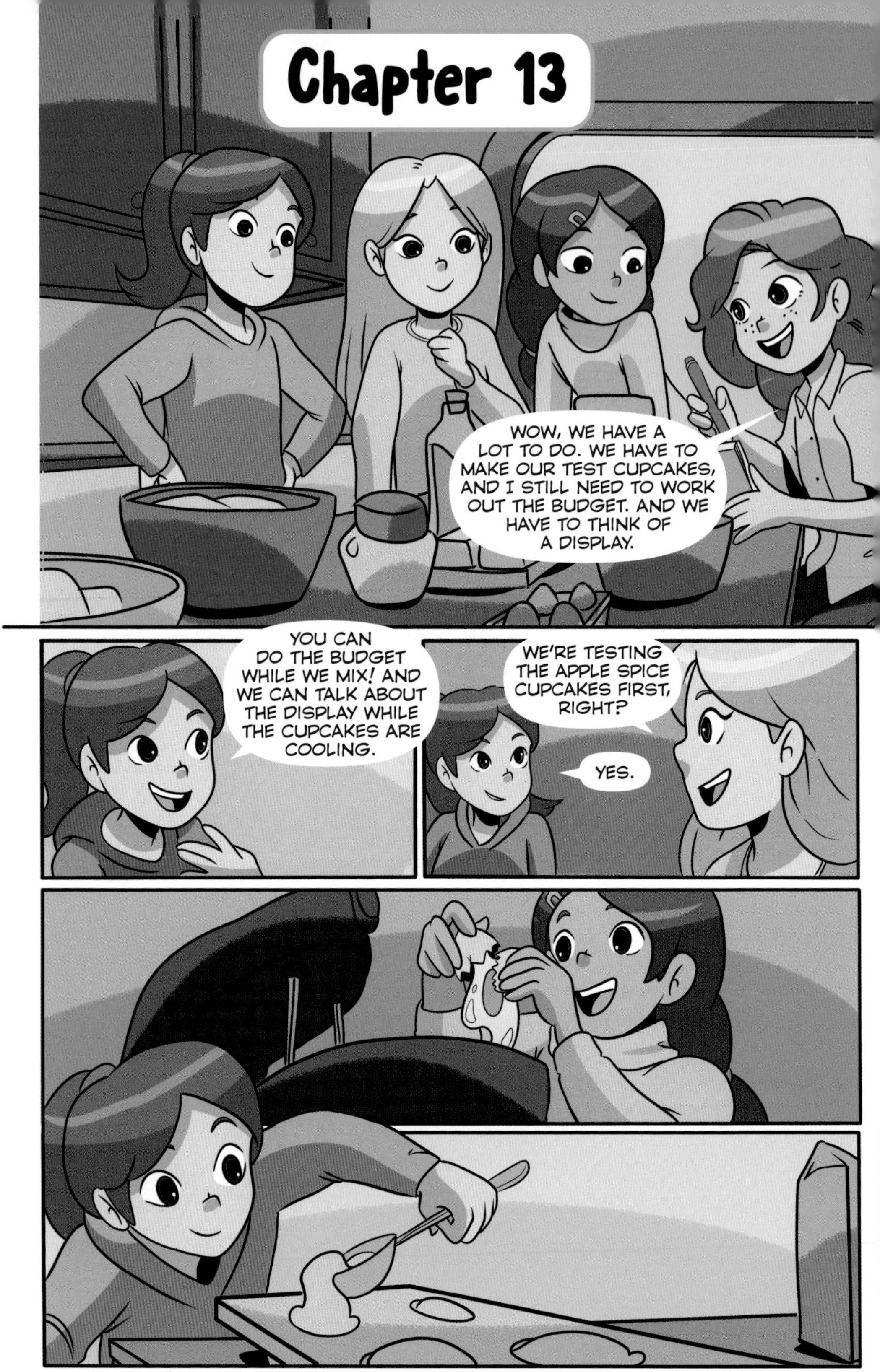
Chapter 13
WOW, WE HAVE A LOT TO DO. WE HAVE TO MAKE OUR TEST CUPCAKES, AND I STILL NEED TO WORK OUT THE BUDGET. AND WE HAVE TO THINK OF A DISPLAY.
YOU CAN DO THE BUDGET WHILE WE MIX! AND WE CAN TALK ABOUT THE DISPLAY WHILE THE CUPCAKES ARE COOLING.
WE'RE TESTING THE APPLE SPICE CUPCAKES FIRST, RIGHT?
YES.

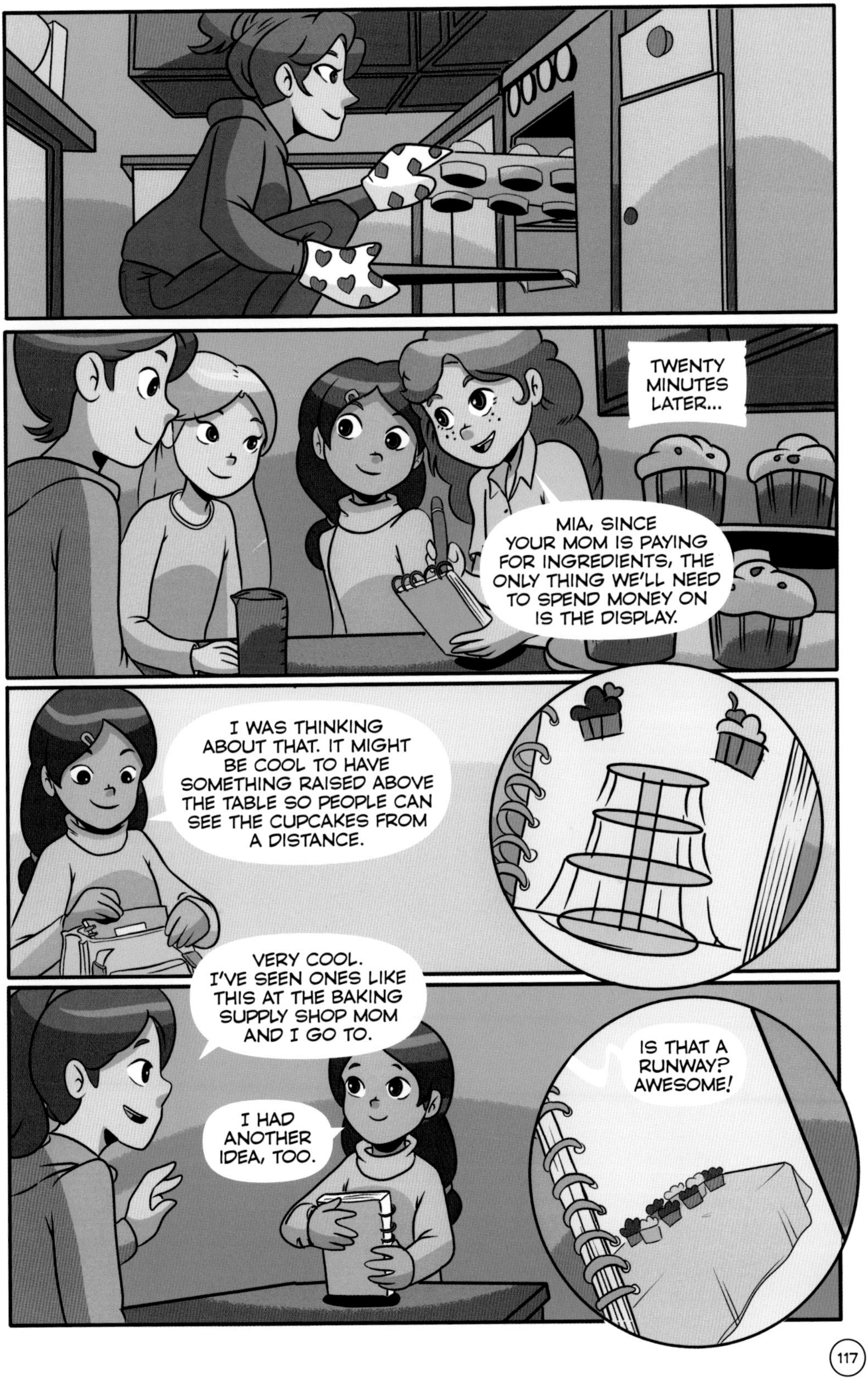
TWENTY MINUTES LATER...
MIA, SINCE YOUR MOM IS PAYING FOR INGREDIENTS, THE ONLY THING WE'LL NEED TO SPEND MONEY ON IS THE DISPLAY.
I WAS THINKING ABOUT THAT. IT MIGHT BE COOL TO HAVE SOMETHING RAISED ABOVE THE TABLE SO PEOPLE CAN SEE THE CUPCAKES FROM A DISTANCE.
VERY COOL. I'VE SEEN ONES LIKE THIS AT THE BAKING SUPPLY SHOP MOM AND I GO TO.
I HAD ANOTHER IDEA, TOO.
IS THAT A RUNWAY? AWESOME!

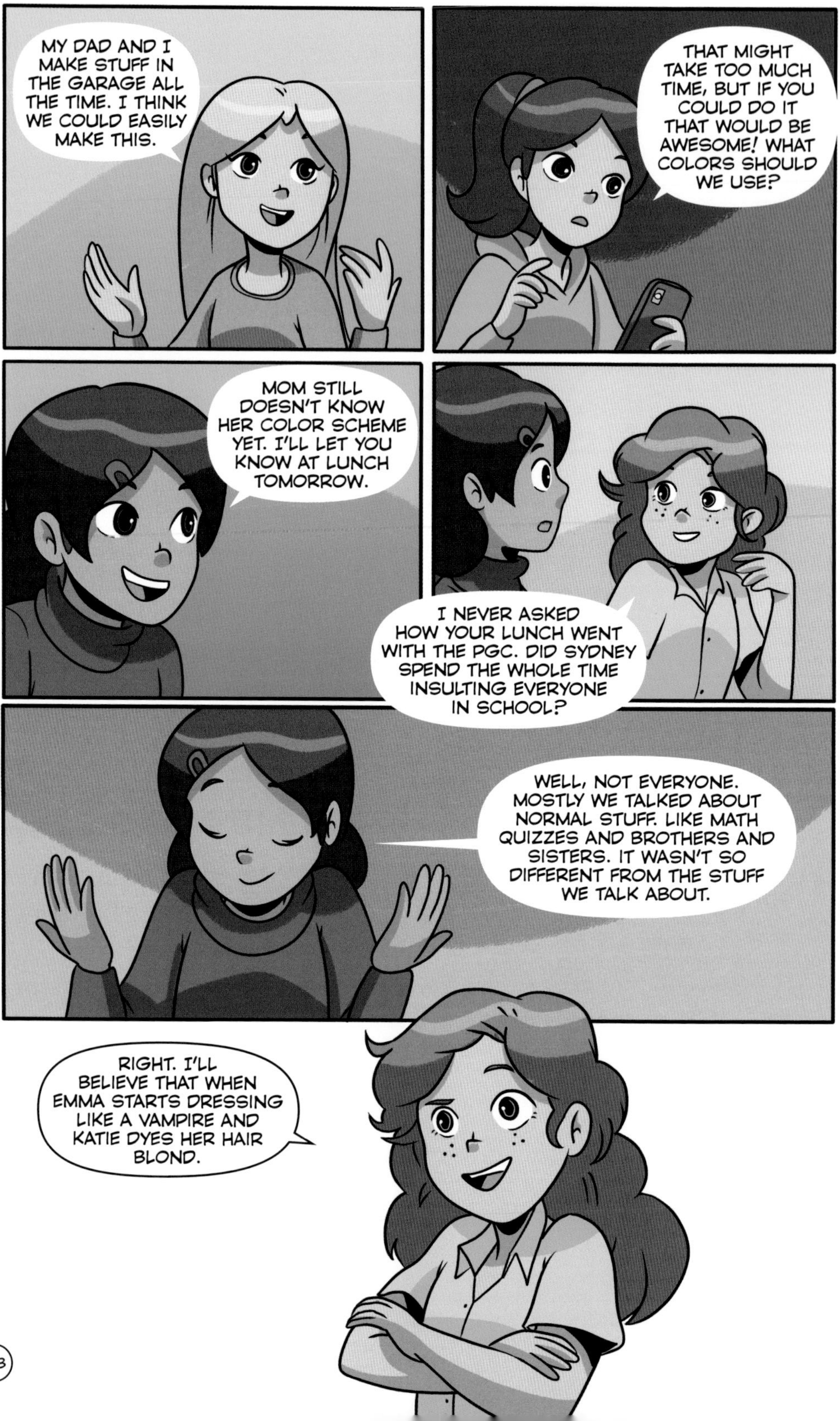
MY DAD AND I MAKE STUFF IN THE GARAGE ALL THE TIME. I THINK WE COULD EASILY MAKE THIS.
THAT MIGHT TAKE TOO MUCH TIME, BUT IF YOU COULD DO IT THAT WOULD BE AWESOME! WHAT COLORS SHOULD WE USE?
MOM STILL DOESN'T KNOW HER COLOR SCHEME YET. I'LL LET YOU KNOW AT LUNCH TOMORROW.
I NEVER ASKED HOW YOUR LUNCH WENT WITH THE PGC. DID SYDNEY SPEND THE WHOLE TIME INSULTING EVERYONE IN SCHOOL?
WELL, NOT EVERYONE. MOSTLY WE TALKED ABOUT NORMAL STUFF. LIKE MATH QUIZZES AND BROTHERS AND SISTERS. IT WASN'T SO DIFFERENT FROM THE STUFF WE TALK ABOUT.
RIGHT. I'LL BELIEVE THAT WHEN EMMA STARTS DRESSING LIKE A VAMPIRE AND KATIE DYES HER HAIR BLOND.

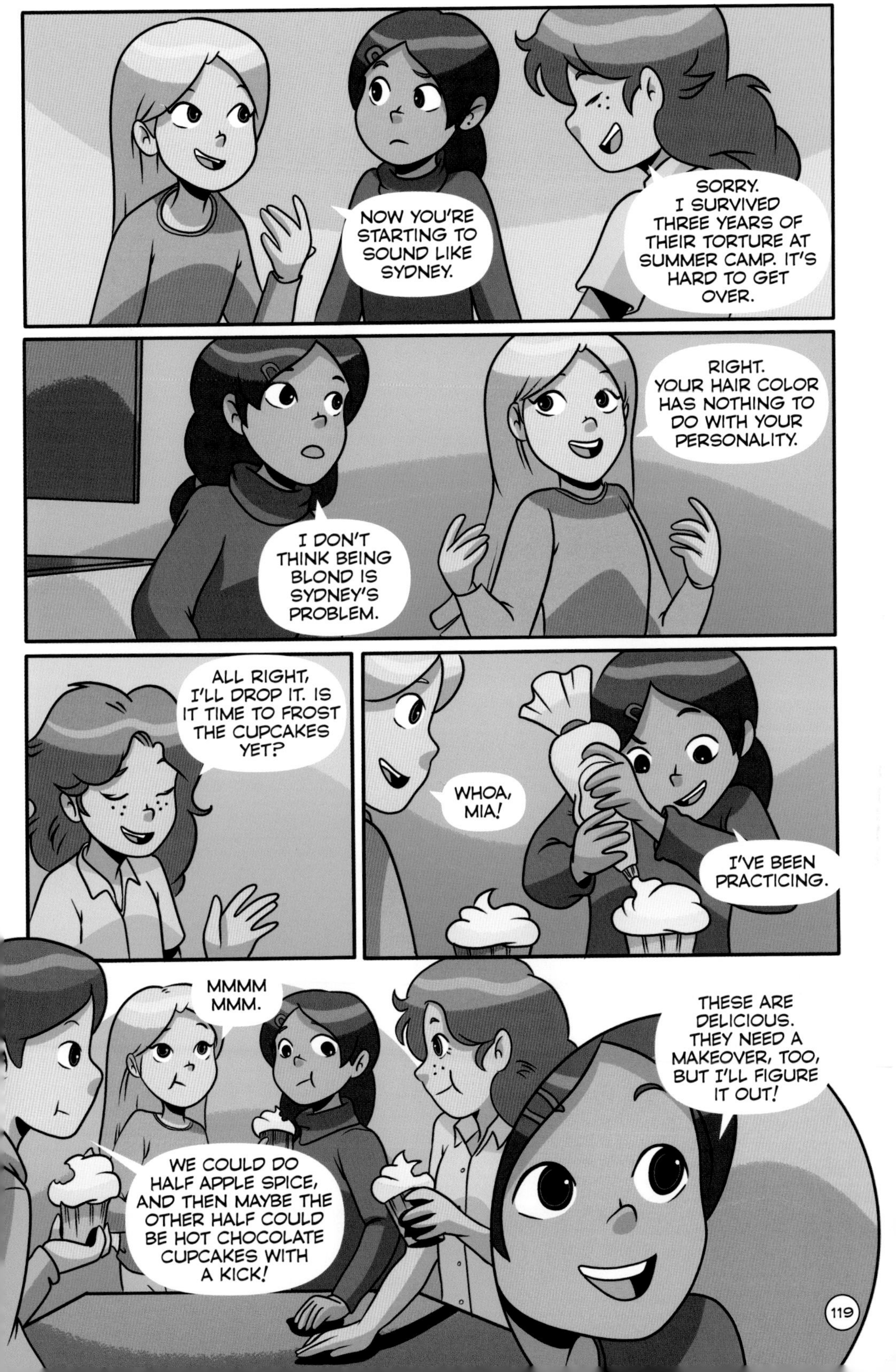
NOW YOU'RE STARTING TO SOUND LIKE SYDNEY.
SORRY. I SURVIVED THREE YEARS OF THEIR TORTURE AT SUMMER CAMP. IT'S HARD TO GET OVER.
RIGHT. YOUR HAIR COLOR HAS NOTHING TO DO WITH YOUR PERSONALITY.
I DON'T THINK BEING BLOND IS SYDNEY'S PROBLEM.
ALL RIGHT, I'LL DROP IT. IS IT TIME TO FROST THE CUPCAKES YET?
WHOA, MIA!
I'VE BEEN PRACTICING.
MMMM MMM.
WE COULD DO HALF APPLE SPICE, AND THEN MAYBE THE OTHER HALF COULD BE HOT CHOCOLATE CUPCAKES WITH A KICK!
THESE ARE DELICIOUS. THEY NEED A MAKEOVER, TOO, BUT I'LL FIGURE IT OUT!

Chapter 14

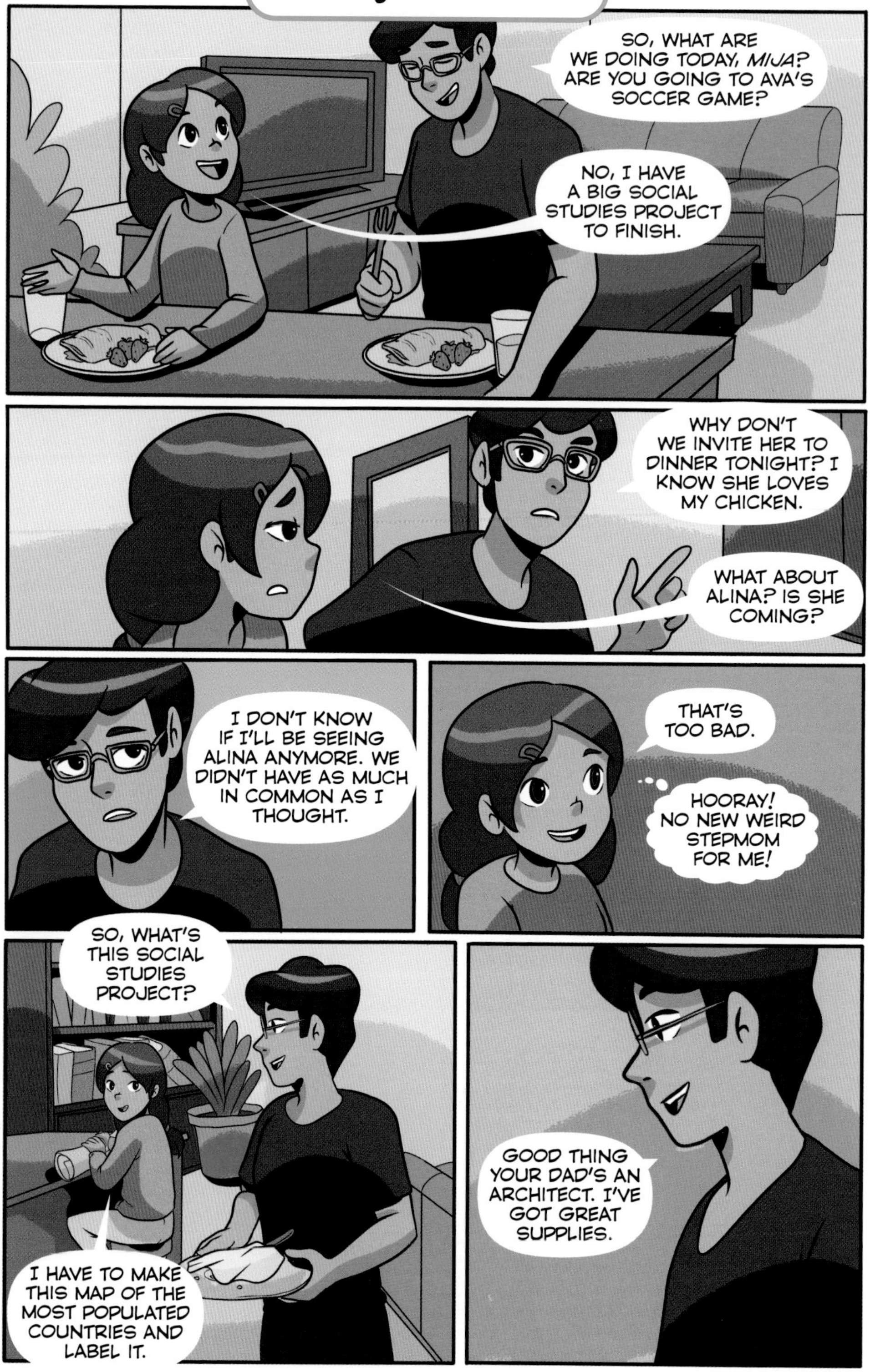
SO, WHAT ARE WE DOING TODAY, *MIJA*? ARE YOU GOING TO AVA'S SOCCER GAME?
NO, I HAVE A BIG SOCIAL STUDIES PROJECT TO FINISH.
WHY DON'T WE INVITE HER TO DINNER TONIGHT? I KNOW SHE LOVES MY CHICKEN.
WHAT ABOUT ALINA? IS SHE COMING?
I DON'T KNOW IF I'LL BE SEEING ALINA ANYMORE. WE DIDN'T HAVE AS MUCH IN COMMON AS I THOUGHT.
THAT'S TOO BAD.
HOORAY! NO NEW WEIRD STEPMOM FOR ME!
SO, WHAT'S THIS SOCIAL STUDIES PROJECT?
I HAVE TO MAKE THIS MAP OF THE MOST POPULATED COUNTRIES AND LABEL IT.
GOOD THING YOUR DAD'S AN ARCHITECT. I'VE GOT GREAT SUPPLIES.

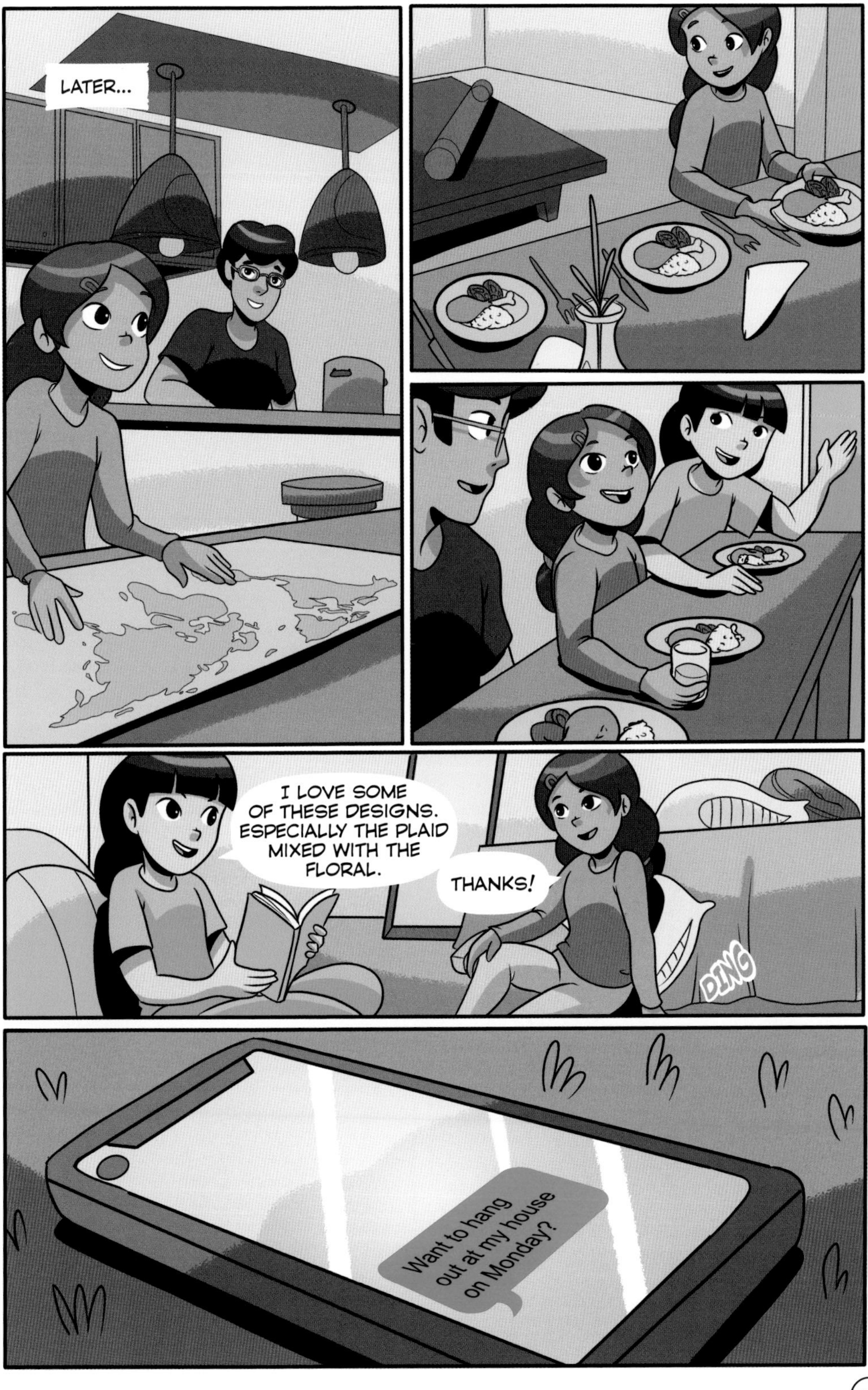
LATER...
I LOVE SOME OF THESE DESIGNS. ESPECIALLY THE PLAID MIXED WITH THE FLORAL.
THANKS!
DING
Want to hang out at my house on Monday?

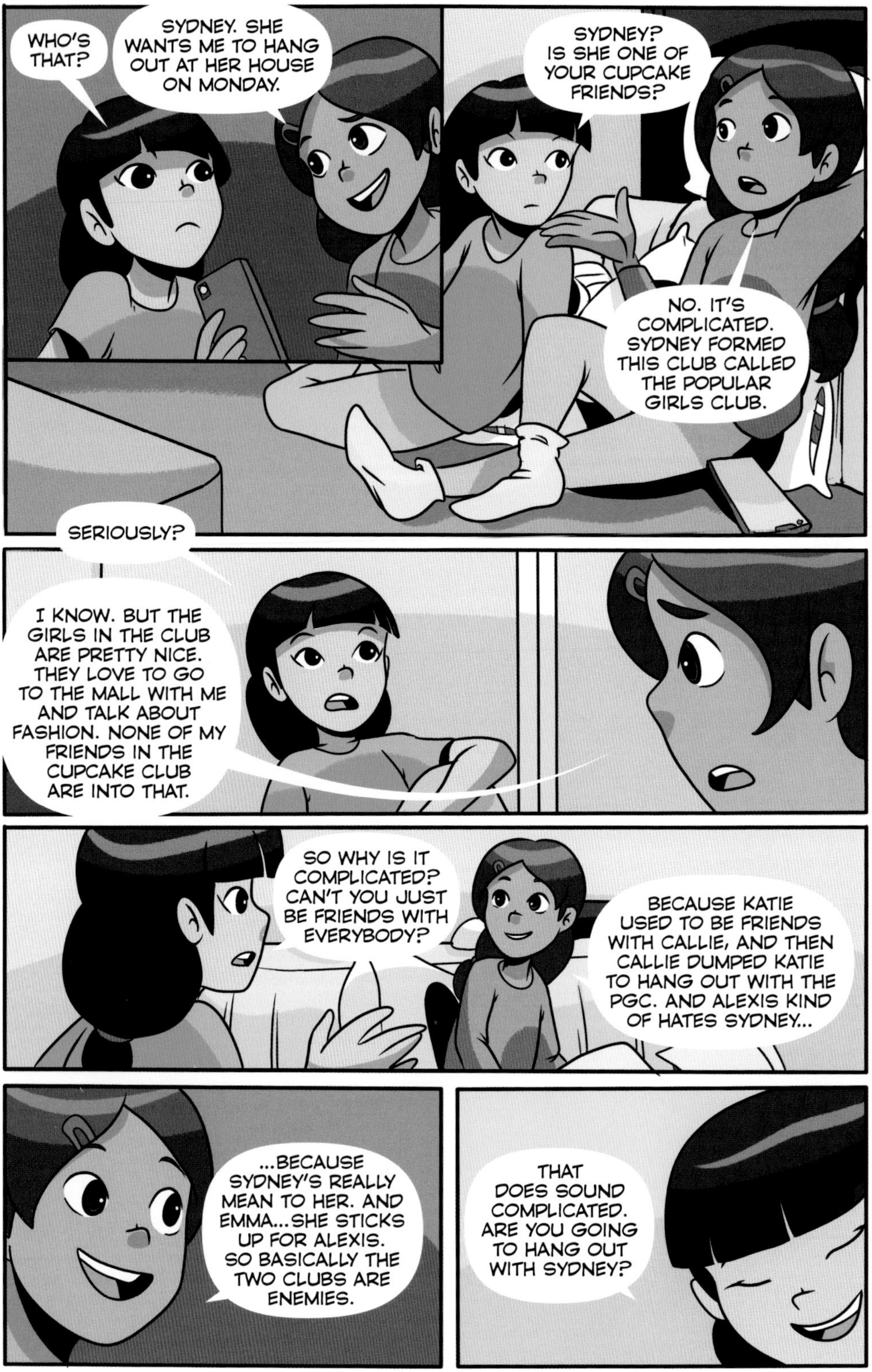
WHO'S THAT?
SYDNEY. SHE WANTS ME TO HANG OUT AT HER HOUSE ON MONDAY.
SYDNEY? IS SHE ONE OF YOUR CUPCAKE FRIENDS?
NO. IT'S COMPLICATED. SYDNEY FORMED THIS CLUB CALLED THE POPULAR GIRLS CLUB.
SERIOUSLY?
I KNOW. BUT THE GIRLS IN THE CLUB ARE PRETTY NICE. THEY LOVE TO GO TO THE MALL WITH ME AND TALK ABOUT FASHION. NONE OF MY FRIENDS IN THE CUPCAKE CLUB ARE INTO THAT.
SO WHY IS IT COMPLICATED? CAN'T YOU JUST BE FRIENDS WITH EVERYBODY?
BECAUSE KATIE USED TO BE FRIENDS WITH CALLIE, AND THEN CALLIE DUMPED KATIE TO HANG OUT WITH THE PGC. AND ALEXIS KIND OF HATES SYDNEY...
...BECAUSE SYDNEY'S REALLY MEAN TO HER. AND EMMA...SHE STICKS UP FOR ALEXIS. SO BASICALLY THE TWO CLUBS ARE ENEMIES.
THAT DOES SOUND COMPLICATED. ARE YOU GOING TO HANG OUT WITH SYDNEY?

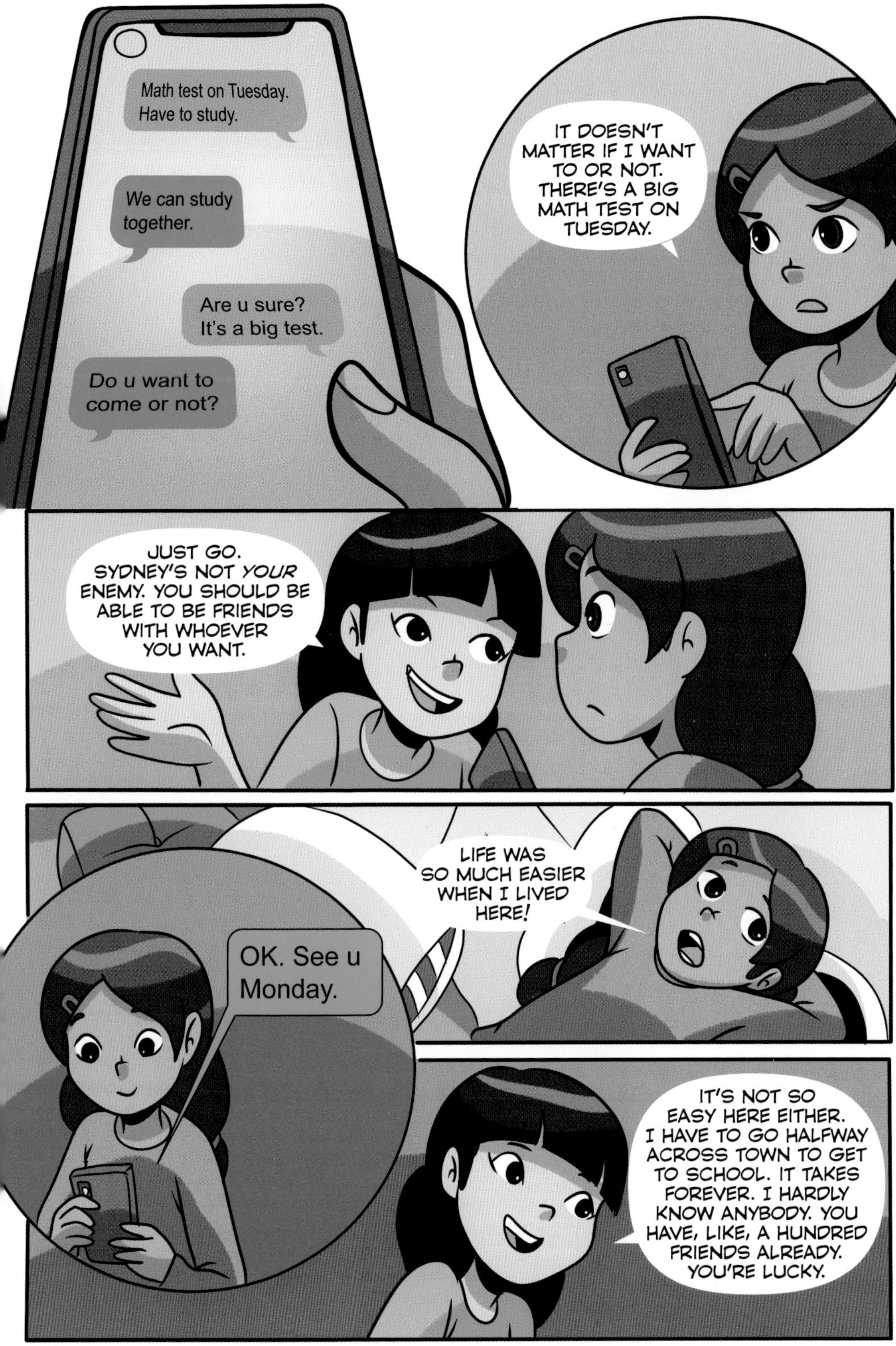
Math test on Tuesday. Have to study.
We can study together.
Are u sure? It's a big test.
Do u want to come or not?
IT DOESN'T MATTER IF I WANT TO OR NOT. THERE'S A BIG MATH TEST ON TUESDAY.
JUST GO. SYDNEY'S NOT *YOUR* ENEMY. YOU SHOULD BE ABLE TO BE FRIENDS WITH WHOEVER YOU WANT.
LIFE WAS SO MUCH EASIER WHEN I LIVED HERE!
OK. See u Monday.
IT'S NOT SO EASY HERE EITHER. I HAVE TO GO HALFWAY ACROSS TOWN TO GET TO SCHOOL. IT TAKES FOREVER. I HARDLY KNOW ANYBODY. YOU HAVE, LIKE, A HUNDRED FRIENDS ALREADY. YOU'RE LUCKY.

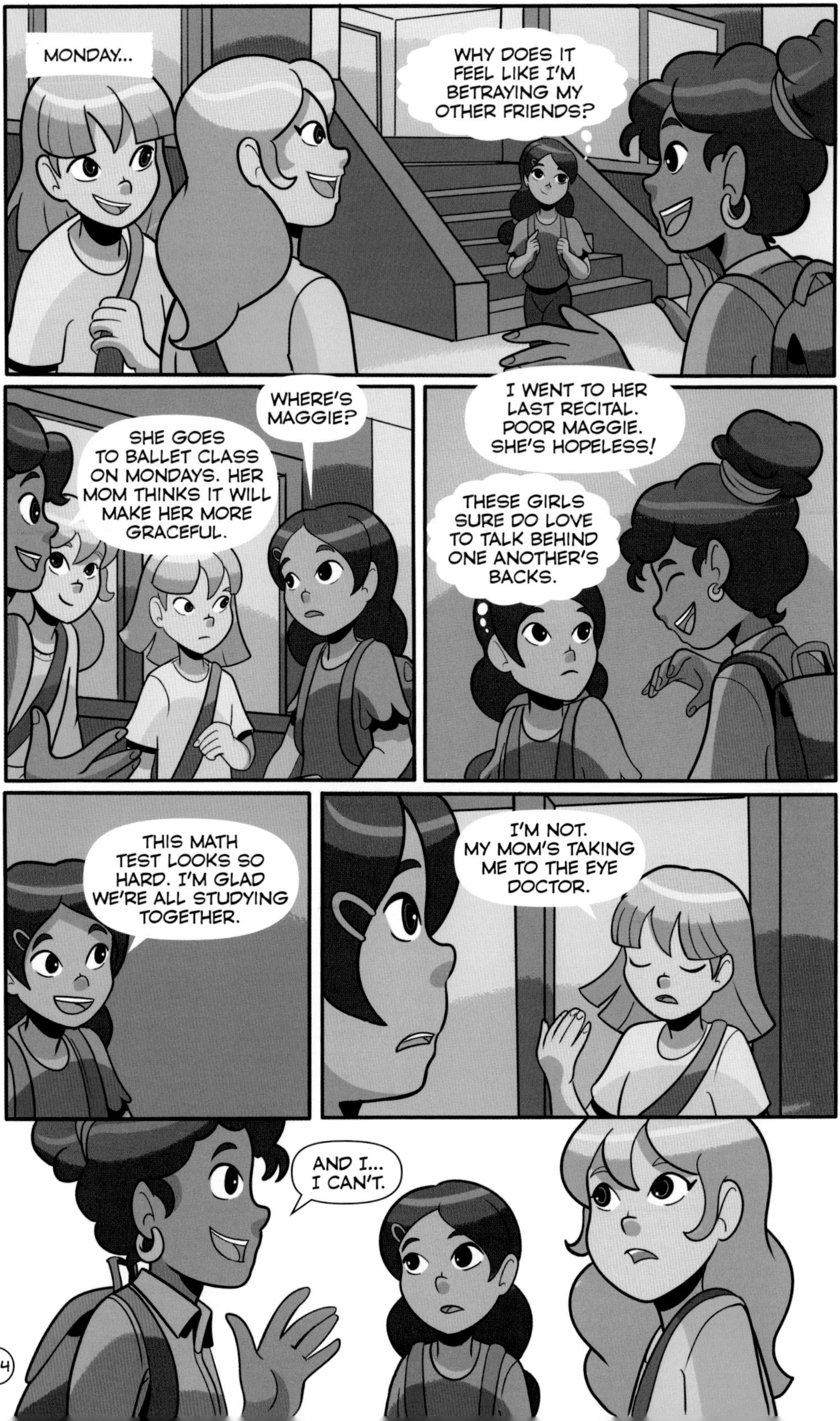
MONDAY...
WHY DOES IT FEEL LIKE I'M BETRAYING MY OTHER FRIENDS?
WHERE'S MAGGIE?
SHE GOES TO BALLET CLASS ON MONDAYS. HER MOM THINKS IT WILL MAKE HER MORE GRACEFUL.
I WENT TO HER LAST RECITAL. POOR MAGGIE. SHE'S HOPELESS!
THESE GIRLS SURE DO LOVE TO TALK BEHIND ONE ANOTHER'S BACKS.
THIS MATH TEST LOOKS SO HARD. I'M GLAD WE'RE ALL STUDYING TOGETHER.
I'M NOT. MY MOM'S TAKING ME TO THE EYE DOCTOR.
AND I... I CAN'T.

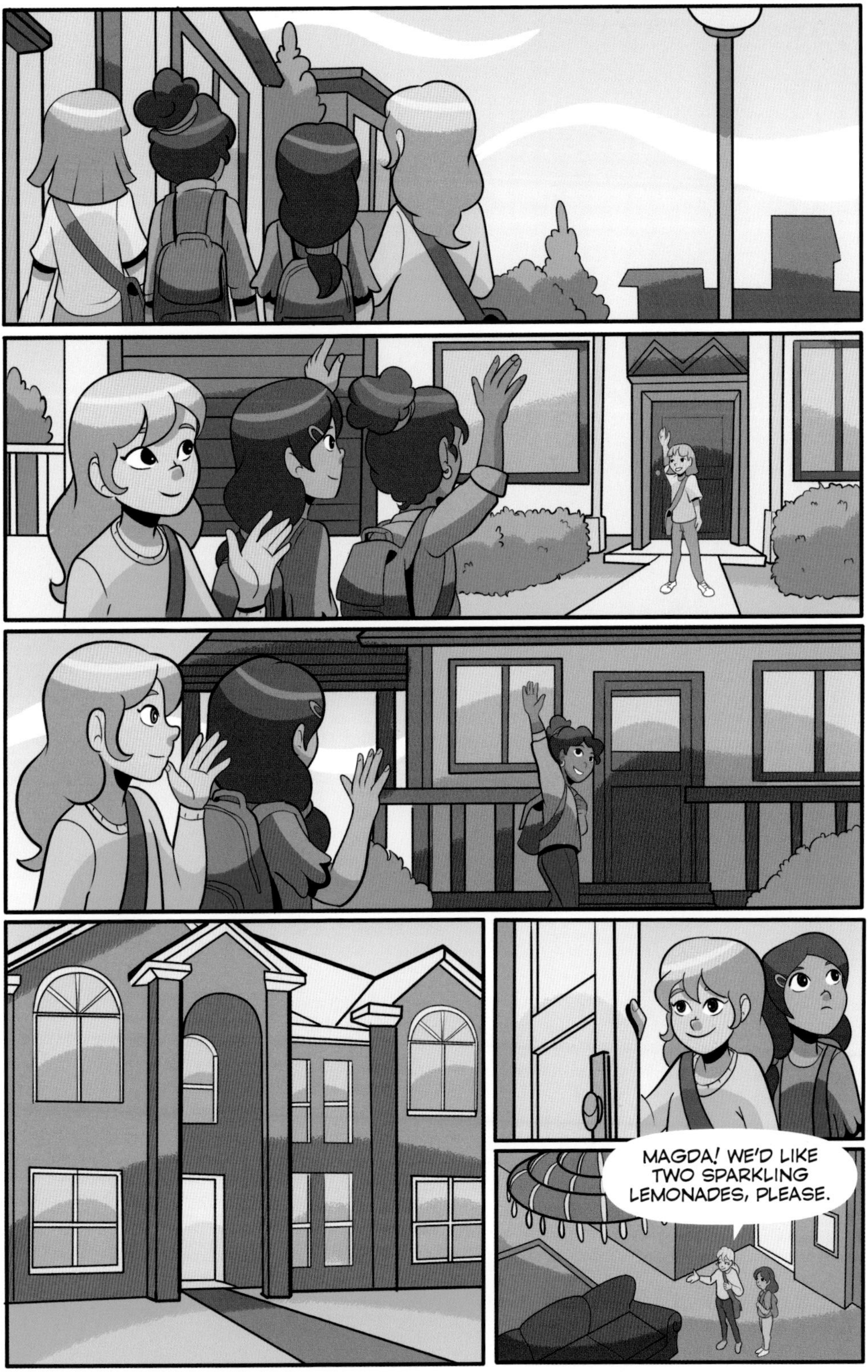
MAGDA! WE'D LIKE TWO SPARKLING LEMONADES, PLEASE.

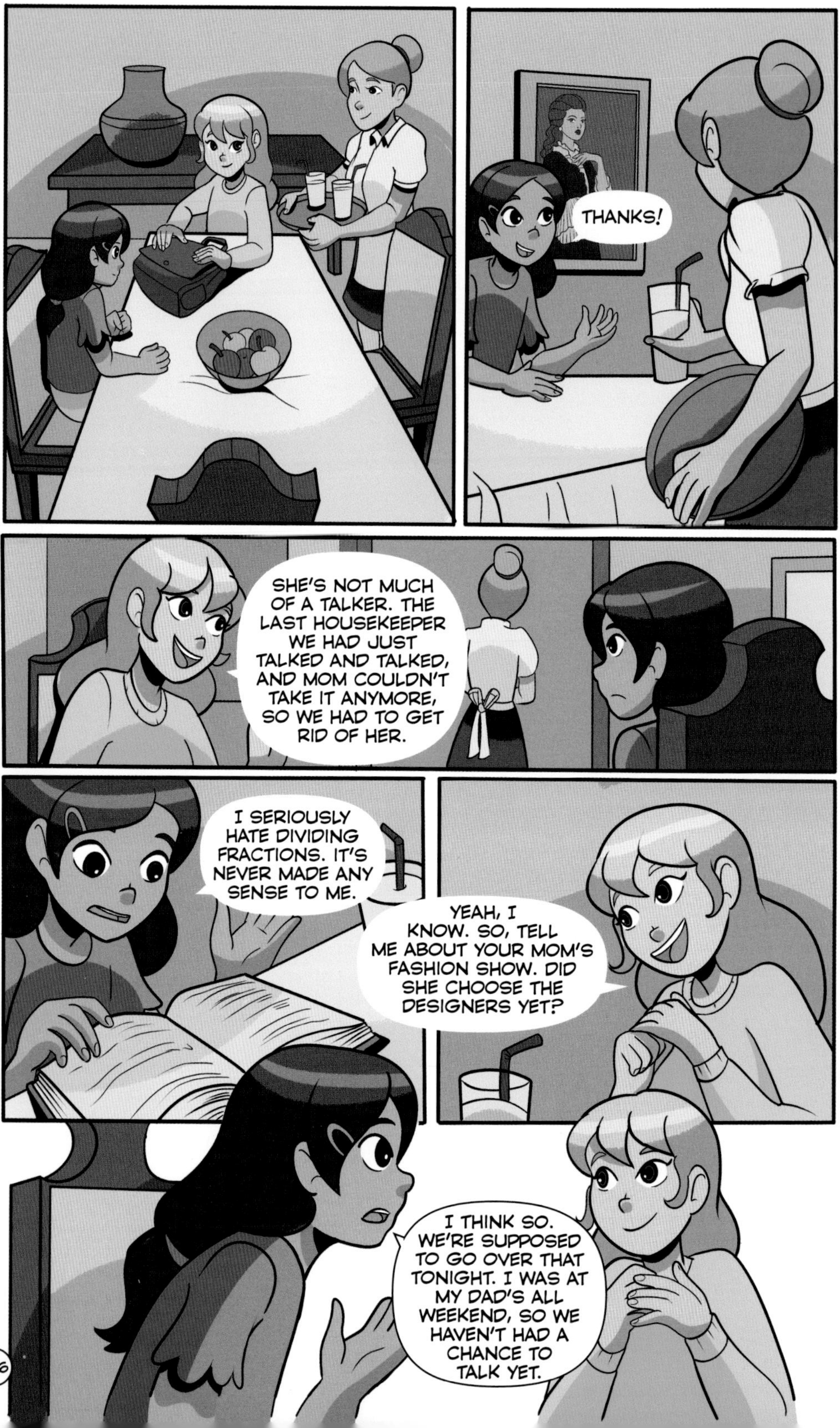
THANKS!
SHE'S NOT MUCH OF A TALKER. THE LAST HOUSEKEEPER WE HAD JUST TALKED AND TALKED, AND MOM COULDN'T TAKE IT ANYMORE, SO WE HAD TO GET RID OF HER.
I SERIOUSLY HATE DIVIDING FRACTIONS. IT'S NEVER MADE ANY SENSE TO ME.
YEAH, I KNOW. SO, TELL ME ABOUT YOUR MOM'S FASHION SHOW. DID SHE CHOOSE THE DESIGNERS YET?
I THINK SO. WE'RE SUPPOSED TO GO OVER THAT TONIGHT. I WAS AT MY DAD'S ALL WEEKEND, SO WE HAVEN'T HAD A CHANCE TO TALK YET.

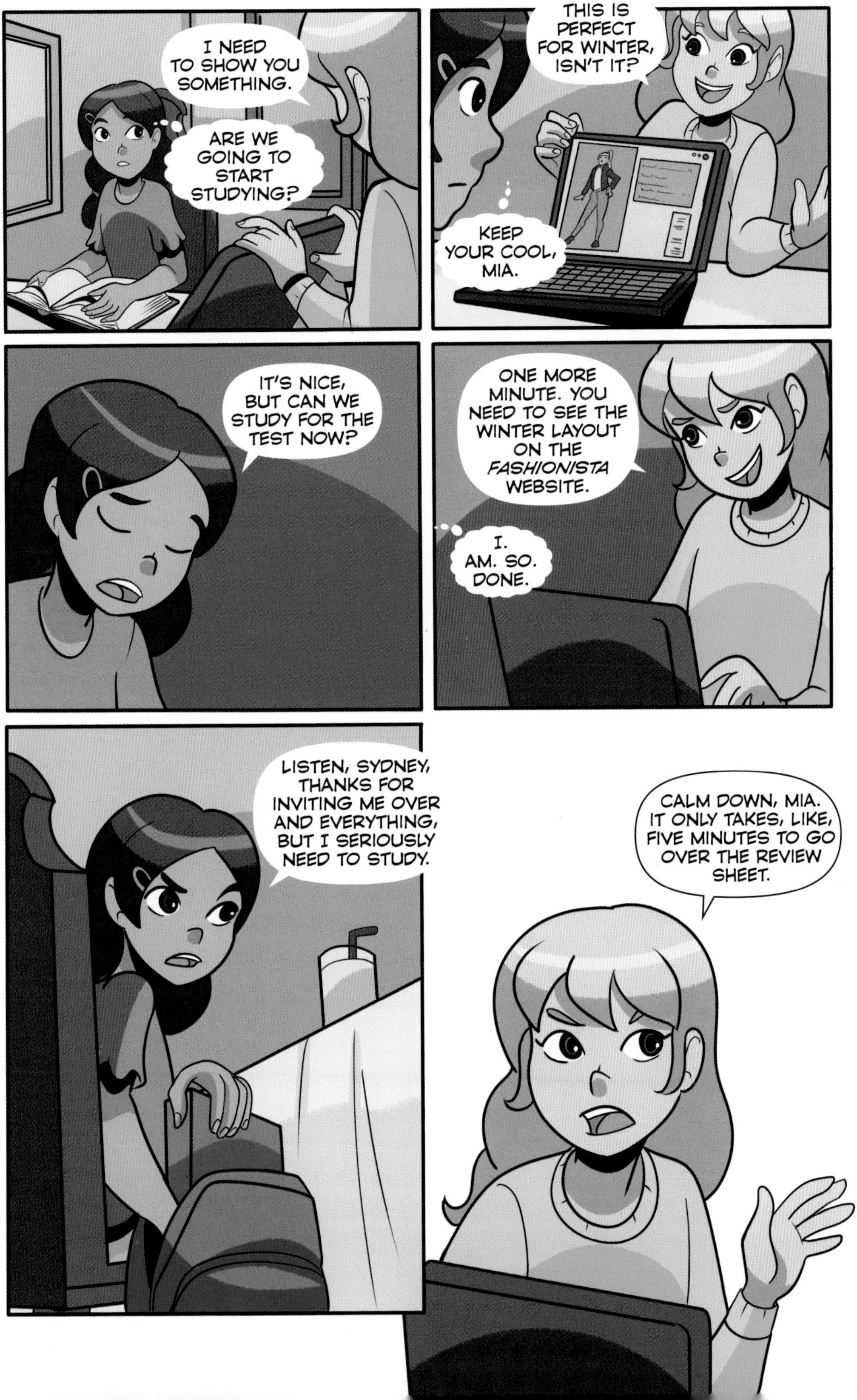
I NEED TO SHOW YOU SOMETHING.
ARE WE GOING TO START STUDYING?
THIS IS PERFECT FOR WINTER, ISN'T IT?
KEEP YOUR COOL, MIA.
IT'S NICE, BUT CAN WE STUDY FOR THE TEST NOW?
ONE MORE MINUTE. YOU NEED TO SEE THE WINTER LAYOUT ON THE *FASHIONISTA* WEBSITE.
I. AM. SO. DONE.
LISTEN, SYDNEY, THANKS FOR INVITING ME OVER AND EVERYTHING, BUT I SERIOUSLY NEED TO STUDY.
CALM DOWN, MIA. IT ONLY TAKES, LIKE, FIVE MINUTES TO GO OVER THE REVIEW SHEET.

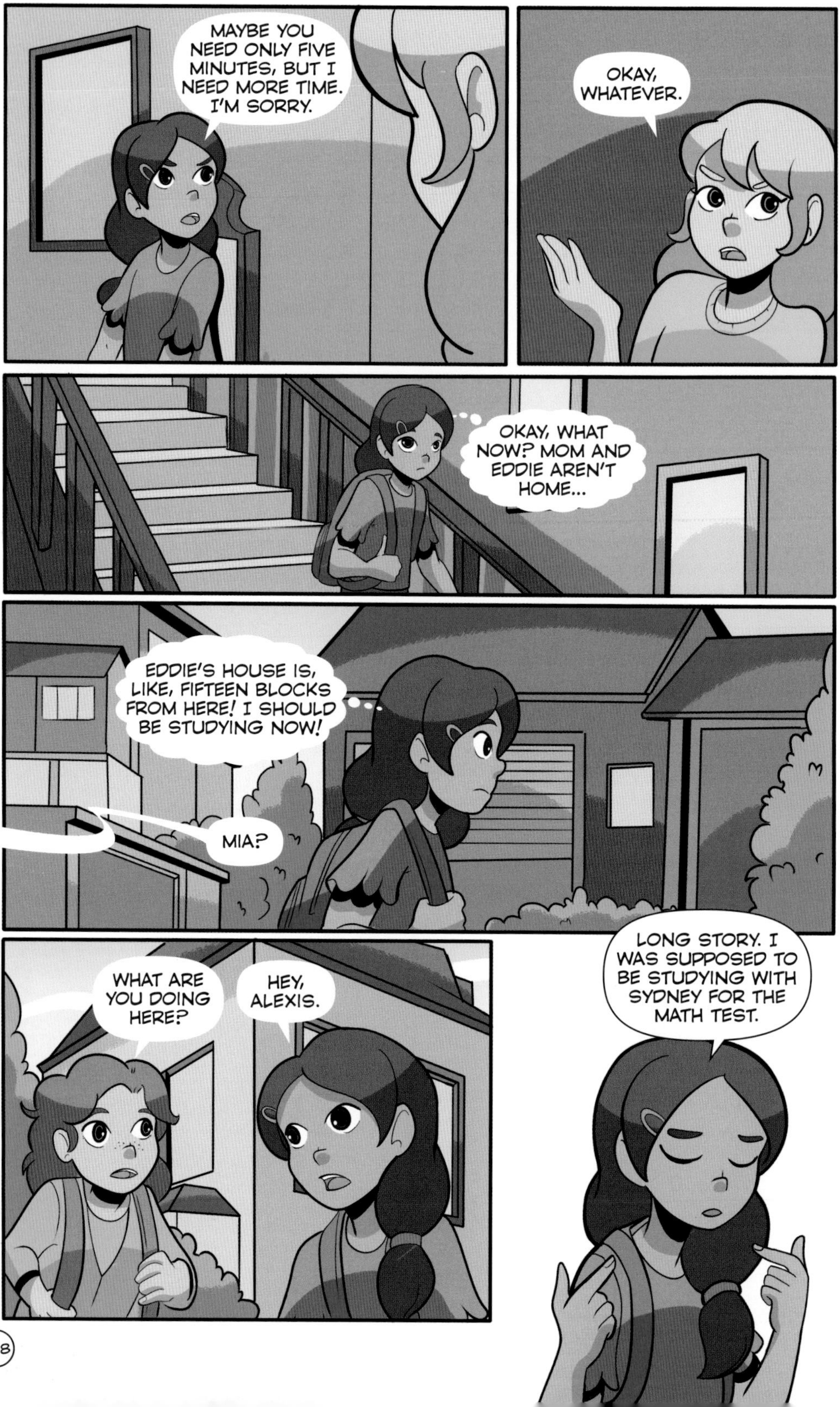
MAYBE YOU NEED ONLY FIVE MINUTES, BUT I NEED MORE TIME. I'M SORRY.
OKAY, WHATEVER.
OKAY, WHAT NOW? MOM AND EDDIE AREN'T HOME...
EDDIE'S HOUSE IS, LIKE, FIFTEEN BLOCKS FROM HERE! I SHOULD BE STUDYING NOW!
MIA?
HEY, ALEXIS.
WHAT ARE YOU DOING HERE?
LONG STORY. I WAS SUPPOSED TO BE STUDYING WITH SYDNEY FOR THE MATH TEST.

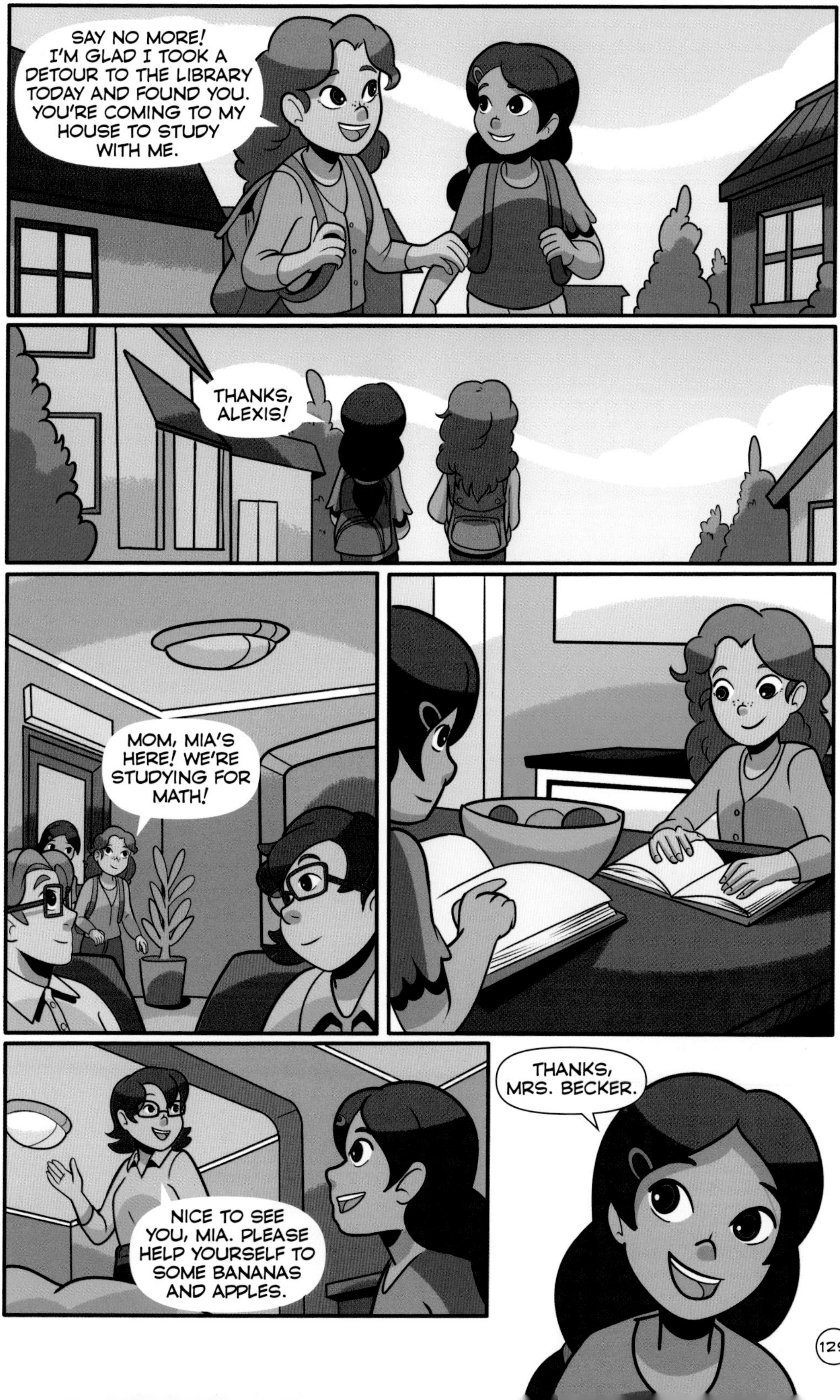
SAY NO MORE! I'M GLAD I TOOK A DETOUR TO THE LIBRARY TODAY AND FOUND YOU. YOU'RE COMING TO MY HOUSE TO STUDY WITH ME.
THANKS, ALEXIS!
MOM, MIA'S HERE! WE'RE STUDYING FOR MATH!
NICE TO SEE YOU, MIA. PLEASE HELP YOURSELF TO SOME BANANAS AND APPLES.
THANKS, MRS. BECKER.

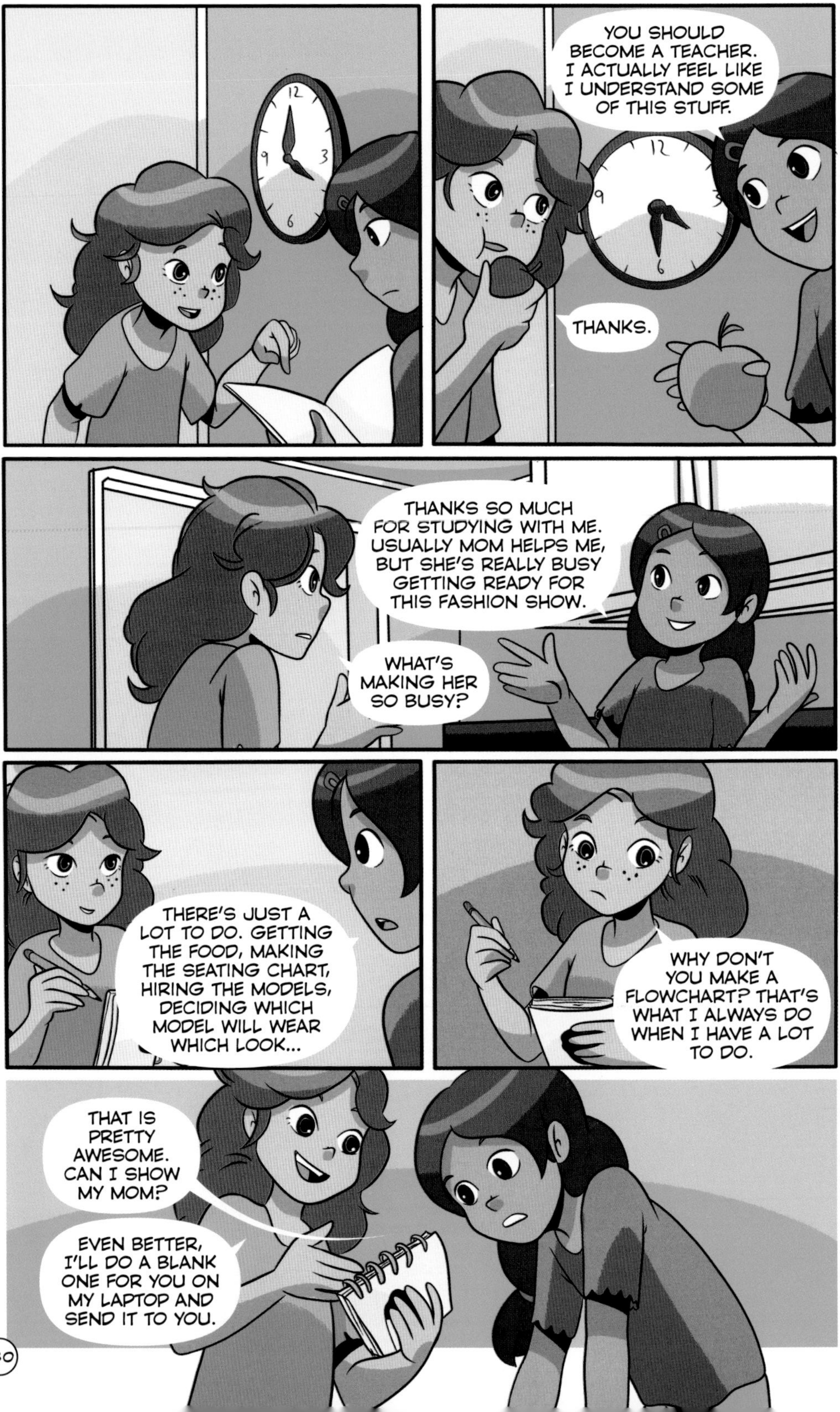
YOU SHOULD BECOME A TEACHER. I ACTUALLY FEEL LIKE I UNDERSTAND SOME OF THIS STUFF.
THANKS.
THANKS SO MUCH FOR STUDYING WITH ME. USUALLY MOM HELPS ME, BUT SHE'S REALLY BUSY GETTING READY FOR THIS FASHION SHOW.
WHAT'S MAKING HER SO BUSY?
THERE'S JUST A LOT TO DO. GETTING THE FOOD, MAKING THE SEATING CHART, HIRING THE MODELS, DECIDING WHICH MODEL WILL WEAR WHICH LOOK...
WHY DON'T YOU MAKE A FLOWCHART? THAT'S WHAT I ALWAYS DO WHEN I HAVE A LOT TO DO.
THAT IS PRETTY AWESOME. CAN I SHOW MY MOM?
EVEN BETTER, I'LL DO A BLANK ONE FOR YOU ON MY LAPTOP AND SEND IT TO YOU.

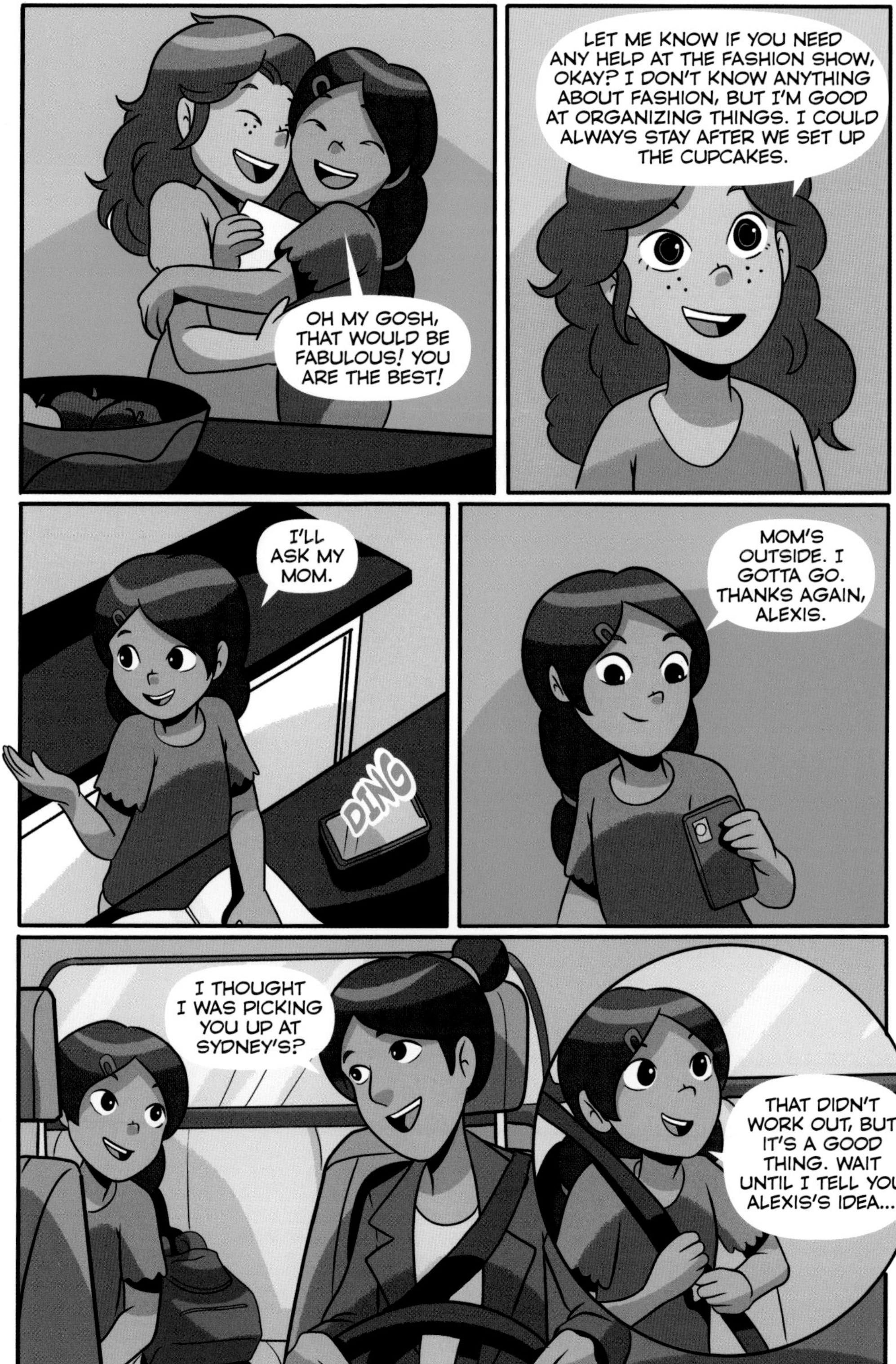
OH MY GOSH, THAT WOULD BE FABULOUS! YOU ARE THE BEST!
LET ME KNOW IF YOU NEED ANY HELP AT THE FASHION SHOW, OKAY? I DON'T KNOW ANYTHING ABOUT FASHION, BUT I'M GOOD AT ORGANIZING THINGS. I COULD ALWAYS STAY AFTER WE SET UP THE CUPCAKES.
I'LL ASK MY MOM.
DING
MOM'S OUTSIDE. I GOTTA GO. THANKS AGAIN, ALEXIS.
I THOUGHT I WAS PICKING YOU UP AT SYDNEY'S?
THAT DIDN'T WORK OUT, BUT IT'S A GOOD THING. WAIT UNTIL I TELL YOU ALEXIS'S IDEA...

Chapter 15

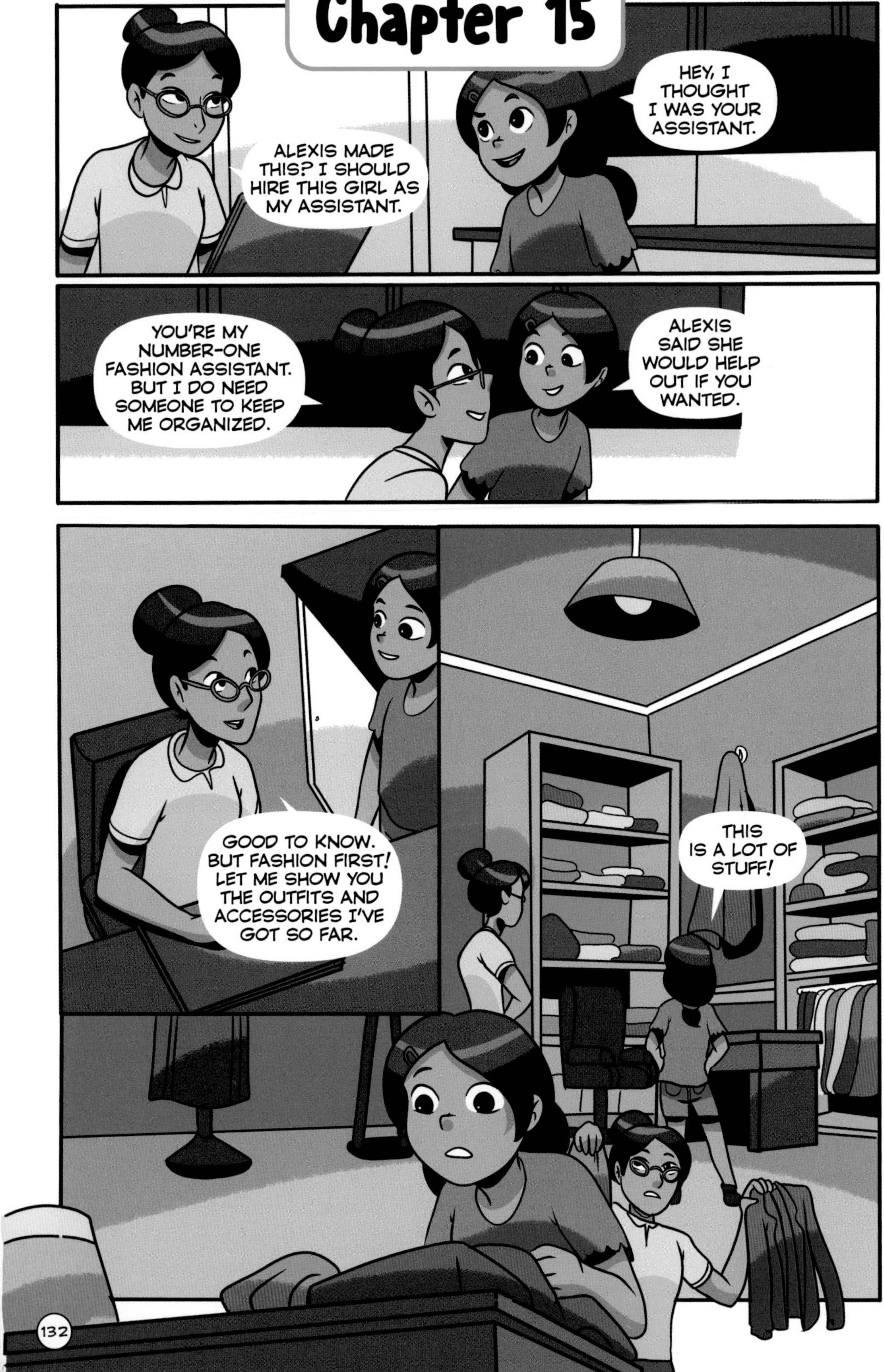

ALEXIS MADE THIS? I SHOULD HIRE THIS GIRL AS MY ASSISTANT.
HEY, I THOUGHT I WAS YOUR ASSISTANT.
YOU'RE MY NUMBER-ONE FASHION ASSISTANT. BUT I DO NEED SOMEONE TO KEEP ME ORGANIZED.
ALEXIS SAID SHE WOULD HELP OUT IF YOU WANTED.
GOOD TO KNOW. BUT FASHION FIRST! LET ME SHOW YOU THE OUTFITS AND ACCESSORIES I'VE GOT SO FAR.
THIS IS A LOT OF STUFF!

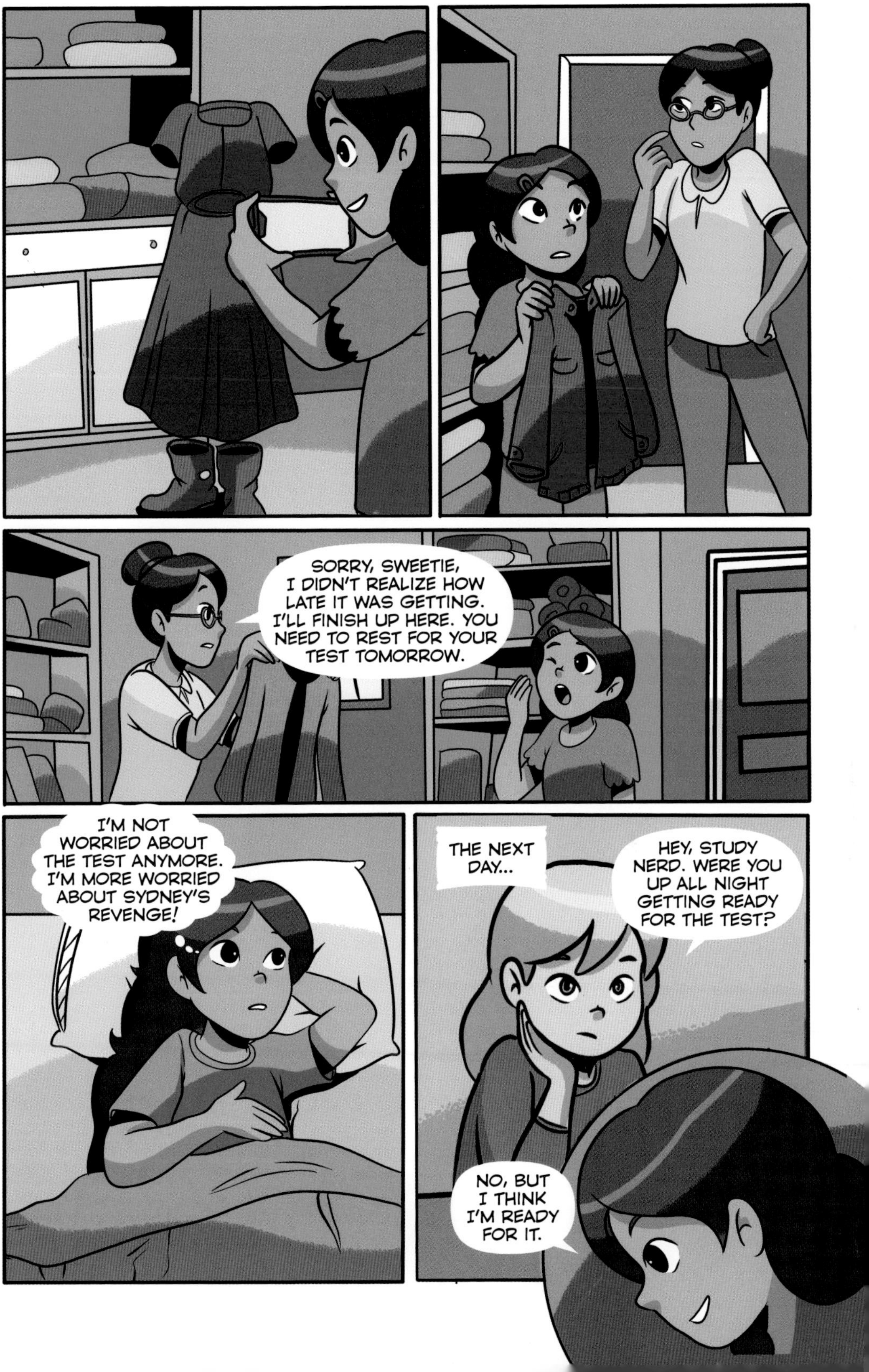
SORRY, SWEETIE, I DIDN'T REALIZE HOW LATE IT WAS GETTING. I'LL FINISH UP HERE. YOU NEED TO REST FOR YOUR TEST TOMORROW.
I'M NOT WORRIED ABOUT THE TEST ANYMORE. I'M MORE WORRIED ABOUT SYDNEY'S REVENGE!
THE NEXT DAY...
HEY, STUDY NERD. WERE YOU UP ALL NIGHT GETTING READY FOR THE TEST?
NO, BUT I THINK I'M READY FOR IT.

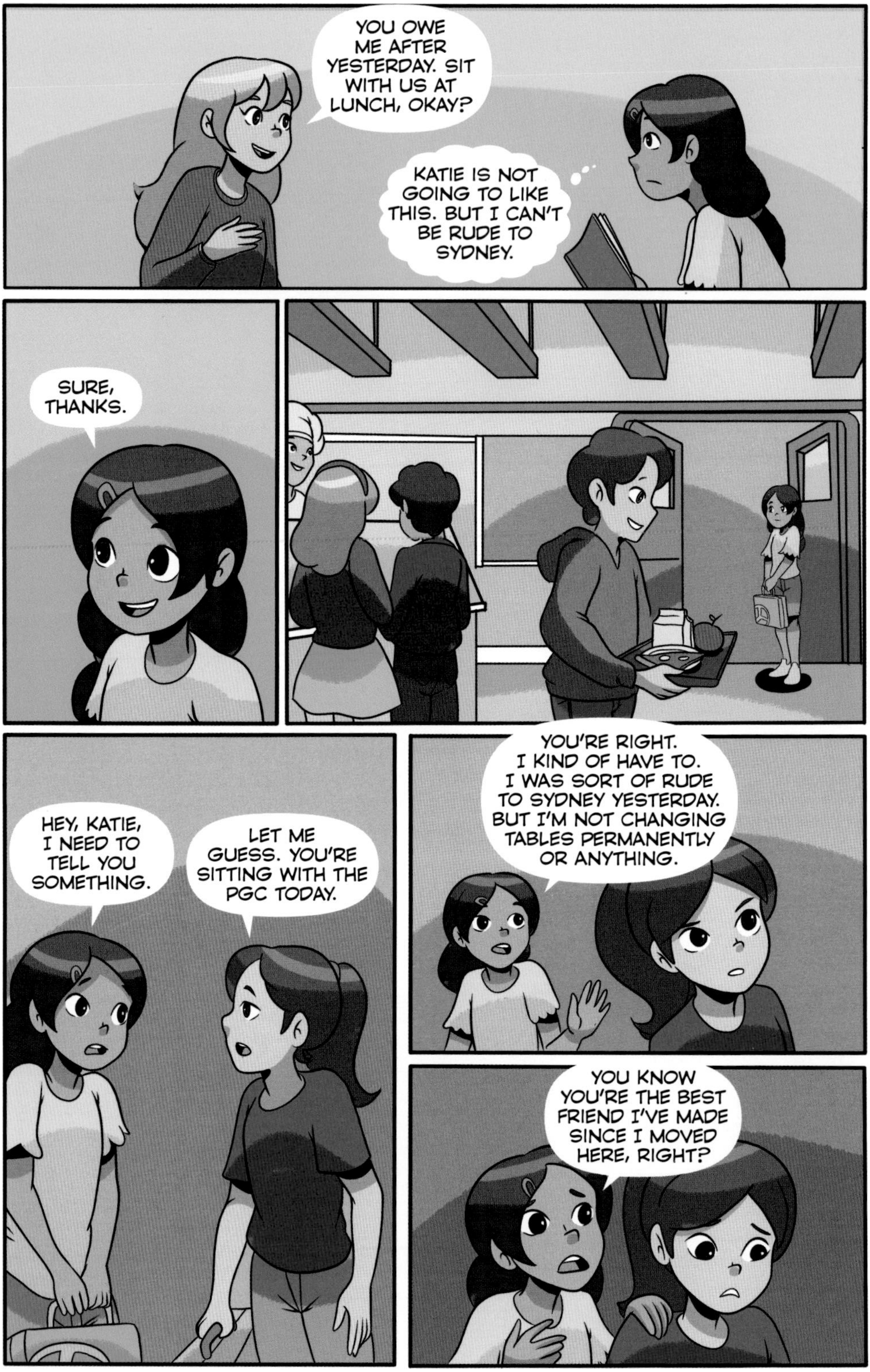
YOU OWE ME AFTER YESTERDAY. SIT WITH US AT LUNCH, OKAY?
KATIE IS NOT GOING TO LIKE THIS. BUT I CAN'T BE RUDE TO SYDNEY.
SURE, THANKS.
HEY, KATIE, I NEED TO TELL YOU SOMETHING.
LET ME GUESS. YOU'RE SITTING WITH THE PGC TODAY.
YOU'RE RIGHT. I KIND OF HAVE TO. I WAS SORT OF RUDE TO SYDNEY YESTERDAY. BUT I'M NOT CHANGING TABLES PERMANENTLY OR ANYTHING.
YOU KNOW YOU'RE THE BEST FRIEND I'VE MADE SINCE I MOVED HERE, RIGHT?

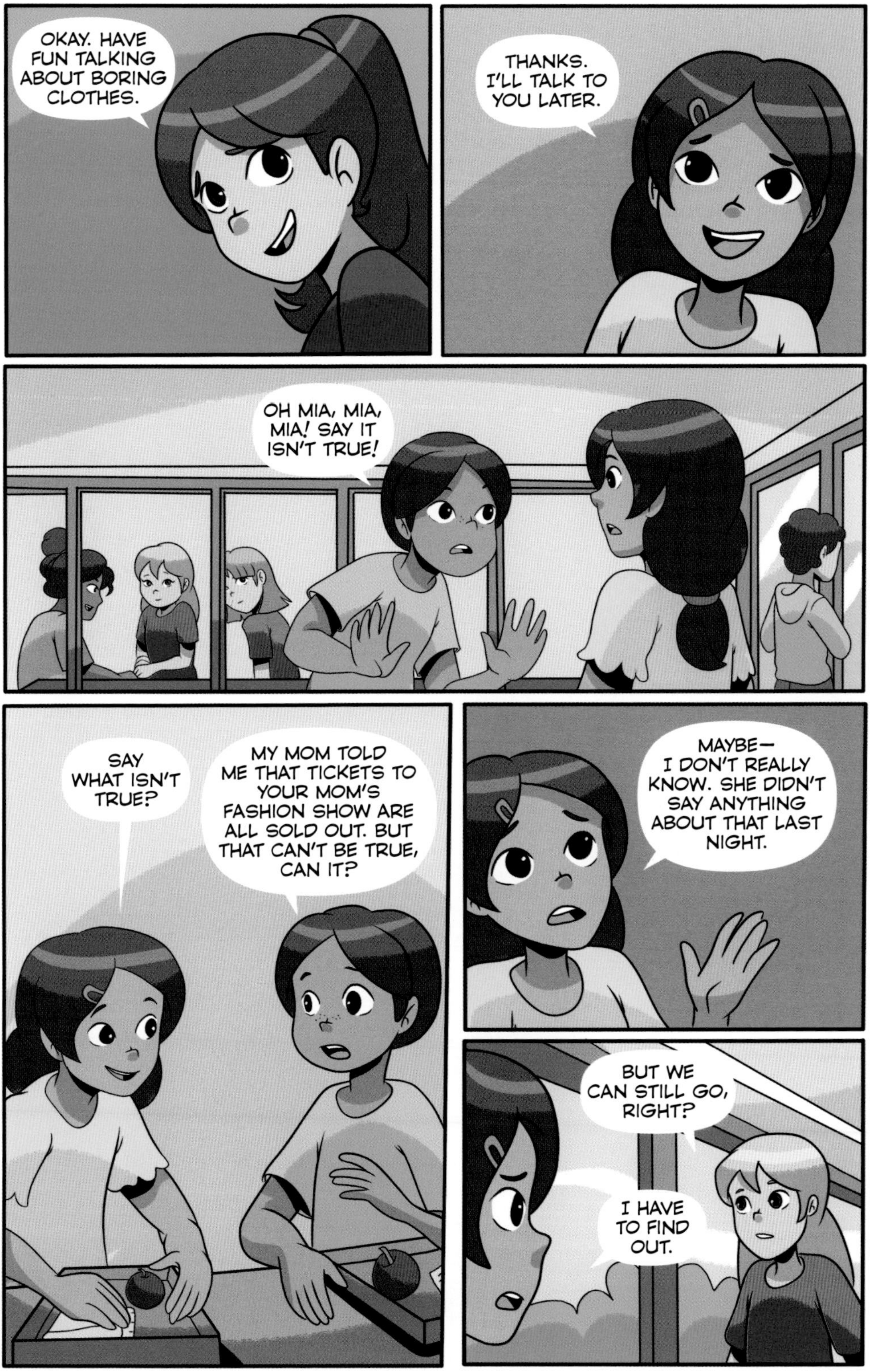
OKAY. HAVE FUN TALKING ABOUT BORING CLOTHES.
THANKS. I'LL TALK TO YOU LATER.
OH MIA, MIA, MIA! SAY IT ISN'T TRUE!
SAY WHAT ISN'T TRUE?
MY MOM TOLD ME THAT TICKETS TO YOUR MOM'S FASHION SHOW ARE ALL SOLD OUT. BUT THAT CAN'T BE TRUE, CAN IT?
MAYBE— I DON'T REALLY KNOW. SHE DIDN'T SAY ANYTHING ABOUT THAT LAST NIGHT.
BUT WE CAN STILL GO, RIGHT?
I HAVE TO FIND OUT.

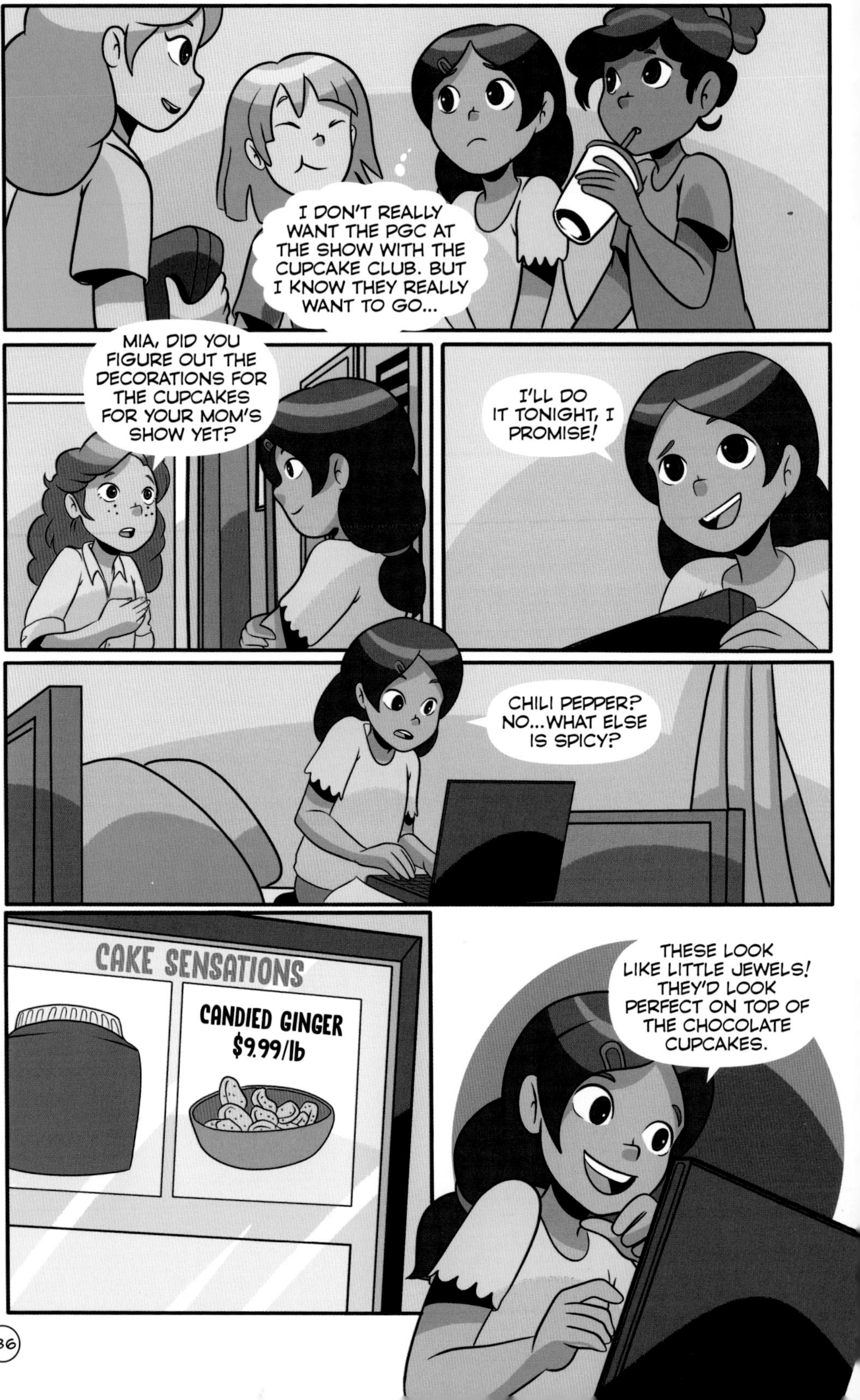
I DON'T REALLY WANT THE PGC AT THE SHOW WITH THE CUPCAKE CLUB. BUT I KNOW THEY REALLY WANT TO GO...
MIA, DID YOU FIGURE OUT THE DECORATIONS FOR THE CUPCAKES FOR YOUR MOM'S SHOW YET?
I'LL DO IT TONIGHT, I PROMISE!
CHILI PEPPER? NO...WHAT ELSE IS SPICY?
CAKE SENSATIONS
CANDIED GINGER
$9.99/lb
THESE LOOK LIKE LITTLE JEWELS! THEY'D LOOK PERFECT ON TOP OF THE CHOCOLATE CUPCAKES.

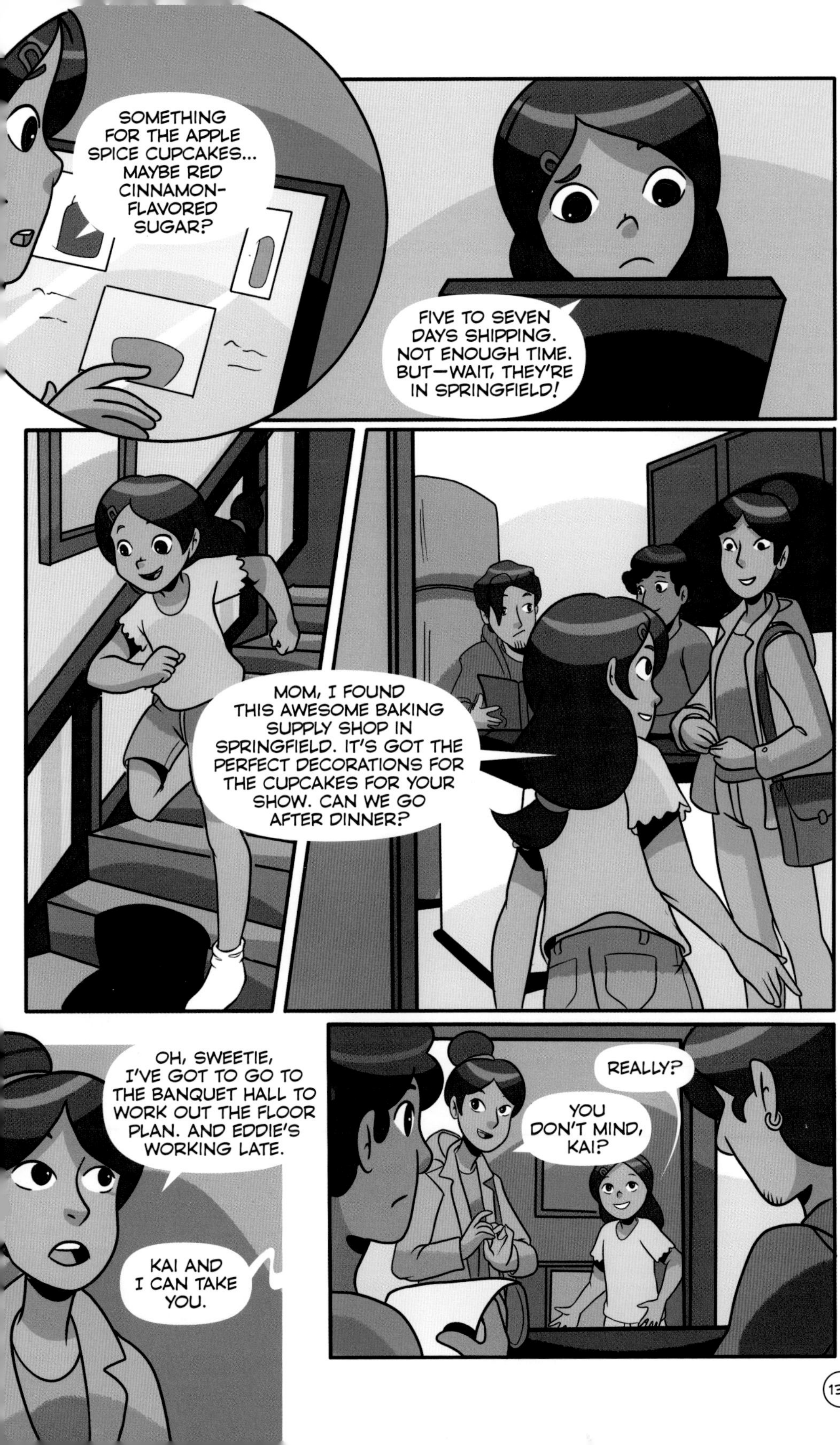
SOMETHING FOR THE APPLE SPICE CUPCAKES... MAYBE RED CINNAMON-FLAVORED SUGAR?
FIVE TO SEVEN DAYS SHIPPING. NOT ENOUGH TIME. BUT—WAIT, THEY'RE IN SPRINGFIELD!
MOM, I FOUND THIS AWESOME BAKING SUPPLY SHOP IN SPRINGFIELD. IT'S GOT THE PERFECT DECORATIONS FOR THE CUPCAKES FOR YOUR SHOW. CAN WE GO AFTER DINNER?
OH, SWEETIE, I'VE GOT TO GO TO THE BANQUET HALL TO WORK OUT THE FLOOR PLAN. AND EDDIE'S WORKING LATE.
KAI AND I CAN TAKE YOU.
REALLY?
YOU DON'T MIND, KAI?

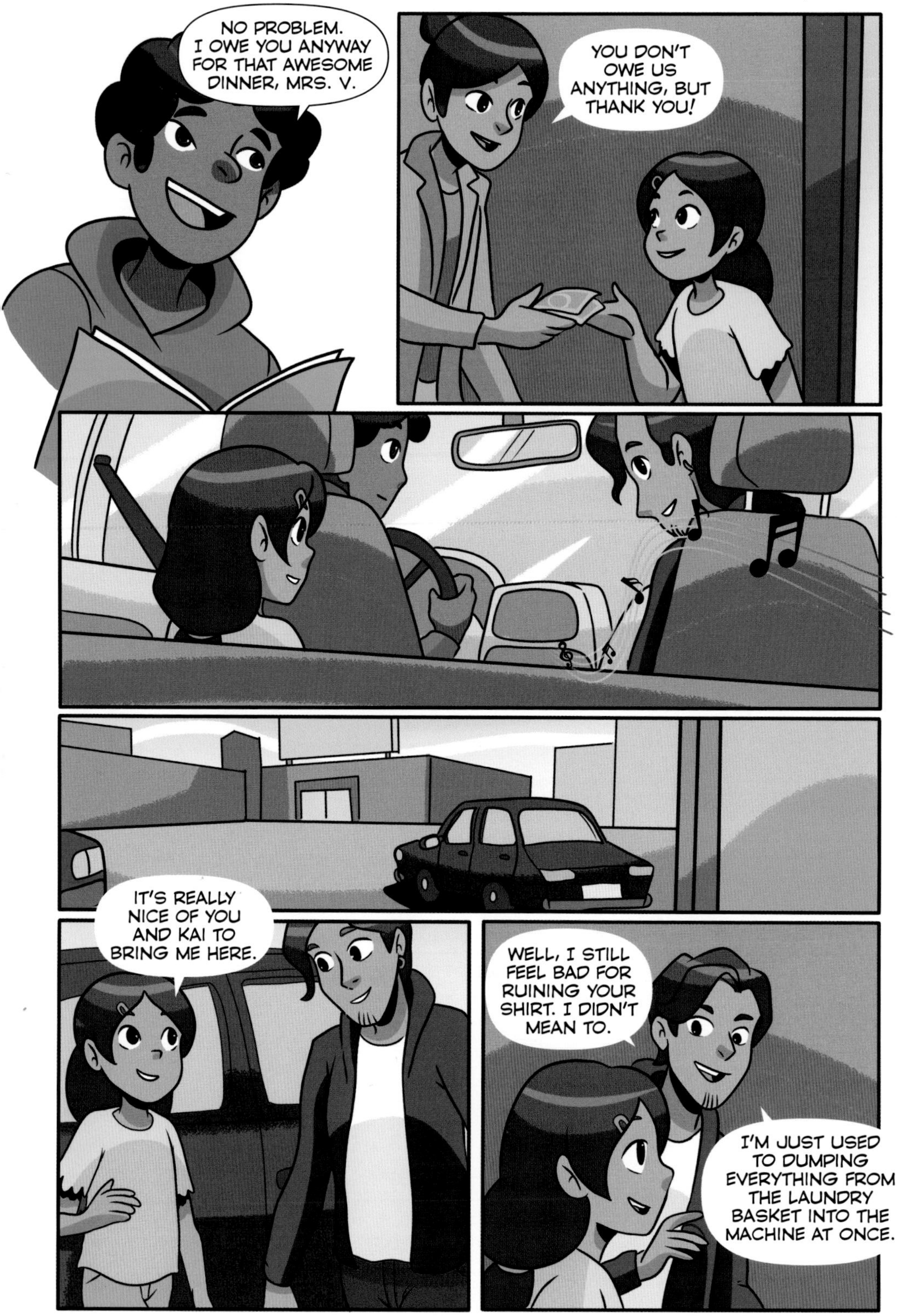
NO PROBLEM. I OWE YOU ANYWAY FOR THAT AWESOME DINNER, MRS. V.
YOU DON'T OWE US ANYTHING, BUT THANK YOU!
IT'S REALLY NICE OF YOU AND KAI TO BRING ME HERE.
WELL, I STILL FEEL BAD FOR RUINING YOUR SHIRT. I DIDN'T MEAN TO.
I'M JUST USED TO DUMPING EVERYTHING FROM THE LAUNDRY BASKET INTO THE MACHINE AT ONCE.

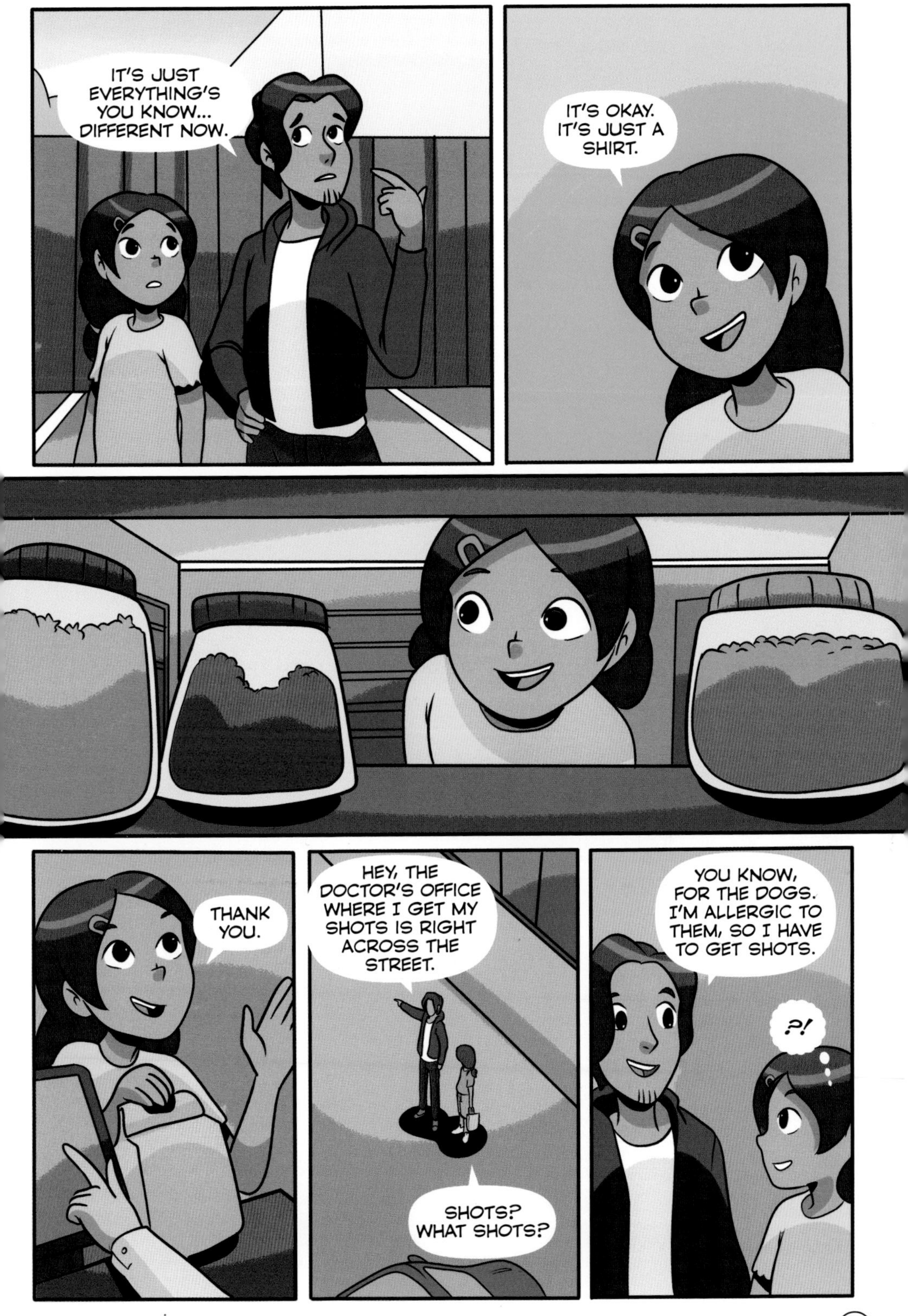
IT'S JUST EVERYTHING'S YOU KNOW... DIFFERENT NOW.
IT'S OKAY. IT'S JUST A SHIRT.
THANK YOU.
HEY, THE DOCTOR'S OFFICE WHERE I GET MY SHOTS IS RIGHT ACROSS THE STREET.
SHOTS? WHAT SHOTS?
YOU KNOW, FOR THE DOGS. I'M ALLERGIC TO THEM, SO I HAVE TO GET SHOTS.
?!

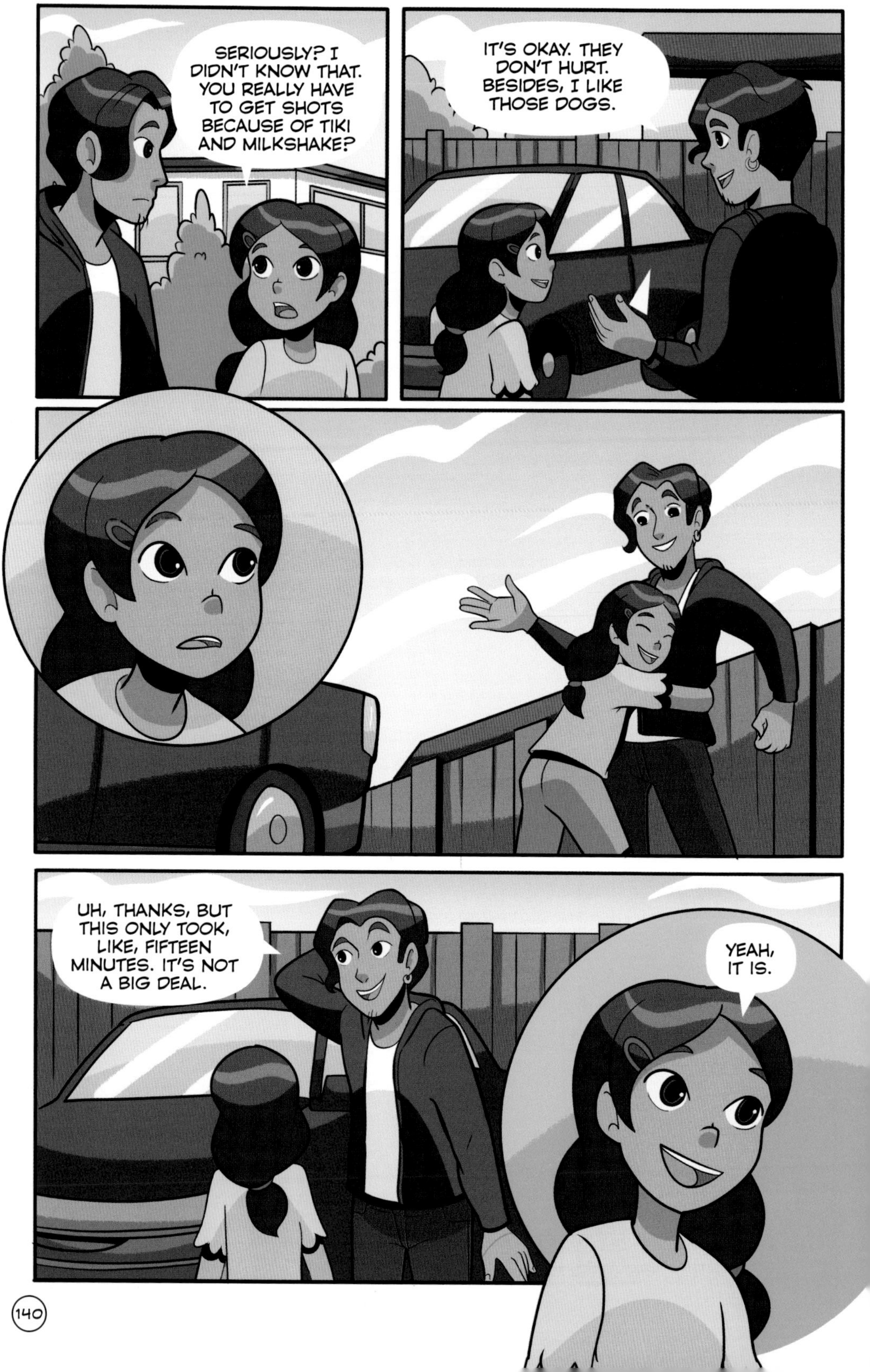
SERIOUSLY? I DIDN'T KNOW THAT. YOU REALLY HAVE TO GET SHOTS BECAUSE OF TIKI AND MILKSHAKE?
IT'S OKAY. THEY DON'T HURT. BESIDES, I LIKE THOSE DOGS.
UH, THANKS, BUT THIS ONLY TOOK, LIKE, FIFTEEN MINUTES. IT'S NOT A BIG DEAL.
YEAH, IT IS.

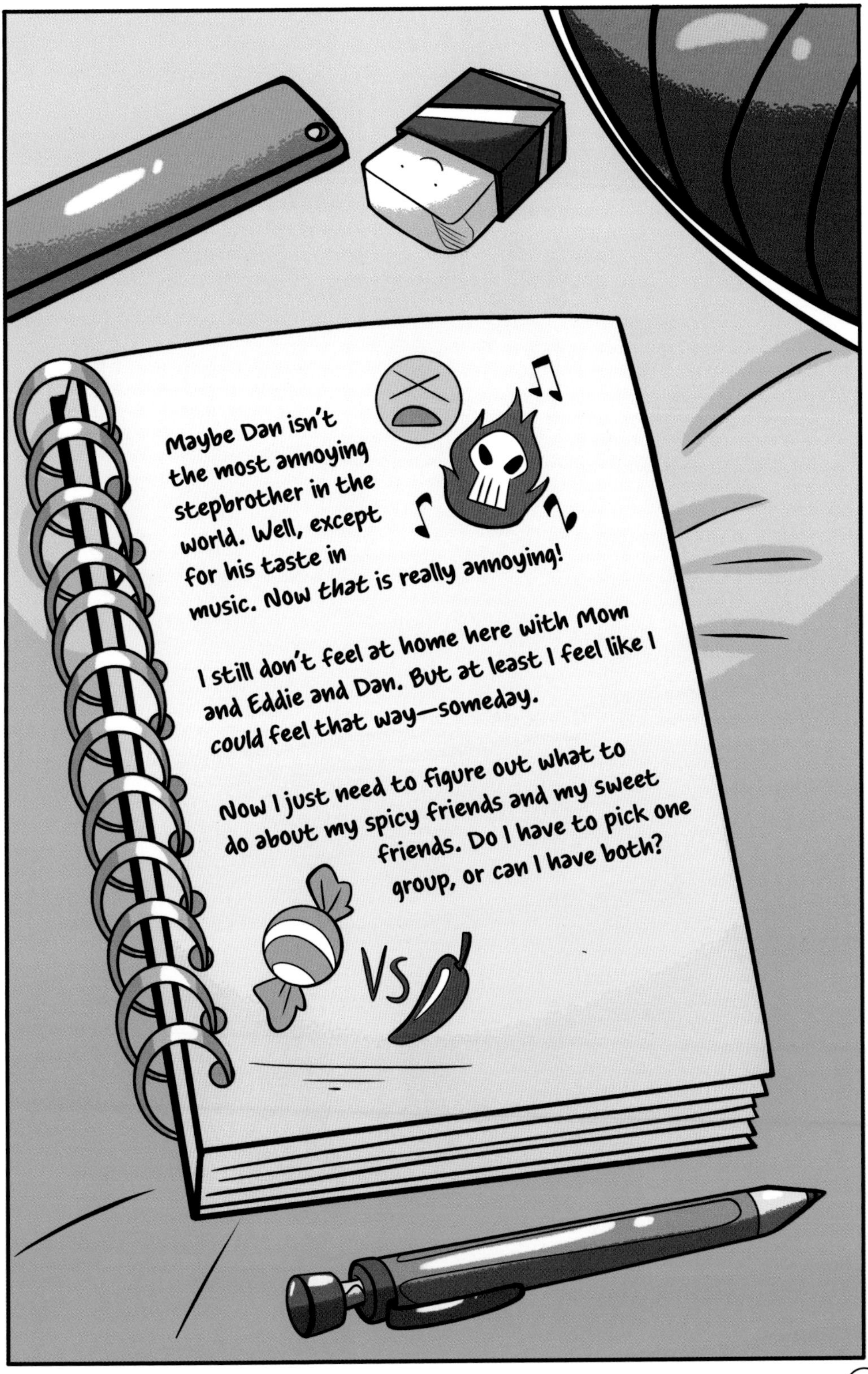

Maybe Dan isn't the most annoying stepbrother in the world. Well, except for his taste in music. Now *that* is really annoying!
I still don't feel at home here with Mom and Eddie and Dan. But at least I feel like I could feel that way—someday.
Now I just need to figure out what to do about my spicy friends and my sweet friends. Do I have to pick one group, or can I have both?
VS

Chapter 16

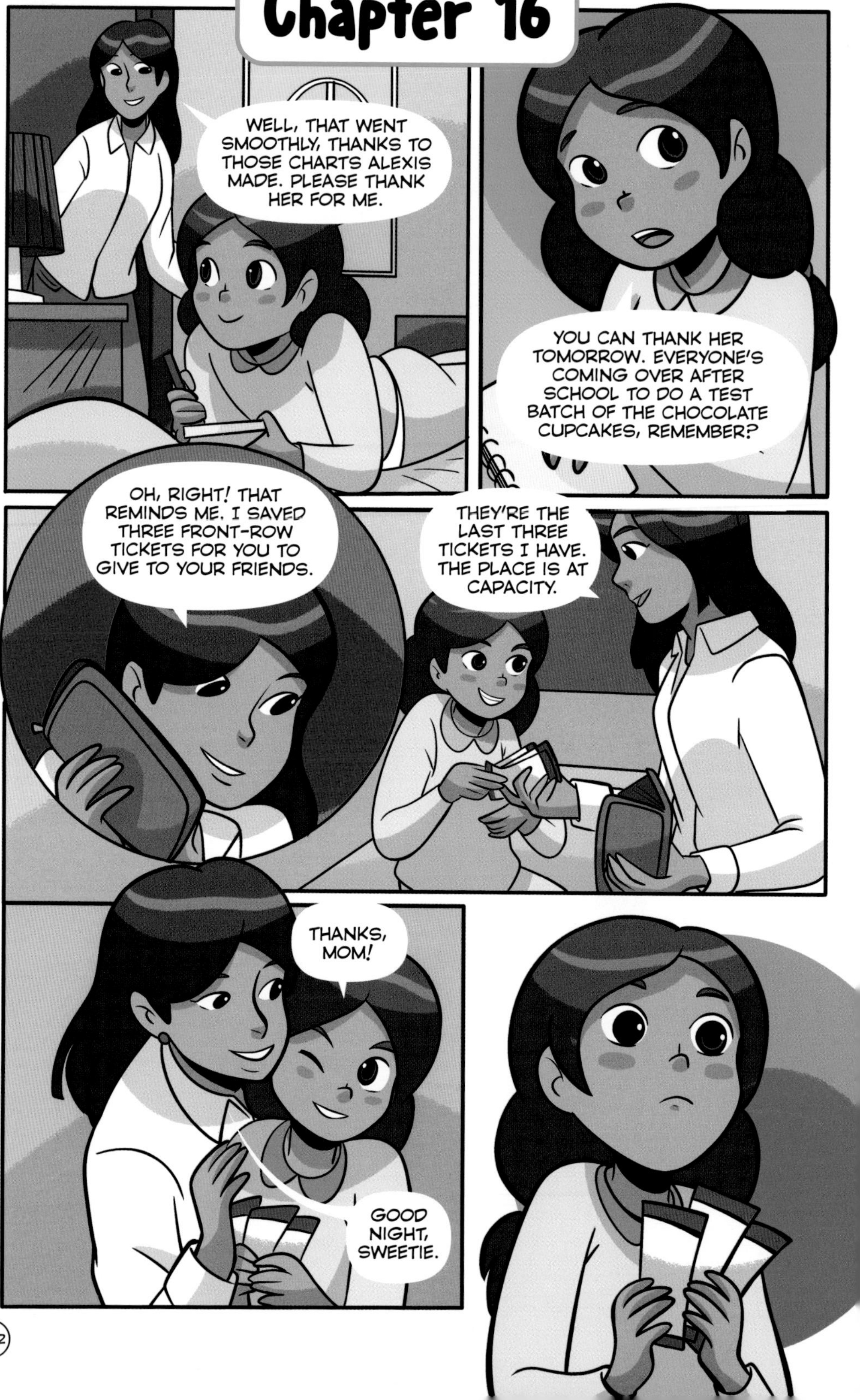
WELL, THAT WENT SMOOTHLY, THANKS TO THOSE CHARTS ALEXIS MADE. PLEASE THANK HER FOR ME.
YOU CAN THANK HER TOMORROW. EVERYONE'S COMING OVER AFTER SCHOOL TO DO A TEST BATCH OF THE CHOCOLATE CUPCAKES, REMEMBER?
OH, RIGHT! THAT REMINDS ME. I SAVED THREE FRONT-ROW TICKETS FOR YOU TO GIVE TO YOUR FRIENDS.
THEY'RE THE LAST THREE TICKETS I HAVE. THE PLACE IS AT CAPACITY.
THANKS, MOM!
GOOD NIGHT, SWEETIE.

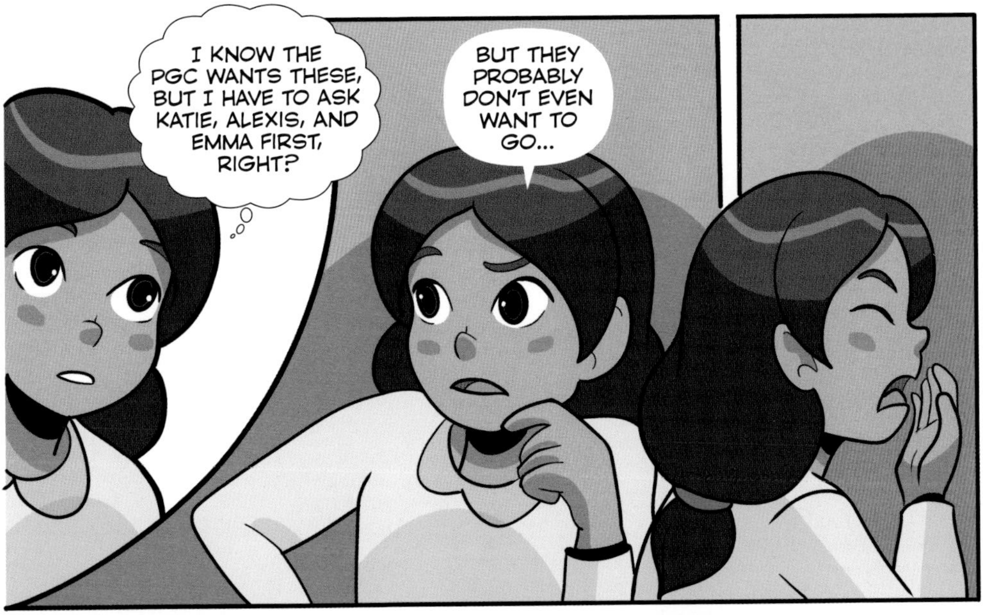
I KNOW THE PGC WANTS THESE, BUT I HAVE TO ASK KATIE, ALEXIS, AND EMMA FIRST, RIGHT?
BUT THEY PROBABLY DON'T EVEN WANT TO GO...

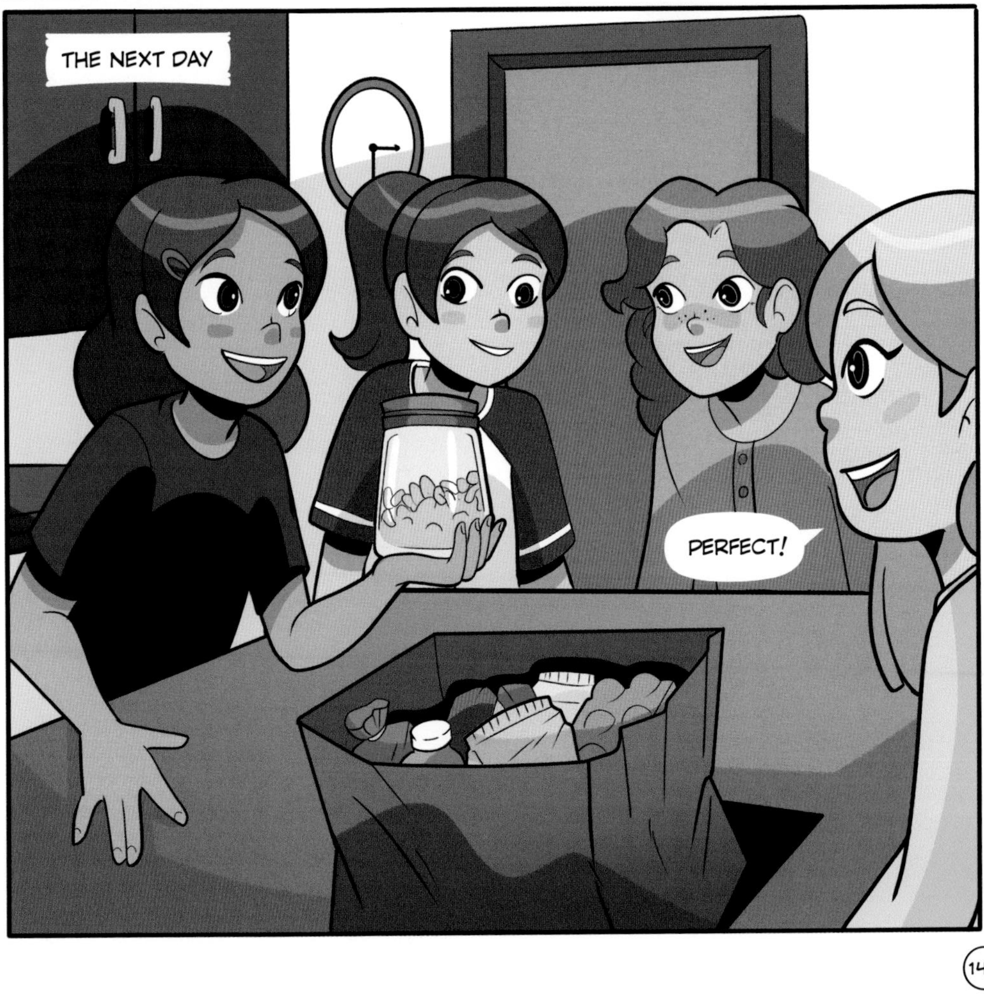
THE NEXT DAY
PERFECT!

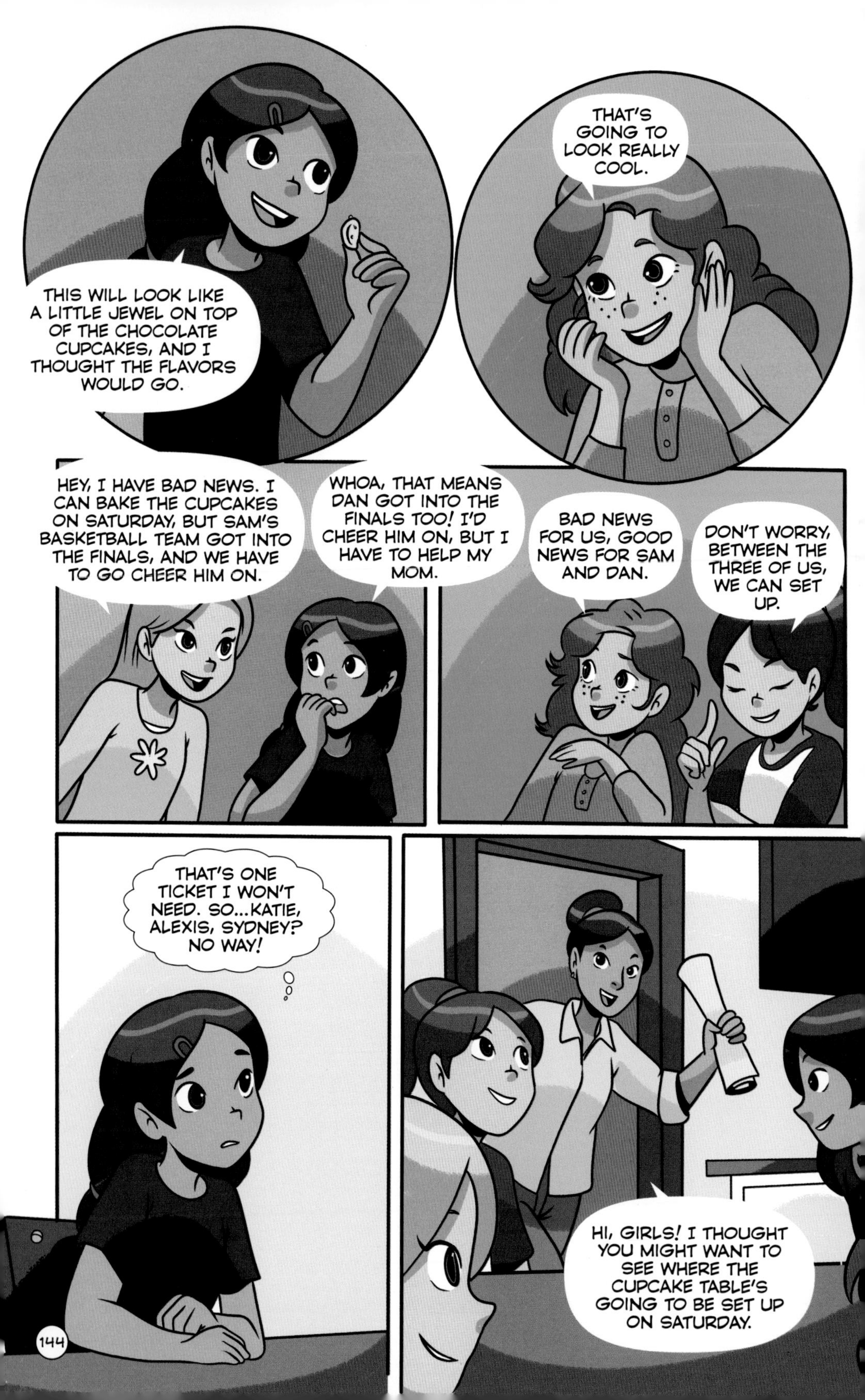
THIS WILL LOOK LIKE A LITTLE JEWEL ON TOP OF THE CHOCOLATE CUPCAKES, AND I THOUGHT THE FLAVORS WOULD GO.
THAT'S GOING TO LOOK REALLY COOL.
HEY, I HAVE BAD NEWS. I CAN BAKE THE CUPCAKES ON SATURDAY, BUT SAM'S BASKETBALL TEAM GOT INTO THE FINALS, AND WE HAVE TO GO CHEER HIM ON.
WHOA, THAT MEANS DAN GOT INTO THE FINALS TOO! I'D CHEER HIM ON, BUT I HAVE TO HELP MY MOM.
BAD NEWS FOR US, GOOD NEWS FOR SAM AND DAN.
DON'T WORRY, BETWEEN THE THREE OF US, WE CAN SET UP.
THAT'S ONE TICKET I WON'T NEED. SO...KATIE, ALEXIS, SYDNEY? NO WAY!
HI, GIRLS! I THOUGHT YOU MIGHT WANT TO SEE WHERE THE CUPCAKE TABLE'S GOING TO BE SET UP ON SATURDAY.

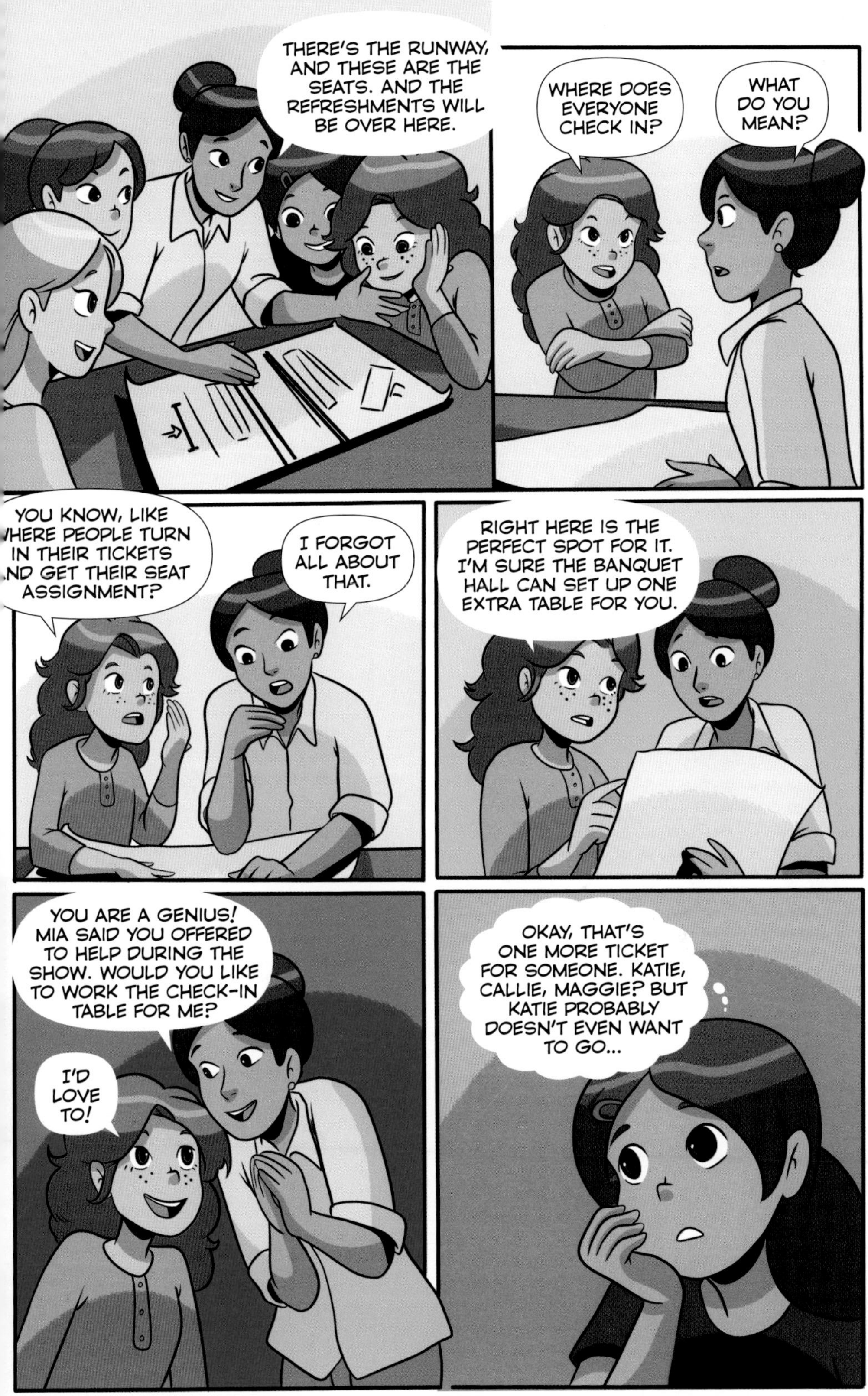
THERE'S THE RUNWAY, AND THESE ARE THE SEATS. AND THE REFRESHMENTS WILL BE OVER HERE.
WHERE DOES EVERYONE CHECK IN?
WHAT DO YOU MEAN?
YOU KNOW, LIKE WHERE PEOPLE TURN IN THEIR TICKETS AND GET THEIR SEAT ASSIGNMENT?
I FORGOT ALL ABOUT THAT.
RIGHT HERE IS THE PERFECT SPOT FOR IT. I'M SURE THE BANQUET HALL CAN SET UP ONE EXTRA TABLE FOR YOU.
YOU ARE A GENIUS! MIA SAID YOU OFFERED TO HELP DURING THE SHOW. WOULD YOU LIKE TO WORK THE CHECK-IN TABLE FOR ME?
I'D LOVE TO!
OKAY, THAT'S ONE MORE TICKET FOR SOMEONE. KATIE, CALLIE, MAGGIE? BUT KATIE PROBABLY DOESN'T EVEN WANT TO GO...

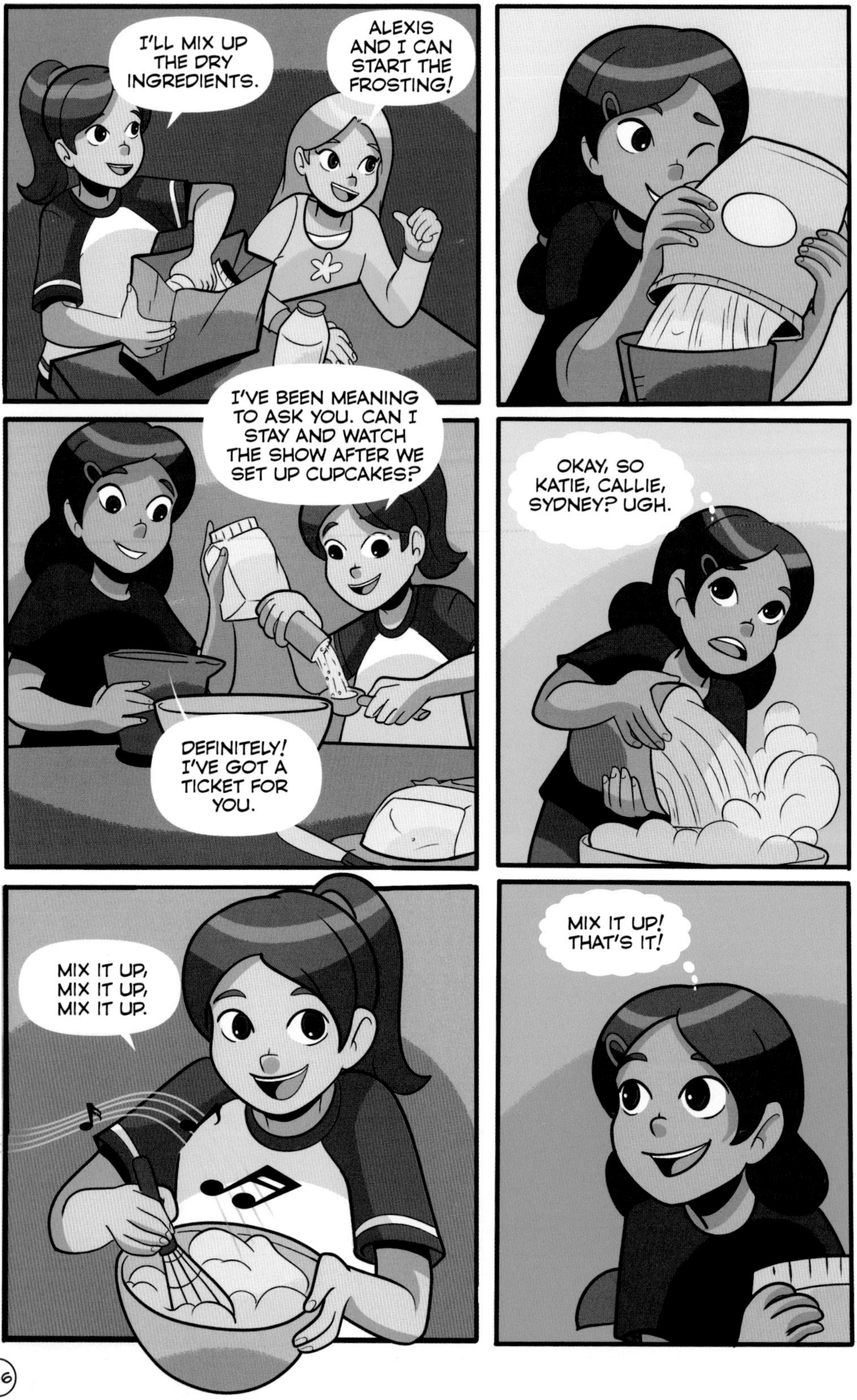
I'LL MIX UP THE DRY INGREDIENTS.
ALEXIS AND I CAN START THE FROSTING!
I'VE BEEN MEANING TO ASK YOU. CAN I STAY AND WATCH THE SHOW AFTER WE SET UP CUPCAKES?
DEFINITELY! I'VE GOT A TICKET FOR YOU.
OKAY, SO KATIE, CALLIE, SYDNEY? UGH.
MIX IT UP, MIX IT UP, MIX IT UP.
MIX IT UP! THAT'S IT!

Chapter 17

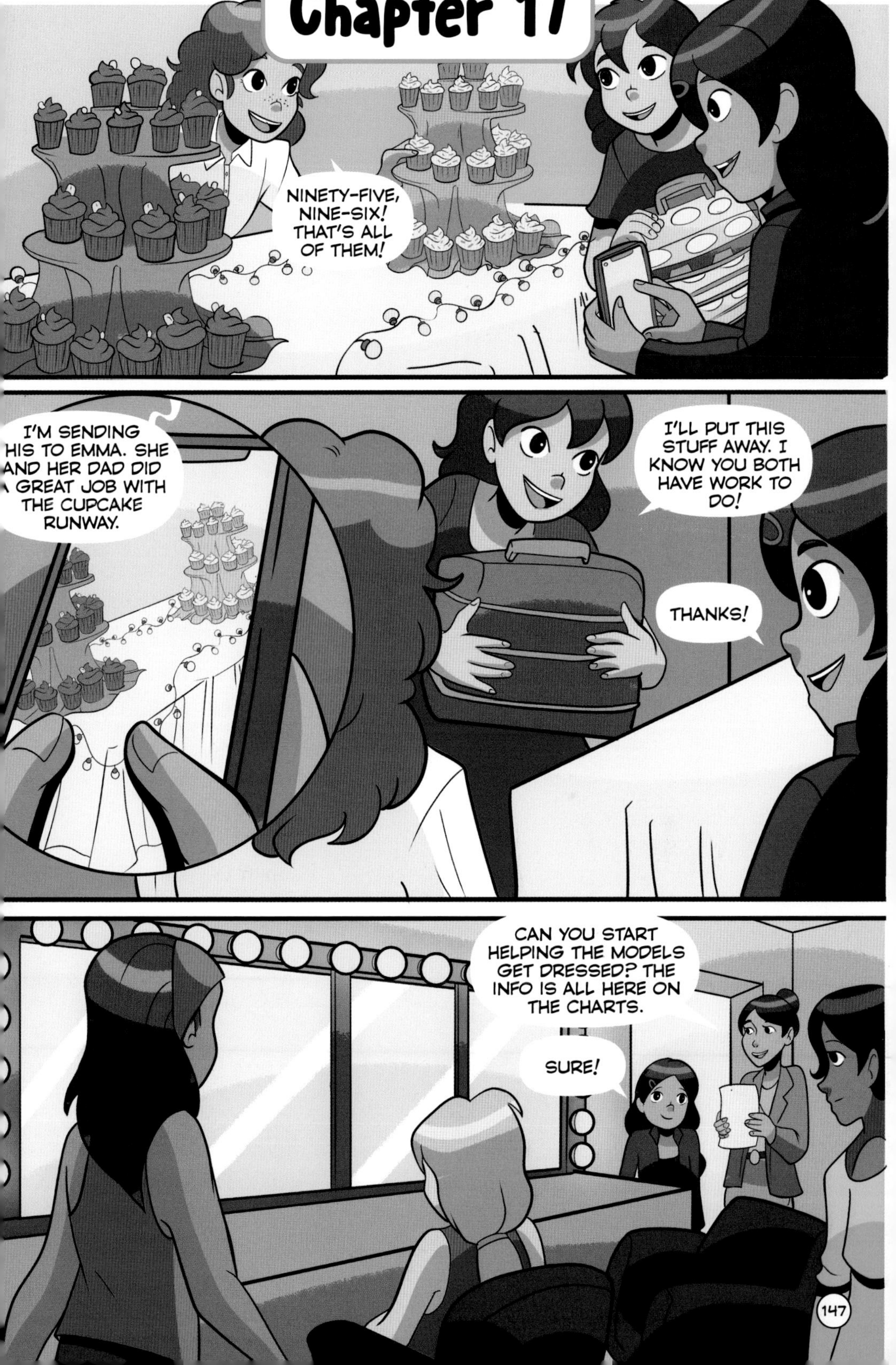

NINETY-FIVE, NINE-SIX! THAT'S ALL OF THEM!
I'M SENDING HIS TO EMMA. SHE AND HER DAD DID GREAT JOB WITH THE CUPCAKE RUNWAY.
I'LL PUT THIS STUFF AWAY. I KNOW YOU BOTH HAVE WORK TO DO!
THANKS!
CAN YOU START HELPING THE MODELS GET DRESSED? THE INFO IS ALL HERE ON THE CHARTS.
SURE!

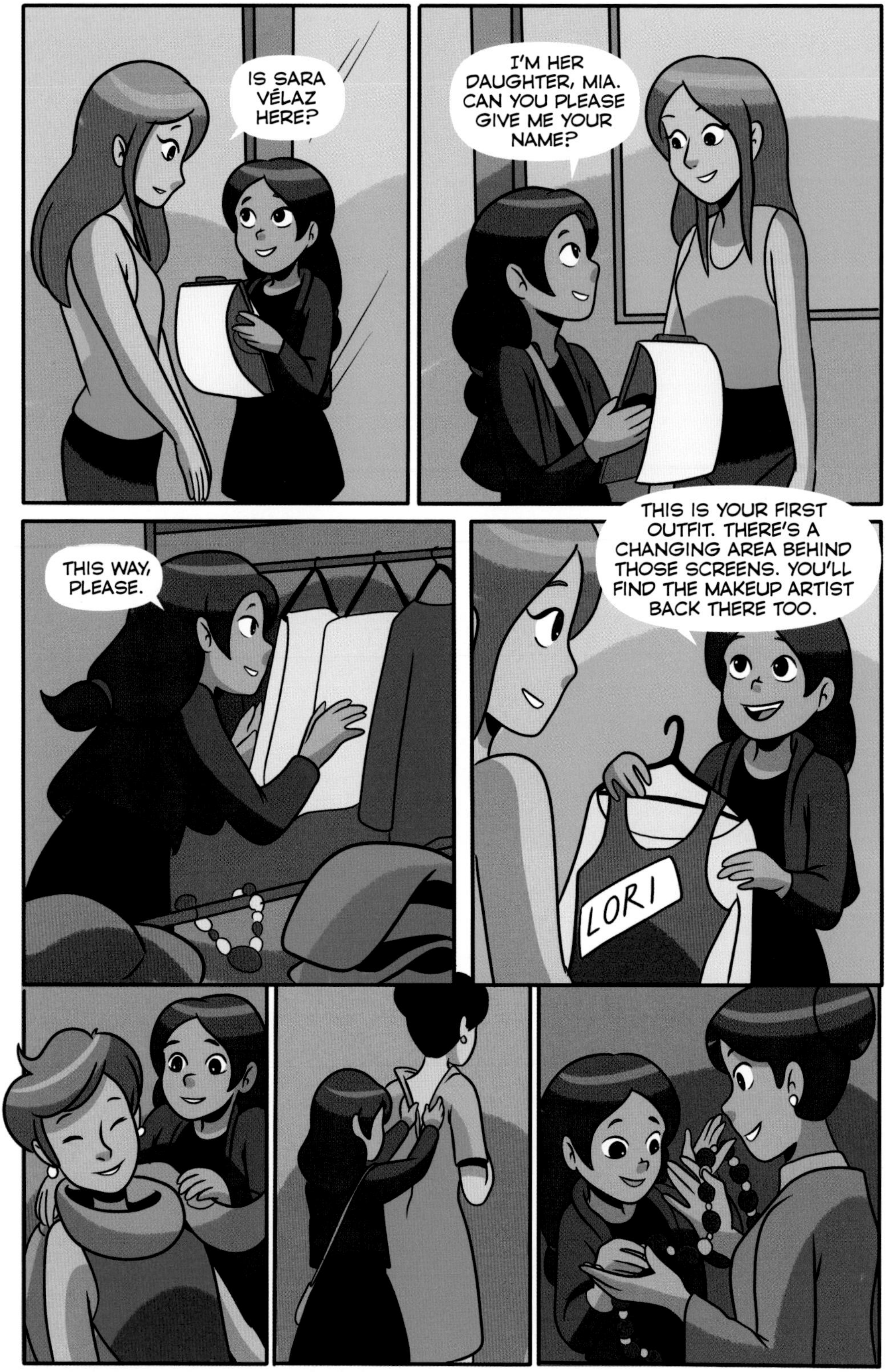
IS SARA VÉLAZ HERE?
I'M HER DAUGHTER, MIA. CAN YOU PLEASE GIVE ME YOUR NAME?
THIS WAY, PLEASE.
THIS IS YOUR FIRST OUTFIT. THERE'S A CHANGING AREA BEHIND THOSE SCREENS. YOU'LL FIND THE MAKEUP ARTIST BACK THERE TOO.
LORI

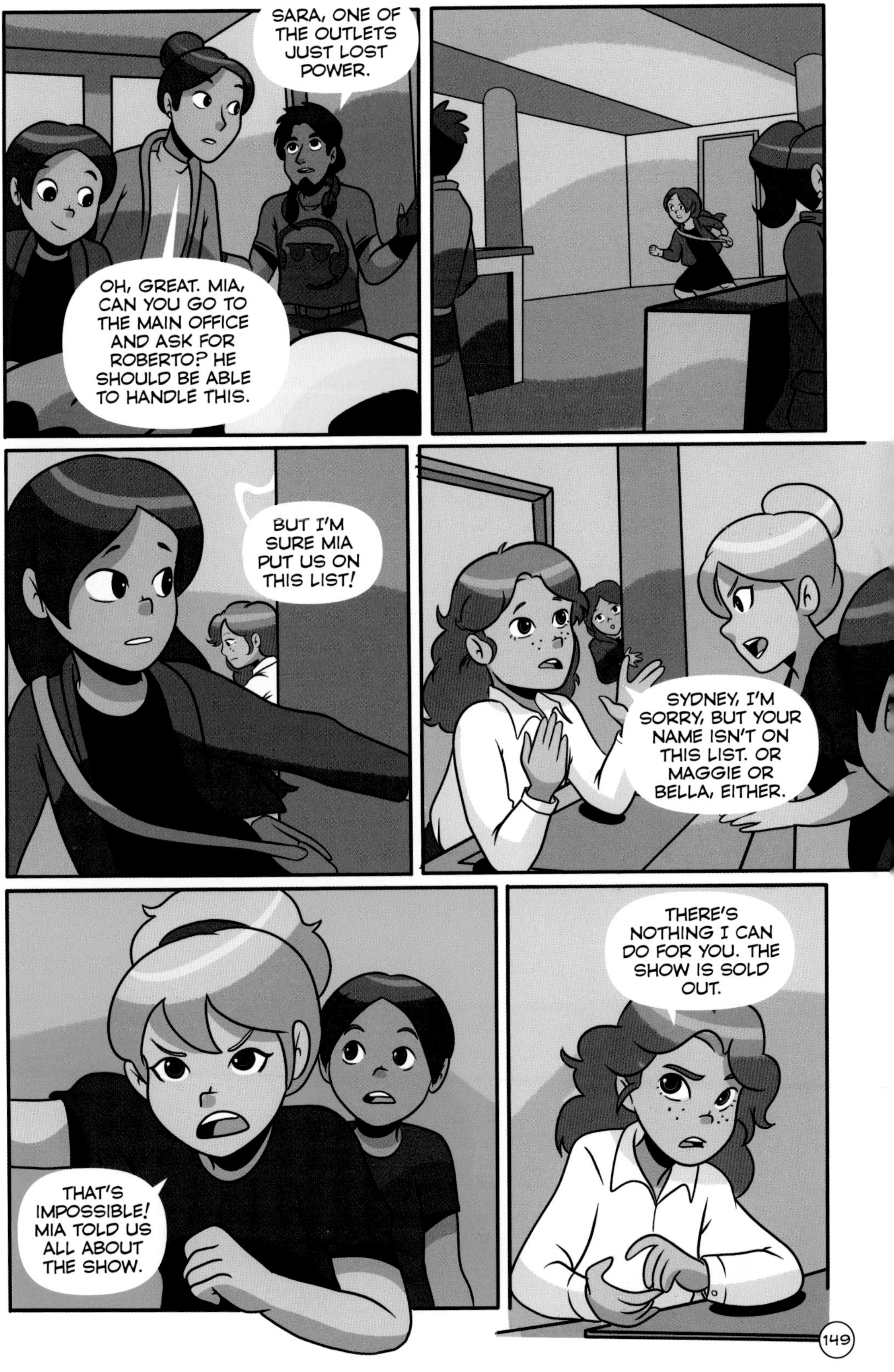
SARA, ONE OF THE OUTLETS JUST LOST POWER.
OH, GREAT. MIA, CAN YOU GO TO THE MAIN OFFICE AND ASK FOR ROBERTO? HE SHOULD BE ABLE TO HANDLE THIS.
BUT I'M SURE MIA PUT US ON THIS LIST!
SYDNEY, I'M SORRY, BUT YOUR NAME ISN'T ON THIS LIST. OR MAGGIE OR BELLA, EITHER.
THAT'S IMPOSSIBLE! MIA TOLD US ALL ABOUT THE SHOW.
THERE'S NOTHING I CAN DO FOR YOU. THE SHOW IS SOLD OUT.

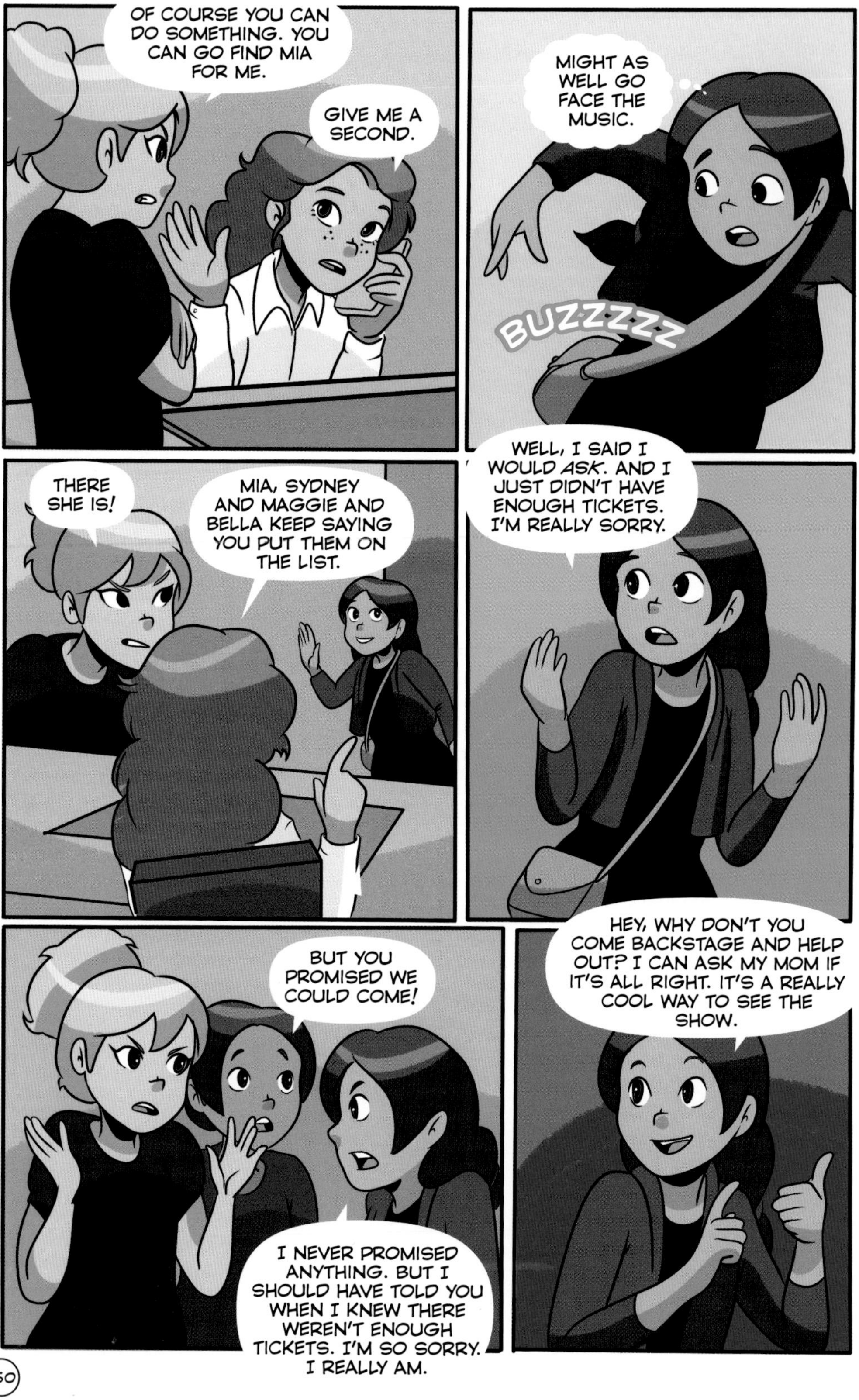
OF COURSE YOU CAN DO SOMETHING. YOU CAN GO FIND MIA FOR ME.
GIVE ME A SECOND.
MIGHT AS WELL GO FACE THE MUSIC.
BUZZZZZ
THERE SHE IS!
MIA, SYDNEY AND MAGGIE AND BELLA KEEP SAYING YOU PUT THEM ON THE LIST.
WELL, I SAID I WOULD *ASK*. AND I JUST DIDN'T HAVE ENOUGH TICKETS. I'M REALLY SORRY.
BUT YOU PROMISED WE COULD COME!
I NEVER PROMISED ANYTHING. BUT I SHOULD HAVE TOLD YOU WHEN I KNEW THERE WEREN'T ENOUGH TICKETS. I'M SO SORRY. I REALLY AM.
HEY, WHY DON'T YOU COME BACKSTAGE AND HELP OUT? I CAN ASK MY MOM IF IT'S ALL RIGHT. IT'S A REALLY COOL WAY TO SEE THE SHOW.

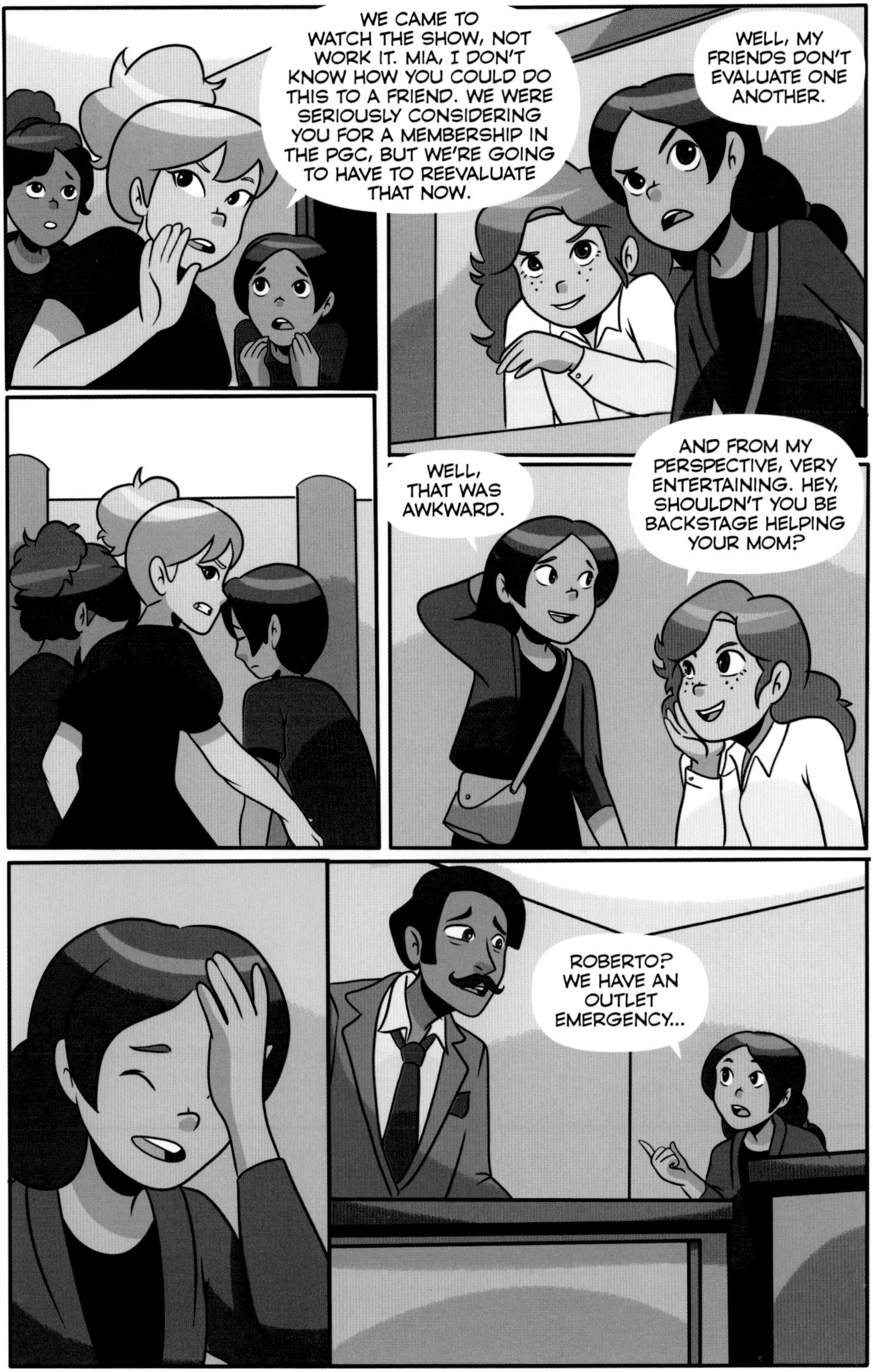
WE CAME TO WATCH THE SHOW, NOT WORK IT. MIA, I DON'T KNOW HOW YOU COULD DO THIS TO A FRIEND. WE WERE SERIOUSLY CONSIDERING YOU FOR A MEMBERSHIP IN THE PGC, BUT WE'RE GOING TO HAVE TO REEVALUATE THAT NOW.
WELL, MY FRIENDS DON'T EVALUATE ONE ANOTHER.
WELL, THAT WAS AWKWARD.
AND FROM MY PERSPECTIVE, VERY ENTERTAINING. HEY, SHOULDN'T YOU BE BACKSTAGE HELPING YOUR MOM?
ROBERTO? WE HAVE AN OUTLET EMERGENCY...

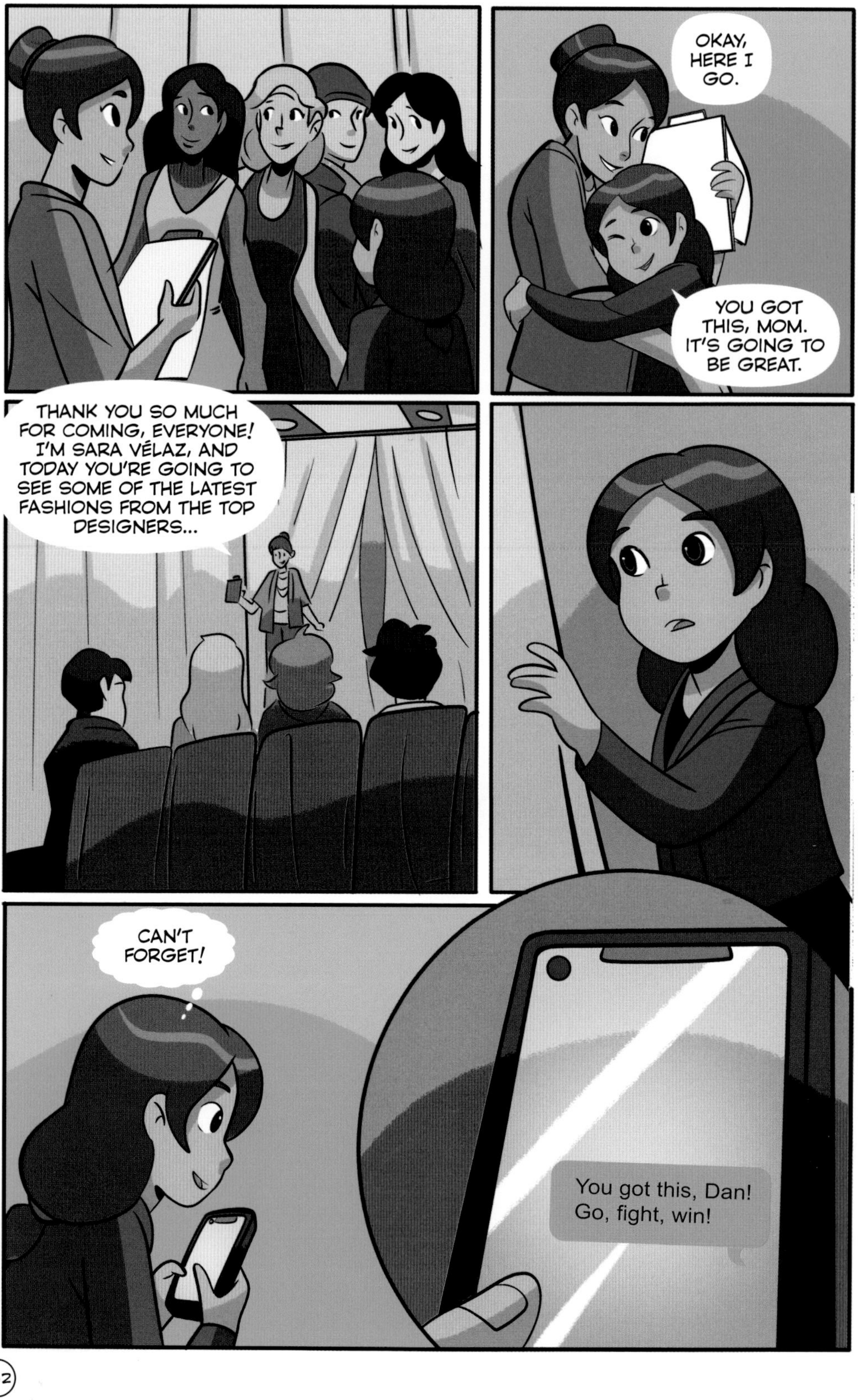
OKAY, HERE I GO.
YOU GOT THIS, MOM. IT'S GOING TO BE GREAT.
THANK YOU SO MUCH FOR COMING, EVERYONE! I'M SARA VÉLAZ, AND TODAY YOU'RE GOING TO SEE SOME OF THE LATEST FASHIONS FROM THE TOP DESIGNERS...
CAN'T FORGET!
You got this, Dan! Go, fight, win!

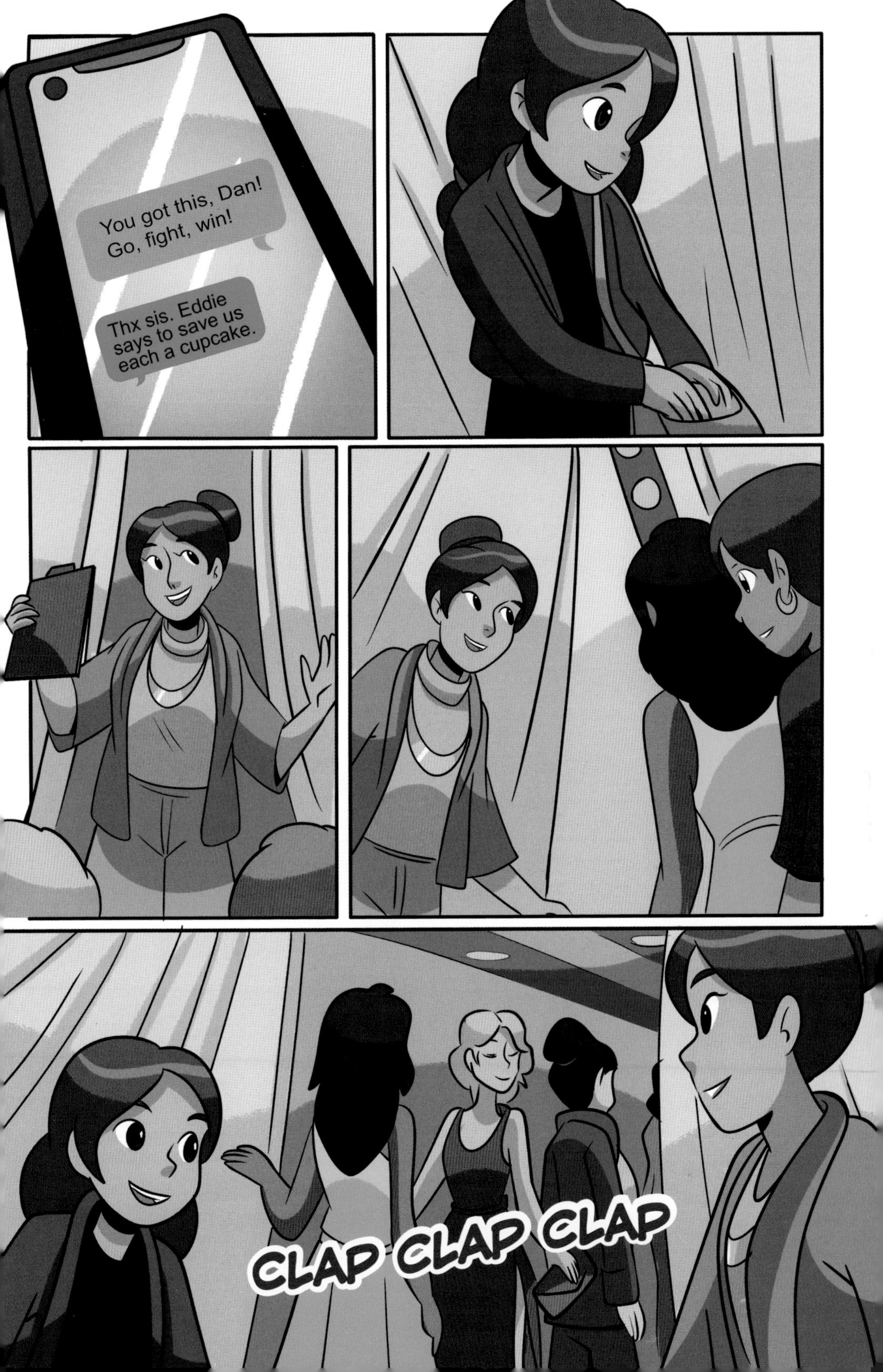
You got this, Dan! Go, fight, win!
Thx sis. Eddie says to save us each a cupcake.
CLAP CLAP CLAP

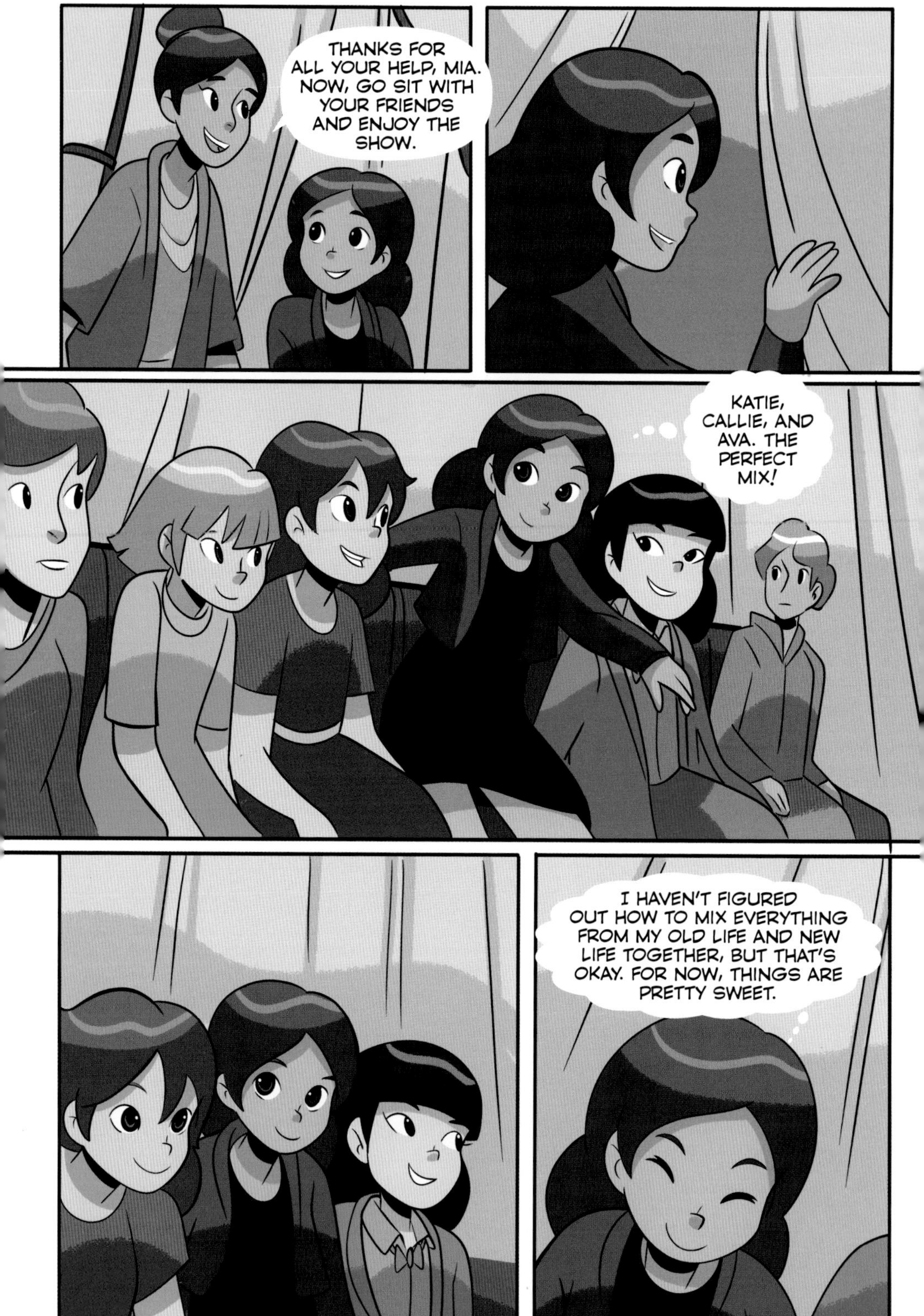
THANKS FOR ALL YOUR HELP, MIA. NOW, GO SIT WITH YOUR FRIENDS AND ENJOY THE SHOW.
KATIE, CALLIE, AND AVA. THE PERFECT MIX!
I HAVEN'T FIGURED OUT HOW TO MIX EVERYTHING FROM MY OLD LIFE AND NEW LIFE TOGETHER, BUT THAT'S OKAY. FOR NOW, THINGS ARE PRETTY SWEET.

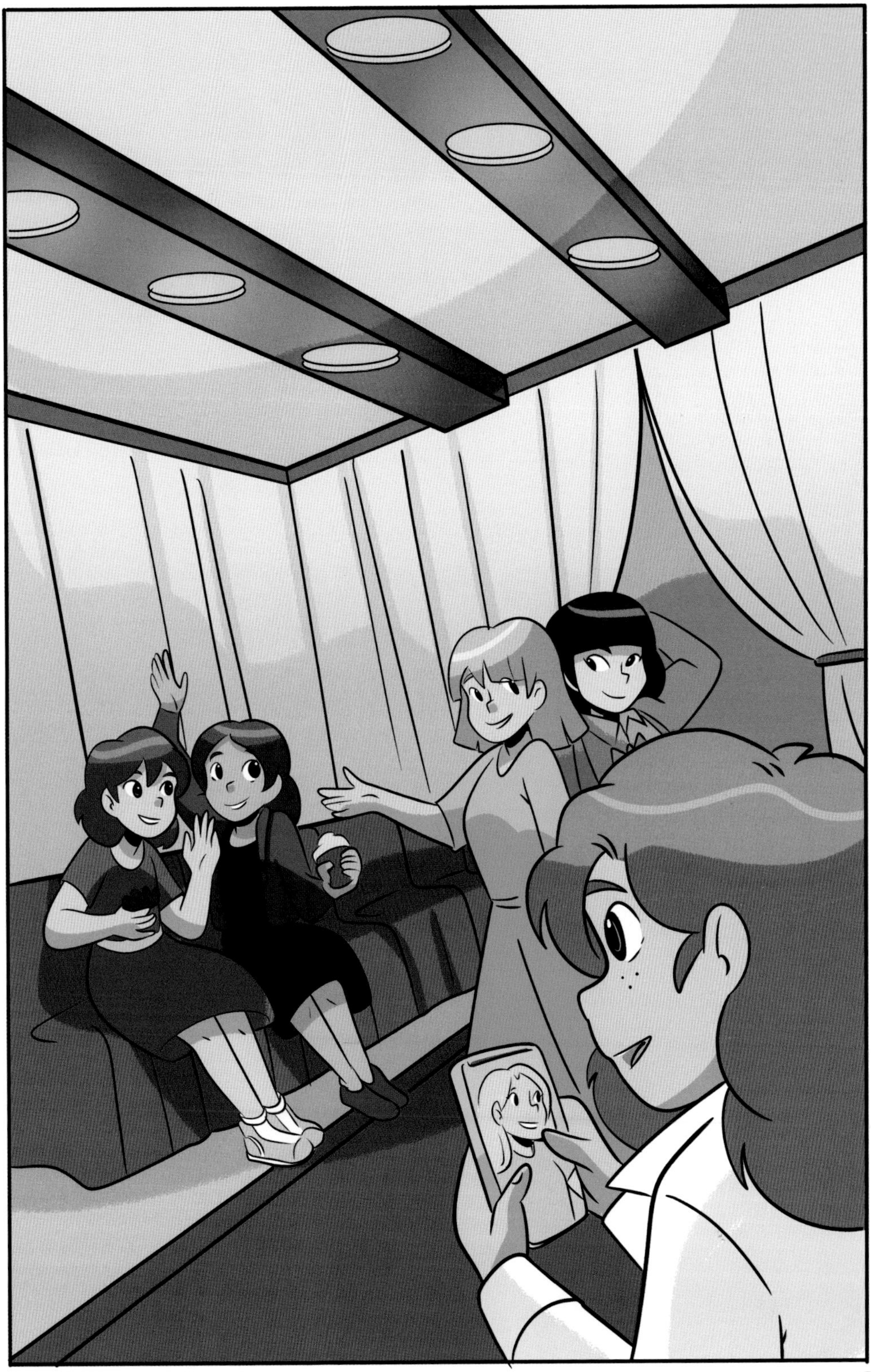

Make sure you read them all!

Cupcake Diaries

Katie and the Cupcake Cure

From the bestselling author of Cupcake Diaries Coco Simon
Cupcake Diaries
#1
The Graphic Novel
Katie and the Cupcake Cure

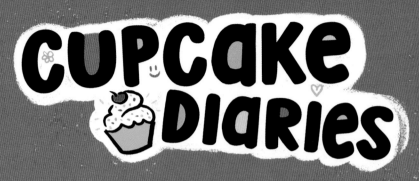

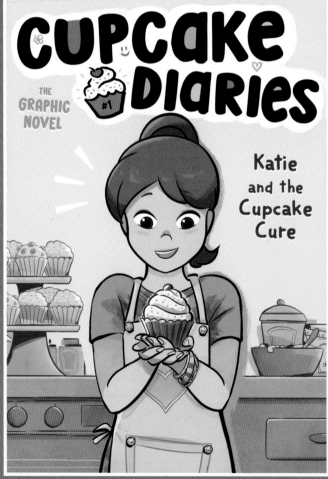

Chapter 1

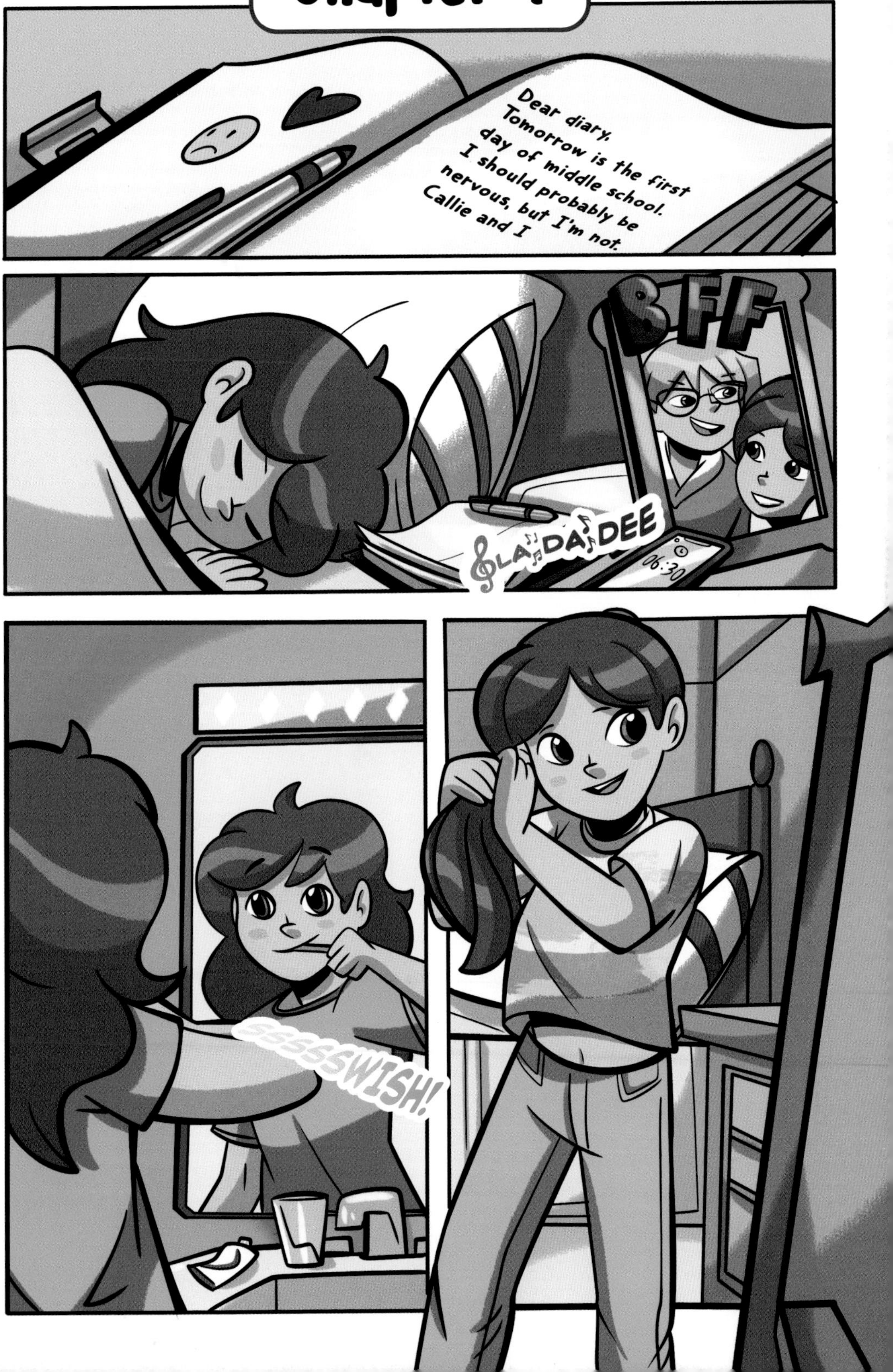
Dear diary,
Tomorrow is the first
day of middle school.
I should probably be
nervous, but I'm not.
Callie and I
BFF
LA DA DEE
06:30
SSSSSWISH!

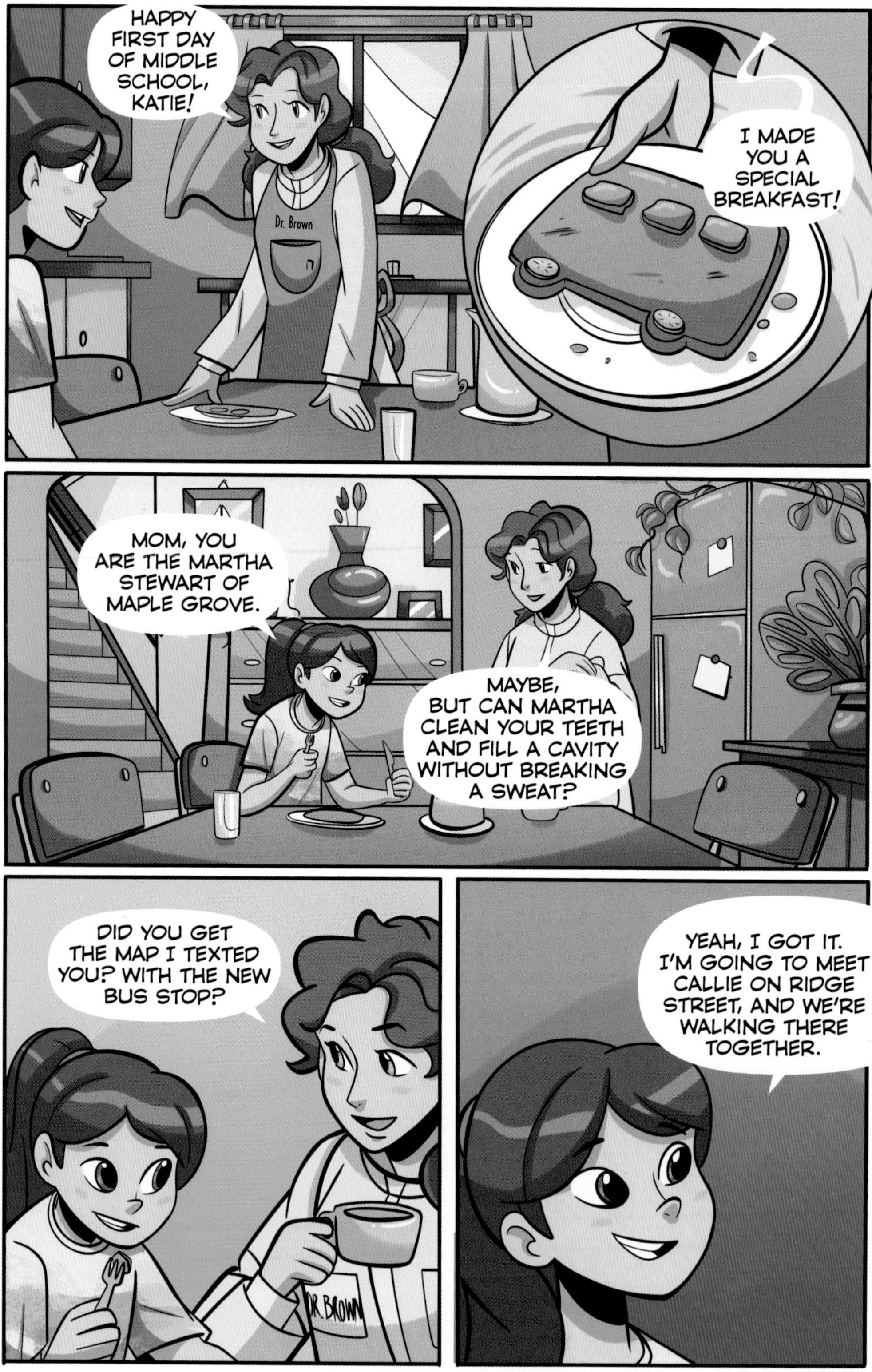
HAPPY FIRST DAY OF MIDDLE SCHOOL, KATIE!
Dr. Brown
I MADE YOU A SPECIAL BREAKFAST!
MOM, YOU ARE THE MARTHA STEWART OF MAPLE GROVE.
MAYBE, BUT CAN MARTHA CLEAN YOUR TEETH AND FILL A CAVITY WITHOUT BREAKING A SWEAT?
DID YOU GET THE MAP I TEXTED YOU? WITH THE NEW BUS STOP?
DR. BROWN
YEAH, I GOT IT. I'M GOING TO MEET CALLIE ON RIDGE STREET, AND WE'RE WALKING THERE TOGETHER.

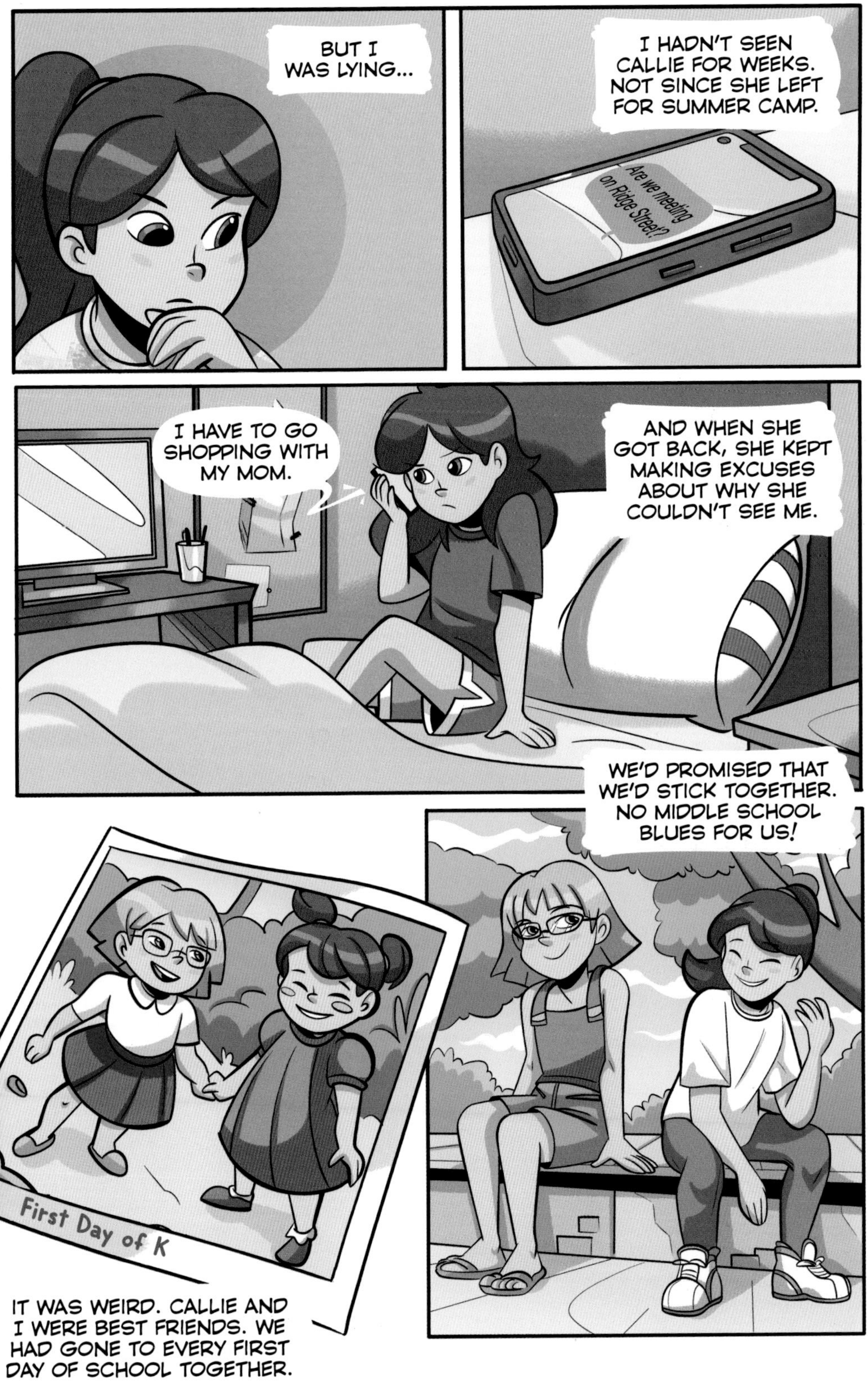
BUT I WAS LYING...
I HADN'T SEEN CALLIE FOR WEEKS. NOT SINCE SHE LEFT FOR SUMMER CAMP.
Are we meeting on Ridge Street?
I HAVE TO GO SHOPPING WITH MY MOM.
AND WHEN SHE GOT BACK, SHE KEPT MAKING EXCUSES ABOUT WHY SHE COULDN'T SEE ME.
WE'D PROMISED THAT WE'D STICK TOGETHER. NO MIDDLE SCHOOL BLUES FOR US!
First Day of K
IT WAS WEIRD. CALLIE AND I WERE BEST FRIENDS. WE HAD GONE TO EVERY FIRST DAY OF SCHOOL TOGETHER.

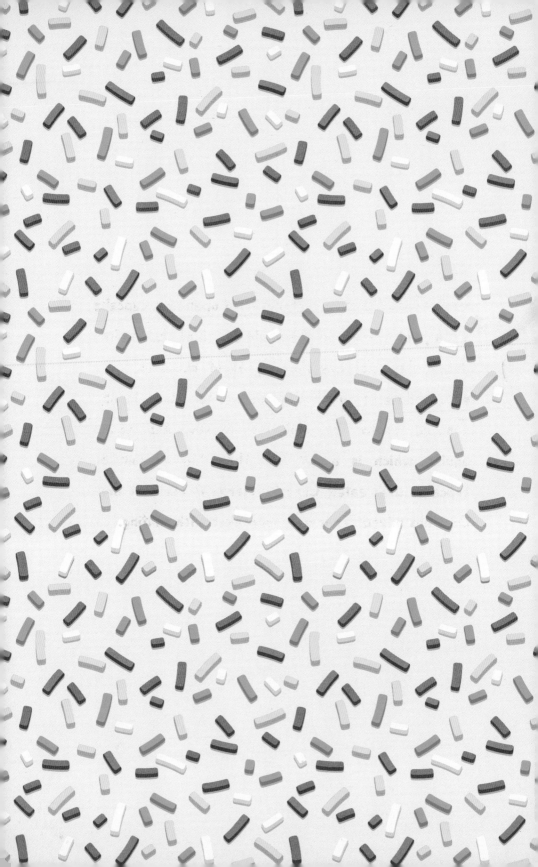